LORENZO

CHICAGO RUTHLESS: BOOK 3

SADIE KINCAID

CONTENT WARNING

This book is intended for mature readers and contains scenes of graphic violence as well as those of a sexual nature.

Triggers include domestic abuse, discussion of terminal illness, and discussion of past sexual assault. Some of the practices depicted in this book can cause injury if safe and proper guidelines are not followed.

To my beautiful Fin,

Know that I would trade it all for one more anything...

PROLOGUE
LORENZO

Rain bounces off the fabric only a few inches above my head. A constant hammering of tiny bullets bears down on the sea of black umbrellas currently sheltering the fake mourners from the driving Chicago rain. The priest stands just a few feet in front of us, yet his words are drowned out by the storm. Or maybe it's the sound of blood rushing in my ears that makes me struggle to hear what he says.

It doesn't matter that I can't hear him. I already know the well-practiced speech falling from his lips. What a kind soul she was. How she was a light in this dark fucking world. Both true.

How God has called her home. Fucking liar. Her home is here. With me.

I step out from beneath the umbrella being held over me and blink up at the gray clouds rolling overhead. I want to feel the rain drip down my face. I want the cold rainwater to soak this goddamn suit—the one that was laid out on the bed for me this morning, as though I'm suddenly incapable of dressing myself. I want to feel anything other than this deep gnawing emptiness that consumes me—eating through my bones and feasting on my soul.

The shadow of the umbrella arches over my head again, and a growl of warning rumbles in my throat.

There's a sigh of exasperation. The shadow disappears.

A snarling order to leave me alone comes from my younger brother who stands a few feet behind me. I close my eyes and tilt my head to the sky, tuning out the priest's voice as he raises it a few octaves to be heard over the hammering rain. Water runs down my face, trickling into my ears and down my neck, soaking the crisp collar of my shirt. What if I could drown in this? Open my mouth and let the rainwater fill my throat and my lungs while everyone stands around crying fake tears and holding handkerchiefs to their faces? Or what if I simply opened her casket and crawled inside with her? Took her in my arms and lay with her for eternity, like I was supposed to.

That was the fucking deal, Anya! Forever! You promised me forever.

I see her beautiful face—etched with so much pain despite the drugs given to help ease her suffering. Her final words ring in my ears—*my dearest love*—and they rip a fresh gaping wound in the center of my chest. If I concentrate hard enough and drown out this entire fucking shitshow of a day, I can still feel her warmth when I held her one last time. As she slipped away in my arms. I felt her passing in every cell of my body, like it was my own death I lived through rather than hers. The devil himself dragged me to hell with the visceral tearing of her soul from this world.

Rage simmers, deep inside my gut, but it's buried by too much grief and guilt and pain to boil over the surface. How could I, the most powerful fucking man in Chicago, not save her? Despite all my money, my resources, and my family's name —a name that can move fucking mountains—I couldn't give her even one more moment. Never have I felt so powerless, so utterly hopeless and alone, as when I watched my wife take her last breath in my arms.

Because I allowed it to happen. I didn't stop it. I couldn't stop it.

Tears run down my face, indistinguishable from the freezing rain if not for the sharp contrast of their heat. Maybe I will join her—wait here until they're all gone and fucking climb in there. Fall asleep and never wake up.

My heart shudders violently, reminding me that it's broken beyond repair. As if I could fucking forget.

Soft fingers curl around my left hand, slender digits threading through my thick ones. My sister, Joey. And now my right; my sister-in-law, Kat. Hands that are slight and nimble against my own, but too strong for me to pull away from, like vines on the trunk of a tree.

I feel the weight of their concern as they watch me, but I keep my head tilted toward the sky. They squeeze my hands tighter, letting me know they're still here. Reminding me that their tears are as real as mine. They loved her too. How could they not? Anyone who was given the opportunity to truly know my sweet, beautiful wife couldn't help but love her. She was the best person I've ever known. The best part of me.

And now she's gone.

And I'm left to endure this life without her. Left with no heart and only half a soul and the knowledge that I'll never love another woman for the rest of my days. I promised her that when she closed her eyes for the final time, and it's a promise I will keep with my dying breath.

CHAPTER

ONE

MIA

TWO YEARS LATER

My husband towers over me, his lips twisted into a cruel sneer as he threads his belt through the loops of his trousers. I rest my throbbing head against the kitchen cupboard and blink away the trickle of blood dripping into my eye, too afraid to swat it away in case he sees the motion as a pathetic attempt at retaliation. I've learned that the best way to handle him when he's like this is to remain as small and as still as possible. Let him think he's won.

"And I want you and this entire goddamn house cleaned by the time I finish my shift tonight," he says, his bared teeth making him look like a diseased weasel. To compare my husband to a dog would be far too kind; dogs are loyal and protective and sweet. He fastens his belt, the metal buckle clattering loudly. "I ain't fucking you in that state."

My faint nod is met with an arrogant snort, and he glances over my almost-naked body, surveying his handiwork. With a final curl of his lip, he turns around, grabs his gun, and strides out of the kitchen—transforming into Sergeant Mulcahy, upstanding and decorated officer of the Boston PD.

As soon as the door closes, I force myself to sit up and run my tongue around the inside of my mouth. The metallic tang of blood seeps into my tastebuds, but at least I didn't lose any teeth this time. I glance at the broken breakfast dishes littering the ground around me. Coffee and cereal are splattered all over the cabinets and the new cream floor tile we picked out together a few weeks ago.

It will take hours to clean the kitchen to meet Brad's exacting standards. Getting my feet underneath me, I wince at the throbbing ache in my head, ribs, and thighs. When I feel steady enough to move, I stumble out of the kitchen and into the downstairs bathroom. With the light on, my gaze is drawn straight to the mirror over the sink, but there's no need to prepare myself for the sight that greets me. How sad is that? I can't remember the last time I looked in a mirror after one of Brad's outbursts and felt shocked or surprised by what he'd done to me. Sad and hurt—that still gets me every time—but not surprised.

I run the water and grab a washcloth, soaking it before placing it over my right eye. Then I repeat the process I've done so many times that I don't even have to think about it anymore. My muscles move of their own volition, like a machine.

I always clean my face before getting into the shower to survey the rest of the damage and to clean his cum from between my thighs. Bruises on my body I can hide, but bruises on my face require more care.

Not that I care as much about that today. Sergeant Mulcahy does whatever he can to keep tabs on me. He tapped my phone to listen in on conversations with my friends, which rarely happens these days, and he combs through my accounts and books to make sure I'm only giving massages to clients he deems appropriate. Brad sees everything—everything except *me*.

He's so focused on controlling my life outside of these walls, he pays little attention to my life within it. So when I occasionally have a spot of car grease on my T-shirt or a scratch on my knuckles, he doesn't even notice. I always have an explanation ready just in case, but I've never needed one.

Done showering, I wrap a towel around myself and look in the mirror. There's a gash above my right eye and the deep purple bruise spreads over my entire cheekbone. Lifting my chin, I study the fingertip-shaped bruises around my neck and touch the cut on my bottom lip. I give myself a confident smile. This is the last time.

After my shower, I feel fresh and clearheaded. I thought it would be different. I thought my hands would tremble, that my heart would race, but I feel surprisingly calm. Calm when I walk upstairs and take the small orange floral suitcase from the bottom of the closet. Calm when I fill it with my essential toiletries, several pairs of clean underwear, and a few changes of clothes. I'm still calm when I walk down the stairs, suitcase in hand, and make my way through the kitchen, littered with the remnants of breakfast. I grab my purse, but I leave my cell phone on the counter. It's little more than a glorified tracker these days.

Opening the garage door, I smile when I see it. My green goddess. The 1986 Mustang that Brad and his brother, Jake, bought four years ago, shortly after their father died. The one they swore they'd fix up and take on a road trip. Neither of them has touched it since, but I've spent the last year fixing it. It's incredible what you can learn online these days. I mean, you can get yourself a degree using only a computer, right? No reason you can't learn to fix an engine that way too.

Humming "Bright Side of the Road," I can't stop grinning as

I pop the trunk and place my bag inside. I climb into the car and, with a deep breath, run my hands over the steering wheel. This is it. My ticket to freedom. It's been a long time coming.

I get her fired up, and the roar of the engine vibrates through my bones. It's the sweetest sound I've heard in my entire life. Excitement and trepidation coil in my gut. After checking my reflection one last time, I put on my sunglasses, hiding the worst of the bruises. Not that it matters where I'm headed, but I don't want some cop seeing my busted face and pulling me over out of concern while I'm getting there. It's a fifteen-hour drive, and apart from bathroom breaks and filling up on gas, I have no intention of stopping until I arrive at my destination.

I've got one shot at this, and there isn't a snowball's chance in hell I'm going to screw it up.

TWO
LORENZO

F ury simmers beneath my skin, like a pot of water on the cusp of bubbling. Always there. Every waking second of every single day. And all it takes is a flash of heat to make it boil over. Sometimes I wonder if the rage I carry deep inside me will ever abate. It's been two long years, yet it grows fiercer every day. It used to be that doing shit like this would give me some release—a few moments relief. But, like an addict who needs more each time to reach that euphoric high, even this has lost its ability to calm the raging demons in my soul.

"P-please, Lor—" the man on his knees before me sputters. I punch him square in the mouth, cutting off the plea for mercy which would have fallen on deaf ears anyway. I am not a man of mercy. Why the fuck would I care about anyone in this world when I have no fucking heart? He falls to the floor like the useless sack of shit he is, blood flying from his mouth and spattering my pants and shoes.

He lies motionless. I look down at the droplets of his blood on my black shoe, and that simmering rage bubbles dangerously close to the surface. They're made from the finest Italian leather, but I don't give a fuck about that. I do give a fuck about the fact that my wife bought them for me a few weeks before she ...

I clench my fists so tightly my forearms feel like they're about to explode, my knuckles turning white. Grinding my teeth, I stretch my neck to alleviate a little of the tension that seeps into every muscle and sinew of my body. Manfred remains prone at my feet, but that won't save him. Molten-hot anger, like the heat from an open furnace, blazes through me, propelling my foot into his head. Not just once, but over and over again. I keep kicking him until his face is unrecognizable as human and my shoes are covered with blood and skull and brain.

"Lorenzo? Please?" Manfred's business partner, Richie, cries from a few feet away, too chickenshit to try to stop me himself. But I can't stop. Can't stop unless some of this deep-seated rage abates. I can't go home to the house where my family lives, where my niece and nephews call me Uncle Loz. Not when I'm this close to the edge. No, I have to leave the worst of it here.

When there's little left of Manfred's head to kick, I move to his body and stamp out as much of the anger as I need to in order to function again. Richie's pleas for mercy diminish with every second that passes, and the sound of him retching and the acrid smell of vomit fills the small room. Instinct makes him rush for the door, despite his former partner blocking his exit. He must know there's no escape, but people tend to lose touch with their common sense when the compulsion to survive kicks in.

Without stopping my assault on Manfred's dead body, I reach out and grab Richard by the throat. He should have left me to it. Maybe then I would have worked out all my anger on his buddy's corpse.

"Lorenzo. Please?" he snivels, tears and snot running onto my hand as I train my glare on him. "I'll get you your money."

"You think this is about the money?" I ask, fascinated by the unadulterated terror on his face. "Your lousy ten grand means nothing to me."

"P-please."

"You and Manfred lied to me, Richie. And that's why you're both going to die in this tiny fucking room and why even your mama won't be able to identify your bodies."

His face pales, which is fitting because he's already a ghost. I throw him across the room, and he stumbles to the ground, trembling as he stares up at me advancing on him. When I force my thumbs into his eye sockets and gouge his eyeballs from his head, his screams for mercy soothe my blackened soul.

I walk down the hallway of my family's mansion. My home. Lessened by her absence, but still the only place I feel any comfort or solace.

"Uncle Loz. Help." The squeals of my three-year-old niece, Gabriella, fill the air as she barrels down the hall toward me in her stockinged feet. Shrieking with high-pitched giggles, she runs right into me, and I scoop her into my arms, holding her to my chest. Okay, so maybe I do still have a heart, but it's shattered into a thousand fragments. The few slivers capable of any positive emotion belong mostly to this little girl and her two younger brothers.

"What are you running from, my little Ella?" She stares up into my face, her dark brown eyes so full of trust and innocence that I sway on my feet.

"Dinosaur Daddy." She lets out another giggle as Dante comes charging down the hallway after her, the pink tiara on his head at odds with his dinosaur-like roar. Gabriella squeals louder, burying her small face against my chest until all that can be seen are her thick curls.

Dante's smile falls away when he sees my knuckles, bloodied and bruised. I cleaned up a little before I came home, but there's only so much gore you can get rid of after you've beaten two men to death. His expression darkens, and the irony of the contrast is not lost on me. Me soaked in blood while I hold onto my sweet niece.

"What the hell, Loz?" he mutters. "I thought you were going to talk?"

I give him a nonchalant shrug. "I didn't like what they had to say."

He reaches for his daughter and plucks her from my arms. She gives a squawk of protest, but he wraps her up and peppers her face with butterfly kisses, making her snuggle into him with another squeal of delight. Something unidentifiable but not unfamiliar settles over me. I shake my head. She's far safer with her father than she is with me—her monster of an uncle.

"Hey, why don't you go find your mom and your brothers while I talk to Uncle Loz?" he says quietly.

She pouts. "I want Uncle Loz to play princess dinosaurs with me too."

"He will soon. He and Daddy just need to talk first. Okay?"

Gabriella turns to me, her brow pinched into a cute frown as she considers his request. She looks so much like Joey; when she pouts, it's almost like traveling back in time to when my sister was her age. "I promise I'll play soon," I assure her.

"Good." After a decisive nod, she squishes Dante's cheeks together and kisses him loudly on the mouth, then wiggles out of his arms and scampers off down the hallway.

With a sigh, I watch her leave and wait for my younger brother's lecture. While I'm the oldest, he's the official head of the family. My father denied me that birthright when I chose Anya Novikov as my bride instead of the Italian woman he picked out for me.

"What the fuck, Loz?" Dante snaps once his daughter is out of earshot.

"I told you, I didn't like what they had to say."

He runs a hand through his hair and sighs. "This shit happens almost every single fucking time you leave the house."

I square up to him. "Why the fuck do you care about those two pieces of shit anyway? I did the world a favor getting rid of Manfred and Richie."

He cocks his head, visibly working to keep a lid on his temper. "I don't give a fuck about Manfred and Richie, but I do give a fuck about you leaving a trail of goddamn bodies in your wake every fucking time you walk out the front door."

I snarl. "I cleaned up after myself. I always do."

He gives my clothes a pointed look. "Not well enough."

Glancing down, I wince at the blood, so much of it clearly visible on my dark suit. Pretty sure some of Manfred's brain matter is spattered on my shoes too. "I'll take care of it now."

"But you drove home like that, Loz. What if some asshole cop with a point to prove had stopped you?"

"The cops don't stop us," I remind him.

"It takes one fucking time, Loz." He holds up his pointer finger, his brow furrowed in a deep scowl. "One fucking time."

I shrug. "I don't fucking care."

"I do, Loz," he shouts. "I fucking care!"

My pulse races, and I suck in a deep breath through my nose. I can't do this right now. I can't—

He grabs my face in his hands, pressing his forehead against mine. "I can't fucking do this without you, brother."

"You can." I choke out the words.

"No I can't. If you don't give a fuck about yourself, think

about us and how we would ever cope without you. Me and Kat. Joey and Max." His pleas pull at some of those tiny slivers, gathering enough together to make my heart start beating again. It's faint but there. "Think about Gabriella and the boys and what they would do if they lost you." Those words act as the final nail in my coffin, and I break.

Tears stream down my face, and he wraps his arms around my head and neck, pulling me into his shoulder. "This has to stop, Loz."

"I know," I admit.

But what if I can't stop?

THREE

LORENZO

Dante fastens his cufflinks and studies me with concern. "You sure you'll be okay? We can stay home."

I roll my eyes and look into the face of his eight-month-old son, Micah, who's nestled in the crook of my arm and drooling while he chews on a teething ring. "Your daddy thinks I can't handle some little punks like you and your big brother and sister?" I bounce him and he giggles.

"Gabriella and Marco are sound asleep," Kat says as she walks into the room. "You sure you don't want me to try and put him down too?"

"We'll be fine. We're going to watch some wrestling. Aren't we, kid?" I wipe the puddle of drool from his chin with a sweep of my thumb.

He goes on happily gnawing on his chew toy like a contented puppy.

"Thank you, Loz." My brother's wife rests a gentle hand on my shoulder. I catch the scent of her sweet perfume, and it stirs up long forgotten memories that I force back down. She gives Micah a soft kiss on his head.

"Dada," he coos in response.

"Ma-ma." She corrects him, enunciating the syllables. Kat keeps hoping he'll repeat that word, but he's stubborn like the rest of the Morettis.

"Dada," Micah repeats, and Kat sighs.

"That's my boy." Dante grins and kisses his son goodbye.

"We'll be back after breakfast." Kat smiles, but I don't miss the concern in her expression. Dante must have told her about the state I came home in today. He tells her everything. She never judges, but their worry is palpable, and it makes my skin itch. I wish I was an easier person to care about, but this is who I am.

"Take your time. We'll be fine. Enjoy the show and the hotel."

"Oh, we'll be enjoying the hotel," Dante says, his grin devious.

"Stop." His wife's cheeks flush red. He wraps his arm around her, silencing her with a kiss.

Sometimes seeing them together forces me to remember how good it felt to have a love like that, and just like I always do, I bury those emotions deep in the hopes of never feeling them again. Otherwise I would be crushed under the pain of it all. If there's one thing I've learned since my wife's death, it's that those memories bring nothing but grief. Better to concentrate on my anger at not having her than any of the love or happiness that we shared. That's the only way I can keep putting one foot in front of the other. The only way I go on surviving for the people who need me. Because the thought of my family having to suffer even a fraction of my torment is the only thing that stops me from giving into the darkness completely.

～

A DEEP VOICE rouses me from sleep. "Boss."

"What?" Sitting up, I wince at the sharp pain that jolts through my neck and jaw. My recently acquired habit of sleeping on the sofa rather than facing the loneliness of my bed has been rough on my body. I hoped that replacing the bedroom furniture would allow me to sleep in there, but it didn't.

"There's someone at the gate."

I check my watch. "It's 2:00 a.m. Tell 'em to fuck off."

I stretch my neck out and the sharp pain turns to a dull ache.

"I would, but ..."

My scowl has him flinching back. "But?"

"She says she's Mrs. Moretti's cousin."

My breath stalls in my lungs. Anya's cousin is here? She lives in Russia and didn't even come to her fucking funeral. "Her cousin is here? Now?"

"Yeah. That's what she said. She asked for Kat."

Closing my eyes, I let out the breath I was holding. Of course he's talking about *that* Mrs. Moretti. After two years, I still think of my Anya when I hear that name. "Tell her to come back tomorrow."

"I would, but ..." He scrubs at the stubble on his chin. God, who the fuck is this guy? Is he new? He's really testing my fucking patience.

"But what?" I snap.

"I told her Mrs. Moretti wasn't home, and she said she has nowhere else to go—"

"So tell her to wait in her fucking car."

His Adam's apple bobs as he swallows.

"You have a fucking problem with that?"

"It's just ... she's kinda beat up, Boss."

I sit up straighter. Kat only has one living relative. Mia, I think. I vaguely recall meeting her at Kat and Dante's wedding. She left early. "What do you mean, beat up?" My short tone matches my patience.

He frowns. "Like someone hurt her real bad. Her face is a mess."

I jump to my feet. What the fuck is going on? "Who hurt her?"

"I-I don't know. I didn't ask. She just asked for Kat and said she has nowhere else to go."

"Fuck," I mutter, slipping on my shoes. "This is all I fucking need."

"Should I tell 'em to open the gates, Boss?"

"Yes," I reluctantly grumble.

He tries to hide his smile by dipping his head and hurrying from the room.

I stalk through the house, my head pounding and my hands balled into fists. Kat and Dante have one fucking night away in two years, and that's when her cousin decides to show up. This is just my luck all fucking over.

By the time I get to the driveway, there's an old green Mustang pulling to a stop a few feet away. Folding my arms across my chest, I wait for the damsel in distress to get out and run crying to the safety of our mansion. If she thinks she'll get any sympathy from me, she's sorely mistaken. I'll show her to the guest room and leave her for Kat to deal with tomorrow. I don't have the time or the energy for emotional women.

The car door opens, revealing one long tanned leg, followed by another. She's wearing a bright yellow dress—the color of sunshine. She turns and spots me, and I frown. Cue the tears, right?

Wrong. She gives me a smile; a huge ass smile that lights up her entire face. Even from here, I can see the dried blood on her lip and eyebrow and the colorful welt covering most of her cheekbone. Assessing for further damage, I allow my eyes to travel the length of her body. Down her neck and the fingertip-shaped bruises partially hidden by her honey-blond hair. Her collarbone. More bruises. My lingering gaze comes to a halt at her chest, where her tits strain against the taut yellow fabric.

"You must be Lorenzo?" Her voice, sweet like nectar, cuts through the quiet night. The guard who alerted me to her arrival returned to his station at the gate, and the others are making their rounds, patrolling the perimeter. She and I are alone. My pulse thrums against my neck, and I swallow harshly.

"It is Lorenzo, right?" she asks again, and I finally manage to tear my eyes from her chest.

"Yeah." My voice comes out an octave higher than usual, and I'm fucked if I know why.

She walks closer. "I'm so sorry about this, but I literally have nowhere else to go." The breeze ruffles her hair, carrying the scent of jasmine and lemon through the air between us. "You might not remember me, but I met you at Kat and Dante's wedding. You and your lovely wife. Anya, right?"

The sound of her name makes me sway on my feet. Nobody says her name. Nobody talks about her for fear that they will unleash the rage that's lived inside me since I lost her. I'd forgotten the power of her name. Forgotten how it's like music to my dark soul.

"I was so sorry to hear about her passing." She continues to approach me, seemingly oblivious to my distress. "She was a beautiful person. We spoke about her illness."

I frown at her, unconvinced. Anya never talked about her cancer with anyone. "You did?"

She gives me a sympathetic smile. "I think it's sometimes easier to talk to strangers, you know? Although I can talk to anyone. I talk too much. I always have. I'm a babbler."

"Yeah, I got that," I mutter, turning on my heel and walking back into the house.

Not bothering to wait for an invitation, she follows me inside. "Will Kat be back tomorrow?"

"Yes. After breakfast. I'll show you to a guest room and you can see her when she gets home."

"Oh, I need to grab my bag." She giggles lightly. "I was so excited to get here and finally pee that I forgot to get it out of the trunk." She's certainly very happy for a woman who looks like she went a round with a heavyweight champ not too long ago.

"I'll have one of my men fetch your bag."

"Thank you. And that bathroom?" Gazing up at me, she chews on her bottom lip.

I frown. "What?" My brain feels like it's misfiring. Maybe it's having my sleep interrupted? Or maybe it's listening to this strange woman talk about my wife like she knows her.

She laughs again. "I need to pee," she reminds me.

"Oh. Sure. Down the hall. Second room on the left."

"Thank you so much." Already darting away down the hall, she calls the words over her shoulder, and I watch after her, curious about how she ended up here and why. It's no leap to assume she got those bruises from a man. A man with big, meaty fists if the size of that black eye is any indication. If I recall correctly, she's married. Is she running from her husband?

Leaning against the wall, I wait outside the bathroom. I can't exactly leave her wandering the halls now, can I? My niece and nephews are asleep, and for all I know, she could be a serial killer who smells like lemons and jasmine.

When she emerges a few minutes later, she gives me another wide smile. Her injuries look worse in the bright light of the hallway, her swollen eye giving way to a purple contusion that covers the entire right side of her face. A drop of blood wells from the cut in her lip. She must have wiped it in the bathroom and caused the wound to reopen. Her tongue darts out to lick the blood, and for some reason, I look away.

"Would it be too much trouble to get a little something to eat? All I've eaten today was a bag of Skittles and some beef jerky." She looks at me with wide hazel eyes—or are they green? It's hard to tell in the glare of the light. "I can fix something myself if you show me the way?" she offers.

Fuck! I shake my head to clear it and motion in front of me. "I'll show you the kitchen."

She falls into step beside me. "Thank you so much. I can't imagine what you must be thinking having me turn up on your doorstep like this."

"That you're running from your husband?" I offer with a disinterested shrug. My tone is clipped and harsh, but if she takes any offense, she doesn't show it.

"Yup. You read me right," she says with a soft laugh. "I guess you're good at reading people in your business."

I arch an eyebrow at her. "And that is?"

She shrugs. "Mafia stuff."

I stop and stare at her. Did she really just say that out loud? "Mafia stuff?"

"You're Cosa Nostra, right? Sicilian Mafia?" she says, turning around when she notices I'm no longer walking beside her.

The corners of my mouth lift into a faint grin. "People don't usually say it so bluntly. Not to my face."

She tilts her head, chewing on the inside of her cheek as she stares at me with a look on her face that I can't quite figure out. Is she fronting or is she really as unaffected by this encounter as she appears to be? "Oh, right. I'm sorry. I thought it was like your job title or something."

Swallowing an unexpected laugh, I move past her and push open the kitchen door, motioning for her to go ahead. "Do you always say what you're thinking, or is it a nervous thing?"

"Oh, almost always," she says, walking past me into the kitchen and leaning up against the massive wooden table. She studies me curiously. "And I'm not nervous.".

I narrow my eyes at her. Who the hell is this woman? "You're not? You're in this house, alone, with a man who does *Mafia stuff*, and you're not even a little nervous?"

"Not even a little." She grins, and her eyes, appearing brown in the softer light of the kitchen, burn into mine.

I take a few steps toward her. Goosebumps prickle her forearms, but she keeps her gaze locked on mine. "Maybe you should be nervous, Mia."

Her face lights up like a Christmas tree. "You remember my name?"

"I-I, uh—"

"Anyway, Kat told me you're a really good guy. Plus, I saw you with your wife. How you acted, you know ..." Her eyes fill with tears, and she swats them away.

I swallow the hard knot of emotion lodged in my throat. I'm going to regret this, but I can't pass up the opportunity to see our relationship through someone else's perspective—it's like getting back a piece of Anya, a piece I never had while she was here. "How did I act?"

"The way you looked at her. Like you would hang the moon for her." She sighs softly. "Every woman deserves a man who looks at her like that. Everyone deserves someone who adores them. Someone who would die for them."

This woman—this stranger could see all that? Fuck, I *still* adore Anya. I would've died for her one hundred times over. Given half a fucking chance, I'd die right now just for one more moment with her. I cough to clear my throat, but it doesn't help. My voice comes out rough. "You got all that from a few hours in our company?"

"Love like that can't be masked. A few moments in your company would have told me the same." Her stomach growls loudly, and her cheeks flush a delicate shade of pink. "Any chance of that food?"

"What? Yes, of course." I was staring again. What the fuck? "We have some leftover risotto, or there's meat and fresh bread?"

"Risotto would be perfect. Thanks."

I've never seen a woman take as much joy in food as Mia does. She closes her eyes to savor each mouthful and lets out a soft moaning sound every time she takes a bite. Our cook Sophia does make an incredible risotto, but still.

I watch her intently, fascinated by this woman who seems to have every reason to be terrified and depressed but might just be the happiest person I've ever met.

In stark contrast to the way she scarfed down her risotto, Mia daintily dabs at her mouth with her napkin when she's done. The bruise on her face has grown darker and her right eye is partially swollen shut. Kat will check her over in the morning, but the sight of her battered features has my ever-present rage bubbling to the surface.

"Who did that to you?"

Her eyes flicker to mine. They're hazel again now. "My husband. Like you said."

I knew it. That fucking bastard. "Why?"

"Why?" The bitter laugh sounds unnatural coming from her lips. "You think there's ever a reason to do this to someone you're supposed to love?"

I silently curse myself for my careless choice of words. "No, but I meant did something provoke him?"

"Umm ..." She presses her lips together as though deep in

thought. "This morning it was because the cereal was too soggy."

My brow furrows. "What?"

"I poured the milk too soon, therefore rendering his cereal inedible," she says with a resigned shrug.

"So this was a common occurrence?"

"If you call once every other month common, then yes."

"And it was always your fault, right? You made him act that way?"

"You know the script?" Her smile is sad but genuine.

I heard it many times with my own parents, but I don't tell her that.

She stares at me so intently that I feel hot under her gaze. "And now you're wondering why I stayed so long."

"I never said that."

"I'd ask me that if I were you. Ten long years I stayed with him. Hoping ..." She shakes her head. "But hope's a dangerous thing, right? Sometimes I think it's the most powerful force in the universe."

"You do?" My words drip with derision.

"Yes," she says, straightening her spine. "We can live without most things, even love. But without hope, well, we have nothing left worth living for." I frown at her, and she laughs softly. "I take it you don't agree?"

I shrug. "I think life is full of hopeless situations, but people keep going without it."

"They keep going because of that little ray of light in the darkness. That's hope," she insists.

My skin prickles with annoyance. "No. There isn't always a ray of light, Mia. Sometimes there's just darkness and nothing beyond it."

She leans forward and gentles her tone. "But there's a ray of light to be found in even the darkest of situations."

Spoken by a person who hasn't had their entire world crash down around their ears. The sound that rumbles out of my chest makes it clear I disagree, but she starts talking again before I can argue.

"It's true. Sometimes you have to look real hard to find it. But it's always there, even if it's just the tiniest speck of light. And when you do find it, well, then it's your job to nurture it until it grows bigger and the light begins to outshine the darkness. Eventually, light will be all that's left."

"That's your philosophy, is it?" I snap, annoyed by her steadfast positivity. If I'm forced to listen to much more of it, she's going to see just how little light I have inside me.

"It's the only one I have," she says in a softer tone.

Feeling the need to change the conversation before she can piss me off with more of her hippie bullshit, I place my palms on the table in front of me and lean forward. "So why did you stay with him?"

If she's bothered by me shifting the conversation back to her abusive marriage, she doesn't show it. "Same reasons everyone stays, I guess. First because I thought he could change. I thought I could change him." She snorts a self-deprecating laugh and shakes her head. "Then I convinced myself it wasn't so bad. That the good times outweighed the bad. The sex was incredible." She arches an eyebrow.

I take a sip of my coffee to distract myself from thoughts of her having sex, because for some reason that I can't identify, the thought of the asshole who gave her those bruises putting his hands on her in any way makes me see red. "You really don't have a filter, do you?"

That makes her laugh again. "Sorry."

"Please go on," I say, annoyed at myself for interrupting her.

"Then when the bad times got more frequent and even the sex became ... well not bad. I just didn't want it, you know?"

Every cell in my body vibrates with tension and anger. What I wouldn't give right now for a few minutes alone with that motherfucker. Who the fuck treats their wife that way? Her voice brings me back from the ledge, and I'm left wondering why her situation is provoking such an intense physical reaction from me.

"Well, I finally decided I had to get out before he killed me, but I didn't think I had anywhere to go. About a year ago, I was talking to Kat and she made an offhand comment about how I was always welcome here, and I realized that I was wrong. I did have somewhere to go. Kat's my family, and she's there for me just like I'd be for her. I hate to be a burden to any of you, so I won't hang around for long, but I knew I was running out of time and that if I didn't get out of that house of my own free will, I'd be leaving in a box."

I fight the urge to lean across the table and brush away the tear running down her cheek. I don't think I've ever met anyone else so willing to bare their soul to a complete stranger. Talking with her is the most intimate thing I've done with a woman in a long time.

"So, I fixed up that old Mustang and left this morning. Sixteen hours and two gas and bathroom breaks and I'm here." The smile that lights up her face makes the hair on the back of my neck stand on end.

I need to break this connection between us, but I can't seem to tear my eyes away from her.

FOUR

MIA

I lie back on the soft pillow and stare at the ceiling. This house is incredible. The guest bedroom is like something from a five-star hotel. I can't believe that my cousin gets to live in this place. Without warning, a tear drips down my cheek. I wish she was here. Trust me to turn up on the one night she's away with her husband. Not that Lorenzo wasn't completely welcoming, despite not wanting me here. He's clearly a good man but seeing the amount of sadness he carries around nearly made me want to cry.

I wonder if Brad's filed a missing person's report yet. Normally, police departments won't file unless the person has been missing for more than forty-eight hours, but I bet he'll use his badge to expedite the process. Imagining his face when he walked through the door and saw the house hadn't been cleaned makes me smile. And then when he saw the Mustang was gone—I almost wish I was there to see it.

Sighing with contentment, I roll onto my side and snuggle into the pillow. This bed is so damn comfy.

Brad's in Boston and I'm here, hundreds of miles away from him. Even if he tries to follow me, I'm safe behind these walls.

I'm not naive enough to be unaware of the Morettis and what they do. Cop or not, Brad wouldn't dare take on the Mafia. And while I'm a pacifist at heart, I'm in a desperate situation. What other choice did I have?

As I start to doze off, images of Lorenzo's handsome face and intense brown eyes flash through my head. It was odd to sit and speak so openly with a complete stranger, particularly one as dangerous as him, but also weirdly familiar and comforting. I feel at ease in his presence. I didn't even babble as much as I usually do, a fact I bet he'd find hard to believe because I talked nonstop. I'm still thinking about his dark, hypnotic gaze and deep, soothing voice when I drift off to sleep.

I MUST HAVE BEEN COMPLETELY WIPED out by my drive from Boston to Chicago because the next thing I know, I'm startled awake by a soft knock on my door followed by my name. Her voice makes my heart swell in my chest.

"Kat?" I throw off the covers and jump out of bed just as she rushes through the door. We run into each other's arms, hugging tightly as tears roll down our faces. After we've embraced for several seconds, we step back and she scans my appearance, her brow furrowed with concern.

"We should get that eye looked at by a doctor. Just to be sure there's no permanent damage."

I shake my head. "No doctors. It'll be fine. It's happened before," I assure her.

"Oh, Mia," she says on a sob, wrapping her arms around me again. "I'm so sorry, honey."

I rub a soothing hand over her back. "Don't be. I hid the worst of it, Kat. Please don't feel sorry for me."

She straightens up, wiping the tears from her cheeks. I

know she understands the deep-seated desire not to feel pitied. Something happened to her a few years ago, and although she never told me what, it changed her. She completely withdrew from life for a time. Then she met Dante, and I've never seen her so happy.

"I'm so glad you came. You can stay as long as you like. We have plenty of room. In fact, stay forever." She brushes a fingertip over my bruised cheek, smiling softly. "He'll never hurt you here. I promise."

"Thank you." I can't stay here forever, and I have no intention of doing so, but the fact that she would let me means the world to me. "I've missed you so much. And I haven't seen those beautiful babies of yours nearly enough."

That makes her laugh. "No, you haven't. Gabriella is three and a half going on thirty. She'll have dozens of questions to ask you, so be prepared."

"You know talking is my thing," I remind her.

She squeezes my hand. "You have no need to be nervous in this house. Dante is really pleased you're here, and I know Lorenzo seems a bit grumpy ..."

"He was quite sweet actually."

She pops a perfectly manicured eyebrow at me. "Lorenzo? Sweet?"

"I mean, I rocked up in the middle of the night looking like this." I wave a hand over my face. "But the guy barely batted an eyelid. Then I talked his ass off and he didn't tell me to shut up once."

"Hmm." She narrows her eyes at me. "Brad set the bar way too low if you think Lorenzo Moretti is sweet."

I nudge her in the ribs. "You left him in sole charge of your three little angels, so he can't be that bad."

"Oh, he's a good guy. The kids love him. I love him. Just ..." She wrinkles her nose. "Sweet?" Laughing, she shakes her head.

"Anyway. Let's go get some breakfast and you can say hi to Dante and my three little angels."

The noise from the kitchen can be heard from the hallway, and the laughter and shouting makes me smile. When we get there, Dante's holding Gabriella upside down and pretending to dip her into a bowl of oatmeal.

"No, Daddy!" she squeals with delight, and he pulls her into his arms and tickles her.

Joey sits on the other side of the table with her husband, Max. I met them both at Kat's wedding, but they weren't together then. Joey shouts to Marco that he needs to save his sister from their monster Daddy while Max laughs at them all. Lorenzo is seated at the head of the table, holding baby Micah in his arms and shaking his head in bemusement. He says something to Micah, who smiles up at him in response, but the kitchen is too noisy for me to hear what he said.

"Our guest of honor has arrived." Kat cuts through the sea of noise, and everyone stops and stares at us. I self-consciously lift my hand to my cheek, aware of how hideous I look right now, but before I have time to wallow in my embarrassment, Joey jumps from her chair and rushes toward me.

"Mia. It's so lovely to see you again," she says, wrapping me in a warm hug.

I squeeze her back. "You too!"

When she steps away, Dante's there waiting for a hug. "I'm glad you came here. Kat's family is our family too," he says, his tone full of genuine affection.

I blink to clear my unexpected tears. "Thank you. I really appreciate you all having me here."

Gabriella eyes me warily until Kat picks her up and explains that I'm her auntie Mia and I'll be staying here for a while. She asks about my face, and I tell her I had an accident, which she doesn't question because she's three and a half. I give Marco a squeeze too, but Lorenzo keeps hold of Micah, so I guess I'll have to get my baby cuddles later.

Dante scoops Gabriella up from the floor. "Time for your lessons, princess."

"Aw. I want to stay with Auntie Joey and Auntie Mia." Her lower lip pokes out, making her look utterly adorable.

"Lessons," he says sternly, even though he's still smiling at her. The love he has for Kat and their kids is so tangible, I can practically touch it. It radiates out of him.

"Do what Daddy says, sweetheart," Kat adds.

"You too, little dude." Dante picks Marco up in his other arm. "I'll be back in five. Don't start without me," he says to Kat before giving her a sweet kiss.

A lady with gray hair who's been standing quietly by the stove shoos me toward an empty seat. "Sit. What would you like for breakfast? We have everything you can think of."

"Waffles, please," Joey announces loudly.

"Sophia makes the best waffles," Kat tells me, giving the older woman a quick squeeze.

I sit in the chair Sophia indicated. "Fruit's fine for me, thanks."

Joey scoffs. "That's like a snack. Not breakfast."

"You only say that because you can't function without coffee and sugar, baby girl." Max teases her good-naturedly, and she flutters her eyelashes at him in response.

"Are you sure I can't fix you anything more substantial?" Sophia asks.

I eye the plates of food on the table. It looks like Kat, Dante, and Lorenzo had bacon and eggs, and even the leftovers look amazing. But my ass will get fatter than it is now if I start indulging in waffles or bacon and eggs for breakfast. And I was so hungry when I got here last night, I inhaled a plate of risotto right in front of Lorenzo. He must think I'm a glutton already.

"Fruit is fine." A flush creeps across my cheeks. "Thank you."

Smiling at me over her shoulder, Sophia goes to the fridge. "Of course."

I glance around the table, and I'm surprised to find Lorenzo staring at me. He doesn't attempt to disguise his scrutiny but continues watching me with a curious expression on his face.

For some reason, the heat from my cheeks travels down my neck and chest, and I shift in my seat. Yep, feeling that heat elsewhere too. What the hell, Mia?

I take a deep breath and flash him my best smile. His eyes crinkle at the corners and one side of his mouth curls up in amusement before his attention moves to the doorway just as Dante walks back into the room.

"So, what's the plan?" Max asks as soon as Dante sits down at the table. "I can be there and back in a day. Make it look like an accident? A suicide?"

Lorenzo scowls. "No. I'll do it."

"You sure that's wise?" Dante asks him.

"You think I'm not capable of handling this?" Lorenzo barks.

I watch them with morbid fascination. They're clearly talking about one of their enemies, but I'm shocked they'd discuss killing someone so openly in front of me. I guess I really am family, huh?

Dante huffs and rolls his eyes. "Don't be fucking ridiculous, Loz. But you have been a little ..." He winces.

"A little what, D?"

"Psycho?" Max offers.

"Not helpful," Joey chides her husband.

"You haven't been your usual levelheaded self is all," Dante says. "And this needs to be clean. The guy's a cop."

"I fucking know that," Lorenzo says with a snarl.

The hairs on the back of my neck stand on end. "A c-cop?"

Everyone turns and looks at me.

"Who are you talking about?" I ask, even as my heart races. I think I know the answer.

"Your piece-of-shit husband," Lorenzo replies, as though murdering a police officer is a normal breakfast conversation.

I push my chair back as bile surges up my throat. "W-what? No! You can't ... I never asked you to ... You can't!"

Kat puts a reassuring hand over mine and shoots her husband a warning look. "I told you she wouldn't want that."

"How else do you expect to stay safe from him, Mia?" Dante asks.

"I-I ..." The words won't come. "I don't know. But I don't want you to kill him."

Lorenzo's jaw ticks as he glares at me. "Shame you don't get a vote."

"Loz," Dante warns.

"Are we killing this guy or not?" Max asks.

Lorenzo scowls. "Yes."

"No," I insist. My heart threatens to burst out of my chest. "That's not why I came here. That's not what—I shouldn't have come."

I turn to leave, but Kat grabs my hand. "No one will hurt Brad if you don't want that, Mia. I promise you."

I look at her husband, the head of the Cosa Nostra, and he nods his agreement. Satisfied, I return to my chair.

"Do you expect him not to follow you here, Mia?" Dante asks softly, his voice thick and smooth like velvet.

"I ... I didn't think. I thought maybe he might, but ..."

Lorenzo sighs. "But what?"

"I thought once he saw where I was, he'd just leave and not bother me again."

Lorenzo snorts. "That's either incredibly naive or incredibly stupid."

"Don't call me stupid." I glower at him.

He narrows his dark eyes and glares right back. "Naive then?"

"Maybe." I shake my head. I clearly didn't think my plan through well enough, and now I feel like a fool.

"You're safe while you're in this house, Mia. But is that what you want? To stay behind these walls forever?" Dante asks.

"No. But I thought maybe just for a little while. Until I can figure out my next move. Then I could start somewhere new. With a new name."

"Just like that, huh?" Lorenzo's voice drips with sarcasm.

"Enough," Kat says with a sigh. "There's nothing that needs to be decided right now, is there? Let Mia think about her next steps, and while she does, she can stay here as long as she needs to." She squeezes my hand again.

"Of course." Dante shoots a look at his brother who closes his eyes and shakes his head.

"You won't hurt Brad?" I ask.

Dante stares at me for a few seconds before he replies. "We won't go looking for him, but if he turns up here and causes any trouble ..."

"We'll give him a pair of concrete boots and toss him in the river," Lorenzo finishes for him, a malicious grin on his face.

Reluctantly, I agree. "I guess I can't argue with that."

FIVE

LORENZO

I pace up and down my study, hands stuffed in my pockets to stop me from punching a hole in anything. We've already had the door to this room replaced three times in the past two years. I'm astounded by Mia's naivete. I guess I had her figured all wrong. Last night she seemed strong and determined, yet today she refuses to take any vengeance against the man who spent the last decade beating the shit out of her. I can't comprehend her thought process. Why won't she let us protect her?

A soft knock at the door snatches my attention. "What?" I bark.

Mia's soft voice carries through the thick oak. "Can I come in?"

Why the hell is she here? "Yes."

She walks in and closes the door behind her. Her right eye looks even worse today, and she blushes when she catches me staring at her bruised face.

"Did Kat check that out for you?"

She brushes her fingertips over her cheek. "Yeah, but it's fine. It usually calms down in a day or two."

The fact that her piece-of-shit husband has done that to her so many times before that she has a *usual* recovery window makes my blood fucking boil.

"Did you need something?" I snap at her, my tone harsher than I mean it to be.

"I just wanted to ..." she chews on her lip. "You seemed angry about me not wanting anyone to hurt Brad?" Her voice rises at the end like she's trying to understand my frustration.

Why the fuck does she care what I think?

She fidgets with a button on her shirt. "I'm sorry. I get why you'd want to do that, I mean, I do, but it's not ..." She swats at a tear running down her cheek. "God, I hate crying."

I resist the urge to ask why she hates crying. She's Kat's cousin, so I will tolerate her presence in this house, but that's as far as our interactions need to go. I open my mouth, about to tell her that she shouldn't concern herself with what I think and then ask her to leave my study, but she starts talking again.

"I'd hate for anyone to get hurt or get into any trouble because of me. Brad's a cop. He has a lot of friends in high places. I just don't think he's worth anybody's time or trouble."

That's not what she means at all. I see it in every movement of her body. Every shadow on her face. What she actually means is that she doesn't think that *she's* worth the time or the trouble. That motherfucker really did a number on her. "What I don't get is why you wouldn't want that sick fuck to feel even a fraction of the pain he forced you to endure."

"It wasn't that bad—"

"Have you looked in the fucking mirror today, Mia?"

She flinches, making me feel like shit for victimizing her all over again, but she squares her shoulders and steps so close to me that I can smell her perfume. "I am well aware of what I look like, Lorenzo. But how is hurting Brad going to change any of what he did to me? You think if I could take back every single bruise, every single scar, every single time he raped me, every single moment I lived in fear that the next time he might kill me, that I wouldn't do it in a heartbeat?" Her breath comes in pants, teeth bared and body shaking with temper. I was right. She is a feisty one.

I glower at her. "I would take all of those things back for you. I'd make him pay a hundredfold for every single thing he ever did to you."

"But why?" She throws her hands in the air. "It would change nothing."

"It would make you feel better," I insist.

"It wouldn't!"

"Fine. Then it would make *me* fucking feel better," I shout.

She blinks at me, her hazel eyes fixed on mine. "Why?" She whispers the word so quietly I almost don't hear it.

I have no idea why. No fucking clue why I care one single iota about making her shitbag of a husband pay for all the pain he caused her. So I ignore the question and try a different tactic. "Wouldn't you sleep easier at night if he was no longer breathing?"

"Knowing that you, Max, or Dante had a man's blood on your hands because of me?" She shakes her head emphatically. "No."

"I have so much blood on my hands, Mia. Trust me when I tell you that ten more pints of it won't make the slightest difference."

She folds her arms across her chest, pushing her ample tits together. "I disagree."

I snort. "What would you know?"

"I know that no matter how many lives a man takes, each one leaves their mark, Lorenzo. And if you were to have that on your conscience, on your soul—because of me—that would hurt more than anything he ever did."

Fuck me, she really means that. It's evident in the defiant tilt of her jaw and the way her hazel eyes sparkle green with fury and determination.

"Well, it seems like you got your wish anyway, because no one is laying a finger on him."

Her face lights up with a smile, like she somehow won.

"He'll come for you though. You know that, right? He's not going to just accept you walking out on him without a fight."

The light falls away from her expression and she nods.

I sit down and indicate she should do the same. "What would be his first move?"

"I thought maybe he'd file a missing person's report, but ..." With a shake of her head, she sinks her teeth into her full bottom lip. "I don't think he'd risk his police buddies finding out who he truly is. He'll track me down himself."

"That won't take long. He knows Kat's your cousin, right?"

She leans back in the chair with a sigh and pinches the bridge of her nose. "Yes. But he doesn't know where she lives."

"Hmm." I rub a hand over my beard. "With his connections, it won't take him long to find this place once he learns she's a Moretti. Is that Mustang yours or his?"

"It's his," she says quietly, sinking deeper into the chair.

"If I were him, I'd report it as stolen."

"I don't think he's as smart as you are." She gives me a faint smile. "But yeah, he probably will."

"We can't have cops turning up here looking for a stolen car."

She gasps. "I'm so sorry. I didn't think."

"I'll have someone drive it back to Boston and dump it near your house."

Looking down at her hands in her lap, she nods. "I'm sorry."

Seeing this strong, fiery woman so defeated and meek

causes something inside me to snap. "That's the third time you've apologized since you walked in here. Stop it."

"I'm ..." She presses her lips together. "It's a nervous tic."

Saying nothing, I stare at her.

"I appreciate you helping me out with this more than you will ever know. Thank you, Lorenzo."

"Like Dante said, you're family." Brushing her off, I grab my phone and make arrangements to have the Mustang picked up and taken back to Boston. She doesn't look like she's buying my feigned disinterest; she's staring at me with an expression full of curiosity and awe—as though I'm some hero who's going to save her. I'm not. I can't even save myself.

CHAPTER
SIX
MIA

Scooping baby Micah up from his play mat, I give him a squeeze. I've been here for over a week now, and I've barely gotten to spend any time with him.

"Hey, buddy. Your Uncle Lorenzo has been hogging my baby cuddles the whole time I've been here."

"Dada," he squeals, showing off his single tooth with a drooly grin.

Kat sidles up behind me, enunciating the syllables of my name. "Mee-uh."

"Dada," he repeats, clapping his hands with delight.

Kat rolls her eyes dramatically. "He's been saying dada for three weeks now, and he still refuses to say anything else."

"That's because his daddy is his favorite person in the world," Dante says, walking straight to his wife and wrapping her in his arms. He gives her a soft kiss on the lips, and she leans into him. The contented look on her face warms my heart. She had a shit time of it before she met him, and she deserves every ounce of happiness coming her way.

Kat looks up at Dante and smirks. "Try telling him that when he's screaming for a boob."

He nuzzles her neck and whispers something for her ears only judging by the way her cheeks turn red and she giggles. After a few seconds, she pushes him away. "We have a guest," she scolds.

"Mia isn't a guest. She's family. Right?" He directs the question to me.

"Right," I agree. "But that reminds me. I want to be helpful while I'm here. You guys have any jobs that need doing? Anyone got any muscle pain they need fixing?" I ask with a self-deprecating shrug.

Dante's brow furrows and he looks from me to Kat. "Muscle pain?"

"Mia's a trained and certified massage therapist," my cousin explains.

"Really? Huh. Lorenzo's had a stiff neck for a few weeks. He insists on sleeping on the sofa instead of in a bed."

Kat turns to face Dante, her features etched with concern. "He's still doing that?"

Dante nods, his brow furrowing.

Why is Lorenzo sleeping on the sofa? I don't ask that question out loud though because it seems impolite to ask them about Lorenzo's sleeping arrangements instead of asking him myself. "I'll see if he'll let me take a look. But is there anything else I can help with? Babysitting? Office work? Cleaning?"

"You don't have to do any of that, Mia. We have an army of staff here." Her cheeks flush. Before she married into the Moretti family, she cleaned office buildings, and she still isn't comfortable with having people pick up after her.

Dante and Kat share a look. "Actually, I think there is something you can help with."

Yes! I knew there must be a way I could earn my keep around here while staying occupied. "I'll do anything."

"We sold our old family home a few months back and a lot

of my mom's old papers, pictures, and books are still in boxes. Lorenzo and I were going to sort through it all, but we never seem to have the time. Could you take a look and try to find everything a new home in our library? The entire place is a bit of a mess to be honest, and you'll probably have to reconfigure the whole room to fit everything in, but there should be enough space."

"It would be my pleasure. That sounds like exactly the kind of project I'd be good at." Organization, books, and photographs are three of my favorite things. "And I'm so impressed you guys have a library here. I feel like I just dropped into Beast's castle." I laugh softly.

"Well, the only beast you'll find in our library is Lorenzo." Dante chuckles. "He usually works in there instead of in our study."

Kat gives me a conspiratorial grin. "Here's a pro tip—if he gets super grumpy, he can be calmed down with a huge slice of caramel cheesecake."

Dante rolls his eyes. "He and Kat have a particular thing for one of the bakeries downtown that I will never understand."

I nod my agreement and flash him a knowing smirk. Oh, I'm well aware of my cousin's cheesecake habit.

"Only because you don't like sweet things." Kat nudges him in the ribs, and he slides his hand down to her ass.

"I like *some* sweet things, kitten."

She blushes beet-red again and I turn away, talking to Micah and peppering his downy head with kisses because his parents look like they're about to need the room to themselves. Kat's voice has me turning my attention back to her. "Anyway, help yourself to the books in there. I added my own special section," she adds with a pop of one eyebrow.

I waggle my eyebrows back. "Oh?"

"You enjoy reading porn too, Mia?" Dante asks with a wicked grin.

I cover Micah's ear with my hand, mouth wide open as I feign my horror at his father's denigration of mine and his mom's reading material.

"It's smut," Kat insists.

"We've been reading cliterature since we were fourteen and we first discovered Anne Rice's Sleeping Beauty series," I say in defense of the finest genre of books to ever be created.

"Cliterature." He snorts a laugh and Kat gives him another dig in the ribs.

We're saved from the rest of the conversation by Max walking into the room. He greets Kat and me then he looks to Dante. "You ready, compagno?"

Dante sighs. "I hate the Strauss brothers."

"I know. But if we send Lorenzo ..."

Dante finishes his sentence. "We'll be cleaning up bits of brain from the casino carpet for weeks."

I press my lips together and squeeze Micah a little tighter to my chest. *Bits of brain?* Surely Lorenzo isn't that crazy? Right?

A FAMILIAR PIANO tune carries down the hallway as I approach the library, growing louder the closer I get. The song is being played so beautifully and hauntingly that it makes the hairs on the back of my neck stand on end. It's only when I'm standing outside the room that I realize it isn't a recording. Someone is actually playing the piano.

Lorenzo? I press my forehead against the door and listen to the soft melody grow louder and more insistent the longer he plays. Tears stream down my face as the pain in the notes, played so perfectly, washes over me.

A sob catches in my throat, and I can't resist opening the door. Engrossed in the tune, he doesn't hear me come in. His fingers glide effortlessly over the keys. Such talent. Where did he learn to play so beautifully? I watch him, transfixed, feeling like a voyeur by intruding on this private moment, but I'm unable to turn away. His head is bent low so I can't see his face, but I feel the anguish in his every keystroke.

I wipe a tear from my cheek and the movement must alert him to my presence because he stops playing and turns to me.

I walk over to him, wringing my hands. "I'm so sorry. I didn't mean to disturb you, but Dante asked me to sort through your mom's books and things. And then I heard you playing, and it was so beautiful and—"

"It's fine," he grunts, waving a dismissive hand and closing the lid of the piano.

"You play beautifully."

He doesn't respond. Instead he glares at me so fiercely that I feel like I might burst into flames.

"It's really hard to play Tchaikovsky. I've tried," I add with a weak laugh.

His eyes narrow. "You know that song?"

"'Flight of the Swans?' Of course. It's from the most famous ballet ever."

Looking down, he rubs a hand over his beard. "It was Anya's favorite."

I pluck up the courage to step closer. "Where did you learn to play like that?"

"My mom taught me."

"She must have been a good teacher."

A faint smile flickers over his lips. "She was."

"You don't have to stop on my account. I can come back later, or you can play while I work. You really do play exceptionally well. It was very"—a sob builds in my throat, and I swallow it down quickly—"moving."

He shakes his head. "I don't play for anyone else."

"Did you play for her? For Anya?"

He looks past me, his Adam's apple bobbing as he swallows hard. Finally, he nods. She was a lucky woman to have the love of a man like him. I'd voice that, but he wouldn't take kindly to me referring to his dead wife as lucky, so I remain uncharacteristically quiet.

He stands abruptly. "I'll leave you to get on with whatever you're doing."

I remain frozen to the spot, staring up at him as I feel a tugging on my heartstrings. It's my fault he stopped playing, and now he's leaving and I desperately want to ask him to stay. I'm sure that his wife's favorite song brings him some comfort, and now he looks so sad and lonely. But I also want him to stay because I feel something in his presence, something I haven't felt in such a long time that I don't even know how to describe it. Safe? Seen?

With a shake of my head, I clear my throat, aware that I'm staring at him like a moron. "I-I'll be working in here for the next few weeks I guess, depending on how much there is to sort through and organize. So, if there's times you like to be alone in here, then I can work around you, or ..." Squeezing my lips shut, I stop babbling.

His brow furrows in a frown. "Or?"

I chew on my lip. "Or, um. I kind of like company when I work, so don't ever feel like you can't be in here just because I am." *Why did I say that? This is his house. Of course he knows he can be in here whenever he wants. Moron!*

His frown deepens into a scowl, and I feel even more stupid than I did a few seconds ago. Without another word, he stalks out of the room, leaving me to let out the breath I was holding.

Well. That was awkward.

I glance around the room, eyeing the huge pile of boxes in the corner. Slipping off my shoes, I flex my toes on the warm wooden floor beneath my feet. I was so focused on Lorenzo, I failed to notice my incredible surroundings when I walked in here. I know I joked about Beast's castle, but this library really is like something from a fairytale. Three walls are lined with floor-to-ceiling shelves, most of which are crammed full of books. There's a ladder on each wall—the kind that has wheels and is attached to the bookcases. I brush my fingers along the spines as I pass by, noting the rare first editions and leather-bound encyclopedias. It's marvelous. I could spend six years here and not get bored. Stepping further into the room, I blink at the sunlight filling the space thanks to the massive sash windows.

Wandering to the large oak desk beneath the window, I run my fingers over the wood and smile to myself, imagining Lorenzo sitting here, head bent low and brow furrowed as he works, while I'm sorting through his mom's things in the corner. Although given the scowl on his face when he walked out of here a few moments ago, that's not likely to happen any time soon.

SEVEN
LORENZO

The library is filled with the scent of jasmine and lemon and it stops me in my tracks. She sits cross-legged on the floor, surrounded by piles of books. I forgot she was in here sorting through our mom's stuff. Before I can sneak out, she looks up and catches my eye, giving me a huge smile like seeing me is the best thing that's ever happened to her.

"Hey! I hope you don't mind me getting an early start, but I couldn't sleep knowing all this stuff needed sorting."

Clearing my throat, I close the door behind me. So she heard me playing piano last night; it isn't like I shared anything meaningful with her. Just because she's in here doesn't mean I can't work in here too. She'll stay on her side of the room, and I'll stay on mine.

"Morning," I say, taking a seat behind my desk.

"Your mom has some incredible first editions in here. Did you know that?"

I switch on my laptop and avoid her gaze. "Yes."

"I mean, some of these are super rare. Did you know she has—"

"I'm well aware of what books my mother owned, Mia." My tone might be overly harsh, but I have shit to do.

"Of course you are." She laughs softly, seemingly unaffected by me snapping at her. "She was your mom." She goes back to sorting through the books, and I open a file on my screen.

Less than a minute passes before she speaks again. "How long has it been since your mom died?"

Twenty-one years and five months. "Too long."

"My mom died when I was twenty-two. Eleven years later, and I still miss her every single day," she says with a sigh.

"Hmm," I murmur, keeping my eyes focused on the screen.

"But your dad only died a couple years back, right? That's why you sold your family home?"

Jesus fucking Christ. "Mia!" I immediately regret looking up when I see that beautiful smile of hers falter. Just for a second. But it's enough to make me feel like a total dick.

"I'm sorry. You're busy. Talking's my thing. It's always getting me into trouble." Looking down at the books in her lap, she sighs. "I'll leave you to your work now. Promise." She glances back at me with an apologetic smile, one that I don't deserve.

Feeling guilty, I return my attention to my screen and open the police report I received a few minutes ago that details the search of one of our warehouses last night. According to the report, the cops got an anonymous tip that we move weapons through there. Like we'd be stupid enough to use our legitimate businesses to move guns. That would defeat the entire purpose of *having* legitimate businesses.

Why did they act on this particular tip-off? We have an unwritten understanding that as long as we don't cause mayhem on the streets of Chicago or go around hurting "innocent" civilians, the police department won't bother us. I stare at the screen, looking for a clue. New cops trying to beef up their reputations? But no, I recognize the names of the officers listed.

The constant noise from the other side of the room makes it hard to focus, and I glance at Mia. She's happily sorting books and mumbling a tune to herself—the same song over and over.

"What the hell are you singing?"

She gives me a puzzled look. "'Bright Side of the Road.'"

I roll my head back and forth on my shoulders, trying to stave off the looming tension migraine. "Don't you know any others? You've been singing that one for the past ten minutes, and it's annoying."

She presses her lips together as though she's trying to suppress a smile. "You have any special requests?"

I twist my head from side to side. "How about silence?"

"How about I take a look at your neck for you?" Before I can refuse, she's already on her feet, brushing the dust from her jeans.

"I'm fine," I assure her.

Ignoring me, she draws closer. "It looks like you're kinda stiff and sore."

"I said it's fine. I have work to do," I bark, hoping my tone will scare her away. It's usually enough to make grown men shit their pants. But not her. No, she keeps coming at me, the smile on her face as bright as her yellow tank top. *What the fuck?*

"I'm a fully qualified massage therapist. It'll take me five minutes and you can go on working. I promise not to look at anything I'm not supposed to."

Her scent of jasmine and lemon scrambles my senses. "What?" What the fuck is she not going to look at? A bead of sweat rolls down my forehead. She doesn't expect me to remove my clothes for this massage, does she?

Laughing, she nods her head at my desk. "I won't look at anything on your computer."

Of course that's what she fucking meant. *For fuck's sake, Lorenzo. Hold it together!*

She walks up behind me and my entire body goes rigid. "Seems to be worse on your left side from what I've noticed?" Her warm, soft fingers brush the back of my neck.

I flinch at her touch.

"Is it sensitive?" Her voice is laced with concern.

"No," I snap, annoyed with myself for reacting the way I am. She's just a woman—no, a professional massage therapist giving me a neck massage. Nothing to get freaked out about.

"I see," she says softly. What does she see? That she's the first woman who's not related to me that I've allowed to touch my skin in over two years?

"It's just a stiff neck."

"I know. Just give me five minutes, and even if it doesn't feel better, all you've lost is a little time. And you'll have made me feel useful."

"Fine," I grunt, leaning forward.

Nimble fingers knead the back of my neck, surprisingly strong for someone with such small hands. Fuck, in fact, she's way stronger than she looks. I snarl when she finds the sensitive spot that's been plaguing me for weeks.

She chuckles. "Don't be a baby." Her warm breath dusts over my skin and a shiver runs the length of my spine.

I try to focus on the screen in front of me, but Mia's touch is too distracting. She presses deep into my muscles, causing waves of pain and relief to roll through my body. It hurts so fucking good ... I close my eyes and clamp my mouth shut so I don't groan her fucking name, because fuck me, her hands are magical.

"So, you're not a Van Morrison fan then?"

My eyes snap open. "Huh?"

"The song? 'Bright Side of the Road?' You don't like it?"

"Not a fan, no."

"It's my favorite," she says with a soft sigh.

Closing my eyes again, I refocus on the sweet relief her hands offer. My neck has been stiff for so long that I've forgotten what it felt like before.

Mia ignores my silence, needing no invitation to keep talking. "I just love the words. So full of hope, you know?" I try to tune her out and focus on her hands instead. That's so much less complicated than conversation. "It's my sunshine song."

Oh, fuck it. "Your what now?"

"My sunshine song," she replies matter-of-factly, as though I should know what the fuck that means.

"What the hell is a sunshine song?"

"Well, I have lots of sunshine things. A sunshine movie. TV show. Food. You know, the kind of thing that always makes you smile no matter how bad your day is? Like sunshine? 'Bright Side of the Road' is my sunshine song."

I frown. This woman clearly lives in a world that is so far removed from mine.

She laughs again. "I guess you don't have a sunshine song then?"

"No."

Her fingers knead deeper into my muscles, and the endorphins that flood my body make me grunt. She dips her head and some of her hair falls onto my shoulder. "I'll let you borrow mine if you like." Her warm breath dances over my cheek and, without warning, all the blood in my body rushes south.

What the motherfucking fuck!

I wrench out of her grip, ignoring the protests of my aching neck and my cock at the loss of her hands. "I need to get back to work," I bark, leaning away from her.

"Okay," she replies breezily, seemingly unbothered by my harsh tone. "Did it help at all though?"

I roll my neck and shoulders. It actually feels a fuckload better than it did a few minutes ago. "Yeah. Thanks."

"Well, give me a few minutes a day and I'll sort it out for you. And it's probably a good idea to stop sleeping on the sofa—"

"What?"

Her cheeks turn pink. "Kat and Dante mentioned you often sleep on the sofa. Isn't that why you have a stiff neck?"

Who the fuck do they think they are, discussing that with her? They know why I sleep on the sofa. They know ... My hands clench into fists. "Where I sleep is nobody's fucking business but mine."

Mia flinches away. "You're right. I'm sorry. I, uh, I'll leave you alone now."

I tell myself I'm relieved that she's finally leaving me alone, but if that's true, why the fuck do I keep stealing glances at her every few minutes? Bathed in sunlight, she sits beneath the window with her head bent low, humming that damn song to herself while she carefully sorts through my mother's most prized possessions. Her honey-blond hair falls in loose waves over her shoulders. She looks just like ...

Just like what, asshole?

Just like a ray of fucking sunshine.

EIGHT

LORENZO

I stalk down the hallway to the study, aggravated for reasons I can't fully explain. It's not my usual simmering anger, but a bone-deep irritation that I'm unable to fathom or fix. What the hell is wrong with me lately? Maybe I need to beat someone to death.

Maybe I need to do something else ... A shiver runs down my spine and my cock twitches at the memory of her hands on me. Her soft voice in my ear. Her breath on my skin ...

"Lorenzo?" I turn in the direction of Max's voice and find him frowning at me. "You okay, compagno?"

"Yeah, why?"

"You blew right by me, and I had to call your name twice before you answered."

Sighing, I pinch the bridge of my nose. "I got a lot on my mind."

"Well, I hate to add to your load, but Joey just called ..."

"What is it now?"

"Cops at the casino. Checking out reports of prostitution and underage drinking and gambling. They're going through the place right now. Joey's handling it, but I wanted to let you

53

know that I'm headed down there. Dante's gone to that meeting for the new shipping contracts."

"With the Benettis, yeah?" I shake my head. "I'll come with you."

"You know we can't kill no cops today, right?" Smirking at me, he winks.

"Damn fucking shame," I say, only half joking. "You know they were in the warehouse last night dealing with another anonymous tip?"

"Yeah, I heard."

"It's no fucking coincidence the casino gets hit the next day."

"Nope. But your sister runs the tightest, cleanest operation I've ever seen. They won't find anything."

"Someone *is* fucking with us though." And I have a feeling I know exactly who it is.

I SPOT my sister as soon as we walk into the lobby of our hotel and casino. She runs this side of the business and does a great job. She's currently arguing with a cop and, from the look on the guy's face, I'd say she's winning. Joey's one of the toughest and smartest people I know. Max sure has his work cut out for him.

Turning to me, he rolls his eyes. "I'll go talk my wife down before she gets arrested for punching a cop in the face."

"Good luck with that, compagno." Giving his shoulder a squeeze, I scan the lobby for a familiar face.

I spot the man I'm looking for. While Max makes his way over to defuse the bomb that is my sister, I head toward the guy scribbling in his notebook near the main desk.

Leo Romano is a good cop. We have plenty of Chicago's

finest on our payroll, but this man isn't one of them, which is why I value his opinion more than most. He and I went to high school together, and I once saved his ass after he kissed the star quarterback's girl at a party. We keep our distance because we live very different lives, but I admire his integrity and he has a grudging respect for my family and the good we've done in this city over the years.

"Lorenzo." Sighing, he shakes his head. "You know I can't tell you nothin'."

"I'm not asking for details, Leo." I lean on the reception desk beside him. "But this is the second raid on my family's businesses in two days. Now, we both know that's no coincidence."

He tilts his head and eyes me with curiosity. "Can't tell you nothin'."

"I think I already know."

"You do, huh?"

"If you're taking these tips seriously, they must be coming from a source high up the chain. Either that or someone who's able to whisper in the right ears."

Leo doesn't answer. His jaw ticks as he stares at me.

"What I can't figure is how a Boston cop has so much sway here in Chicago?"

Leo shakes his head, a grin tugging at the corner of his mouth. "You're fuckin' unbelievable."

Looks like my instincts were spot on; Mia's husband somehow has a hand in this mess. "You know I'll find out anyway."

"Well, not from me. I ain't sayin' a damn thing."

I edge closer, crowding his personal space. "He have links to your department or something?"

He shakes his head, every bit as pissed about being here, going through these motions, as I am about having the Chicago fucking PD in my family's casino.

I look around the lobby, counting the number of cops I can see. "You know this is a waste of your goddamn time, Leo. You know our warehouses and our casino are clean, yet you and three of your—"

"Four," he interrupts me, tone full of annoyance. "Four of my guys they got on this."

I arch an eyebrow. Looks like I'll need to push his buttons a little more. "You and four of your guys are wasting time in here when you could be doing some actual police work. So tell me what the hell this cop has on your captain to make shit like this happen?"

Leo scowls. "Not the captain." As far as Leo is concerned, Captain Ortega is a fucking modern-day hero.

"The chief?"

He hikes his thumb up, indicating this goes higher.

I frown. "Superintendent Keane?"

"His deputy." He gives me a wry smile. "But you ain't never heard that from me."

I choke down a laugh. "You're a closed book, Leo."

"Yeah? Well I got work to do, Mr. Moretti," he says as one of his officers wanders over.

Taking the hint, I step back. "Of course, Detective. Please make sure you and your men clean up after yourselves when you leave my family's establishment."

My jaw clenches at the sight of Max and Joey huddled together near the elevators. Whatever he whispers in her ear makes her laugh, and the sound of her joy has me grinding my teeth. What the fuck is wrong with me? She's my baby sister, I want her to be happy. Fuck, I threatened to feed Max his balls if he ever did anything to make her unhappy. But why the hell must I be constantly surrounded by couples so sickeningly in love?

Seeing me approach, Joey gives me a triumphant smile.

"They're clearing out of here in a few minutes. They found nothing. Assholes."

"Yeah." I glance around to make sure none of the officers are within earshot. "It seems a certain Boston cop has the ear of the deputy superintendent, and that's why we've had two raids in two days. We need to double-check that everything connected to Moretti Holdings is one hundred percent clean. Once they realize we have nothing to hide, they'll back off. There's only a finite amount of manpower they can waste on leads that go nowhere."

Max nods. "Everything's clean, but I'll make some extra checks."

"A Boston cop?" Joey says with a frown. "You think Mia's husband's behind this?"

"Absolutely. He somehow has the ear of the deputy super, and I want to know why."

"I'll look into it," Max assures me.

Deep in thought, Joey chews on her lip. "Do you think Mia knows anything about their connection?"

"No, I think she'd have mentioned it. Either way, she doesn't need to know about this yet. She'll only worry herself sick."

Joey and Max share a fleeting look that makes me feel like they know something I don't.

"What?" I bark.

"It's just you, uh ..." Joey presses her lips together.

"I what?"

"You don't usually give a fuck about anyone who's not one of us, Loz," Max finishes for her.

Rage bubbles beneath my skin, and I snarl. What the fuck does that mean? "She's Kat's cousin, that makes her one of us."

Max holds his hands up in surrender. "Calm down,

compagno. Just nice to know you're not completely dead inside, that's all."

Is he suggesting that Mia and I ...? That I'm— "And just what the fuck does that mean?"

My kid sister reads the murderous expression on my face and, shooting a warning look at her husband, wraps an arm around my shoulder. "He only means that it's nice to see you care about someone, Loz. Nothing more than that. We all care about Mia. You're right. She's one of us."

Glaring at my best friend, I crack my neck. "Hmm."

Max arches his eyebrows at me, the corner of his mouth tilted up in amusement. I swear, I'd punch the fucker in the face if the cops weren't still hanging around. "I guess I'll get to work on finding the link between Mia's ex-husband and the deputy."

"Yeah, you do that," I snap and walk away.

Taking my cell out of my pocket, I dial the number of an old friend.

Lionel Hart answers with his distinctive smooth Southern drawl. "Mr. Moretti. It's been a long time." He sucks in a breath, taking a heavy drag on the cigarette I can picture dangling from his lips.

"I need a favor." I glance at Max and Joey, making sure they didn't follow me.

"Off the books?"

"I wouldn't be calling you if it wasn't."

He takes another drag of his smoke. "I'm retired, Lorenzo."

"Yeah, right." I roll my eyes. "It's nothing big. Nothing that'll get your hands dirty."

"Shame," he says with a soft chuckle. "So what is it?"

"I need some information on a guy. A cop."

"Ah." He laughs again. "I see."

"No point in knowing a former FBI agent if he's no use to me occasionally." Jaded by the whole system, Lionel left the bureau twenty years ago and has worked freelance ever since. He's sixty-six and swears every year that he's going to retire, but the hunt is in his blood. "So, can you help me out?"

"Sure. I'm working a case for some oil tycoon right now, but I can do a little digging in my downtime. Send me his details. I'll see what I can find."

"Great. Check in when you have something for me."

I end the call and slip my cell back into my pocket. Catching Max's eye, I jerk my head at him, letting him know I'm ready to get the fuck out of here.

NINE

MIA

Running my hands self-consciously over my hips in front of the mirror, I study the way the orange material stretches across my frame. "You're sure this isn't too tight on me?" I ask Kat.

She places her hand on my upper arm and checks out my reflection. "It looks stunning. Everything looks stunning on you." She curls a lock of my hair between her fingers before letting it fall over my shoulder. Then she gives me a playful swat on the behind. "You're a knockout."

I roll my eyes, dismissing her compliment. "My ass and boobs are way fatter than yours though," I insist, trying to pull the material up over my straining cleavage.

Kat wrinkles her nose. "Not really. Maybe a cup size bigger than me, but the dress fits you beautifully." She slaps my hand away. "Now stop fidgeting."

I drop my hands to my sides. There's no way she's looking in the same mirror I am. Kat has an enviably slim figure, while I'm always at least ten pounds overweight. "It's not too revealing for the dinner table?"

"It's a wrap dress, Mia," she says with a dramatic eye roll. "Not a bodycon mini."

I didn't bring much with me, and I'm running out of things to wear. Dinner at the Moretti mansion is a semiformal affair most evenings, and I don't want to embarrass my cousin by wearing jeans and a tank top when everyone else is dressed up. "Thanks for the loan."

"You should keep it. That color is perfect on you." She wrinkles her nose and I see where Gabriella gets that very same expression from. "It doesn't suit me."

"I can't take this. I bet this dress cost more than my last car!"

She grins at me. "All the more reason you should have it. It's like an asset."

I laugh. "I could sell it if I ever have to go on the run."

"Seriously though, it looks incredible on you, Mia Melon." She wraps her arm around me, and her use of my childhood moniker warms my heart. "I'm so glad you're here."

"I'm glad I'm here too, Kat Cabana," I reply, resting my head on hers. We stand like that for a few beats, smiling at each other in the mirror the way we used to when we were thirteen years old and life was so much simpler.

JOEY JUMPS up to give me a hug when I walk into the dining room with Kat by my side. "Wow! You look hot." She pulls back and looks me over from head to toe. "That color's amazing on you."

Kat takes a glass of wine from Dante and turns to Joey. "Isn't it?"

My cheeks flush pink at their praise.

"Yeah. I never did like it on you, but on Mia ..." Joey's face lights up with a wicked grin.

"You were the one who persuaded me to buy it!"

"I know." Joey winces. "It looked good on you in the store, but I think it was the lighting. Green and blue are definitely more your colors."

Kat gives her sister-in-law a look of mock-betrayal and shakes her head. "Remind me to never take you shopping again."

"I did help you choose that incredible green dress you wore for your wedding anniversary." Joey wiggles her eyebrows. "The one you said Dante tore in half because he—"

"Enough, Joey," Dante says good-naturedly, shooting Kat a smoldering glance that makes her blush. Then he turns his attention to me and hands me a glass of wine. "You look very nice, Mia."

"It's a beautiful dress," I reply self-consciously, smoothing the fabric over my thighs. I turn to the table and notice Lorenzo sitting by himself, nursing a glass of Scotch. He's looking down at his drink, but my skin tingles like his eyes had been locked on me only seconds before.

"Do you have to cause trouble everywhere you go, baby girl?" Max asks Joey as he pulls out her chair.

"You know I do," she replies with a soft giggle, and the sound he gives in response makes me smile. Everything about being around this family makes me happy. They're so close-knit and care about each other so much. I'm privileged to have been allowed inside their little bubble, if only for a short while.

"Speaking of trouble, I heard there was some at the casino today?" Dante asks as he takes his seat at the head of the table.

Max and Lorenzo share a brief glance, but it's Joey who answers. "The cops received a tip that we had some underage patrons and were also running hookers out of the place. Obviously it wasn't true. It's handled."

"Yeah. All sorted," Max agrees.

Dante turns to his older brother. "Loz?"

"Dealt with," Lorenzo replies.

Dante frowns and takes a sip of his wine. Everyone remains silent for a few seconds, and when he speaks again, I see Lorenzo roll his eyes in my peripheral vision like he's annoyed that his younger brother won't let this drop. "Why did the cops act on such a bogus tip-off? Where did it come from?"

"We'll discuss it later," Lorenzo says, fists and jaw clenched.

Dante glares at his older brother. "I'd rather we discuss it now."

Lorenzo glares back at him. "It's handled."

Dante's hand balls into a fist on the table. "Why are the cops acting on tip-offs about our casino instead of speaking to us about it?"

"Because it came from a source they deemed reliable."

Dante seems to take Lorenzo's tone as a signal to stop asking questions, but my heart sinks through my stomach. "It was Brad, wasn't it? He's been making trouble for you?"

"It's handled," Lorenzo repeats sternly.

Dante's nostrils flare. "Did it have anything to do with that fucker?"

"I'm so sorry," I whisper, wishing I'd never come here at all. The last thing I wanted was to cause trouble. I should have known Brad would try something underhand.

Joey squeezes my left hand. "You have nothing to be sorry for, Mia. We dealt with the cops and Max and Loz are looking into Brad's connection to the deputy superintendent."

"He's connected to the deputy?" Dante asks with a frown.

Max speaks up. "It seems so, but we don't know how yet. We're looking into it."

Dante growls. "This is all we need."

Oh, god. "I'm so sorry," I say again.

"You have nothing to apologize for, Mia," Kat assures me. However, her husband looks like he's about to start foaming at the mouth.

"I do. I'm so sorry I brought this trouble to you all. I'll leave first thing in the morning. I'll find somewhere to go. I'm so sorry. I had no idea that Brad had any connection to anyone high up in the Chicago PD, because if I had—"

"Mia!" Lorenzo's deep voice cuts through my breathless chatter and a deafening silence falls over the room, broken only by me sucking in air. My blood thunders in my ears. "None of this is your fault," he says, his tone calm and reassuring.

"He's right, Mia." Dante sighs. "Please don't think my anger at your ex-husband is in any way directed at you."

"B-but I—"

"Enough," Lorenzo barks, and this time his tone slices through me like a hot knife through butter, rendering me speechless, but not in an unpleasant way. I can't explain the feeling that settles over me, but I sit back in my chair and shut my mouth, content not to speak for the moment.

"I'll have some information by tomorrow," Max says.

Dante nods approvingly. "And last night, Joey? Max told me there was some trouble?"

Joey takes a sip of her wine before she replies. "Iman and his crew turned up, which isn't a big deal. But they got pretty wasted on the complimentary drinks at the high rollers' table and insulted two of our biggest female investors. Security dealt with them, and the ladies said they were fine, but I don't like women getting hassled in our casinos."

I listen to the ongoing discussions about the casino and the Moretti business empire, thankful for a distraction from Brad even if the amount of drama this family deals with on a daily basis sounds exhausting. Still conscious of Lorenzo's earlier command, I refrain from apologizing again about adding to their stress.

"Max and I will pay Iman a visit tomorrow," Lorenzo says, which earns him a grin from Max.

Dante raises his eyebrows at the two of them. "Just try not to kill anyone, eh?"

Before either of them can answer, two housekeepers walk into the room carrying dinner and all talk of murder and mayhem is put on ice.

CHAPTER
TEN

LORENZO

Max stretches his neck, his dark eyes fixed on the man currently lying on the floor at my feet with blood running from his ears and a piss stain on the crotch of his pants.

"I don't think he knows anything, Loz."

I kick the piece of shit in the chest and he coughs blood onto the floor. "You hear anything from Iman and you'll let me know?"

He sputters some more.

"Pretty sure he can't hear a fucking thing you said after you burst his eardrums," Max says with a dark chuckle.

"Hmm." I look at the two metal kebab skewers on the ground, coated with his blood. This dog turd and his boss are the least of my problems right now, but they disrespected one of our biggest investors at our own casino, and for that they must pay. I crouch down on my heels, grabbing his jaw in my hands and squeeze hard, forcing him to meet my glare. "Tell Iman I want to see him." I mouth each word carefully so he can read my lips. "Or you both die. Understand me?"

He nods furiously, aware that the fact he's still breathing is nothing short of a miracle. I'm not usually such a man of mercy, especially these days. I don't know what the fuck's gotten into me.

I stand up, brushing the creases from my suit pants and follow Max out of the restaurant.

"You had some kind of epiphany or something, Loz?" Max asks me as we climb into his car.

"Fuck you," I mutter, making him laugh.

"Hey, I'm happy not having to help dispose of dead bodies every other day."

"Yeah, well don't get used to it." I lean back in my seat, close my eyes, and pinch the bridge of my nose. I'm so fucking agitated. I have no idea why I didn't kill that stupid fuck in there. I barely slept at all last night. Every damn time I tried to doze off, all I could see were dangerous curves wrapped in orange fabric. Holy mother of fucks, why did she have to come to dinner dressed like that? Not that it was inappropriate, but it was way too distracting.

My cock twitches.

Fuck! I scrunch my eyes tighter, trying to rid my brain of the memory of her in that goddamn dress. And why is her seat at the table directly opposite mine, where I have no choice but to look at her all fucking night? Is it not bad enough that she's invaded my library? Now she's invaded my every waking thought. And that ass ... so fine it should have its own national holiday.

"I got some information on Deputy Superintendent Hayes," Max says.

My eyes snap open and I turn to him, thankful for an entirely different kind of distraction.

"Seems he was a beat cop back in Boston when Brad was a rookie. They were partners for a year before Hayes applied for a transfer. He moved to Chicago and rose up the ranks pretty quick."

"So they're old partners? Buddies?"

"Not buddies from what I hear. Seems like Hayes's move was related to some kind of fallout between him and Brad."

I run a hand over my beard. "You learn what that was about?"

"Not yet."

"If they're not buddies, Brad must have something on Hayes."

"Makes sense."

I grind my teeth. My jaw ticks. "Find out what it is, Max."

He doesn't ask me if I'm going to ask Mia if she knows anything about it, even though I can tell that's what he's thinking. But after my reaction at the casino yesterday, he holds his tongue, for which I'm grateful. Mia Stone brings out my protective streak, and I'm not prepared to consider why.

And I'm certainly not ready to have anyone else think about it either.

MY THOUGHTS ARE STILL on Deputy Superintendent Hayes and what Brad Mulcahy might have on him when I walk into the library. Her sweet scent fills my nostrils, and I stop in my tracks. Of course she's in here. She's always in here. Fuck. I need space from her. Space to think clearly.

"You okay?" she asks breezily as she continues to pull papers from a brown cardboard box.

I realize I'm still standing in the doorway, probably looking like I forgot what I came in here for. "Yeah." I stride over to my desk, refusing to glance in her direction with the hope that she'll take the hint that I'm busy and don't have time for her endless chattering.

"It's beautiful out today, right? I know it's cold, but it's so bright and fresh. I took a walk in the gardens earlier, and I had no idea—"

"Mia!" Squeezing my eyes shut, I rub my temples. "Do you have to talk all the goddamn time?"

Even from here, I see her throat constrict and her cheeks flush pink. A pang of guilt slices through my chest. I'm annoyed and frustrated, and yes, a lot of that has to do with her, but that's not exactly her fault.

"I'm s-sorry," she says softly, wringing her hands in front of her. God, I'm such a fucking prick. She continues before I can apologize for snapping at her. "I know I talk way too much. Brad always told me that too. He hated it ..." She shakes her head like she's trying to dislodge an unwanted memory. Curling my fingers into fists at my sides, I curse silently, annoyed at myself. "I'll give you a little peace and quiet." She bows her head and walks silently from the room, leaving me to stare after her, feeling like the world's most insensitive asshole. I despise him for making her feel bad for being who she is. But I despise myself even more for having anything in common with that motherfucker.

I should go after her and apologize. Tell her she doesn't need to change a single thing about herself for anyone. But I don't. Better she knows what an insensitive, heartless bastard I am than think there's anything but anger, despair, and bitterness inside me.

∾

WITH MY EYES closed and my palms flat on the tiled wall, I stand in the shower. Usually, the scalding water takes the edge off a little, but not today. Nothing soothes me lately. Pent-up tension and rage bristle beneath my skin. My muscles are tense as fuck. My cock is rock hard and has been for the past hour. After Mia left the library, I kept seeing that tormented look I put on her face. The hurt I etched there. And then I imagined her gazing at me like that for an entirely different reason. What if I could give her a completely different kind of hurt? The kind that walks the thin line between pleasure and pain.

No! I shake my head and bang my fists on the tiles and imagine Anya's face. Blue eyes and ash-blond hair. High cheekbones and pale pink lips.

I squeeze the base of my shaft hard, waiting for the relief to seep into my bones, but none comes. I pump fast, hoping some of the tension will start to dissipate as a climax builds. But it doesn't. Nothing helps.

Screwing my eyes tightly shut, I comb through the memories I have saved for moments like these. The thousands of times I fucked my wife. But they all elude me. All I can see is Mia's face. The pain. The way she smiles even when she's hurting. Heat sears in my chest, tightening my balls. Would she smile like that if I …

"Fuck!" I roar, banging my clenched fist against the wall.

I can't think about anyone but Anya while I'm jacking off. Can't think about anything but her beautiful body. That's the way it's been for as long as I can remember. That's the way it will always be. But when I close my eyes again, even her face eludes me.

I press my forehead against the cool tiled walls and release my grip on my aching cock. It throbs painfully, but there's no relief for me if it's not with her.

ELEVEN

LORENZO

"You'll be around for dinner, right?" Dante asks as we walk down the hallway to our study. "We missed you the last two nights."

I answer with a grunt. It's true that I've been avoiding dinner since I snapped at Mia a couple of days ago. But I guess she's been avoiding me too because I've barely seen her. I know she's been in the library—boxes have been moved and her goddamn scent hasn't faded. But she must be sticking to times when she doesn't think I'll be there.

Dante arches an eyebrow at me. "You been going anywhere in particular?"

My muscles tense. "Working."

His brow wrinkles with concern. "On anything I should know about?"

My phone rings, saving me from having to answer my brother. I check the screen; it's Lionel's number. "I have to take this."

Dante narrows his eyes and nods. "Go ahead then."

I glance between him and the phone. We never keep secrets from each other, but for some reason, I don't tell him who's calling. Not even when the look he gives me makes me think he believes this is something personal, which it's definitely not.

The corners of his mouth curl up in amusement. "Dinner? Tonight?"

"I'll be there," I snap.

"Good." With a satisfied grin, he walks off down the hallway, leaving me to answer my call in private.

"Yeah?" I push open the door to the library, both annoyed and relieved to find it empty. It's been two days since I last spoke to her. Surely she's not still pissed at me.

"Lorenzo, you there?" Shit. How long has he been talking? I once again allowed myself to become distracted by thoughts of Mia when I should be thinking about anything but her.

"You got something for me?"

"That guy you asked me to look into, you know he had a sister?"

I'm one hundred percent sure Mia never mentioned a sister-in-law. "No."

"Hmm, thought as much. I don't got a lot on her. Her records are sealed—"

"Sealed?"

"Yep."

I attempt to rub away the persistent throb in my temples with my knuckles. "Why would that happen?"

"Any situation where a minor's the victim of a crime would account for sealed records, but this seems to go deeper than that. I couldn't access most of it."

"You can usually get to that shit though, right?" I frown. I've never known Lionel to be unable to access information, even high-level stuff. It's why I use him. "Why can't you get this?"

"I figure it involves someone important."

I run a hand through my hair. This is all I need. "So, what exactly do you know about her?"

"Name's Michaela Mulcahy. She was born in 1989 to Mike and Janice. She has two older brothers, Bradley and Jake. Then there's nothing of note on the entire family until she turns thirteen. Something happened that caused her to be removed from the home the same year her mom died. Apparent suicide."

My chest tightens. Did Mia's ex-husband learn everything he knows about beating women from dear old dad? "Apparent?"

"Yeah. I looked over the police reports and there was some controversy, but ultimately the coroner ruled suicide."

"How did she die?"

"Hanged."

"Fuck."

"But that's not the most disturbing fact about this case, Lorenzo." The tone of his voice sends a chill down my spine. He continues. "Michaela's aren't the only records that are sealed. There was evidence of recent sexual activity after Janice was found hanging from the back of the bathroom door."

"That doesn't seem so unusual, especially if the husband did kill her."

"It wasn't the husband's DNA they found inside her, Lorenzo. It was the son's."

Bile burns the back of my throat. "What the fuck? The son? Brad raped his own mother?"

"Well, this is where it gets patchy. These records are sealed tighter than a nun's cunt," He gives a dark laugh at his own wit but clears his throat when I remain silent. "Bradley would have been seventeen at the time, and the other son, Jake, he'd have been fifteen. Most of what I got is conjecture and witness testimony, but the official story is mom and Bradley were having sex, and when the father found out, mom killed herself to avoid the scandal and possible prosecution."

I hiss out a breath. I thought my family was fucked up.

"However," Lionel goes on, "Janice had a sister, Minerva, who refused to accept the coroner's verdict. Convinced Janice was a victim and was murdered to cover up the whole disgusting affair. She continued to campaign for her sister's death to be investigated for another two years, but then she died in a car accident."

"Suspicious circumstances, right?"

"Yup. Quiet road late at night. The other car was never found."

Dammit! "And the daughter? Michaela? What happened to her?" The sister could be the key to nailing that sick fuck once and for all.

"No fuckin' clue. She disappeared without a trace."

"So find her, Li. If the records are sealed, unseal them." Rage courses through my veins and turns my voice into a growl.

"Spent the last few days trying, buddy. If I could, I would. This case has me more intrigued than anything I've worked on in the past ten years. This involved someone real high up to seal these records the way they did. They're watertight. Way above my pay grade."

"What about the father? Mike Mulcahy? Where is he now? Does he have that kind of pull?"

"He died four years back. Massive heart attack. He was a police chief, highly decorated and respected. But still, he definitely didn't have that kind of sway."

My hands clench into fists and sink into the huge leather chair behind my desk. "For fuck's sake."

"Sorry I ain't got more for ya, buddy. I'll keep digging, see if there's anything else I can come up with."

"Yeah," I say with a sigh. At least I know more now than I did an hour ago. And not that I needed further proof that Brad Mulcahy needs to be wiped from the face of the earth, but I sure have it. Sick, twisted fuck. I can't even imagine what happened to his kid sister.

"I have to go to Abu Dhabi for a few days," he says with a dramatic sigh. "That oil guy is making me work for my money. But I'll get right back on it as soon as I get home."

I thank him and end the call, my mind racing with more questions than ever. I need a fucking drink. Or maybe I need a completely different kind of distraction.

Mia opens the door, her eyes widening when they land on me. "I'm s-sorry." Her cheeks flush pink and her voice gets quieter. "I thought you were out. I'll come back later."

"Don't be ridiculous, Mia," I snap, harsher than I intended, but Lionel's revelations have me on edge.

She frowns, rolling her shoulders back before stepping into the room. "You don't have to be so rude. I was being polite," she replies, her tone clipped. She walks to the pile of boxes where she's been working, her movements stiff and her whole demeanor cold and detached. Nothing like the woman who's spent the last few weeks in this house. The Mia I've gotten to know is always full of warmth, rarely seen without a smile on her face.

A wave of guilt rolls through my gut. How many times has she forced herself to be a lesser version of who she is to placate a man?

I push my chair back and wander over to her side of the room. She barely glances at me, focusing instead on the pile of books in front of her. "Have you been avoiding me, Mia?" The flush on her cheeks creeps down her neck.

For a few seconds, I wonder if she's going to brush me off, but she looks me square in the face, full of confidence and a defiance that makes all the blood in my body head south. "I've been giving you space, is all. I assumed you were happier working in here alone."

My jaw clenches. I should tell her that's true. It should be true. Except it's not. "Actually, I kind of missed you."

Her eyes spark with the kind of unrestrained happiness that should make me turn around and walk out of this room without looking back, but I can't pull my gaze from hers. There's something magnetic about those hazel-green eyes. But this is strictly platonic. What's wrong with enjoying the company of a beautiful woman when nothing will ever happen between us?

"You did?"

"I guess I've gotten used to your background noise," I say with a shrug. "It's quiet in here without you."

I watch her throat bob as she swallows. "I know I talk way too much," she says. "Brad hated it. He was always telling me to shut my yammering. Sometimes I think that made me worse." Her laugh is full of self-deprecation and humility.

That simmering anger bubbles beneath my skin. I fucking hate that her prick of an ex-husband talked to her that way. I hate that he ever made her feel like she's anything less than perfect just the way she is. "You talk the exact right amount, Mia."

She sinks her teeth into her full bottom lip, her eyes crinkling at the corners. "Now I know you're just being nice." She laughs softly. "I'm aware that I'm a chatterbox, so you can tell me if I'm talking too much. I don't mind, honestly."

"Maybe I should be a little less of an ass about it in future," I suggest.

"I really wasn't avoiding you, Lorenzo. Not in the way you think, anyway. I just thought you didn't want me in here and this is your space. I'm a guest. Besides, you haven't been at dinner the past few nights. Were you avoiding me?"

I don't particularly want to tell her that I've been feeling guilty about the way I spoke to her, so I lie. "I've been busy."

"Well, I kinda missed you at dinner," she says softly, that flush on her cheeks deepening further.

My heart rate kicks up a notch. I clear my throat and change the subject. "Do you know anything about Brad having a sister?"

Her brows pinch together. "No. He doesn't have a sister."

"It seems he does. She was a few years younger than him. Looks like she was removed from the home when she was thirteen, but I can't find the reason."

Her frown deepens. "Brad never mentioned a sister to me. Neither did his brother or his dad. Are you sure?"

"I'm sure. So there was never any mention of her anywhere? Any old pictures with a girl you didn't recognize maybe?"

She shakes her head. "No. But they didn't have any family photos. Brad told me his dad burned them all after their mom killed herself."

"She hanged herself, right?"

"Yeah. So sad," she says softly. "Poor Brad and Jake never really got over it."

I tilt my head, cracking my neck. Maybe I should tell her about *poor* Brad and what he did to his own mother, but it would bring her no peace, so I keep quiet.

Mia stares at me intently, her lips pressed together like she's deep in thought. "You have any idea where this sister of theirs is?"

I shake my head. "No. Nothing."

"How strange."

"Yeah, well families are strange, right?"

She smiles up at me. "Your family is wonderful though."

"That's because you've only met the nice ones," I assure her.

That makes her laugh. "I like talking to you, Lorenzo. Or at you." She grins at her own joke. "It's been a long time since I've had a friend." Tears prick at her eyes, and she gives her head a brief shake.

A friend. The tension in my shoulders loosens a little. That's all we are and there's no need for me to fear being alone in her company. I hold out my hand. "Friends?"

"Friends." She curls her delicate fingers around mine, and I try to ignore the warmth that spreads through my forearm at her touch, curling itself like a snake through my veins.

TWELVE

MIA

I feel his presence in the room before I even see him, and my heart flutters in my chest at the sight of him sitting alone at the kitchen table. I'd like to say I have no idea why I enjoy his company so much, but I'd be lying to myself. Lorenzo Moretti is a complex and wonderful man, and he's become a true friend to me the past three weeks. It's been two days since he admitted that he missed me in the library. Two days since I felt the strange fluttering in my stomach—when he looked at me like that. When he made me believe, just for a second, that there might be another reason he missed me besides having grown used to my background noise.

But he's just a friend. Nothing more. He's clearly still grieving for his wife, and I'm still married.

I take a seat opposite him and pour myself a mug of coffee from the pot on the table. My eyes are drawn to the delicious-looking cheesecake he's eating, and the scent of sweet caramel makes my stomach growl.

"I'm sorry. I took the last piece," he says with an apologetic shrug.

"That's okay. I had a snack earlier. Some carrots and cucumber sticks."

His top lips curl with disgust. "You call that a snack?"

I smirk at him. "You don't like vegetables?"

He tilts his head as though deep in thought. "I like them just fine, as an accompaniment to a meal. Except cucumber. That stuff's the work of the devil."

"Noted," I say with a soft laugh. He's funny even though he doesn't mean to be. "Anyway, I don't eat dessert."

His eyes narrow in suspicion. "Why not?"

I blink at him. "What?"

"I asked you why not."

I shift in my seat. "What kind of a question is that?"

A frown furrows his brow. "A straightforward one. Why don't you eat dessert?"

Old memories and lingering shame cause heat to creep up my neck and cheeks. I don't want to answer, but Lorenzo stares at me, patiently waiting for my reply. "Sugar and fat go straight to my ass. I'm always ten pounds heavier than I should be, and dessert does not look good on a body like mine."

His jaw ticks. "Who told you that?"

"What?"

His frown deepens. "Are you having trouble hearing today? I asked who the hell told you that?"

I swallow a lump of emotion. Years of being belittled for my size and my tendency to put on a few pounds during the holidays, constant monitoring of what I ate and thinly veiled criticism if I ate even the slightest bit of anything sweet—all of that left a mark. "Brad told me—"

Lorenzo snarls.

"But it's true. I am really susceptible to gaining weight if I don't eat healthy."

He snorts and looks down at the cheesecake in front of him.

I dip my head, so not wanting to have this conversation. A large bite of cheesecake appears in front of me. "What?" I look between him and the gooey dessert two inches from my face.

"Eat."

I blink at him. *Is he for real?* "I-I can't."

"Yeah, you can." He inches the fork closer to my lips, and despite my embarrassment, I find myself opening my mouth and allowing him to feed me. As soon as the flavor hits my tongue, the sweet taste floods my senses, making me moan softly in appreciation. My eyes flutter closed. Oh! This is so good. My tastebuds are overwhelmed by rich, tart cream cheese, velvety caramel, and the slightest hint of salt, and I'm reminded how much I love dessert. This cheesecake is divine.

Lorenzo pulls the fork from my mouth, and I lick my lips before swallowing. "Thank you," I whisper.

"You're welcome." He takes a bite for himself, licking the fork—the one that was just in my mouth—clean before scooping up another chunk and holding it out to me.

Raising my hand, I shake my head. "No, you enjoy it."

The corners of his mouth curl upward. "I'm gonna enjoy watching you enjoy it."

Holy crap! I open my mouth again and he pushes the fork inside slowly, as though he's savoring the moment. It feels so intimate. Too intimate. Heat coils deep in my core.

I suck the cheesecake from the tines, sweeping my tongue over every nook to savor the sweet, delicious substance. Lorenzo keeps his gaze fixed on mine, making no attempt to pull the fork from my mouth. I'm hyperaware of the fact that he licked it clean only seconds earlier, and a throbbing ache builds inside me.

Why does this moment feel so sensual? His fork is in my mouth, but it may as well be his tongue for the way my body reacts. Pulse thrumming against my pressure points. Skin flushed. Wet heat pooling between my thighs.

His eyes darken as he pulls the fork from my mouth. His attention remains locked on me while he takes another bite for himself, repeating the process again and again until he's feeding me the last morsel. I keep my lips closed around the fork a little longer than necessary, wanting to prolong whatever this is. I don't remember the last time a man looked at me with the kind of hunger I see in Lorenzo's gaze.

When he pulls away a few seconds later, I almost groan with frustration. He was simply sharing his dessert with me. That's all that was. He places the silverware on the plate and it clinks against the china.

"Was that good?" he asks, his voice smoother than the caramel we just shared.

Is he talking about the cheesecake or the way he fed it to me? "Yes," I reply to both, my cheeks flaming brighter.

"It's a pleasure to watch a beautiful woman enjoy her food."

I blink at him. *He thinks I'm beautiful?* My heart flutters in my chest like a bird trapped in a cage.

His eyes narrow again as he searches my face. I wish I knew what he was looking for so I could give it to him. The sound of his throat clearing brings me out of my fantasy. "I should get back to work."

I'm struck silent for the first time in my life. *Say something, Mia!*

"Of course, can't keep all those mobsters waiting." *Oh, bananas. Anything but that.* The puzzled look on his face makes me wince.

I stare at my hands, picking at a loose piece of skin near my thumbnail while he washes his plate. I steal a glance at him. His broad frame obscures my view of the sink. With every motion, his thick biceps strain the seams of his crisp white shirt. He places the wet dishes on the drainer to dry, and I'm struck by how comfortable he looks doing such a domestic chore. Sure, this is his house, but he has a bunch of servants and he still washes his own dishes. Brad didn't wash a single thing the entire time we were together, not even at the beginning when he was sweeping me off my feet. That probably should've been a sign, huh?

When he spins around to face me, I realize I'm staring and avert my gaze. He walks past me, headed for the door, but he stops as he reaches me, and I inhale the familiar masculine scent of him. "For the record, I think your ass, and the rest of your body, is fucking perfect."

My jaw nearly hits the table as I watch him walk out of the room. Perfect? Lorenzo Moretti thinks my body is fucking perfect? Holy goddamn bananas. I might have just fallen head over heels in lust.

THIRTEEN

LORENZO

"Futtuto idiota!" I mutter under my breath, stalking down the hall and as far away from Mia as possible.

I just told our temporary house guest that her body is perfect. Why the hell did I say that? Maybe because I felt bad that her asshole ex-husband made her feel so shitty that she denies herself the pleasure of a food she so clearly enjoys?

Yes, that was why. Not because my gaze drifts far too often down to her juicy round ass or her tits that strain against the fabric of the various dresses and tops she wears. My pity for her is the only reason I said what I did. The only reason I spent five minutes feeding her cheesecake and watching her pretty lips wrap around that fork. I sure as fuck did not imagine those lips wrapped around my cock, her soft tongue sweeping over the tip and collecting the precum collecting there.

My balls feel heavy and hot. I haven't jerked off for over a week, and I need to cum before I implode. That's all this is about. Once I blow my load, I'll forget about the way that distracting yellow dress hugs every inch of her body and shows off her tan, toned legs. I need to get off to the memory of my wife. The only woman I will ever love. The only woman I can ever want.

A few moments later, I'm standing in the shower with piping hot water streaming over my face and chest. Gripping the base of my shaft, I squeeze hard and groan as blessed relief rolls through me. I picture her. My sweet Anya. Her ash-blond hair and ice blue eyes. The curves of her body. My tiny ballerina.

My thighs tremble with the desperate urgency for release coursing through me. One hand on the tiled walls to hold myself steady, I tug harder, grunting as my balls sear with the need to come. Water drips down my face. I close my eyes and grant myself permission to remember her. Running my tongue along that scar over her hipbone. How she could take my entire cock inside her tiny little body. The way her pale skin marked so easily when I punished her.

I pump harder. "Fuck!" Thighs burning and eyes stinging, I allow the memories to take hold. They swirl around my brain like the water around the drain.

Honey-blond hair. No! Ash-blond hair.

I recall the sweet scent of her. Jasmine and lemon—no, vanilla and almond.

Her tits straining at the buttons of the clothes she wears.

Small pink nipples and tiny breasts dwarfed by the palms of my hands.

How her sweet round ass looked in that yellow dress today. Her pink lips wrapped around my shaft. Hazel eyes gazing up at me while I sink my cock into her.

No! I slam my fist into the tiled wall of the shower and shout my frustration at the ceiling. "Fuck!"

Anya. My beautiful Anya. Where are you, passerotta? Wiping the water from my eyes, I try to picture her face, but all I see is the siren downstairs. My cock weeps, and I squeeze harder, forcing myself to focus on my wife's pale blue eyes and her sweet smile. How her delicate fingers brushed my skin. The pleasing way she would dip her head whenever she spoke to me. Her collar. Her cunt. The way it rippled around my cock.

Heat sears up my spine, and I continue to pump my shaft as new images and old memories fight for dominance, blurring into each other as they flash through my head. My hand flattens against the cool tile. I press up onto my toes. My balls draw up, all fire and fury as I work my cock more firmly. When I lose control, coming so hard and fast that my knees buckle, it's to the vision of shining hazel eyes, full pink lips, and a pair of beautiful big tits encased in a yellow dress.

CHAPTER
FOURTEEN
LORENZO

"You've reached me but I ain't here." Lionel's Southern drawl drones down my ear. "Leave me a message after the beep. If I haven't been abducted by aliens or taken away from it all by a rich heiress, I'll get back to you."

With a sigh, I slip my cell back into my pocket. It's been three days since I spoke to him. He must still be in Abu Dhabi. I glare at my laptop screen, hoping I'll find a message from him telling me he's found more information about that twisted piece of shit, but my inbox remains empty except for a spam email about erectile dysfunction.

"Only dysfunction I have is a boner that won't go away," I mutter under my breath. Every single morning, I wake with a raging hard on, and every single morning, I try to jerk off to the memory of Anya's face, only to be plagued by images of Mia. Inevitably, I give up and spend the next half hour beneath the icy spray of a cold shower.

I've had a semi-permanent hard on for the past three days, and I swear that if I don't bust my nut again soon, I'll have a coronary.

The sound of the intercom buzzing snaps me from my train of thought. Dante and Kat are out with the kids. Mia's in the kitchen with Sophia, learning to make fresh pasta—a skill she claims to have wanted to learn her entire adult life but never gotten around to. Fuck, that just leaves me.

Pressing the button, I bark at the guard on the gate. "What?"

"There's a guy here, Boss …"

"And?"

"He says he's a cop."

"He says he's a cop or he is a cop, Jimmy?" I snap, too wound up for riddles.

"Well, he showed me his badge, but he's not Chicago PD."

"So where is he from?" I already know the answer.

"Boston."

"Fucker," I mumble, balling my hands into fists. I've wondered how long it would be before he came for her.

"He says you've kidnapped his wife," Jimmy adds.

I chuckle humorlessly. "I'll be right out."

Leaving my desk, I straighten my jacket and roll my neck and shoulders, trying to relieve a modicum of the tension currently squeezing every muscle in my body. Cop or not, I will shoot Brad Mulcahy where he stands before I let him anywhere near Mia.

I walk down the expansive driveway of our family's mansion and spot the black Chevy idling right outside the gates. A tall sack of shit with a buzzcut leans against the driver's side door, running a hand through his mousy brown beard. Two of my armed guards stand on either side of his car, but he stares directly at me and pays them no attention.

"You have a problem fuckface?" I ask as I come within a few feet of him. I can smell his stench from here. Unwashed clothes and sweaty pits, stale cigarette smoke and junk food. Either he was punching way, way above his weight class with the little firecracker in my kitchen, or he's really let himself go since she left him. I suspect it's both, but mostly the latter. He has that drawn, haunted look of a man who had it all and lost it in the blink of an eye.

He spits onto the ground near my feet. Disrespectful prick! "I've come for my wife."

I fold my arms over my chest and glare at him, watching the bead of sweat run down his forehead, belying his cocksure facade. This man knows who I am. He's aware that I could put a bullet in his brain right now and there's every possibility I'd get away with it. There's every possibility that I wouldn't too, given he's a cop and it's broad daylight, but he doesn't know which side of the coin his fate lies on today.

"I said I've come for my wife," he repeats, spittle forming on the corners of his mouth. Jesus fuck, how did Mia ever even kiss this disgusting fucker?

I go on glaring at him, refusing to confirm that she's here—for now at least. I'm enjoying watching him work himself into a fit.

He balls his hands into fists by his sides and stamps his foot, a toddler throwing a tantrum. A chill runs down my spine. I've known plenty of men like Brad Mulcahy, with the emotional maturity of a child but the body of a heavyweight boxer. It's a fucking miracle Mia didn't leave that house of theirs in a box. I glance at his hands. Not as big as mine, but they're big. I imagine them wrapped around Mia's neck. Slamming into her face. Hitting her. Restraining her. Forcing her. He's a fucking dead man walking.

Rocking my head side to side, I pop my neck and step closer, biting back a smirk when he flinches.

"Hand her over now and we'll talk no more of it," he says, his voice taking on a desperate whine. "I'll tell my buddy Superintendent Hayes to back off, and you can return to whatever it is you do."

"Seems Hayes isn't really your buddy though, is he? You have something on the deputy, isn't that right?"

He shrugs, trying to appear casual while sweat beads on his forehead and his arms remain rigidly clenched by his sides. "Even more powerful to have a superintendent in your pocket than as your friend, as I'm sure you know."

"*Deputy* superintendent," I remind him.

His lip curls with contempt. "He can still make your life very difficult."

"He could." With a shrug, I edge closer. "But he's not. A few raids on my family's businesses. Is that the best you got, fuckknuckle?"

He bares his teeth, barely able to contain his anger now, so I push him a little further, hoping he'll make a move and give me a reason to beat every breath of life out of him. "I said, is that all you got?"

"Just give me my wife." His voice is half snarl, half whine. "Bring her out here and you'll never see either of us again."

"Now just why the fuck would I want to do that?"

He barks out a laugh. "Because she's not fucking worth it, man. Trust me."

I take another step closer, and he shrinks back before he remembers that he's supposed to be a tough guy cop and squares his shoulders. We stand toe to toe, eye to eye, and I grin with delight. "I happen to think she's very worth it. Every delicious inch of her."

That sparks something in him, and he bounces on his toes, anger radiating from him in waves. A thick vein pulses by his temple and he raises one fist.

"Do it, fuckface," I goad. "Please fucking do it."

"Take all three of you on?" He sneers at my guards.

"I give you my word they won't touch you. They won't fucking have to, but just give me a reason to, you sick fuck."

"Fuck you!" he spits.

"You heard anything from your kid sister lately, Brad?" I ask with a grin, and the color drains from his face in an instant.

His entire face twists with malice. "What the fuck are you on about?"

"I know all about Michaela. And your mom." I hope my lie will get him to reveal something more, but he stays silent and glares at me. Fuck, I want to punch him in that ugly mug. Knock him to the ground. Jump on his fucking head. Want to make him bleed the way he made her bleed and hear him plead for mercy the way she must have so many times.

With impeccable timing, Dante's car comes to a stop behind Brad's. He rolls down the window and eyes me with concern. "Everything okay, brother?"

I keep my attention glued to Brad. "Everything is just fine. Bradley here was just leaving."

The asshole snorts, but his knees shake as he takes the few steps to his car.

Before he opens the door, I grab onto his forearm, digging my fingers into his taut muscle. "You ever set foot in Chicago again and I will kill you in the most painful way imaginable. You ever try to contact Mia in any way ever again and I will tell the entire world about you and your whole fucked-up family. You got me?"

His nostrils flare.

I squeeze tighter, enjoying the pain that flashes across his face. He deserves so much more than that, but we are where we are. "I asked you a fucking question."

"Yes," he hisses.

I release my grip and let him climb back into his shit-box car. All the while, I feel Dante's eyes on me, willing me not to waste a cop in front of our own house with my niece and nephews a few feet away. For their sake, and their sake alone, I don't.

FIFTEEN
LORENZO

Anger courses in my veins like it's my lifeblood as I stalk back through the house, leaving my younger brother alone in the study. I explained what happened with Brad today, but I kept Lionel's findings to myself for now. No point telling only half the story. Dante talked me out of my plan to dispose of Brad Mulcahy. He thinks we should play it smart and wait for Brad to fuck his own life up, but I can't help feeling like we'd be doing the entire world a favor by ending that piece of shit's existence.

I walk into the library, hoping for a little quiet, but she's here. Of course she's here. She's fucking everywhere.

"Are you okay?" she asks, her voice full of concern.

I pace up and down the room, running my hands through my hair. Do I tell her that her sack of shit husband was just here? No, I can't. She might decide to run, and if she left ... I don't know what the fuck I'd do, but I do know I like having her here. Despite her being a constant source of tension and distraction.

"Lorenzo?"

Thick knots of tension build in my muscles. She's close

enough that her scent washes over me. Too close. My dick strains at my zipper, pulsing and aching for relief. Every drop of blood rushes south, making it hard to breathe, and when I do manage to draw air, she fills my lungs. I can taste her, like a python senses its prey. I need to get the fuck out of here. Away from her soft body and her intoxicating scent.

Mia smiles sweetly. Is she aware of the effect she has on me? If she is, she should run. Instead, she comes closer. So fucking close, I swear I can hear her heartbeat. Or is that mine? I can't even think straight anymore.

I stop pacing and stand still, chest heaving as I stare at her. She places her hand on my chest, right over my hammering heart, and leans close. So goddamn close. Her breath dusts along my neck and my cock twitches, letting me know he's running the show from here on out. My brain checks out, happily handing over the reins.

"Tell me what's wrong. What do you need?"

I suck in a breath, lazily looking over her curves. Her fingers twitch and my very last shred of restraint snaps. "What if what I need is you, Mia?" The words rumble out of me like a growl.

"You know you can have me any time you want, right?" she whispers.

Blinding light flashes in my eyes, and a surge of adrenaline propels me forward. My hand is around her throat, pushing her back until she's perched on the edge of the desk, her fingers splayed out on either side of her hips. She spreads her thighs, allowing me to step between them and press my body flat against hers. She holds my gaze, daring me to keep going.

I can't.

I shouldn't.

But I do.

I fist my free hand in her honey-blond hair and hold her head still. My other hand slides down her body, over the pillowy curve of her breasts, eliciting a needy moan from her lips. Those lips. Fucking plump and begging to be wrapped around my cock. I crash my mouth down on hers, swallowing her sounds as my hand travels lower, over the arc of her hip and around to her ass. I squeeze hard, and her soft flesh yields to my touch as though it's been lying dormant waiting for my fingertips. She parts her lips, allowing my tongue inside to explore the recesses of her mouth. She tastes so fucking sweet, and suddenly she is everything and everywhere.

My heart beats frantically against my ribcage, like it's trying to break free and remind me that we're broken and we can't do this. But I am lost in the feel of her soft flesh beneath my hands, her delicious scent in my nose and her taste on my tongue. How good would the rest of her taste?

She rocks her hips forward, grinding her pussy on my cock, and precum weeps from the crown. If I don't come soon, I will die from a fucking heart attack. She pulls back, panting for breath as she runs a hand through my hair and tugs, tilting my head so that I'm staring into her hazel eyes.

"Fuck me," she breathes out the words.

Holy mother of fucks. I almost choke on air, swaying on my feet as violent waves of desire crash over me. My head pounds, my cock aches. I lift her onto the desk and slide a hand between her thighs, my fingertips kneading her soft flesh as I work my way up to the apex. The place where I can lose myself in her.

Pulling her panties aside, I brush my knuckles over her slick folds. So fucking hot and inviting. I want inside her. I want to feel her.

I want to feel.

It's been so long since I've enjoyed the pleasure of a woman. So fucking long.

Her breaths come hard and fast, and her eyes burn into mine. Then her hand is between us, fingertips brushing over my aching shaft as she lowers my zipper and slides inside my boxer shorts. She grips me at the base, squeezing hard, and I groan like a thirteen-year-old boy about to get his first handjob. I yank her arms behind her back, easily circling my fingers around both of her wrists and pinning them in place while I free my cock.

I roughly tug her panties down with one hand. Kicking them off, she wraps her long legs around my waist and pulls me closer. The tip of my cock presses against her wet heat, and nothing exists except for me and her and this moment.

I slide in and her hot pussy squeezes my dick like a vise. "Holy. Fuck!" I grunt, burying my face in her neck. Grabbing a handful of her ass, I rail into her like an animal. My cock pulses and throbs as I drive in and out of her wet pussy. She's dripping, coating my shaft in her sweet juices and making it possible for me to sink balls-deep into her tight-as-fuck cunt. And she feels so fucking good. Pure relief seeps into my bones, and with every thrust inside her, I get closer and closer to the edge that's been eluding me for so long.

"Oh, god, Lorenzo." She breathes out the words, hot against my ear. Her cunt ripples around me, pulling me deeper and deeper. I never want to stop. I want to bury myself right here and feel nothing but her and this pussy for the rest of my days.

"Your cunt, Mia ..." I release her wrists so I can hold onto her hips and drive harder and deeper. "Feels so good."

"Yes," she moans, wrapping her arms around my neck and clinging to me. I slam into her, my balls burning with the need for release. Harder and faster with each roll of my hips, my fingers digging into her soft ass cheeks, kneading and pulling and taking. I need her so fucking much.

"So." Thrust. "Fucking." Thrust. "Good."

She tips her head back, whimpering as I nail her. I run my nose over her sweet-smelling neck and sink my teeth into her flesh. Her pussy squeezes me harder, and I can't hold off any longer. I'm going to come, fill her up, and I'd rather die than stop now. Gripping her ass tighter, I drive inside her one last time, making her cry out as I empty my myself into her. I close my eyes and almost black out from the force of my climax.

I fill her tight pussy until my cum drips out, overflowing from her channel. Three days' worth of cum. Two years' worth of anger and guilt and frustration and sadness. And she took it all.

I pull my cock out of her, and although she does her best to hide it, she flinches. I was too rough. Too hard. I didn't even get her off. And now it's over, the rush of endorphins already leaving my body, replaced by more guilt and anger.

Zipping up my pants, I avert my eyes, unable to look at her.

"Lorenzo?"

"I'm sorry, Mia." There's nothing else I can say. I still don't look at her as I walk away, leaving her alone in the library.

SIXTEEN

I find Dante in our study, reading over a stack of contracts Joey gave him earlier. Glancing up, he gives me a concerned look and sits up straighter in his chair. "You okay?"

Do I look as angry and distraught as I feel? I sink into the chair across from him and scrub a hand over my face. "I cheated on her, D."

He blinks at me, confused. I should have known he wouldn't understand. "On who, Loz?"

"Anya," I snap, barely able to keep the anger surging through me under control.

He leans forward, folding his arms on the desk. "You didn't cheat—"

"I fucked a woman who isn't my wife." Jaw aching with all the tension I'm holding inside, I slam my fist down on the arm of my chair.

"Okay," he says in that calm, soothing tone he's so good at, but it's not working today. He leans back, eyeing me warily. Like I'm completely insane. Maybe I am.

"I fucked someone else, D." I hang my head, dropping it into my hands. All I hear is the sound of my own heartbeat in my ears. How the fuck did I let this happen? Making decisions with my dick, that's how. I'm a better man that that. Anya deserves better than that.

He finally responds. "It's been two years, Loz."

I lift my head, and he's still staring at me with worry etched on his face. "It could be two hundred years, it wouldn't matter. Anya is my wife."

"But she died ..."

"You think I don't fucking know that?" I spit the words, directing my rage at him because I have nowhere else to put it. "You think I don't remember every single second of every single fucking day that she's dead?"

He winces. "I know."

"No, you don't know, Dante. You don't have any fucking idea."

"I miss her too, Loz."

"Of course you fucking miss her. Everyone misses her. But do you feel like every single day is an effort just to open your fucking eyes in the morning because you no longer have the one person who made your life what it was?" I don't give him time to answer. "What if it was Kat? Would you be okay after two years?"

My words cut him deep; the pain is evident in his voice when he manages to speak. "I never said you should be okay, Loz. But you didn't cheat on your wife."

"So, why do I feel like I did?"

"Is this the first time you've ... In two years?"

I scowl at him. "Of course it fucking is."

"Wow." He rubs a hand over his jaw. "I just assumed—"

"No." I shake my head, guilt and shame eating away at my insides. "I've never even looked at a woman like that ..." Until Mia.

"So, what happened. Who was this woman?"

Guilt clogs my throat, and I look down at the floor, unable to meet his eyes.

"Mia?"

I don't confirm or deny, but he takes my silence as an admission of guilt. "For fuck's sake, Loz. She's my wife's cousin."

"It won't happen again," I assure him.

"Does she know that?"

I blink at him. That's a good question. I have no fucking idea. I zipped up my pants and walked away, leaving her alone with my cum dripping down her thighs. Did she enjoy it? Fuck. I didn't even ask if she was okay, didn't stop to consider the fact that we weren't using protection.

"Loz?"

"What?"

"Of all the women, why her?"

"Why not?" I snap, although I know he's right.

"She's my wife's cousin. She's not …"

I frown at him. "Not what?"

"In a good place?" he offers with a shrug.

"Mia is one of the strongest, most together women I've ever met."

My instinct to defend her takes us both by surprise.

"I'm not suggesting otherwise, but you two together …"

"We're not together, D. I told you it won't happen again."

He stares at me, and I will him to argue with me, because maybe raging at him will make me feel better. Maybe I'll get a few shots in and the ache in my knuckles will distract from the churning shame in my gut. But he simply nods, giving me no outlet for all this impotent rage.

A vein in my neck twitches. I'm so fucking conflicted. I hate myself for even thinking about touching another woman, let alone fucking one. But I can't stop remembering how good she felt. How soft her skin was. Her sweet scent. How her tight hot, wet cunt made me think of nothing but the incredible relief of being buried inside her. How for a few moments I forgot ...

"You did nothing wrong, Loz," Dante assures me.

"So why do I feel so fucking bad?"

"Because you love your wife."

I do.

"That will never change. No matter how many women you fuck, it doesn't change how much you love her."

I grind my jaw. I know if things were reversed and he had lost Kat, I would say the exact same thing. But I can't bring myself to believe it. Anya and I were different.

SEVENTEEN

My mind races with unanswered questions. What the hell just happened in the library? I take a seat on the wooden bench in the kitchen, and the slight ache between my thighs tells me that I didn't imagine any of it. All those weeks of pent-up sexual tension, and now it's over. I guess it's not that unusual—unfortunately—for a guy to not care about a woman's pleasure as long as he finds his own, but Lorenzo didn't strike me as that type of guy at all. But the worst part is that he walked away without even checking if I was okay. It seems so at odds with the man I've been getting to know.

I shake my head. We shouldn't have gone there. I mean, it was great sex—hot sex—right up to the point where he left me hanging. I was literally on the verge of a mind-blowing orgasm, and he just stopped. Everything about Lorenzo Moretti screams sex wizard, but that's the problem when you fantasize about someone for so long—the reality never measures up.

The sound of the door opening interrupts my inner chatter, and a flush creeps across my cheeks as Lorenzo walks into the room. Well, holy shit, this is awkward.

"Mia," he says gruffly, his brow furrowed.

"Lorenzo." I give him a forced smile, wondering how I can extricate myself from this room and avoid having this conversation.

He clears his throat. "About earlier."

I wave my hand dismissively. "We don't have to—"

"We need to talk about what happened," he insists and sits on the bench opposite me.

I swallow the ball of anxiety lodged in my throat.

"I'm sorry," he says, his expression so full of guilt, sadness, and pain that I want to wrap my arms around him.

"You don't have to apologize," I assure him. "We're both adults."

"We didn't use"—he clears his throat again—"protection."

"Well, we were kind of in the moment," I remind him.

"Do we need to do anything about that?" His eyes scan my face, full of concern now too.

"No, I have an IUD. Also, just FYI, Brad was such a sleazebag that I had regular STI checks. The results of my last one came through just after I left Boston. Clean as a whistle."

He nods and lets out a long breath. "I'm clean too. There's been no one since Anya."

Holy bananas! I'm the first woman he's been with since his dead wife? I had no idea. No wonder he rushed off the way he did. Unsure what to say, I nod and look around the room for a means of escape. This is torture; I'm such an idiot. "So, we're all good then," I say, infusing my tone with all the chirpiness and indifference I can muster while I sit here with his cum dripping out of me.

"It can't happen again, Mia," he says, his voice deep and solemn. "I'm sorry."

Wow! The arrogance of men with huge dicks. I'm technically still married and not exactly looking for a deep committed relationship here either, buddy.

He frowns. "What?"

I shrug. Shut up, Mia. Don't say it!

"Mia?" he presses.

"It's bold of you to assume I want it to happen again, is all," I blurt. *Idiot!*

His frown deepens into a scowl. "I just ..." His Adam's apple bobs.

"You assumed that I'd be addicted to your giant penis after one quick liaison in the library?" I arch my eyebrow. *Oh, for the love of god, shut up, Mia!*

He flinches. "No. I just meant ..."

"It's not like we had great chemistry, is it?" Yeah right. The chemistry between us is scorching hot, which was why the end result was so disappointing. I hoped my lie would defuse the situation, but that huge vein starts to throb in his temple and tells me I only made it worse. "I mean, I guess not all sex has to end with both parties coming. That doesn't necessarily mean it was bad," I babble. From the low growl that rumbles in his chest, I'm pretty sure I just poured a can of gasoline all over this little pickle we've found ourselves in.

He plants his giant hands on the table, jaw clenched tightly shut and rage visibly simmering beneath the surface of his skin. "So we're in agreement then?" he barks. "Never again."

"Never." I offer him my most genuine smile, trying to lighten the mood and convey that we can still be friends despite what happened earlier, but he glowers at me.

Goddammit, Mia! I need to get out of this room before I inadvertently push another button and make him implode.

"Glad we're on the same page."

He storms out of the room, and I rest my forehead on the table, letting the cool wood soothe my flushed skin. How the hell did my day end this badly? With a deep breath, I push myself up and roll my shoulders back. Tomorrow is a new day, and it will be a better one than this.

Lorenzo and I can be friends again. Lorenzo and his rough hands and sinful tongue. The way it danced over the skin of my neck before he claimed my mouth with a smoking hot kiss. Warmth pools in my core at the memory. So much promise, only for him to leave me wet and needy.

Gah! Stop it, Mia. It was mediocre sex at best. He fucked you and left you hanging.

But what if—

"Mia?" Kat says, popping her head into the kitchen. "That movie we were talking about is on soon. You wanna watch it with me?"

Watching a movie with Kat sounds like the perfect distraction. As much as I'd love to talk to her about what happened with Lorenzo, sleeping with her brother-in-law—who's clearly still grieving for his wife—isn't the wisest move I've ever made. And it's not like it's going to happen again. I'll file it with all my other stupid mistakes I never speak of and leave it there.

EIGHTEEN

"Holy fuck, Loz." Max gives a dark laugh and watches me wipe blood from my shoe with the T-shirt of the man groaning at my feet.

"What?" I snap.

He looks down at the man on the ground and shakes his head. "You just used that guy's face as boot scraper."

"So? He'll live. Barely scratched him."

Max blinks at me, a smile on his face but confusion in his eyes. "He only asked you where the fucking restrooms were."

"People who use restrooms in shitholes like this are likely to get dysentery." I shrug. "I did him a favor."

"Dysentery? What is this, the 1600s? We were only supposed to ask questions about the deputy superintendent," he reminds me.

I look around the whorehouse, my nose wrinkling in disgust. It's not an upmarket place where the hookers are looked after; it's a shitty old house where drugs are cheap and hookers are cheaper. It makes my skin crawl to even be here.

"I want this place fucking shut down, Max. It's fucking unhygienic."

"And what about the women and men who make a living here?"

"Find them somewhere nicer to work," I suggest.

"Fuck me. Like I have nothing better to do with my time," he grumbles as we head out the door.

"Shall I ask Joey to do it? She'd have this place turned over in a fucking day," I snap.

"The fuck you will. I'll fucking handle it."

I crack my neck. "Good."

Max glares at me as we climb into the car. "Threatening to have your baby sister deal with pimps just to prove a fucking point isn't fucking funny, jackass."

I glare right back, spoiling for a fight. "Sort it then."

Max slams his hands on the steering wheel. "What the fuck is wrong with you? You're always a pain in my ass, but you're in rare fucking form today."

"Just drive, Max."

"Not before you tell me what the fuck is going on," he snaps back, folding his arms over his chest. "You've been acting like a bear with a hornet's nest up its ass all fucking day."

"Have not." Fuck, I sound like a child.

"On top of your little outburst back there, you punched a fucking steel door and almost broke your hand, and you smashed the butcher's window with a meat cleaver because he didn't have any prime rib left. What the fuck's going on with you?"

I let out a long breath. This asshole isn't going to let up. "I slept with Mia."

He gapes at me.

"Max?"

"Fuck, Loz." He shakes his head. "How was it?"

"What the fuck, dipshit?"

"What?" He frowns, face a mask of hurt. "She's the first since Anya, right? It's normal for me to ask how it went."

"That is not a normal response, Max."

He finally starts the car. "It is. That's what I was expecting you to ask me after you found out I banged your sister," he says, deadpan.

I turn in my seat, ready to unleash hell on him, but he's bent over the steering wheel, laughing so hard that I can't help but laugh too—just a little. "I should fucking cut your throat for that, you know."

Wiping his eyes, he sits up and shoots me a wink. "But you won't. Your sister would kill you in your sleep, and you know it."

I shake my head and stare out the window while he pulls out into traffic.

"Seriously though, Loz. How was it?"

"The fuck, Max?"

"I don't mean how was the actual sex, fuck-nugget. How was it"—he waves a hand around—"like after and stuff. How were you? Is it an ongoing thing?"

"Never happening again."

"And is she good with that?"

"More than good," I snap.

"Oh?" He glances at me before turning his attention back to the road.

"I don't think she ..." I swallow.

"Don't think she what?"

I scrub a hand down my face. "Enjoyed it," I mumble.

"Sure she did," he insists. "You're like a top fucking Dom or something. I see those women drooling over you whenever we go anywhere near one of those clubs you used to go to." He arches an eyebrow at me.

"I didn't make her come, Max," I blurt out and immediately wish I could take the words back.

"Well, uh, it's been a long time." Giving me an awkward look out of the corner of his eye, he clears his throat. "You didn't expect there to be anyone after Anya. That's some deep shit to process."

I rub a hand through my hair. "I feel so fucking guilty."

"About Anya?"

"And Mia. I should've shown some fucking restraint."

"She's a beautiful woman, Loz. You're both grown-ass adults. And I know you don't want to hear this, but—"

I cut him off before he can finish the platitude. "Don't you dare fucking tell me Anya would have wanted me to move on."

"Okay. I won't tell you then. Does Kat know?"

"I don't think so. It meant nothing. I told Dante it won't happen again, and I'm pretty sure Mia won't mention it."

He's quiet for a few moments before he speaks again. "You did nothing wrong, Loz."

I don't answer. If that's true, why do I feel so fucking torn up about it? Why can't I stop thinking about how I betrayed my marriage vows?

Would I feel better if it truly had meant nothing? What if I had fucked a random woman? Because the only thing that consumes me more than my guilt is the memory of being buried inside Mia. Her taste. Her scent. The way her soft flesh yielded beneath my fingertips. How her hot pussy molded itself to my cock like it was made for me. The way it almost ripped my fucking heart out when she told me we had no chemistry—the knowledge that if I still had a heart, she would have eviscerated it.

NINETEEN

MIA

I sip my hot chamomile tea, eyeing Lorenzo as he stalks through the room toward the refrigerator. His brow is furrowed, dark eyes hooded and unreadable. The sleeves of his white shirt are rolled up to his elbows so that all the beautiful art on his forearms is on full display. He's wearing his light gray suit pants today, the ones that hug his magnificent ass like he was poured into them. I mean, no man has any right to have an ass that looks *that* good. I stare at his perfect posterior while he rummages in the fridge.

"You looking for anything in particular?"

"Dinner," he grunts.

Placing my mug onto the counter, I wander over to him. "Sophia made lasagna and I know she saved you some." I sidle up beside him so that we're both looking into the cavernous refrigerator.

"I can find it myself," he huffs.

"And you're doing such a good job," I say with a smirk after he picks up the same tub of yogurt for the third time.

I reach into the back for the glass container with the green lid. My arm brushes against his, and my breath catches.

Warmth spreads across my skin, despite the cool atmosphere. He pulls away like he's been burned by a hot poker. Did he feel that too?

"Here it is." I hand him the food, my voice barely a whisper.

"Thanks," he replies gruffly, snatching the container from my hand. It's only now that I notice his knuckles are bleeding. Again.

"You want me to fix you a little salad to go with that?"

He narrows his eyes at me.

"It'll only take me a minute while you pop that in the microwave." For reasons I can't fully explain, I want to soothe away some of his pain, do something to make him feel cared for, even if it is just a salad. "You like all vegetables except cucumber, right?"

"Yeah," he says, his face softening a little.

"Because it's the work of the devil," I tease.

The faintest flicker of a grin tugs at the corners of his mouth. "Exactly."

I grab the salad from the crisper drawer and place it on the kitchen counter. Then we stand side by side, me chopping vegetables and him staring at the microwave.

I glance sideways at him. "What did you do to your hand?"

"Work," he says with a dismissive shrug.

"You should ask Kat to take a look at it."

He shakes his head. "It's fine."

We edge closer to each other. Heat radiates from him like a furnace. He smells so good—fresh air and cologne—and my mouth waters. I chew on my lip, aware of my breath growing increasingly heavier, my pulse thrumming against my skin.

While I'm chopping a tomato, a sudden memory of his tongue in my mouth makes me falter, and the knife slips, cutting my finger. "Ouch!"

"Are you okay?" He grabs my hand, sending rivulets of pleasure coursing through me. Caressing the tip of my finger, he inspects it for damage.

"It's just a tiny scratch," I insist, pulling my hand away. Goosebumps prickle along my skin.

His eyes darken to black orbs. "You should be more careful, sunshine."

Sunshine? He's never called me that before. My throat constricts. "I will," I whisper hoarsely as the tension sizzles between us.

He nods, his gaze fixed on mine so intently that I worry he can read my thoughts. Thoughts of him and what it would feel like to have him kiss me again. His tongue darts out, running over his bottom lip, and I swear I feel it between my thighs.

I suck in a shaky breath.

His dark eyes narrow.

The damn microwave pings, and just like that, the spell is broken. He turns away to retrieve his lasagna, and I arrange his salad and place it on the countertop in front of him.

"Enjoy your dinner," I say with a forced smile, but he doesn't turn back to me. The closeness we shared has already vanished.

"Thanks," he mumbles.

I swallow down the knot of regret that sticks in my throat. Why is this so awkward?

I turn to leave the kitchen, but he grabs hold of my wrist and tugs me forward. Our bodies are barely an inch apart. My heart races. Blood rushes south. My mouth is so dry that I can't even swallow. Then he dips his head, hot breath dusting over the skin of my neck and making me shiver.

"You seriously think we don't have chemistry, Mia?" he asks with a low growl that travels directly between my thighs.

"M-maybe it was a poor choice of words."

"Maybe?"

"Yes. Clearly, we have something, but ..."

"But what?"

"Well, it should have been fireworks, but it was more like a fizzle."

He glowers at me, jaw ticking. "A fizzle?"

I should stop talking. Right now. But I am Mia freaking Stone, and talking when I should shut the hell up is my lifelong curse. "It's okay, not every guy can make every woman come."

Holy crap, Mia. Why?

Lorenzo snarls, his muscles vibrating with pent-up rage. Towering over me, he picks up his plate, gripping it so tightly his knuckles turn white. I wince at my own stupidity. I basically accused the most dangerous man I've ever known of not being able to satisfy a woman. "I didn't mean— I meant me. You couldn't make *me* come," I babble on, embarrassing myself further. What the hell is wrong with me?

His nostrils flare as he draws in a deep breath, probably trying to stop himself from throttling me. Then he storms out of the kitchen, muttering something in Italian and leaving me to stare after him.

TWENTY

My cock throbs painfully as soon as I open my eyes, just like it has every morning for the past two weeks. I stalk through this house in a constant state of semi-arousal, feeling like I'm going to tear someone's head off. Only now I can't jerk off because Mia is all I can see when I do. Incessant thoughts of her fill my mind. Her sensuous curves. Her smile. The way she smells—so sweet and tempting. The memory of her hot, wet cunt squeezing my cock. The way she looked at me when she said I couldn't make her come.

Throwing back the covers, I jump out of bed, cursing under my breath as I stalk to the bathroom. I've never been so insulted in my whole fucking life. Couldn't make her come! I could make her come so fucking hard she'd still moan at the memory when she's a hundred years old.

Rubbing my temples in an attempt to stem the ever-present throbbing, I make my way to the library. She's here. Of course she is. I can't avoid her—or maybe I can't stay away from her.

CHAPTER TWENTY

I walk to my desk, and she sashays past me, her perfectly round ass swaying seductively in that little yellow dress she's wearing—the same one she wore the night she arrived. My cock twitches in my pants at the sight and the thought of all the filthy, depraved things I'd like to do to her.

"Oh, bananas," she mutters, stooping to pick up the pen she dropped on the floor. Holy fuck! Does she do this to me on purpose? Get some sick kind of thrill from making me walk around with a constant erection? I try to avert my eyes, but they're glued to her. Fixated on every sumptuous curve, every single movement of her sexy body.

She stands up straight and spins on her heel to face me, and I almost throw out my goddamn back trying to make it appear like I'm not staring at her ass. The grin that tugs at the corners of her full pink lips tells me I wasn't fast enough.

"You need any help there?" she says, glancing down.

I frown at her, and it takes me a few beats to realize she's talking about the papers in my hand, not the bulge in my suit pants.

"No, it's fine."

"If you're sure." She sinks her teeth into the pillowy cushion of her bottom lip and flutters her eyelashes. She's fucking with me, right? Nobody can look that fucking seductive just being their regular self. Everything about this woman drives me crazy. The way she tucks her hair behind her ear. Her scent. The way she smiles—all the goddamn time. Her perky tits and how they heave and jiggle when she takes a deep breath. How she hums along randomly to tunes that pop into her head. Even the way she talks far too much. "I guess I'll just get out of your way then," she adds as she sashays across the room toward me, her hips swaying seductively. Like a hypnotist's pendulum, they draw my entire focus.

Yes, she should get out of my goddamn way. She should fucking run from me before—

Her scent hits me, jasmine and lemon, and my mouth waters. All I need is one little taste. Before I can talk myself out of it, my hand darts out and catches her wrist. I squeeze tight, but she doesn't flinch, and when I close the gap between us, her breath hitches.

I dip my head low, brushing my lips dangerously close to her sweet-smelling skin. "I could make you come, Mia."

She shivers, but her dark eyes fix on mine. They're more brown today, her pupils blown wide as she glares at me in challenge. She licks her lower lip and every single cell in my body screams for her. Her full pink lips part, and she breathes out two words. "Prove it."

TWENTY-ONE

MIA

I have never seen Lorenzo's eyes so dark and full of heat. They blaze with fire, searing into my skin and making me squirm under the intensity of his gaze. I swallow hard. Did I completely misread the situation?

The hell I did. He's the one with his hands on me, telling me he could make me come. I'm hyperaware of his fingers circling my wrist. Heat spreads from where he touches me, seeping into every part of my body and setting my skin ablaze. I go on glaring at him. Daring him. His jaw ticks. That thick vein in his temple pulses, and I grow wetter with each passing millisecond. Then he closes his eyes, momentarily breaking our connection. He draws a breath through his nose, his hand still on my wrist, and an animalistic growl rumbles in his throat. Then he picks me up, wrapping my legs around his waist and carrying me across the room to the piano. His hard cock presses against my pussy, and I stifle a moan as I instinctively rub on him.

The corners of his mouth twitch into a smirk, so I smirk right back. He places me down on the piano with a thud before taking a seat on the stool. "You sure about this?"

I arch an eyebrow, unable to resist teasing him a little more. "Sure you can't make me come? Yep."

He gives a single shake of his head, lips pressed together in amusement. His hands glide up my bare calves, his touch soft and warm. I shiver with anticipation.

My voice drops to a whisper, my bravado waning. "What are you going to do?"

Amusement dances in his expression. He's the hunter and I am the prey. Just how he likes it, I bet. "Make you come," he answers, deadpan. His hands coast higher up my legs, brushing over my knees and beneath my dress before skating along my outer thighs.

"But how?"

His dark eyes gleam dangerously. "Does it matter?"

I swallow harshly. "I guess not." But I'm lying. From our position, it seems like he's going to eat my pussy, and for me, that's the most intimate thing a man can do. How the hell will I ever look him in the face again once he's had it buried all up in there?

That arrogant smirk is back again. "Surely you're not nervous, sunshine? Not after you just threw down that gauntlet?" His hands move to the waistband of my panties.

I harden my glare. "No."

He tugs my panties down my hips and wetness pools in my core. Oh god. I lean back on my elbows, and my breathing grows heavier as Lorenzo's strong hands glide over my skin. He places the underwear in his jacket pocket, and I swallow hard at the sight of his predatory gaze, the way his nostrils flare with desire. He reaches for the edge of my dress, pushing it up over my thighs. My heart rate increases with every inch of bare flesh he exposes.

He breaks eye contact, but only to trail his wickedly delicious lips up the inside of my legs. My legs shake, skin sizzling with electricity. Edging closer to the apex of my thighs, he groans softly and pushes my dress higher until it's bunched around my waist. I'm completely exposed to him, my pulse thundering in my ears.

A blush creeps over my chest, racing up my neck and cheeks. His gaze locks on the space between my thighs, and his eyes darken even further. A tremor runs through my entire body as he stares at my pussy like a starving man let loose on an all-you-can-eat buffet. His soft kisses turn to tiny bites, moving higher.

I suck in a breath as he gets closer to the spot where, despite my lingering embarrassment, I'm desperate to feel him. His fingers skate up my inner thighs, leaving trails of fire everywhere they touch. My back arches and I moan softly.

"I can smell your sweet pussy, sunshine," he says with a low, rumbling growl that vibrates against my sensitive flesh. "So fucking wet for me, huh?"

"Holy mother of god," I murmur, letting my head hang back between my shoulder blades.

"Mmhmm," he mumbles, nipping at the skin at the very top of my thighs. "So fucking beautiful."

"Lorenzo!" I plead with him, but he just goes on teasing me, avoiding the place I want to feel him most. I buck my hips, and he rewards me with a dark chuckle.

"Don't be so impatient, Mia. I've waited a long time to taste this pussy. I'm going to savor every second."

He has? I look up at him again and his gaze meets mine as he blows a stream of cool air over the length of my wet slit, making me cry out. It's so intimate. Too intimate. We shouldn't be doing this, and definitely not here on the piano in the library. But if he stops right now, I might die. "Please?" I whimper, desperate for more.

He arches an eyebrow. "Begging, sunshine? You have no idea how much I enjoy that."

"I thought you were going to make me come?" I pant, growing needier and wetter the longer he torments me.

He doesn't answer. My snark seems to have zero effect on him as he continues leisurely kissing the tops of my thighs and brushing his fingers over my skin. I writhe on the piano, and the more desperate my whimpers become, the slower he goes. Damn him.

"Lorenzo, please?" I whine.

He skims his hands all the way down to my ankles, and I whine. Why must he torture me by moving further away from where I want him? But then he grabs my ankles and lifts my legs. "Lie back," he orders, planting my feet on his shoulders.

With trembling limbs, I do as he tells me, hyperaware that I'm spread wide open and his face is only inches from me. I feel so self-conscious.

"You have a beautiful pussy, Mia," he says with an appreciative groan. "I'm gonna enjoy eating it so fucking much."

I bite down on my lip as he inches closer, his warm breath dancing over my sensitive flesh. When he finally kisses me there, his mouth pressed against my wet folds, I moan his name so loudly and wantonly that it makes him groan. His lips dance along my center, making heat sear deep in my core, and then his tongue darts out, warm and wet and soft, licking a path from my entrance up to my clit.

"Holy Moses," I gasp.

"So. Fucking. Good." His tongue swirls over and around my clit, lapping up my juices, animalistic grunts and growls rumbling from his throat. Warmth spreads through me as he coaxes wave after wave of pleasure from between my thighs, feasting on my pussy with skill and finesse. I was right. Lorenzo Moretti *is* a sex wizard.

A familiar pulling sensation in my abdomen and tingling in my thighs builds as he goes on sucking my clit, rimming it with his tongue but concentrating the pressure on one spot. My back arches off the piano and I grind myself against his face.

"Oh, fu-oh," I whimper. My climax builds to a crescendo. I reach the peak, and he maintains his steady yet relentless pace, and soon I'm bucking like a rodeo bull and screaming his name. Even after my hips still and I'm panting from the strength of my orgasm, he continues to suck and lick, wringing every last drop of pleasure from me. Blinking, I stare up at the ceiling, all the bones in my body turned to Jell-O.

Only when I've stopped whimpering and trembling does Lorenzo let up. Despite the incredible orgasm he just wrung from my body, I groan at the loss of him. That was so much, yet not enough. I lift my head, and he catches my eye and winks, making my cheeks flush pink. His beard glistens with my arousal. *Holy banana-balls.*

He won.

I push myself up onto shaky elbows and open my mouth to speak, but no words come out. What can I say? Beg him to keep going? Plead with him to fuck me? Because that's what I want more than I've ever wanted anything in my life.

My pussy aches with a carnal longing to feel him deep inside me, and my eyes brim with tears as I stare at him, silently begging him not to leave me like this. Not after what he just did. After what we just shared.

He stands and my heart stutters but resumes its rhythm when he plants his hands on the piano, bracketing my hips. His dark eyes burn into mine, searing into my soul. "You gonna let me fuck you, Mia?"

Holy mother of bananas. "Yes please."

CHAPTER
TWENTY-TWO
LORENZO

I lick my lips, stifling a groan as I taste her sweet cum again. Swiping a hand over my jaw, I wipe her juices from my beard and the scent of her on my skin makes my cock throb harder. She smells fucking incredible. Tastes even better.

I look down at her, spread open on the piano for me, her cheeks flushed pink. I love the way her pussy glistens and her perfect tits heave with every breath she takes. I'm practically fucking feral with the need to drive my cock inside her, but establishing her consent is a big deal for me. Thank fucking god she said yes.

She stares at me, sinking her teeth into that juicy bottom lip, her eyes pleading as she waits for me to fuck her. It makes me hard as stone to know she's as desperate for me as I am for her. I unzip my pants, sighing with relief as my throbbing cock gets a little more room. Pulling it free from my boxers, I give it a quick tug to alleviate some of the pressure. Precum beads along the slit and I find Mia staring down at it with a ravenous look on her face. Her tongue darts out and moistens her lips.

I bite back a chuckle. "You like what you see, sunshine?"

"Yes," she says with a soft purr.

I rub the pad of my thumb over her bottom lip, pulling down so her mouth opens. "These pretty lips would look so good wrapped around my cock."

My little siren takes my thumb into her mouth, swirling her tongue over it and sucking softly. "If your cunt didn't look so damn inviting right now, I'd put you on your knees and fuck your mouth instead."

She releases my thumb with a wet pop, and she gives me a wicked grin. "I have no gag reflex."

Holy fuck! I arch an eyebrow at her, trying to determine whether she's screwing with me or telling the truth, but my instincts say it's the latter. "I'll be sure to test that theory some time."

I press my cock at her soaking entrance, and she gasps in a breath, her eyelids fluttering as I push the tip inside her.

She moans my name, her jaw slack. "You want this?" I give her a little more, wishing I could savor this but desperate to sink all the way inside her. Her hot pussy feels so good squeezing me.

"Yes! Yes, please!" The sound of her pleading floods me with the insatiable desire to claim her. Grabbing her hips, I hold her still and fill every inch of her tight, wet channel.

"Jesus fuck!"

"Oh, god," she moans at the same time, her back arching off the piano. "That feels ... Oh! It feels so—"

I pull out slowly and thrust inside her again, cutting off whatever she was going to say. Damn right it feels good. Relief seeps into every part of my body as her cunt ripples around my cock.

She reaches for me, clawing at my skin.

"Nuh-uh, little firecracker." Grabbing her wrists, I pin them above her head with one hand. I like her this way, lying beneath me and taking everything I can give her. "Let's see how hard I can make you come with my cock."

She sucks her bottom lip between her teeth and her eyes roll back in her head while I plow into her. I run my free hand over her breasts, squeezing each one hard and eliciting a sharp gasp. With a mumbled curse, I yank her dress down, then her bra, exposing the stiff peaks of her nipples. She grinds her hips against me, mewling and whimpering as I continue pulling out slowly before driving back in, savoring the way every inch of her pussy milks my cock.

I dust my lips over a pebbled nipple. "You love being fucked, don't you, sunshine?"

Biting down, I make her cry out. "Y-uh."

I roll my hips, rubbing the crown of my cock over her G-spot, and she hisses out a breath as I trail kisses across her collarbone. "And you're such a good fuck," I grunt in her ear, and her pussy squeezes me like a vise, making me grin. She'd make an amazing sub.

She whimpers my name, bucking on the piano beneath me as she chases another orgasm. I consider making her earn it and a sick thrill fires through me. How sweet it would be to make her work for her pleasure, to have her luscious body coated in perspiration while I kept her on the edge. God, it would be fucking glorious.

But I don't do that anymore. It's enough to have her completely at my mercy. Pinned down and helpless, so desperate for me to let her come that she'd do anything. She digs her heels into my ass, pulling me deeper and bucking her hips.

"Please let me come, Lorenzo." My cock throbs, balls searing with need, and her words are my undoing. Spine tingling, I give her everything she desires.

"Oh, god," she screams as she falls over the edge.

I graze my teeth over the shell of her ear. "Lorenzo will do fine." With a grunt, I empty myself inside her, my release tearing through me with the force of a hurricane.

Working to catch my breath, I release her wrists. Her arms wrap around my neck, and the euphoria melts away.

"We can't do this again, Mia," I say quietly, unable to look her in the eyes.

She curls her fingers in my hair, her warm breath tickling my ear as her heart races against my own. "I know."

It's almost midnight by the time I head to bed. Passing Mia's room, I see the faint glow of a lamp from beneath her door. Is she awake, or does she sleep with the light on? It wouldn't be surprising, given her history.

I pause outside her door. She's probably asleep, but I rest my forehead against the cool oak and knock as softly as I can.

I'm about to walk away when the door opens and she's standing there in a tiny tank top and panties. She smiles at me, like she knew I'd be here. Maybe we both did.

"Everything okay?" She purrs the words, and they bypass my brain and travel straight to my dick.

My eyes rake over her body and I'm already hard. "I figured ..." Studying her face, I try to determine whether I'm pushing too far. Can we both walk away if we do this again? She sinks her perfect white teeth into that lush lower lip, and all reason goes out of the window. "If it's still the same day, it counts as the one time, right?"

Her perky tits jiggle as she lets out the sexiest little laugh. "I think that's right," she agrees, stepping back and allowing me into her room. I follow, closing the door behind me and herding her toward the bed.

Later in the night, while I'm fucking Mia way into the next day, I tell myself that it's still the one time. It definitely won't happen again.

CHAPTER
TWENTY-THREE
LORENZO

"You're not going to do anything stupid, are you?" Max asks with a wicked glint in his eyes. Max DiMarco might have mellowed in recent years, since he married my kid sister, but he's as unhinged as I am. Even more so in some respects.

Tension seeps into my pores and I roll my shoulders and crack my neck to try and ease a little of it. "Is this why you tagged along? Did Dante send you to babysit me?"

He laughs and shakes his head. "Just keeping you company, buddy."

I look across the parking lot at the motel, the one where Deputy Superintendent Hayes fucks his mistress every Thursday morning. "Like I believe that."

"Number twenty-six, right?"

"Same every week."

After scanning the buildings, he gives me the side eye. "You sure this is a wise move?"

"I'm not going to fucking kill him. But whatever Mulcahy has on this prick is something no other fucker seems to know about, so how else do we find out unless we go straight to the source?"

We come to a stop outside the motel room. "And we can't ask Brad," Max says, eyes narrowed as he holds my gaze.

"No. Mia specifically asked us not to."

His mouth curls up in a smirk. "That's what I just said."

I press my ear to the door. "I know what you're thinking. Fucking cut it out."

He laughs again. "Mind reader now, huh?"

Ignoring him, I listen to the sounds coming from the room. A man's voice and a high-pitched giggling. "We have no reason to go after Brad right now. The raids on our businesses have stopped, and he's leaving Mia alone." Although I'm still not convinced we shouldn't wipe the piece of shit from the face of the earth. But Dante said we should respect Mia's wishes, and I agreed, albeit grudgingly.

"So, why are we about to bust into Hayes's motel room?" Max asks with a devious grin.

"Because I still want to know what the fuck Mulcahy has on this slimy prick." I drop my shoulder and ram it against the door, breaking the cheap-ass lock and bursting into the room.

The woman screams, clutching the sheets to her chest to maintain her modesty, as if we're interested in seeing her tits.

Max picks up what looks like a dress and a bra from the floor and throws it at her. "Get dressed and get the fuck out of here." Shrieking, she scrambles off the bed.

"Who the fuck do you think you are?" Hayes shouts, pulling the covers over himself.

"Private detectives. Your wife hired us." Max chuckles as he pulls up a chair and takes a seat.

"Pete?" The woman scrambles to pull on her clothes.

"Shut the fuck up and get out, Candice," he barks at her. "I'll call you later."

She throws him a look that would melt steel, but then she glances at Max and me and hurries from the room.

As soon as she's gone, Pete Hayes climbs out of bed, his limp dick swinging between his legs, and pulls on the boxers he grabs from the floor. "When I asked who the hell you thought you were, it was a rhetorical question." He sighs, running a hand through what's left of his hair as he sits back down on the bed. "So, Mr. Moretti"—he fixes his blue eyes on me—"perhaps what I should have asked is what the hell do you think you're doing bursting into my motel room the way you just did?"

I pull up the remaining chair and take a seat. Despite who I am, even I would think twice about taking out the deputy superintendent of the Chicago police department in broad daylight, and he knows it. We have an amicable, if somewhat strained, relationship with Chicago's finest—meaning that we stay out of each other's way.

"I just need a little information and then I'll leave you to your day, Deputy."

He bristles at the disdain in my tone, but he shakes it off. "Since when do you and your ilk come to me for information?"

"Since it pertains to you."

His Adam's apple bobs and he glances toward the door, which Max promptly goes to stand in front of.

"You should've known we'd respond to the spate of raids on our businesses. Did you think we'd sit back and not look into that?"

"It was a few raids. Nothing was found." His nostrils flare and his fists clench by his sides. "You're really coming at me over this?"

"I want to know why you allowed a piece-of-shit cop from Boston to pull your strings like that."

A muscle ticking in his jaw, he shakes his head.

"Don't mistake my calm demeanor, Deputy Hayes. Yes, we

have an uneasy truce, but I will happily peel your skin from your body and roast your cock and balls on a barbecue before forcing you to eat them if you don't tell me what I need to know."

Face turning pale, he flinches. Hayes has heard the rumors, it seems, and believes me fully capable of committing such a violent act. But I've been around the block long enough to know that fear doesn't motivate all men. "Look, I have no interest in you. My family and I are happy with the way things operate in this city, and we have no desire to change that. But I do have an issue with Mulcahy."

"You won't come after me?" he asks, and I suppress a grin. I knew self-preservation would be his downfall. That's how Mulcahy was able to use him in the first place.

"I only want Mulcahy," I assure him. "So, tell me what that fucker has on you."

He takes a deep, shuddering breath. "She was his girlfriend."

Girlfriend? What the fuck is he—oh, fuck no. Every muscle goes rigid. Max senses it and takes a step toward me.

"That prick set it all up," Hayes continues. "Told me she was into role-play and that they'd planned it all out. He said she was supposed to say no. The screaming was all part of the act. She was supposed to fight back."

Bile burns the back of my throat.

Max places a reassuring hand on my shoulder. "Fight back?"

Looking down at his feet, Hayes nods. "He told me it was all part of the fantasy. He even told me her safe word, but she never used it."

My growl echoes around the tiny room. "Stop talking in riddles, Hayes, and tell me what that fucker has on you."

He blinks up at me, tears forming in his eyes. Tears for

himself. "He filmed it all. That twisted piece of shit filmed it all."

"Filmed what?" I shout.

"Me f-fucking his girlfriend. He t-told me she had a rape fetish. I knew her. I knew that she'd toyed with the idea of it a few times. So one night ..." He swallows hard, eyes darting between me and Max. My blood boils in my veins. "He arranged for me to h-have sex with her. He said it was the fantasy." He wipes sweat from his brow, and his voice drops to a hoarse whisper. "So she screamed at me. She scratched me and she c-cried, b-but I thought she wanted it." He looks thoroughly ashamed, as he fucking should. But it's not enough. All I can think about is my beautiful Mia being pawed by this sack of shit. Her cries and screams as she tried to fight him off. I don't care who the fuck he is, he's going to die a painful death for what he did to her.

He looks up at me, eyes wide and pleading. "I fuck around, and I like it when women fight back, but only consensually. You have to believe that. I'm not a rapist. I swear I thought she wanted it." He drops his head in his hands.

Stepping forward, I ball my hands into fists, but Max squeezes my shoulder and pulls me back. "You were partners in Boston, right? Thirteen years ago?"

Hayes sniffs. "Yeah."

Thirteen years? Mia met Brad ten years ago. I let out the breath I was holding.

"What was her name? His girlfriend?" Max asks.

"Sherrie Jackson." The name trips easily off Hayes's tongue, like he's never forgotten it. "She's married with three kids now. I hope she doesn't think about that night as much as I do."

Relief that it wasn't Mia washes over me in a wave, but the fury doesn't dissipate completely. It may not have been someone I care about, but no woman deserves that shit. "Pretty sure she thinks about it every damn day," I snap.

"I thought she was into it!" he insists. "I mean, what kind of animal allows their girlfriend to be raped?"

My clipped fingernails dig into my palms as I fight against the urge to punch him in the face. If I start, I'll never stop. "What kind of animal doesn't establish enthusiastic consent before he engages in a rape scene?"

Covering his face with his hands, he sobs into them. Max gives me a warning glance, and I nod my head, giving my assurance that Hayes will live.

Seemingly satisfied that I'm not about to start a war with the Chicago PD, Max takes his hand off my shoulder and turns his attention back to Hayes. "And you said Mulcahy recorded all of this?"

After several moments of sniffling and scrubbing his face, Hayes finally answers. "Yeah. He has it all on video. I'd lose everything. My career. My wife and kids. Everything."

I sit back in my chair and motion for Max to keep going.

"Why would he do that to you? You were partners? Buddies, right?"

"We were. But I guess he saw me as a way to get to the top. I was always going places. Youngest sergeant in my precinct."

"Or maybe it was more about Sherrie than you?" I suggest, knowing what a twisted fuck Brad Mulcahy is. "What happened to the two of them after?"

"They split up. I heard later that he'd caught her cheating on him."

I snarl. "So he had his girlfriend raped as punishment for cheating on him?" I'm going to kill that sick fuck if I ever see him again.

Hayes shrugs. "I guess."

"So, how does this work? Mulcahy just comes to you when

he wants a favor?" Max asks, his face furrowed in a frown as his mind ticks over.

"That was how it worked, but I hadn't heard from him in years. Not since I gathered enough information that could hurt him too. I told him that we were done." Hayes runs a hand through his sparse hair and sighs. "Then he showed up last week with a final ask. He wanted me to 'ruffle the Moretti's feathers.' I figured sending my men on a few raids would satisfy him without causing too much trouble."

"Why give into him when you'd told him you were done?" Max asks.

"He seemed different." Hayes stares at the window for several moments. "Frantic. Like he'd lost his mind. He threatened to show my wife and the superintendent the video, even though I could bring him down just as easily as he could me." I sit forward in my seat, but I don't interrupt. "He didn't give a shit. Said he was happy to take us both down, so I did what I could, while ..."

I narrow my eyes. "While?"

He rolls his neck. "I have enough information on him to get him kicked off the force for good. I just need to get that tape."

"But you haven't yet?" I ask.

"No. Prick up and disappeared. I spoke to his captain back in Boston, and he's been on sick leave for three weeks. Apparently his wife left and he went completely off the rails."

"But you're looking for him?" Max says.

Hayes nods.

"Officially?" I ask.

He shakes his head and avoids my gaze.

I lean forward, my interest piqued. "So, you plan on recovering the tape and then what?"

"Don't get excited, Mr. Moretti. It's nothing quite so

exciting as anything you'd have in mind. I'll turn over the evidence I have on him to Internal Affairs."

My mouth curls into a grin. "And exactly what evidence do you have on him, Deputy?"

"Intimidating witnesses. Mishandling investigations. Tampering with evidence. That kind of thing. Again, nothing quite in your league," Hayes replies.

"Shame," I mutter under my breath.

"So?" Hayes grabs his pants off the floor and holds them in the air. "You gonna let me get back to work before anyone notices I'm gone?"

"You're an asshole, Hayes, but you got balls of steel, I'll give you that. You hear anything from Mulcahy, you let me know."

"His wife's with you, right? Her cousin married your brother?"

I fix him with a glare. "Miss Stone's whereabouts are none of your concern."

He doesn't break eye contact when he replies. "Of course not."

The fucker really does have balls of steel.

"We need to deal with him, D, before he becomes a liability. He's holding us partly responsible for Mia leaving him. He's already proven he's prepared to tank his career. He won't stop until he has her back. Even without the threat to Mia, allowing him to live isn't good for business or our reputation." Talking to Hayes confirmed my initial gut feeling that Mulcahy is a problem we need to rid ourselves of.

Dante's deep sigh communicates his reluctance to go against Mia's wishes. Kat is firmly on her cousin's side, and he's rarely willing to do anything that displeases his wife. But he knows I'm right about this.

I lean against the edge of my desk. "I'm prepared to do it myself, quietly, if that makes things easier," I suggest.

"I'm not lying to my wife, Loz," he says with a frown. "I told her I killed her own brother, I think she can handle this."

"Tell her then. Tell them both. Mia might be pissed, but she'll learn to live with it." I don't understand why—and I don't wish to explore my reasoning—but I hate the thought of doing anything to cause her any degree of unhappiness. Still, I'll take her displeasure if it means keeping her safe from that fucker. Family is everything, and Kat is my family. At least that's what I'm telling myself to justify my commitment to Mia's well-being.

Dante glances between Max and me. "I don't want either of you running around the country looking for this sack of shit," he says with a shake of his head. "Mia's safe here, and she has no plans to leave. When Mulcahy comes back to Chicago for her, do whatever the fuck you want with him. In the meantime, let Hayes do his thing. The man might be a slimeball, but he's smart and ruthless. If luck's on our side, he'll solve the problem for us. An ex-cop is easier to deal with than a cop."

I don't have to like it, but his reasoning is sound. My baby brother has grown up a lot—he didn't have a choice. Dante was never meant to be the head of the Cosa Nostra, but his ability to curb his impulses and look at the big picture makes him the best man for the job, and I respect him enough to follow his lead.

"You okay with that, Loz?"

"Fine. But as soon as he comes back here ..." My chest tightens.

"Do whatever the fuck you like with the slimy prick," Dante finishes with a cruel smile.

TWENTY-FOUR

MIA

I thumb carefully through the well-worn copy of Little Women, wondering who read this book so many times that some of the print has faded. How many times did their hands caress these pages while being absorbed in another world? That's the true beauty of reading—being able to be anywhere you want while staying right where you are.

Closing the cover, I lift up on my tiptoes and slide the book into its proper space on the shelf. The door opens, and even with my back to it, I know it's him. It's been a week since he fucked me on top of the piano in this very room, and despite our agreement that it wouldn't happen again, it's happened at least once a day. And again every night. Lorenzo comes to my bedroom every evening after I go to bed, but he never stays, always leaving once I fall asleep.

The room charges with electricity and sexual tension. Every cell in my body responds to his presence, and my breathing grows faster, my heart rate kicks up, as he draws near.

I feel his warm breath on the back of my neck, and I shiver with anticipation. Strong hands slide over my hips, pulling my backside against his hard cock.

"You're a distraction, sunshine," he says with a low throaty growl, lips dusting over my ear and making goosebumps prickle along my forearms.

A smile spreads across my face. "I am?"

"An addictive distraction. You look good enough to eat."

"So eat me," I offer, wiggling my ass against him.

He sinks his teeth into the delicate skin of my neck, biting down and making me yelp from the combination of pain and pleasure. His fingers dig into my hips as he sweeps his tongue over the sensitive flesh, soothing the sting of his bite. Then he presses his mouth against my ear. "Be careful what you wish for, Mia."

Wetness pools between my thighs. "You could bite every inch of my body like that and you wouldn't hear a single complaint from me."

His deep groan rumbles through my bones. "Yeah?"

"Please?" I gasp out the word, pushing my body back against his and letting his heat warm me from the inside. In moments like these, I'd give anything to feel his hands and his mouth on every part of me. To have him fill me up completely.

He grinds forward, his thick cock pressing against my lower back. "Fuck!" Dragging his teeth along the column of my throat, he feeds my desperate need for him with each passing second. "You know what hearing you beg does to me."

I do know. It drives him wild, and I love it. "Please, Lorenzo," I whine.

Without warning, he spins me around and sets me on the third rung of the ladder beside us, then drops to his knees, a wicked look on his face. His tongue darts out to lick his full lips, and I nearly pass out from anticipation.

Holy bananas!

With a trembling grip, I grab onto the handrail while Lorenzo slides his hands over my ankles, gliding up my calves and past my knees. He slips them beneath my dress, pressing his palms on the inside of my thighs and spreading them wide open, forcing me up to my tiptoes. His fingers trail higher, and I whimper as he brushes over my panties, softly rubbing my clit through the fabric. I bite down on my lip, my eyes fluttering closed at the warm waves of pleasure radiating from that spot between my legs.

"So easy for me, sunshine." He releases a dark chuckle. I don't correct him, too busy shivering as he slowly tugs my panties down my legs.

"Hands behind your back," he orders as he leans forward.

I do what I'm told but struggle to maintain my balance on the small step. Thankfully, his huge frame keeps me in place while he loops his arms around the back of the ladder, grabbing hold of my wrists and pulling them through the rungs before binding them together with my own panties. He pulls the material taut, and it bites into my skin, making me wince. He presses a kiss on my collarbone that elicits a soft moan from me. He's so right. I am easy for him.

Then his hands slide down my thighs again and he lifts my ankles high in the air, causing my knees to press into my chest. He places my feet on the handrails on either side of my ass, making it easier to stay perched on the narrow step.

"If you move those feet, you won't be coming. Understand?"

From the way he has me folded up like a pretzel, I'd have difficulty moving them anyway. I imagine this isn't the most flattering position I've ever been in, but from the fire in Lorenzo's eyes, he's sure enjoying it. "Y-yes," I whimper, waiting for him to touch me as I sit with my dress bunched around my waist and my pussy on full display, tied up and completely at his mercy. A flush creeps over me at the realization of how wet I am and how clearly he must be able to see that.

He drags his pointer finger down my soaking center and I

suck in a breath, my back bowing. "So fucking ready for me." His growl vibrates through my core. "My fingers." He slips one inside me and I release a rush of arousal. "My mouth." A trail of heat follows his tongue from my collarbone up to my ear. "My cock?" He arches an eyebrow at me.

"Yes," I pant, needy and desperate.

He rubs a hand over his beard and stares at me. "But something's not quite right."

I frown. "W-what?"

He fists his hands in the material at the front of my dress. "I want to see this beautiful body when I play with you." In one swift move, he tears my lovely blue dress down the middle. "Much fucking better."

I feign a scowl. "You owe me a new dress."

"I'll buy you twenty."

I open my mouth to give him a snappy comeback, but he kisses me, stealing my words with his sinfully delicious tongue. He slides his hand between my thighs, toying with my swollen clit, and heat coils deep in my belly.

I moan into his mouth, unable to rock my hips against his hand because of the position he put me in. My moans turn to frustrated whimpers, and he chuckles. "I wonder how many times I can make you come with just my fingers?" His eyes search mine as he presses two thick digits inside me, causing a desperate groan to pour from me. "You feel how easily they slide into your tight cunt? So fucking wet and loose for me. I think you like being tied up, huh?" He pushes deeper, sweeping the pads of his fingers over my sensitive flesh and finding nerve endings that I didn't even know existed.

My legs tremble. I pant for breath. My eyes squeeze shut as I fight to control the tremors rippling through my body.

Lorenzo brings his lips to my ear. "And if I press right here ..." Going deeper, he curls the tip of his middle finger against a spot inside me that has never been touched before. It makes me want to howl like a prairie dog. Instead I shout his name as an orgasm more intense than anything I've experienced in my entire life barrels through me with the force of a neutron bomb. "Oh, there she is."

My body quakes with aftershocks. "W-what did you just do?" I whimper.

"I found your G-spot is all, sunshine," he says with a wicked grin while he continues to massage my inner walls.

"It was ... like nothing ..." I blow a strand of hair from my face and smile dreamily. "It was incredible."

He eyes me with amusement. "Wait until I make you squirt."

"What?" I gape at him.

His fingers move gently in and out of me, giving my body time to recover. "You heard me."

"I c-can't do that. My body doesn't do that." I mean I've never done that. I've seen it on the internet, but I'm not entirely sure it isn't just pee.

"We'll see." He winks and sucks one of my hard, aching nipples into his mouth. Biting gently, he prompts a fresh rush of arousal to pour over his hand. He picks up the pace, thrusting faster. The sound of my wet pussy being fucked by his skilled fingers is loud in the quiet library—and so hot I feel like I might pass out.

"You hear how much your pussy loves my fingers, Mia?"

"Y-yeah."

"You ready to soak us in your cum, sunshine?"

"I can't," I insist.

His eyes narrow and he licks his lips, murmuring something in Italian. Then he places his free hand flat on my lower abdomen, directly above my pussy, and presses firmly.

Aching pulses of pleasure sear through my core. "Oh!"

"Oh," he parrots with a devilish smirk and curls the tip of his finger along my G-spot again, rubbing firmly. I feel it more intensely because of the pressure of his hand. Holy shit! As if that wasn't enough to turn me into a gibbering wreck on the verge of melting into a puddle of cum, he straightens out the thumb of his hand pressed on my stomach and rubs the pad over my clit in slow, teasing circles.

I buck against him. With my feet stuck in place and my hands bound to the ladder, I have nowhere to go. "L-Lorenzo, please!"

"You gonna squirt for me?" he teases me.

"I t-told you I c-can't." I scream as my back nearly bows in half.

His dark eyes narrow and he drives into me harder and faster, maintaining steady, delicious pressure on my stomach while he rubs my clit. "You sure about that?"

Oh. My. God. My body will explode if he doesn't let me come soon. "It f-feels too ..." I draw in a sharp breath and let it out on a wail. "I don't feel in control," I whimper as my eyes flutter closed.

"Look at me, Mia," he commands, his tone so deep and authoritative that it makes the hairs on my body stand on end. I have no choice but to obey. I force my eyes open and press my lips shut to keep from babbling nonsense. Pleasure fights to take over completely. "You don't have to be in control here because I am. I've got you, sunshine. Nothing bad is going to happen when I have my hands on you. Understand?" His voice soothes every frayed nerve and every doubt in my mind. Doubts that have plagued me for as long as I can remember.

Why do I trust him more than I've ever trusted anyone in my life? Lorenzo Moretti is not a good man. He's a killer. A broken man, still in love with his dead wife. But I find myself nodding.

His gaze burns with fire and longing. "So, relax and give me everything you've got, tesoro."

Tesoro. I have no idea what that word means, but the way it rolls off his tongue feels warm and familiar. I stop fighting the overwhelming sensations flooding my body and allow myself to give in to them. Lorenzo works his fingers faster and deeper, pressing down on my abdomen until the pressure builds to a crescendo.

Oh mother of holy banana fucks!

"I-I c-can't ... hold on."

"So let go," he orders. "Let go and come for me."

Resting my head on the ladder, I arch my back and press the soles of my feet against the metal handrails as an orgasm even more intense than the last one—more intense than anything the world has ever seen—crashes through me like a freight train. I cum so much that I'm sure I drench us both. Every cell in my body trembles with the force of my release, and the wicked devil with those magic hands finger fucks me through it, grunting his appreciation as he does.

"Did I ...?" I gasp when I can find my voice again.

"You sure did. You've soaked my goddamn pants."

"Wow!" I pant. I squirted. And it was definitely not pee.

He gently slides his fingers out of me. "Told you."

I smile at him, my eyes still rolling back in my head, and tug at my restraints on my wrists. "Can you untie me now?"

A smirk plays across his lips as he unzips his pants. "No."

TWENTY-FIVE

LORENZO

Mia groans. The position I have her in showcases her pussy to perfection, but her arms and legs must be starting to ache, which is too bad because she'll have to remain there a little while longer. Her hazel eyes flash with desire as she glares at me. The fire in her is such a fucking turn-on. I love stoking those embers and igniting that spark.

Grabbing the base of my shaft, I squeeze hard and groan at the instant relief. My gaze falls to her spread thighs that are literally dripping with her cum. So fucking beautiful. I bend my head and lick a drop trickling from her pussy, and she whimpers—desperate for more even after what I just did to her. I could train her so well ... Except I no longer do that.

"Fuck!" I grunt. She tastes so damn good. Part of me wants to bury my head between her legs and eat her until she comes again, but my cock's so hard I'd probably blow my load doing it. I'd rather come inside her than anywhere else.

She breathes my name, and it makes my aching cock weep. I need inside her before I explode.

I place the tip of my cock at her dripping entrance, and she sucks in a breath that makes her beautiful tits shudder. I take in every perfect curve of her body. So helpless and in need of a good fucking. My balls draw up into my stomach at the thought of sinking all the way inside her wet cunt. She cries out as I give her a little more, and I relish the sight of her stretched wide around me.

Cupping her juicy ass with one hand, I give her more, making her thighs tremble. I dust the tips of my middle and pointer fingers over her swollen clit, and she keens, her body bucking on the ladder but pinned in place. So fucking beautiful. So fucking desperate for my cock.

"P-please?" she begs, but I go on teasing her, drawing out our pleasure for as long as I can. Only when I can't bear the exquisite torture of not being balls-deep inside her tight cunt for another second do I allow myself to drive all the way in, filling her with my cock and making her scream my name so loudly it echoes around the library.

Her pussy squeezes around me, hugging my dick as she coats me in her slick, silky juices. "Holy fuck!"

"Oh, god," she pants, her gorgeous tits heaving with every breath.

I wrap my free hand around her slender throat, squeezing just enough that she can feel the pressure on her windpipe but not enough to hinder her breathing, which is as fast and ragged as my own. I pull out and sink back into her again, overcome with the sweet relief of being buried deep inside her.

Tears run down her face, and her pussy grips my cock like a vise. I'm so close to losing myself in her sweet scent and her tight, wet heat. I'm so close to losing myself in her. My sunshine —burning me up from the inside out.

"Oh, Loren—" The rest of my name is cut off by her cries of pleasure as she's taken under the wave of another orgasm. She comes loud and hard, soaking my cock with her cum and milking me so thoroughly with her hungry squeezes that she tips me right over the edge with her. I bury my face in her neck, rolling my hips and grinding out every single drop of my cum. Unable to move, my body sags against hers, my hands still on her throat and her ass.

When I finally look up, she has the sweetest smile on her face, as though I haven't just tied her up and fucked her relentlessly. "You okay?" I work to free her feet from the handrails. She winces as I do, stretching out her legs and rolling her ankles.

"Mia?" I ask softly.

"Okay is not a word I'd use to describe how I feel right now, Lorenzo," she says with a soft laugh.

"So what is?" I reach behind her to untie her wrists.

"Umm." She presses her lips together, deep in thought. "I can't even ..." She shakes her head. "That was incredible. I feel like I could sleep forever and run a marathon all at the same time."

I pull her hands free and rub mine along her forearms to help the circulation. "You're not in any pain?"

"I ache." She sighs dreamily. "But no, I'm not in any pain."

She's moving her arms and legs freely and has that goofy smile on her face. My ray of sunshine can take the kind of fucking I enjoy without even breaking a sweat. But I guess I already knew that. Mia Stone might just be the strongest woman I've ever known.

"Good." I stand straight and pull her up with me.

"I do, however, have nothing to wear to get out of this library and back to my room without raising an eyebrow or two." She holds up the remnants of her dress. "And this was one of my favorites by the way."

I wrap her in my arms and kiss her forehead. "I told you I'll buy you twenty more."

Her body leans into mine, fitting perfectly, as though it belongs there. "Just one will suffice."

"I'll buy you twenty, then I won't have to feel guilty when I tear the next one off you." I chuckle.

She gasps, but the wicked glint in her eye tells me she can't wait for next time. She looks around the library and back at me. "But seriously. What am I going to wear?"

I untangle myself from her and unbutton my shirt. "You can wear this."

She watches me, eyes trained on my fingers as I unfasten each button. "And what will you wear?"

I hand her my shirt and look down to appraise my own attire. "My pants."

She pulls off her torn dress and places it on the ladder behind her before sliding my shirt over her arms. Something about her wearing my clothes makes a primal instinct take hold, but I shake it off. She's not mine. This is just sex. Mind-blowing sex, but just sex.

She arches an eyebrow. "You in your pants and me in your shirt? People will know."

"The only people who matter probably already know," I remind her.

She smiles wider. "I guess that's true. But actually I have some work to finish up here first."

"So do I. I did actually come in here to work before you distracted me with this ass." I squeeze it for emphasis.

"I was simply putting books away when I was accosted from behind."

"Is that so?" I silence her with a kiss. She tastes so fucking good. My cock twitches again, and I force myself to pull away from her before we end up fucking on the floor. "Finish your work in here and then I'll escort you to your room to make sure to protect your modesty."

CHAPTER TWENTY-FIVE

She flutters her eyelashes at me. "Such a gentleman."

"We have work to do, sunshine. So behave yourself." I give her one hard smack on her ass, making her squeal.

WHENEVER MIA REACHES for a high shelf, my shirt rides up and reveals a glimpse of her perfect ass encased in those white cotton panties, and by the time I finish what I'm working on, I'm once again hard as fucking stone. I can think of nothing but burying myself inside her.

I shut down my computer and make my way over to where she sits cross-legged on the floor, poring through a stack of old letters written by my great-grandparents.

She looks up when I approach, her eyes shining. "These letters are truly beautiful. Have you ever read them?"

I hold out my hand. "No. Come to bed."

She bites her lip. "I haven't finished what I was planning on doing today. I got caught up in these." She holds out a letter as evidence.

"So you can catch up tomorrow. You're helping us out, Mia. There's no deadline on this stuff."

"It's a good thing you guys aren't paying me." She places the letter to one side and grabs my hand, allowing me pull her up. "Because I'd definitely get fired," she adds with a soft laugh. "This stuff is all so fascinating that it's going to take me forever to get through it all."

Wrapping my arms around her waist, I pull her body close to mine. "I'd much rather pay you in other ways, sunshine." I trail my lips over her neck and she shivers.

"Me too," she murmurs, melting into my body like hot wax. "You could pay me in orgasms."

"Hmm." I bite down on her neck and suck, causing her to

gasp, before soothing the sting with my tongue. "How many are you owed for today's work?"

"At least another two, I think," she purrs, snaking her arms around my neck and curling her fingers in my hair.

"I thought I might have a credit after those three I gave you earlier. Remember? When you drenched the floor with your cum?"

Still kissing her neck, I feel her skin heat up. "Well, they were back pay." She giggles.

The corners of my mouth curl up. "Back pay?"

"For all those times you made me stare at your hotness all day but didn't even so much as kiss me." She tilts her chin up, giving me better access to her neck.

"In that case, you owe me at least half a dozen blowjobs."

That makes her laugh out loud. Then she fixes her beautiful hazel-green eyes on my face. "You'd better take me to bed so you can collect then."

A couple of hours later, I lie back with Mia's body draped over me, completely spent and satisfied. She made good on her blowjob promise, and I fucked her twice as a reward. I don't want to get up, but I always leave after she falls asleep. Sleeping in the same bed would make this feel like something more than it is. Something more than sex, which is all it can ever be.

She sighs contentedly and snuggles into the crook of my shoulder. "Tell me about being a Dom," she says, taking me completely by surprise.

"What?"

"You were a Dom, right? *Are* a Dom?"

"I was. Not anymore."

She lifts her head, the spot between her eyes pinched in a frown. "How does that work?"

"How does what work?" I snap unintentionally, but I have no clue where this conversation came from and I don't particularly want to have it.

"You were a Dom but now you're not? I just assumed if you were into that, it would always be your thing," she says with a shrug.

"I was Anya's Dom. I won't ever be anyone else's." Hopefully that's enough to shut down the conversation.

"So, you never had other submissives before her?" she presses.

I close my eyes and lick my lips, trying to stem the annoyance bubbling inside me. "Yes, I had other submissives."

Her frown deepens. "So, you're a Dom, not just Anya's Dom."

"I will never be anyone else's Dom, Mia," I bark at her. "That part of me died with her."

She blanches at my tone, but she's relentless. Propping her chin on her hand, she tilts her head. "But why?"

I swallow a thick knot made of guilt, sadness, and regret. "Because I swore I'd never be that for anyone again. Not after her. That part of my life is over."

She opens her mouth as though to reply but quickly closes it. "What?" I demand, against my better judgment.

"I just ... I guess that's all good if it's something you have no interest in anymore, but if you're only closing that part of yourself off because you think it's the right thing to do ..." She looks at me with eyes full of pity and I can't fucking stand it. "Well, that makes me sad for you."

Tension hardens my muscles. "I don't need your fucking pity."

"I never said I pitied you, Lorenzo. I don't."

I glare at her. I've never known anyone to be so infuriatingly difficult to argue with. She never takes the bait. Like she's programmed to defuse situations. Fuck, I guess she is.

"Why are we even talking about this?" I ask with a sigh.

"Because I was interested. The BDSM lifestyle fascinates me."

It does? She lays her head back down on my chest, snuggling close to me again like I didn't just berate her. "But if you don't want to talk about it, that's okay. I understand." She yawns loudly, and her breaths even out as she falls asleep.

Instead of leaving immediately, I hold onto her and think about her fascination with the lifestyle and what a good submissive she would make. I had half a dozen subs before Anya, each different from the other. They all required a different kind of Dom, but no matter what the nature of our relationship, they all fulfilled the same need in me—the need for complete control.

Gazing down at Mia's sleeping form, I wish that I could give her more. I push the envelope every damn day with her as it is. Every day I let her in just a little further, let her see more of my shattered soul. Someday soon that's going to have to stop.

Or her heart will end up looking like mine.

CHAPTER
TWENTY-SIX

MIA

I close the laptop Kat loaned me with a snap, not wanting Lorenzo to see what I've been looking at. Not that I have anything to be embarrassed about—I'm entitled to my curiosity—but after the way he reacted last night, I figure he might be pissed to learn that I've spent the entire day researching the Dom/sub lifestyle. I just find it all so intriguing. And a little thrilling. If only I could get him to unlock that part of himself again.

Lorenzo walks straight to the piano and takes a seat. It's getting dark out and I haven't switched the lights on, but surely he saw me sitting in here. He lifts the lid and his fingers brush reverently over the keys, but he doesn't play.

Setting the laptop aside, I approach him. He remains still, staring at keys as though they might start playing of their own accord. I run a hand over his powerful back muscles that flex beneath his white cotton shirt. His sleeves are rolled up and thick veins wind down his forearms as he clenches his fists.

I lean down and press my lips against his ear. "Would you please play for me?" I whisper.

His jaw tightens, the muscles in his forearms flex. Then his hands dance over the keys, and he plays a few notes of a song I don't recognize. I curl myself around his body, sliding my leg onto his lap, and he stops playing for a second to allow me to straddle him.

"Thought you wanted me to play for you, sunshine?" he asks, his voice a deep growl.

I roll my hips, lining my pussy up directly along his thick cock, and dust his ear with my lips. "I do, but I'm going to play too." My fingers trace the buttons of his shirt while his hands move swiftly and effortlessly over the keys, playing the beautiful song. His muscles tense as I drag my teeth along the fresh-smelling skin of his neck, and I resist the urge to bite and suck. For now. I nuzzle his throat, inhaling his masculine scent. Warmth pools in my core, and I squeeze my thighs together so they're snug against his hips.

As I work my way from one side of his throat to the other, a soft groan rumbles in his chest, spurring me on. He doesn't miss a single note, not even when I unbutton his shirt, but with each inch of skin I expose to the air, he grows tenser. My hands glide over his pecs, down every muscle and groove of his chiseled abs, sinking lower and lower.

I pop open the button of his pants, and he growls and misses a note, making me smile against his skin. To my surprise, he picks the tune back up perfectly, and the haunting song fills the library once more. I pull down his zipper, and he groans as I slide my hand into his underwear. My core contracts with a deep aching need to have him inside me. I can barely think straight, distracted by the burning desperation to have him fuck me. His ability to continue playing so smoothly impresses the hell out of me. How does he maintain such ironclad control?

I tug his boxers down and stroke my fingertips over his smooth, rock-hard length. He misses another note, and I grow braver. Lashing my tongue against a spot on his neck, I wrap my hand around the base of his shaft and squeeze.

"Holy fuck!" he growls, his arms and shoulders tense, but the music stays steady.

"Your cock is so beautiful," I purr against him.

He misses another note. "So sit on it." And another.

"If that's what you want." I fight my base urge and stop short of adding the word *Sir*. Wet heat slicks between my thighs, and I pull him free from his pants. Lifting my hips, I tug my panties aside. The soothing melody fills the room, but the tempo speeds up as I shift myself to the perfect angle for his crown to nudge my entrance.

His eyes burn into mine and my entire body shivers. He looks so tormented. But as I sink down onto him, allowing him to stretch me wide, his mouth goes slack and his eyelids shutter closed. He misses a few more notes, and when he reopens them, they're full of a different kind of desperation. A kind that mirrors my own.

"Mia." He follows my name with something in Italian, and I imagine they're words of desire and longing because those emotions pour from him in waves. His fingers clash and clang on the keys before he stops playing altogether. Banding his arms around my waist, he pulls me in tight, burying his face against my neck while I ride him. My pussy walls squeeze him, trying to draw him deeper, but he's already so far inside me that I feel him everywhere. It's pleasure bordering on the brink of pain. And when he fists a hand in my hair, pulling my head back so that he can feast on my neck, I whimper and allow him to take full control. He drives his hips upward and devours my flesh, all teeth and tongue and lips over my skin.

My skin blooms with heat. Pleasure shuttles around my body like lightning. I'm so close. I squeeze his cock and he groans loudly. Then he's talking to me in Italian again, whispering soothing words that call to my soul.

I rock my hips as he pistons his, thrusting himself deeper and deeper inside me and making light flicker behind my eyelids. Pleasure coils in my gut, snaking through my thighs and up into my ribcage before bursting out of every single part of my body. I scream, hanging onto him and grinding out my release. I'm unable to catch my breath while he holds me tight, pushing into me until he comes with a harsh grunt of my name.

I rest my head on his shoulder. Our breaths come labored and heavy. "What were you saying?" I whisper. "In Italian?"

"I don't remember." The lie falls right off his tongue so easily.

I swallow the sob that wells in my throat. "Shall we go to bed?" *Please.* I want to hold onto our closeness, but it's already ebbing away into the night.

"I can't tonight. I have too much to do." He brushes the hair back from my face and presses a soft kiss to my forehead.

"Are you lying to me, Lorenzo Moretti?" I ask, but I already know the answer, and I prepare myself for another lie.

"No, sunshine. I'm just busy. Promise. Go to bed and get some sleep and I'll see you at breakfast." He's already untangling himself from my arms and pulling his dick out of me before he even finishes the sentence.

Perhaps I pushed him too far by asking him to play for me. Perhaps it was too soon? I climb off him, tugging my panties back in place. "Can you at least tell me the name of the song?"

"Tchaikovsky's sixth symphony."

The final symphony.

"One of history's most famous goodbyes," I say quietly. If he hears me, he doesn't respond.

TWENTY-SEVEN

MIA

Lorenzo glances up at me as I approach, greeting me with a subtle nod before returning to his work. I slept fitfully last night without him beside me as I drifted off. Despite him leaving after I fall asleep, I find comfort in him being there until I do. I stand behind him, running my hand over his back, caressing his strong shoulders through his white cotton shirt. His muscles flex beneath my fingertips. Such a powerful, formidable man. He should frighten me, but instead he intrigues me. I can't help but wonder what it would be like to truly belong to him. To be his submissive. Wear his collar and have him own me.

"You're very distracting, sunshine." His throaty growl rolls through me, making me wet and needy for his touch.

I move around to the front of his desk and take a seat, crossing my legs and smiling when his eyes are immediately drawn to the bare skin of my thighs. "Well, it's so much fun distracting you, Sir," I purr the word, hoping it will shred his last sliver of restraint.

It has the opposite effect. His entire body tenses. A muscle in his jaw ticks, and a deep furrow appears between his eyebrows. "What did you just say?" His tone is full of aggression, and the hairs on the back of my neck bristle.

"I j-just ... I'm s-sorry, I was playing around."

His lip curls into a snarl. "Do you think my previous lifestyle is some kind of joke, Mia?"

"What? No! I just wondered how it would sound."

I wait for his face or his tone to soften, but neither happens. "I told you that part of my life was over. I told you nobody would ever be that for me again."

"I know. I was just reading about it and ..." I shake my head. I'm not sure what I expected to happen, but it certainly wasn't this.

He plants his hands flat on the desk. "To call me Sir is a privilege that no one will ever earn again. Nobody. Not even you. This thing between us—whatever you think it is—will end soon. You know that, right?"

My lower lip trembles, but I refuse to cry.

"Am I making myself clear?" he barks.

I stand. My throat swells with emotion, but I swallow it down and look him in the eyes. "Crystal." Spinning on my heel, I march out of the room.

I don't look back, and he doesn't ask me to stay. Just like that, I know exactly what the next stage of my life must be.

A FEW HOURS LATER, and after some research, I find Kat and Dante in the den with the TV on. She's curled up against him and he has an arm wrapped protectively around her. Smiling, I watch them for a few seconds. They're so happy and in love. Surely that's out there for me somewhere, right?

"Are you okay, Mia?" Kat asks when she notices me in the doorway.

CHAPTER TWENTY-SEVEN

"Yeah, I just wanted to talk to you both about something. But if it's a bad time—"

"No not at all," Kat says, her tone laced with concern. Dante switches off the TV and they both stare at me as I take a seat in the armchair opposite the sofa.

I take a deep breath. "I think it's time for me to leave."

"What? No!" Kat protests, as I knew she would.

"Yes. I've loved being here and getting to spend time with you all, but I'm ready to start the next part of my life. Seeing you and Dante so happy and in love makes me want that for me. And I need to branch out on my own if I'm ever going to have the chance to."

Kat glances at her husband who shrugs in response. How can either of them argue with what I just said? "But where will you go? Brad will find you."

"That's where I was hoping you could help me." I gesture awkwardly at Dante. "You can get me a fake identity, right? Let me start somewhere new as a different person?"

"Of course," he replies with an assured nod. "It would take a few days."

"But Mia ..." Kat makes a sad face.

"I have to do this, Kat. I'll miss you like hell, but I can't stay here forever. I need to go or I might never want to leave." I laugh, making a joke of that even though it's true. Dante regards me warily, and I pray that he doesn't push me for more details.

"Is this about Lorenzo?" Of course Kat's the one to ask that.

"This is about me needing to live my life," I tell her, avoiding any mention of her brother-in-law's part in my decision.

"You've always been a free spirit, Mia Melon," she says with a sad smile.

Tears clog my throat and I cough to clear it. "I'll always be just a phone call away."

"You have anywhere in particular you'd like to go or anyone you'd like to be?" Dante asks.

"If possible, I'd like to be a few hours' drive from Chicago. I found a few jobs in Iowa. But if you can just get me the ID, I can take care of the rest. I'm pretty resourceful when I need to be."

Dante promises me that he'll have everything by the end of the week. Kat gets up and pulls me into her arms. Embracing my cousin, I'm overwhelmed by loneliness, and a sob wells in my throat. Am I doing the right thing here? I remember Lorenzo's harsh words, how he's been pulling back from me. Yes, this is the right choice. I need to get away from him before he breaks me completely.

TWENTY-EIGHT

My mouth is dry, my chest heavy and tight. Last night at the piano was a huge mistake. I shouldn't have played for Mia, but she has me under some kind of spell. She's gotten too close. I feel her beneath my skin, creeping through my veins and forcing her way into my heart. That's what I said to her in Italian. How much I need her. How I can't go a single minute without thinking of her. And when she asked me what I said—how could I tell her the truth? Whatever's between us must come to an end before it goes any further than it already has. Before I lose what's left of my goddamn mind.

And then she called me Sir this morning. The word burned me, seared my soul. So many emotions boiled up inside of me, not all of them unpleasant.

No matter how good it felt or how natural the word sounded falling from her lips, I can't be that for her. And I was clear with her about that, yet she pushed me on it anyway. What the fuck did she expect me to do?

My neck and shoulders ache with tension. I slept on the sofa again last night, too stubborn and possibly too afraid to go upstairs because then I would have had to pass her room, and I might not have had the strength to walk on by. Maybe I would have let her curl up on my chest and fallen asleep right next to her.

My phone rings and I focus on the screen, thankful for the distraction. I sure hope Lionel has something useful for me— something that might take my mind off the siren down the hall.

Answering the call, I wait for some good news.

"I still can't get access to them records, Lorenzo," Lionel says with a sigh. "I even tried my old buddy at the bureau."

"You called me to tell me you have nothing?" I snap, taking the opportunity to direct my frustration at him.

"I called to tell you I'm out of options. And if my contact at the bureau can't help, this mess involves someone high up with deep pockets and a lot of strings to pull."

"Fuck!" The intel on Brad isn't essential to me, but I still want to know what the fuck I'm dealing with. I hate not being able to get the information that's certainly out there but out of my reach. It's not a situation I encounter often.

"I know this isn't how things usually play out for you," Lionel says as though reading my mind, "but this is the United States government. It's gonna take someone with a lot more firepower than me to get what you need. Maybe that girl not being found is a good thing, huh? Who knows what hell she went through that put her where she is?"

Looking up at the ceiling, I consider his words. Dammit, he's not wrong. No good can come from dredging up the past for her. But I don't fucking care. It might make me more of an asshole than even I thought, but Mia's safety is tantamount. "I have no interest in making her life difficult, Li, but I want to know what that sick fuck is hiding."

"I hear ya, I do. But my hands are tied. I do have some good news for ya, though. Your guy left the country."

"To go where?"

CHAPTER TWENTY-EIGHT

"Got himself a one-way ticket to Panama. Had a buddy of mine keep tabs on him and his passport pinged last night."

The knot in my shoulder throbs, and I tilt my head to stretch it out. "Doesn't mean he won't be back."

"Well, I'll let ya know when he comes back."

As we end the call, I mentally sift through my list of contacts, wondering who has the necessary pull to get their hands on those sealed records. If I utilize any of the obvious choices, I'll have to explain to Dante what I've been doing. I guess that's not such a big deal now that he knows about Mia and me.

I'm setting my phone back on my desk when Dante walks into the room, and the look on his face makes me wish I wasn't here. How many more problems want to fuck up my day?

"What is it?" I ask him with a sigh.

"Did you know Mia wants to leave?"

A wave of fresh guilt tinged with intense rage washes over me, stealing the breath from my lungs. I sit up straighter in my chair and take a second to compose myself, hoping my younger brother doesn't see how much his news affects me. "She what?"

His eyes narrow with suspicion as he takes a seat opposite me. "She said it's time to move on. Asked for a new ID to start fresh."

My hands ball into fists by my sides, and I grind my teeth so hard I figure they're about to turn into dust.

"I figured you must know something about it, seeing as how you and she are so"—he arches an eyebrow—"close."

"I knew nothing about it," I admit through gritted teeth.

"You want me to tell her I can't do it?"

Closing my eyes, I will myself to calm down. The blood rushing in my ears is so fucking loud that I can't hear my thoughts. Through my panic, Dante's words hit me, and I'm overwhelmed with love for my brother. He really would do that for me; he'd keep her prisoner here if I asked him to, no matter how much it might piss off his wife.

But no. I can't keep her. I knew that all along, didn't I? She's better off without me. We all know that. Can't believe she doesn't have the guts to talk to me about it though. The fact that I'm hearing about this from Dante instead of her has me wanting to track her down and demand answers, but I take a deep breath and refocus on the conversation. "Let me handle it."

Standing up, he shrugs. "Whatever you want, brother."

TWENTY-NINE

LORENZO

My blood is damn near boiling when I walk into the library and slam the door closed behind me. She spins around, her face a mixture of shock and surprise. Like she didn't know this would happen. This is exactly what she wanted, right? To provoke me enough that I'd beg her to stay?

She opens her mouth to say something, but I don't allow her the courtesy. "Is this some kind of punishment?" I ask with a snarl, crossing the room in a few strides until I'm standing so close to her that I can smell that damn sweet scent of hers. Jasmine and lemon.

Her forehead wrinkles with confusion. "What?"

"You heard what I fucking said, Mia."

She puts her hands on her hips. "I heard you, but I don't understand what you're talking about."

"It's a pretty simple fucking question. You asking Dante to get you a fake identity. Is that payback for what happened yesterday?"

"Don't be ridiculous," she huffs.

I fold my arms over my chest so I don't put my hands on

163

her. If I touch her, it's likely to only end one way. "So what the hell are you playing at? Because it feels like you're doing this to prove some kind of point. Were you hoping I'd ask you to stay?"

Backing up, she scowls. "I need to leave. That's why I went to Dante."

"If this is truly about you leaving, why not ask me to get you the fake papers?"

"You seriously have to ask me that?" Mia scoffs.

"I just fucking did, didn't I?"

"Ugh! For a man who's so intuitive, you're incredibly blind."

What the fuck is she talking about?

"I didn't ask you because I wouldn't have been able to go through with it. You would've looked at me that way you do and I'd have completely lost my nerve. I had to ask Dante or I never would have done it. I couldn't have summoned the courage to leave and I need to."

"Why? Because I snapped at you?"

"Mother of bananas, give me strength," she mutters, pinching the bridge of her nose.

Why do I feel like I'm missing something here? "Mia!" I shout, frustrated.

She flings her arms down by her sides and yells, "I'm leaving because I'm in love with you, Lorenzo."

I stagger backward, feeling like I've been sucker punched.

She softens her tone. "And I know that you can never love me like that." Closing the space between us, she places her hand on my cheek, and her touch soothes me in a way nothing else ever has. For the first time in two years, the constantly simmering rage dissolves, as though her light traveled through her fingertips and seeped into me, just enough to smooth the edges of my fractured heart and soul. "And I would never ask you to. But if I stay here, I'll convince myself that I can survive on any scraps of affection you throw my way. Don't I deserve more than that, Lorenzo?"

She does deserve more than I can give her. She deserves every-fucking-thing. "Yes." The word burns my mouth like acid.

"I want the whole package. I want kids and maybe even to get married again one day. I want a man who looks at me like he'd hang the moon if I asked him to. And if I stay here much longer, I'll never summon the strength to leave and find that for myself."

I stare at her, wanting her to stay but knowing that I must let her leave. She's far too good for an angry, black-hearted monster like me. She has too much to offer this world to waste any of her love on me. "I'm sorry, sunshine."

She gives me a smile that would melt my fucking heart if I had one. "You have nothing to be sorry for. I will never be sad about loving you, Lorenzo Moretti. I'll never regret a single second that I've known you. Just because this is the end of our story doesn't mean that it has to be all tears and sadness. I'm seeing it as the start of a new adventure. A chance for me to begin again, with a better understanding of myself and the kind of love that I've discovered I want."

There's a deep, gaping wound in my chest. Is she talking about the submissive lifestyle? About the things I've done to her body that she's realized she enjoys now? Why does the thought of her finding that with someone else shred through every single part of me like shards of glass?

"What about Brad? He's still out there," I remind her.

"He always will be." She shrugs. "I refuse to live in fear of him forever. I'm going to start a new life with a whole new identity, and I'll do what I can to keep myself safe, but existing in terror behind these four walls isn't what I want. Being a prisoner here wouldn't be all that different from the life I left in Boston."

She's right. She's too free-spirited to be contained. For the past few weeks, I've been a curious child who caught an exotic bird and kept her in a cage to admire her beauty. It's time to let her go and watch her fly. "And besides," she adds as she looks around the library, "I've finished sorting through your mom's things. It seems like the perfect time to move on. I hope it feels less cluttered when you're working in here now ... and I hope you think of me sometimes."

I glance around the library, and a ball of emotion wells up from my chest, sticking in my throat. I will surely think of her every time I set foot in this room. I'm selfish enough to ask her to stay. And if I asked, she'd let me lock her in this gilded cage.

But could I live with myself if I clipped her wings by denying her the life that will allow her to soar? I can never offer her what she needs, or what she deserves—

Mia's mouth opens and promptly snaps shut, and she looks down like she's afraid to say what's on her mind. But this is Mia—keeping her thoughts to herself when she's got something to say isn't her strong suit. "I know you think you're some tough guy with these walls you've built, but you're letting fear hold you back. It takes real bravery to open your heart and start again."

"You think I'm afraid? Of what? You?"

"I think you're afraid of feeling anything for anyone, Lorenzo. Of loving again. But love is always worth the risk. Even if your heart gets broken in the process. What's the point of living if you won't let your heart soar?"

"I could never love anyone the way that I loved her."

Sorrow clouding her hazel eyes, she shakes her head. "I know you believe that."

THIRTY

MIA

TWO WEEKS LATER

Dante hands me my new passport and driver's license. "Who are you?"

I answer without looking down. "Amelia Donovan from Phoenix, Arizona."

He nods his approval. "The house is all paid for—"

"I wish you'd at least let me pay rent."

"We've discussed this, Mia. We own plenty of property. The house is an investment for us, and it's yours for as long as you need it." I swallow the emotion welling in my throat and hug him goodbye. He wishes me luck and goes inside, leaving me alone in the driveway.

Kat and I said goodbye in the house; she said she couldn't bear to see me drive away. We stayed up way too late last night, watching movies and reliving our teenage dramas. We cried and laughed, then cried some more. But she and the kids, and their army of bodyguards, are coming to visit me next month.

I can do this. Any life I build now can't be any worse than what I left behind in Boston. Tossing my purse into the passenger seat, I grin at the blue Mustang that's almost identical to the one I drove when I fled Boston. I appreciate the gesture, and I'm certain it was Lorenzo's doing.

I've barely seen him since I announced I was leaving, and if I'm being honest, I'm glad. The time apart convinced me that I'm making the right decision. As much as it hurts to leave, and as much as I'll miss Kat and the kids and everyone here—*especially him*—this is the best thing for me.

I loved Brad once and he destroyed it. He almost destroyed me too. But what I felt for him pales in comparison to what I feel for Lorenzo. To stay here and risk never being loved that way in return makes my heart ache. As much as I love him, I would rather live alone with hope than live a hopeless life with him.

I thought he'd be here to say goodbye, but I guess I never meant all that much to him.

Looks like there's nothing left for me here. With a heavy heart, I pull open the car door, wishing I'd at least written him a note.

The front door of the house opens and he steps outside, dressed in one of his finely tailored suits. Without thought, I run toward him and throw my arms around his neck. Because despite it being over, what we had meant something, even if that something wasn't enough for him.

"I'll miss you, sunshine. Take good care of yourself, okay?" he says, his voice hoarse and shaky.

I close my eyes and breathe him in, savoring the familiar warmth of his embrace—all for the last time. It hurts to let him go, but he was never really mine to begin with. I press my lips to his ear. "Thank you so much for everything, Lorenzo Moretti, but most of all for making me remember how it feels to be alive."

With every ounce of willpower and strength in my body, I

untangle myself from his arms and walk to the car without a backward glance. Forward is the only direction I have any interest in now.

I hit play on the stereo, and the first bars of "Bright Side of the Road" fill the car. Singing along, I exit the gates of the Moretti mansion and drive toward my new life, leaving behind the man I foolishly hoped could be my forever.

THIRTY-ONE

LORENZO

I t's not an unfamiliar feeling that settles over me as I walk toward the study. The house seems quieter and darker than before, although I'm aware it's exactly the same.

I shake my head, annoyed that I'm wallowing in a misery of my own making. So, I miss her. It means nothing. She inserted herself into my life from the moment she arrived here—of course I fucking miss her. I threw myself into the arrangements for her new identity in Iowa because it was the perfect distraction and because it made it easier to let her go if I knew she'd be safe. According to Lionel, Brad's still in Panama, and Mia now has a secure house in a quiet neighborhood where nobody will ask questions about a woman who just moved from Arizona for a change of pace. I avoided her too. Under the misguided notion that not being around her would make her absence less difficult to bear.

None of that helped with the loss I feel today. It hurts just as much as if I'd held her in my arms up to the last second. Even when I was avoiding her, she was still here. Her laughter echoed around these walls, her scent filled every room she left. She made this house a home for me again.

But it was all an illusion. She can't replace Anya's position in my life or in this house. No one can.

MAX WALKS INTO MY OFFICE, his expression full of anguish. Oh, fuck. "What's wrong? Is it Joey?"

"No. Everyone's fine," he assures me, and a wave of relief washes over me.

"So what the fuck's wrong with your face, compagno?"

His Adam's apple bobs. He wasn't this fucking nervous when I caught him at his cabin with my sister. "I'm sorry, Loz." His voice cracks with emotion, and adrenaline thunders around my body. "I should've seen it." He places his large hands over his eyes, like he can't bear to look at me.

"What the fuck are you going on about, Max?" I ask with a snarl, a million different scenarios running through my head.

"This." He pulls a white envelope from the inside of his suit pocket. "She asked me to give it to you when the time was right, but I didn't know it was the right time. You told me it was just sex. She was the first woman ..." He shakes his head again, nervous energy radiating from him. "I didn't realize how much she meant to you until I saw how miserable you've been since she left. It's almost like when—" He coughs.

"Are you talking about Mia?" It's been a week since she left, and I've barely slept or thought of anything but her. I'll get over it. It's nothing compared to Anya.

I glance at the envelope in his hand. A letter from Mia? That doesn't make sense. It must be from— My heart races and I struggle to catch my breath. "What is that? Who asked you to give it to me?"

He holds out the white envelope and I see her distinctive writing. Tears well in my eyes. I slam my hands on the desk and everything on it shakes violently. "You had a letter from my wife, and you've kept it to yourself for over two years?" My voice is quiet. Calm. Deadly.

"She made me promise, Loz." He places the envelope on my desk. "I fucking hated keeping it from you, but she made me ..."

I stare at my name written in her beautiful cursive hand-writing. He had a letter from *my wife*, and he kept it from me. Anger wells up like a volcano and I glower at him, ready to tear his head off his fucking shoulders. "You kept it from me."

"She made me—"

"I don't fucking care!"

"Read it and you'll see why," he says, his eyes brimming with tears. "I'm not sorry I kept it from you, Loz, but I am sorry I didn't give it to you weeks ago. So you can hate me all you want, but you'll never hate me as much as I'll hate myself if I fucked this up for you."

"Get the fuck out!"

He blinks at me.

I snarl, lip curled and nostrils flaring as indescribable rage courses through me, blurring my vision and rendering me immobile.

"Now." My chest heaves with the effort of not killing him.

"Nobody else knew, Loz. I didn't even tell Joey." With that, he walks out, leaving me alone. I glance at my desk, at the innocuous-looking white envelope that just turned my whole goddamn world upside down. With trembling fingers, I pick it up and lift it to my nose, inhaling deeply. I hoped for her scent, but it smells of Max's cologne.

Placing it back down, I sit and stare at it. Once I open it and read her words, they'll be gone. I'll know them and there will be nothing new of her left.

I have no idea how much time passes while I sit and look at the damn thing, wondering why the hell she gave it to Max and not me—or even to Dante. He never would have been able to keep this from me. Is that why she chose Max?

My hands shake as I pull it open. It's not sealed, and I recall Max's words. *Read it and you'll see why.* How dare he read her final words to me!

My rage is washed away by a wave of bone-crushing sadness at the sight of the pale pink pages that spill from the envelope. I hold these to my nose also and sob when I find her sweet vanilla scent.

I open the pages slowly, careful not to tear or blemish the delicate paper, and I read.

MY DEAREST LORENZO.

I know you hate surprises, my darling. This is the last one from me, I promise. If Max has given you this letter, it must be time. Asking you not to be mad at him for keeping it from you is like asking the sun not to set, but please know that I chose him because he loves you like a brother, yet he's strong enough to see you in pain and still do what's best for you. Don't spend too long punishing him for only doing what I asked. I trust him to know when the time is right. He won't let either of us down.

So, you've met someone, right? I hope she is everything you need and want. I hope she makes you smile again, my dearest love. If I know anything though, it's that you'll be fighting your feelings, pushing her away and letting guilt consume you for loving her after you promised to only love me.

My Lorenzo, my darling. My everything. Our love was timeless. Perfect. It will never be replicated or repeated.

That doesn't mean you can't find a whole new kind of love. She might be exactly like me or nothing like me—all that matters is that she makes you happy.

My greatest regret in leaving you comes from my fear that

you will spend the rest of your life in darkness. Please don't, my darling. It would break my heart a million times to think of you never again experiencing all the joy that life has to offer. Your love for another does not diminish your love for me, and you honor my memory by allowing your heart to beat for another.

I wish that I could write more, but you know how easily my hands tire now. Besides, you are a man of few words.

So I'll leave you with this—grief is the price we pay for love. Would you trade any of your pain if it meant we lost even a second of our time together? I know you well enough to know your answer. You would endure a thousand years of torment for one more kiss, one more dance, one more anything. Do not let fear of loss stop you from living, Lorenzo. And know, that no matter what you do, I will always be proud of you.

So go live enough for both of us, content with the knowledge that the piece of your heart you gave me is safe in my hands for eternity.

Until we meet again, my dearest love,

Anya x

CHAPTER
THIRTY-TWO

MIA

FOUR WEEKS LATER

I have my back to the door when it opens. I smile, ready to turn and meet my newest client.

"Hey, sunshine." Oh dear god. That voice. The deep throaty growl I know so well. My legs tremble. My knees almost buckle

Spinning around, I gape at him and drink him in. And dammit, he looks so good. His beard has been neatly trimmed, his thick hair combed to the side. He's wearing dark gray suit pants and a white shirt with his sleeves rolled up. Those forearms—my kryptonite. A dull ache builds between my legs, and I clench my thighs together. I haven't had enough time away from him to stop responding to his presence. I wonder if it's even possible for enough time to pass for me to forget the pleasure this man's body can wring from my own.

He laughs nervously. "Surprised to see me?"

I finally find my voice. And my backbone. Damn right I'm surprised to see him. I've worked hard to start a new life here in Iowa. I love my job at The Relaxation Rooms and if he thinks he can just walk in here … "What the hell are you doing here, Lorenzo?"

He rocks his head from shoulder to shoulder. "I have that twinge in my neck again."

I fold my arms over my chest and fix him with my fiercest glare. "There are plenty of good masseurs in Chicago."

He starts unbuttoning his shirt. What the hell is he doing? "I drove five hours to have you give me a massage though. So hadn't we better get started? You charge by the hour, right?"

Charge by the hour. Jackass!

"Yes, and you got fifty-eight minutes left."

A smirk plays across his lips, and he shrugs off his shirt before placing it on the chair in the corner. "Pants as well?" he asks with a cock of one eyebrow.

I sigh. "Just your shirt is fine." He's actually going through with this?

"Where do you want me, sunshine?"

Back in Chicago? Or with your head between my thighs? I can't decide. I go with neither of those responses though. "On the bed. Face down, please."

He mumbles something unintelligible and lies on the bed, arms above his head and his face in the small hole in the bench. Without him watching me, I take a moment to check out his body while I rub massage oil into my hands. His powerful back is covered with eye-catching tattoos. Every muscle taut and toned and begging me to touch. And then there's that ass. I could sink my teeth into it, even when I'm pissed at him for intruding into my new life, especially when I've done my best to move on and get over him. Right now all I can think about is how I'd much rather be getting *under* him.

Stop it, Mia. He's a client. Nothing more. *You can do this.*

I slide my oiled hands over his back and his muscles flex beneath my palms. "Is it just your neck you're having trouble with?" I ask, biting on my lip as warmth spreads through my core.

"My back and shoulders too." He lets out a deep groan as I work my fingers into the muscles between his shoulder blades.

"You still sleeping on the sofa?" I ask and immediately regret it. I don't need to know where he's been sleeping. I don't need to know anything about his life.

"Uh-huh." He really has the most beautiful body. So big and powerful. Hard and toned and ...

"Are you okay?" He cuts through my internal chatter, and I wonder if I said any of that aloud. Or did I stop massaging him while I was thinking about how good his body feels?

"Yes. I'm sorry, did I stop?"

"No. It's fucking perfect." He groans again. "But are you okay here? In Iowa?"

What the hell kind of question is that? "Why are you here, Lorenzo?"

"I told you, my neck."

"Yeah, right." I stop massaging him. "Tell me why you're here or you can leave now."

He's quiet for a few beats. "I had to make sure you were okay, that's all. I just needed to see you and ..."

"I'm okay." I resume his massage. "It's nice here. I like my new job. My house is lovely and it's in a quiet neighborhood. Dante did a great job picking it out," I say, although I suspect Lorenzo had a hand in it too.

"I'm glad."

"You could've asked me all of this over the phone, you know. It would've saved you a trip."

"I told you, I needed to see you."

I swallow down a lump of sadness. "I wish you hadn't," I admit, dropping my hands to my sides.

He turns over and sits up on the bed, and I can't fail to

notice the huge erection he's now sporting. I guess it's not just my body that remembers, huh? "I've told you before that I don't offer those kinds of services," I say with a nod to his groin, trying to add a little humor to defuse the increasing tension.

He swings his legs off the side of the bed. "I swear I didn't come here for that, Mia."

I nod, glancing at the floor. I should be pleased about that, but for some reason it hurts.

"That's not to say I'm not currently thinking about pinning you up against the wall and fucking you so hard you pass out," he adds with a shrug. "But I came here to talk to you."

I look up at him and find his dark, pain-filled eyes fixed on my face.

"I wanted to say I'm sorry for being such an asshole when you said you were leaving. It was the right thing for you to do, and I should've supported you instead of pretending like you didn't exist."

"You should have," I agree.

"I need you to know why I acted like that," he says, his voice thick with emotion.

Tears prick at my eyes. "Okay. Why?"

"Because it hurts so fucking much to lose you. I need you to know that it wasn't all one-sided. You told me you loved me and I let you believe you meant nothing, when you mean more to me than I thought anyone ever could again."

He takes my hand in his and lets out a long breath. Bastard's about to break my heart all over again, isn't he?

"But?"

His face tightens, so full of anguish and pain and heart-break. "I care about you, Mia. I really do. But I can't let her go."

A tear runs down my cheek. I don't bother swatting it away. "That is why we would never work, Lorenzo. Not because you still love your wife—of course you do—but because you have no idea who I am. For a man so intuitive to my emotions and my physical needs, you don't actually know me at all."

His brow furrows. "I know you, Mia."

"No." I shake my head. "If you knew me, you'd know that I believe every person we love makes their mark on our hearts, shaping us into the people we become. You are the man you are because of Anya. Who knows if I would've even liked the man you were before her? But I love the man you are now. And if you *truly* knew me, you'd know that I would *never* ask you to let her go."

I pull my hand from his. "I'm going to the store. When I come back, I'd like you to not be here." I walk out of the room.

Don't look back. If I risk even one glance, I might break. I might accept the crumbs of affection he offers me. But I deserve more, and he was the one who helped me realize that. I close the door behind me. Closing it on him. On us.

WITH TREMBLING HANDS, I open the door to my treatment room. I'd be lying if I said there wasn't a part of me hoping he's still in here, waiting to tell me that he can't live without me. I suck in a deep breath, and I'm flooded with both relief and sorrow when I find the space empty. His scent and his essence remain. The memory of him. And a note, in his handwriting.

I'm sorry I can't be the man you deserve, sunshine. But I will always be here if you ever need me. No matter what or when or why, call me and I'll come. X

His cell phone number is scrawled at the bottom.

Tears rolling down my cheeks, I crumple the note in my hand. Damn that man!

THIRTY-THREE

LORENZO

ONE MONTH LATER

My fingers glide over the keys of the piano, playing the final notes of the song. It only took me a week to master, and now I can play it from memory. I guess Van Morrison isn't as difficult to learn as Tchaikovsky—or maybe that damn melody is just permanently etched in my mind. Her sunshine song, she called it. She hummed it all the goddamn time, and after she left, I couldn't get the fucking tune out of my brain. Who the fuck has a sunshine song anyway?

With a heavy heart, I close the lid. I should have learned this while Mia was still here and played it for her. I should have done a lot of things while she was here. Like never let her fucking leave.

I take my phone out of my pocket and, like I do every single day, check it, hoping for a message or a call from her. And just like every day that's passed, there's nothing. Of course there isn't. She's living her life and moving on without me.

She hasn't met a guy yet. I know that because I keep tabs on her via her cell phone and the security guard who works near her job. I don't know what I'll do when she does. Probably have him taken out by a sniper so nobody knows who's responsible. And then I won't be forced to admit that the idea of Mia being with anyone else fills me with jealousy that burns me from the inside out.

I scroll through my contacts and bring up her number. My heart races in my chest at the thought of pressing that green circle on the screen and hearing her voice. As it turns out, I still have a heart after all. It seems Mia Stone put it back together so quietly and carefully that I didn't even notice until I felt it break all over again.

I lock the screen and slip it back into my pocket. She made it clear when I saw her last that she didn't want to hear from me. Not that I blame her. I went there to tell her how much I missed her and that I wanted her to return to Chicago, but once again I let my doubts—guilt over Anya and fear of fucking Mia's life up more than I already have—stop me from saying any of that.

I need to delete her number. Need to stop checking up on her, other than to make sure she's safe from her prick of an ex-husband. I need to let Mia Stone go. She was never mine to begin with.

THIRTY-FOUR

LORENZO

THREE MONTHS LATER

The sound of my cell phone vibrating on the nightstand rouses me from a fitful sleep.

"What the fuck?" I grumble, fumbling in the dark for the offending item. Whoever's waking me up at buttfuck o'clock in the morning better have a great fucking excuse.

Every ounce of anger in my body is replaced with dread when I see her name on the screen. If she's calling me, especially this early, something's wrong. I've imagined this moment at least a million times, all the things I'd say to her to make her come back to me, but now I'm only filled with panic.

"Mia? What's wrong?"

A loud, guttural sob echoes in my ear, and every muscle in my body tenses. I fist my free hand in the sheets but keep my voice calm. "What is it, sunshine?"

"I-I ..." She sobs again. "I k-killed him."

Adrenaline courses through my body. "Brad?"

"Y-yeah," she stammers.

He's not even supposed to be in the country. I'll kill Lionel when I get my damn hands on him. I take a deep breath. "Are you hurt?"

"I-I don't th-think so."

I throw back the covers and jump out of bed, putting her on speaker so I can keep talking to her while I get dressed. "Where are you, Mia?"

"H-home."

"Is anyone else there with you?"

"N-No. I ..." She cries louder, and my heart seizes in my chest.

"I'll be there as soon as I can. Don't leave the house. Don't call anyone. You wait for me, okay?"

Her gut-wrenching sobs are her only response. Fuck!

"I have to make some calls. Then I'll call you back and keep you on speaker till I get to you, okay?"

After several seconds of silence, she sniffs loudly. "Y-yeah. Okay."

"I'm going to hang up now, tesoro. I'll call you back as soon as I can."

She doesn't reply, and I reluctantly end the call. I throw on a pair of sweats, my sneakers, and a clean T-shirt as fast I can. As soon as I get to my car, I dial Max's number.

He answers on the sixth ring, his voice thick and heavy with sleep. "What's wrong, Loz?"

"I need you to pay attention, Max."

"I'm here, buddy. What is it?" he asks, his tone laced with concern.

This man never fails to have my back, and that's why I couldn't stay mad at him for keeping Anya's letter from me. It took me a few days to get my head out of my ass, but once I did, I realized that he was right. I wasn't ready until I met Mia. Until I fell for her. And now she needs me and—fuck!

I quickly explain what happened while I head to my car. In

the background, I hear him telling Joey to go back to sleep, then the sound of clothing rustling over the receiver.

"What do you need?" Max asks.

"I need you to get four of our best men and a removals truck over to her place in Iowa."

"I'm on it." He sighs. "She okay?"

"She will be. I'm on my way there now. I need you and the guys there as soon as you can."

"I'll make the calls now. We'll be there an hour after you. Tops."

"Can you call Dante too? I know they're on vacation, but he and Kat will want to know. If you'd heard her … she was …" An image of Mia, broken and alone, makes anger and terror burn through my veins. I press my foot down on the gas. I need to get to her.

"I'll call him. You focus on getting where you need to be. I got it all covered."

I keep my eyes on the road and take a deep breath. "Thanks, compagno."

THIRTY-FIVE

MIA

I stare at Brad's lifeless body. His cold, dead eyes stare back. Unblinking. Accusatory. Deep red blood pools around him. Spreading out across the tiled floor like raspberry sorbet left out in the sun. Its coppery tang fills my nose and throat. I can taste it when I swallow.

I pull my knees closer to my chest and curl my toes into my feet so the growing puddle of blood doesn't touch me. It continues to reach for me, like his essence wants to drag me down to hell with him. Even in death he can't leave me alone. A deep sobbing sound echoes in my ears, and it takes me a few seconds to realize that it's coming from me.

A sudden vibration in my hand jolts me. I tear my eyes away from Brad's and glance down at my phone that's covered in bloody fingerprints. An unknown number flashes on the screen. Oh yes, I called him, didn't I?

The phone goes on ringing, and I blink at the screen until it stops. A second later, it starts again. The persistent vibrations travel through my palm and along my forearm. My thumb keeps slipping as I fumble to answer the call, but I finally manage it.

"Mia?" His deep soothing voice fills my ear. "Talk to me, sunshine."

"I-I'm here." I sob out the words as my gaze drifts back to Brad.

"Are you okay?"

I stare at the body of the man who made my life a living hell. A shudder runs down my spine. I can't take my eyes off him for too long. What if he's just messing with me? What if he isn't really dead? "I st-stabbed him."

"You did good, Mia. Are you still alone?"

"Y-yes."

"Does anybody know he's there with you? Did he come alone?"

Did Brad just wink at me? Did his eye move?

"Mia?" The soothing timbre of Lorenzo's voice calms the tremors fighting for control of my body.

I take a gulp of air. "He came alone. I d-don't think anyone knows he's here."

"Did he hurt you?"

I look down at my torn clothes and note the fingertip-shaped bruises blooming beneath the skin on the tops of my thighs. "N-not really."

"I'm on my way, sunshine. I'll be there as soon as I can."

"What if he's not really dead?" I whisper, scared that if Brad can hear me, he'll choose this moment to strike. I'm no longer holding the knife in my hand; my only weapon is this cell phone.

"Is he moving? Breathing?"

"N-no."

"Are his eyes open or closed?"

I shiver. "Open. He's staring at me."

"Have his eyes moved? Has he blinked at all?"

"I don't ... I don't think so."

CHAPTER THIRTY-FIVE

"He's dead, Mia."

"He looks dead, but what if ...?"

"Have you checked for a pulse?"

"N-no. I don't want to touch him."

"Mia, listen to me." He speaks slowly and softly. "You need to check for a pulse."

The thought of touching his body fills me with terror. "I c-can't."

"You can do anything, sunshine. You're the toughest woman I know. Do you know where to check on his neck for a pulse?"

"Uh-huh."

"Go on, sunshine. I'm right here with you."

Taking a deep breath, I creep forward, watching intently for any sign of movement. My fingers hover over the spot on Brad's neck. "What if I touch him and it wakes him up?"

"He's not sleeping or unconscious. If he was, his eyes would be closed. But if the man has no pulse, he's most definitely dead. Check and then you can know for sure too."

I nod. Logically, I know he's right, but fear has its icy grip clamped around my heart. All rational thought and reason seem to have left me. I fumble with his collar, exposing the skin I need to touch, and press two fingers against his throat. He's still warm, still feels alive. But his body remains motionless. Applying more pressure, I stare at Brad's face and wait. Nothing.

"You okay, sunshine?" Lorenzo asks softly.

"Yeah." I wait for a faint pulse to thrum against my finger-tips. Still nothing.

"You feel anything?"

Relief rushes through me, and I close my eyes at last. "No. Nothing at all."

"That's my good girl."

My heart finally begins to calm down. I lean back against the cupboard and hug my knees to my chest once more, feeling safe now that I know he's gone but still unable to find the courage to get up and leave him here alone.

"I have to make a few more calls. Will you be okay while I'm on my way to you?"

"I-I'm fine," I lie.

"I'll be there soon. Call me back if you need anything at all. Don't answer your phone unless it's me calling. And don't answer the door until I get there. Promise me."

"I promise," I whisper.

He hangs up and I press the phone to my chest. Right now it feels like my lifeline. My only link to the real world outside this nightmare in my kitchen. Brad goes on staring at me with his cold, dead eyes. It's a look I'm used to from him.

A slideshow of images from earlier flicker through my mind, and goosebumps break out along my arms. *Please hurry, Lorenzo.*

WRAPPING my hands around my mug of chamomile tea, I smile at the view from the window overlooking my little yard. A feeling of contentment settles over me. I love it here. It's still dark out, but a string of fairy lights illuminates the cluster of exquisite rose bushes grown by the previous owner. They've started to bloom alongside the jasmine I planted a week after I moved here.

My phone lights up beside me, the flashing battery indicator reminding me that I forgot to charge it last night. Putting it in my pocket with a mental reminder to plug it in while I get showered and dressed for work, I open the back door and step outside. The gentle morning breeze dances over my skin, and the sweet scent of jasmine drifts through the air. My stomach growls, so I return to the kitchen, take a large knife from the drawer, and place it on the counter. I open the refrigerator, searching for the strawberries I bought yesterday. Darn it! I got home late and was so exhausted that I ate them for dinner. A banana it is, then.

I close the refrigerator door.

My heart stops.

He's here. His face.

Right outside my window.

I scream.

He smiles.

My heart starts beating again. No, it gallops.

He's closer to the back door than I am. I'll never make it. I run for it anyway, desperate to close it before he can make his way inside. It's like I'm running through molasses in wintertime. He's inside before I can even reach the doorway. He closes the door behind him. The deadbolt clicking into place echoes around my small kitchen like a death knell.

I scramble backward and bump into the kitchen counter.

"Hey, honey, I'm home," he sing-songs, like he just came home from a shift.

"B-Brad?" My blood freezes in my veins and my heart tries to beat its way out of my chest.

He licks his lips, leering at me like I'm his last meal. There's a crazed look in his eyes. "You really thought you could hide from me, Mia?"

"I-I—" My words are stolen by the thick knot of terror lodged in my windpipe.

He edges closer, his expression growing more crazed as he nears me. His face is unshaven, his appearance unkempt. A sour stench fills the space between us, making me gag. My chest aches from the pressure of my racing heart.

I'm going to die right here in this spot before he even puts a hand on me.

"Faking a panic attack again, are we?" he says with a cruel laugh, mocking me.

"P-please," I beg, despite knowing the futility of it. He never showed me any mercy before, and now …

His face contorts with hatred. "Please?" He snarls. "You think I give a single fuck about you anymore, Mia?" He spits out my name like a curse. "Eight months I've been looking for you. Waiting for you to see sense and come back to me. You had your chance to beg me for forgiveness, but it's long gone, honey."

He takes another step closer, and my hands and legs tremble violently. Watching me, he gives a vicious laugh.

Fucking asshole.

I suck in air and lean against the counter for support, trying to regulate my breathing and calm my stampeding heart. Nothing I say will have any effect on him. Brad Mulcahy doesn't have one decent bone in his entire body. Why the hell would I give this sack of elephant dung the satisfaction of seeing me cower in fear? Never again. This might be the end for me, but I won't make it easy for him.

"Beg your forgiveness?" I find my voice, and while it's little more than a croak, he falters. His nostrils flare as he glowers at me. "I should have left you the first time you hit me." My voice grows stronger. "The first time you raped me. The first time you made me question my own sanity."

"Ungrateful bitch," he spits, cracking the back of his hand across my face. His signature move. My head snaps back and pain blooms on my cheekbone, but I stand tall and glare at him.

"You are a coward and a bully, Brad Mulcahy."

He bares his teeth, like a rabid animal. "Did he tell you that?" His face contorts with disgust. "The guy you were fucking in Chicago?"

The reminder of him gives me a fresh shot of adrenaline. Even in the face of certain death, Lorenzo Moretti would stay strong until his last breath. "Lorenzo is a far better man than you will ever be, Brad."

His body vibrates with rage. "Fucking whore." He makes a grab for me, and I'm not fast enough to dodge him. Vicious hands tear at my clothes. I struggle against him. My shirt rips down the middle, exposing my breasts. That only seems to drive him into a deeper frenzy.

He rages at me. Calls me a slut and a whore while he tries to tear off the rest of my clothes. I scratch and claw at him, but he's bigger and stronger and his determination to take what he wants rivals my resolve not to let him. Survival instinct kicks in, and I lash out, kicking him in his knee. He howls but remains undeterred. Slamming me back against the counter, he tugs at my pajama shorts, almost making me topple over as he wrenches them off my legs.

"I don't want you, you fucking animal!" I screech, but he only laughs.

"Tough shit, honey. I'm going to fuck you so hard you'll forget about ever having another man between your legs." He wraps a hand around my throat, his grip brutal. Thick, ugly fingers probe the tops of my thighs, leaving bruises everywhere he touches. I need a weapon. Something. Anything. He brushes the edge of my panties and bile surges from my stomach, burning my esophagus as I'm forced to swallow it down.

Strawberries!

I reach behind me, scrabbling for the knife in the sink. My hand curls around the smooth handle, and I'm filled with a rush of adrenaline. Brad's disgusting fingers slip into my panties, and I swing my left arm, plunging the blade into the column of his throat. His gray eyes widen; his grip loosens. Blood bubbles from his lips and he staggers back, reaching for the knife embedded in his neck. He pulls it free and blood gushes from his wound, spurting all over me as he lurches forward, grasping at my clothes.

This time he's the one begging. His eyes plead for mercy, full of terror and the knowledge that he's about to die. I wrench from his grip, and he stumbles back and crumples to the floor, choking on his own blood.

I gulp for air. *What the hell have I done?*

I killed a cop. Holy fuck! My cell phone vibrates in my pocket, and I pull it out. The red indicator flashes, reminding me that the battery is low. A hysterical laugh bubbles out, and it tumbles from my hands as I lift them to my lips. The battery symbol continues to blink at me from the floor, almost like it's trying to tell me something ...

Ten digits pop into my head. A phone number I memorized from the wrinkled piece of paper that I read more times than I could count. Sinking to the floor, I send up a prayer that he picks up, and I use my trembling, blood-soaked fingers to call Lorenzo.

THIRTY-SIX

LORENZO

Throwing the driver's side door open without bothering to turn off the engine, I bolt from the car and race up the small path that leads to Mia's little house in this idyllic neighborhood that I chose especially for her. I called her back after I finished speaking with Max, but it went straight to voicemail. I've spent the past four hours thinking of every possible worst-case scenario while praying that her phone just died.

The front door is locked, but that's not about to stop me. Using my shoulder as a battering ram, I splinter the wood around the frame and stumble into the entryway. The scent of jasmine and lemon fills the air.

"Mia?" My heart pounds so hard in my chest I'm certain it will explode if I don't know that she's okay in the next ten seconds. I head for the kitchen, crossing the small hallway in two strides, and I see her piece-of-shit husband first. Lying face up, his body sprawled at an unnatural angle in a pool of congealed blood.

My eyes dart around the kitchen, heart hammering and

blood thundering in my ears until I see her, curled up in a ball a few feet away from him, her attention fixed on his dead body.

I say her name again, but she doesn't respond. Stepping over him, I crouch down in front of her. She stares right through me and offers no resistance while I check her to make sure she's okay, running my hands down her arms and pulling them away from her body to check for damage. There's a small cut above her eye and red marks on her neck, and she's covered in blood, but it doesn't look like any of it is hers.

Her T-shirt is torn, her shorts are in the corner. Every sinew in my body threatens to detonate with pent-up rage. This is my fault. I should have killed that twisted fuck when I had the chance.

I never should have let her leave.

"Mia," I say calmly, swallowing down all the rage that's bubbling to get out of me. I snap my fingers in front of her face and she blinks, so I cup her jaw softly, tilting her head. Her hazel eyes fix on mine. "I'm here, sunshine."

"Lorenzo?" she croaks, tears welling in her eyes. They're full of confusion and terror and panic, and my heart is fucking breaking in two. How the fuck could I let this happen to her? I should have done better. I should've looked after her and protected what's mine.

Mine.

I pull her into my arms, wrapping them around her as I press my lips against her hair. "I'm here, sunshine. I got you."

Heaving sobs wrack her body and I hold her until they subside enough that I can speak to her. Brushing her thick hair back from her face, I kiss her forehead and inhale her sweet scent. "Let's get you cleaned up and get you out of here. Okay?"

She nods meekly. I've seen this before. She's numb from the shock of what she did, and from the realization of what might have happened if she hadn't killed him first. I scoop her into my arms and stand, noting the fresh bruises on the tops of her thighs. Bile burns in my gullet, but I swallow it down and carry her from the kitchen, closing the door behind us so the stench of her ex-husband's corpse doesn't follow.

I set her on her feet in the bathroom and she wobbles unsteadily. Grabbing her waist to steady her, I try not to think about all the other times I've had my hands on her. And how that disgusting fuck had his hands on her again—which I allowed to happen.

Keeping one hand on her waist, I reach behind her and turn on the shower. "You need help getting undressed?"

After shaking her head, she peels the torn T-shirt from her body and stands before me in only her panties. I glance away while she tugs them down her legs and kicks them off her feet. Once she's undressed, I look into her hazel eyes, more brown today than green. "You want me to wait outside for you?"

She shakes her head again, but then she just stands there, like she's forgotten what to do next. "You're going to get into the shower and wash the blood off," I say, gently coaxing her.

"Yeah," she says absent-mindedly, her voice little more than a whisper. She steps gingerly into the walk-in shower and stands beneath the hot running water. I wait for her to wash herself clean of that fucker's blood, but she remains still, her only movement the gentle shuddering of her shoulders as she starts to cry.

Fuck!

I kick off my sneakers and step into the shower behind her, turning her around and pulling her into my arms. She buries her face against my T-shirt, sobbing softly as the water runs over us both. I have no idea how long I stand with her, holding her while she lets everything out, but I do know that I will hold her for the rest of my life if that's what she needs.

CHAPTER

THIRTY-SEVEN

MIA

I lean back against Lorenzo's strong chest as he lathers shampoo in my hair. He's surprisingly gentle for a man with such powerful hands. I love the feeling of his skin on mine. I'd forgotten how much I missed it. He climbed in here with me fully clothed, but now his T-shirt and sweatpants lie in a soaking heap in the corner of my bathroom floor.

"You okay there, sunshine?" His lips trail over the sensitive skin on my neck. Despite the circumstances, my core contracts with heat at the memory of his mouth on my body.

"I'm better than I was," I reply honestly. At least I can think clearly now that I'm no longer trapped in a daze of panic and fear. Lorenzo is here. Lorenzo can make all of this go away, right? Maybe I can go back to my nice little life that I was building here in Iowa. He rinses the shampoo from my hair and adds conditioner before squeezing body wash into his palms.

"Are you hurt anywhere?" he asks in his deep, soothing voice as he starts to wash my arms.

"My face is a little tender, but it's okay."

He clears his throat. "And what about anywhere else? Is there any place you don't want me to touch you?"

CHAPTER THIRTY-SEVEN

I turn in his arms and stare up into his handsome face.

"You have some bruises on your thighs," he says, by way of explanation, and the fear in his eyes makes my heart ache for him.

"They don't hurt. And I stabbed him before he could ..." My cheeks burn with anger and irrational shame.

"I'm sorry I didn't kill him for you myself. I should have." His soapy hands glide over my stomach.

"I asked you not to," I remind him. "I honestly thought he'd let me go. That once I was gone, he'd see that we had nothing left together." I shake my head at my own naivete.

He kisses my forehead and washes the blood spatter from my chest. "You're a very difficult woman to let go of, Mia."

Not all that difficult. Not for you. I don't say that though, because it's petty and childish. Lorenzo came when I called. He's taking care of me, and he'll do that right up to the point he has to leave. I close my eyes and focus on the sensation of his strong, comforting hands washing me clean. Finished with my top half, he drops to his knees and washes my ankles, snaking up my calves to my thighs. He's extra gentle when he soaps the tops of my legs, careful not to apply too much pressure to my bruised skin.

His knuckles brush my pussy lips, and my knees almost buckle at his touch and the rush of memories he invokes. He moves on quickly, and I remind myself that this isn't about that. This is simply him helping me out because he cares. I need to stop clinging onto hope for more.

I step out of my bedroom, towel drying my hair. Lorenzo paces up and down my hallway with a towel wrapped around his waist, and he's speaking into his phone in Italian. I don't understand a word of what he's saying. However, I can tell from his tone and the scowl on his face that he's annoyed. Seeing me, he stops pacing and quickly ends the call.

"You feeling better, sunshine?" he asks, his eyes narrowed in concern.

"A little, but ..." I swallow the ball of anxiety that has made a permanent home in the space between my chest and throat.

"I'll take care of all this." He steps toward me. "It'll be like you were never here. Brad too."

"Me?" I assumed I'd stay here, although living in this house after what happened this morning doesn't exactly fill me with joy.

"Yes, you. You can't stay here now. Max is on his way with a team. They'll move all your things back to Chicago. Amelia Donovan has returned to her old life in Phoenix, and Mia Stone has been with me in Chicago since you left Boston."

My head spins. I must still be in shock. "You're taking me back to Chicago with you?" Before I can ask why or what that means, there's a knock at my front door.

"That'll be Max and the guys. You have nothing to worry about, sunshine. They'll take care of everything and I'm going to drive us home."

He opens the door, and Max steps inside first, not even batting an eye at Lorenzo only wearing a towel. "I got some spare clothes in the truck." He gives his friend a quick hug and moves around him.

Max approaches me with a sympathetic smile. "Hey, Mia. How're you doing?"

Four men dressed in coveralls with the name *Tommy's Removals* printed on the front file into my small hallway, each of them greeting Lorenzo. None of them show any surprise at his lack of clothing.

I glance back to Max. "I guess I've been better."

Max wraps an arm around my shoulder and gives me a brief squeeze. "You did the right thing."

"Tommy, take that fucker's car and drive it to the pound in Michigan. Leroy will turn it into a pile of scrap metal before the day's out."

A tall man with gray eyes and a gray goatee nods. "Will do."

"Any of your furniture you have a particular fondness for, Mia?" Lorenzo asks me.

I shake my head. I don't have a lot of attachment to material possessions.

"Then pack up her personal belongings and burn everything else," Lorenzo orders.

"What? Some of that stuff is nice. At least give it to goodwill," I insist.

"Burn it," Lorenzo repeats. "The less evidence there is of Mia being here, the better."

I frown at him, but he goes on barking orders to Max and the other men. They're going to make this look like Amelia Donovan never existed at all. Max will check the security footage, including doorbell cameras, in the nearby area and erase anything that shows Brad's car. When they've finished discussing the plan for my house and my things, they move onto the body.

"So, we cut him into pieces, stuff him in a couple of suitcases and then we drive him to Chicago and turn him into ash?" Max says with a wicked grin, like this is his favorite part of his job. Like they aren't talking about a man whose heart beat steady in his chest just a few hours ago. A vile man, but still a man. My stomach rolls and I fight the urge to be sick.

Sensing my discomfort, Lorenzo steps up beside me and slips his arm around my waist, giving me a reassuring squeeze before adding, "Then you scatter him in the river."

I stand frozen in my hallway while Max and the other guys

get to work. A million thoughts and questions race through my head. What about my job? My clients? The friends I was starting to make? My life here in Iowa?

"Mia?" Lorenzo's deep voice cuts through my internal chatter, and I realize he's been talking to me.

I gape at him. "This is …" I swallow a sob. What the hell did I expect? I just killed my cop ex-husband in my kitchen. "It's a lot."

He pulls me close and wraps his arms around me. I hate that he feels so much like home. I hate that within an hour of him being here, I'm already so dependent on him for comfort. "I know, sunshine. We'll be home soon though and you can put all of this behind you."

Home? Chicago isn't my home. "But what about my job?"

"You'll need to call your boss and tell her you can't come back. Tell her your mom is sick so you've had to rush home to Phoenix to take care of her. That's all you need to say."

He makes it all sound so easy. Like we can just erase everything that happened here. Like he erased everything that happened between us? Another sob wells up in my throat. I'm overly emotional, but he's right. I need to leave here. I can figure out where to go next once I'm safe in the Moretti mansion. Once I'm back with Kat, the only family I have left.

Nodding my agreement, I roll back my shoulders and look him in the eye. "I'll call Gina and tell her."

"Good girl."

I ignore the way those two words make goosebumps prickle out all over my body, and I hope that Lorenzo doesn't notice either.

CHAPTER
THIRTY-EIGHT

LORENZO

I end the call to Max and lean back in my chair. It seems Lionel Hart died of a heart attack two Saturdays ago. Alone in his apartment, drinking a beer and smoking a cigarette. No wonder the guy didn't tell me Brad had returned to the States. I hope he at least went out with a smile on his face.

Brad's ashes have been tossed into the river, his car crushed, and every trace of him and Mia has been forensically removed from her little house in Iowa—the house I found for her, thinking it would keep her safe. The house she never should have even moved to because I never should've let her leave the protection of these walls.

The door to the study is open, and Ed, one of the men who helped today, strolls in. "Anything else you need before I leave, Boss?"

I rub my temples, trying to stave off the inevitable headache. "Are all of Mia's things here?"

"Yep. Moved them all in myself."

"Then yeah, you can go. I need to call Dante. Tell the guards I'm not to be disturbed."

"Will do, Boss." He pulls the door closed behind him.

Dante answers on the second ring as though he's been waiting for my call. "Hey, Loz. How is she?"

"She's okay. Shaken up. Has a few bruises, but she's here now and she's safe."

He relays the information to Kat. Mia called her cousin herself on the drive back to Chicago, but she'll have been waiting for confirmation that Mia made it home safely.

"And how're you doing?" Dante asks, his voice laced with concern.

"Fine."

He gives a faint laugh.

"I never should have let her go, D." He doesn't try to correct me or make me feel better about the fact that I failed her, which I appreciate. "I should've ..." I run a hand through my hair and stare up at the ceiling.

Dante remains silent.

"If I make her stay ... She's like a ray of fucking sunshine, and I'm a huge fucking black hole. I'll consume her with my darkness, D. I'll fuck up her life, just like I fucked up Anya's."

"You are not the reason Anya got sick, Loz," Dante snaps. "She loved every fucking second of her life with you. She loved *you*. Don't start rewriting history because you're feeling sorry for yourself."

I suck on my bottom lip, mired in thoughts of my dead wife as well as the woman who calls to my fucking soul like she was born to be a part of me. Dante's right, but I don't need to tell him that.

"Mia loves you too. It's not too late to fix whatever it is you think you did wrong."

"Yeah," I murmur absent-mindedly.

"Anyway, tell me what happened. Is everything taken care

of?" He brings the conversation back to business, and I give him a rundown of the day's events.

THIRTY-NINE

MIA

T open the door to my old room, expecting to see stacks of boxes, but it's just as I left it four months earlier—full of tasteful furniture but none of my things are in here. Frowning, I wander over to the closet. Perhaps someone put everything away? No, it's empty too, aside from a few blankets and spare pillows.

Where the hell is my stuff? I want to take a long hot soak, and I need my clean clothes and toiletries. Wandering back into the hallway, I look around for one of the housekeepers.

Hearing footsteps in the hallway below, I lean over the rail and recognize one of the men who arrived with Max earlier today.

"Hey?" I call, unaware of his name.

He looks up at me and smiles. "Yeah?"

"Do you know where my things are?"

"Sure. We put everything in the boss's room."

I frown. "Oh?" They must have misunderstood our relationship. "Do you know where he is?"

"He's on a call with Dante. Not to be disturbed."

"Oh. Okay. Um, thanks."

CHAPTER THIRTY-NINE

"You're welcome, ma'am."

What the hell should I do? I need my stuff, but I don't want to interrupt his call. Maybe I can sneak into his room and quickly grab what I need. Then I can tell him there's been a mix-up and get everything put in the right place.

My heart beats fast as I push open the huge oak door that's as imposing as he is. Stepping inside, I suck in a shaky breath. I've never set foot in here; it feels like a violation of his privacy.

The space is very *him*. Dark and masculine and fresh smelling. A four-poster super king-sized bed with navy bed linens dominates the room. The wooden floor is warm underfoot as I pad over to my boxes stacked in front of a large oak dresser.

I find the box labeled *toiletries* in thick black pen. Everything is packed neatly inside, and tears prick at my eyes. Lorenzo and Max and their men looked after me so well today. I move the make-up bag from the top of the pile, searching for my bubble bath.

"Where the fig are you?" I mutter as I dig deeper.

The door closes behind me and a shiver runs along my spine. Oh crap!

I spin around, heart beating wildly from being caught in Lorenzo's private space. He stares at me, his hands stuffed in his pockets and stretching the material taut over his thick thighs.

Words get caught in my throat, and for an awful moment I wonder if I've lost my ability to speak. "I'm s-sorry." I dart my tongue out, moistening my dry lips. "Your men put my things in here by mistake."

He crosses the room in three giant strides. Wow, he smells so good. My body instinctively leans toward his, the memory of the comfort I found in his arms earlier dominating my thoughts. Being near him made everything better; he made me feel so safe and cared for.

"Not by mistake, Mia. I asked them to."

My racing heart flutters like a butterfly trapped in a glass jar. "But why?" The words come out so quietly, I wonder if he heard them.

He brushes his fingertips over my bruised cheek. "Because I want you in here with me."

My head spins. I'm still so confused. "For tonight?"

"For every night." He cups my chin in his hand. "But I should have asked. You can have your own room if you'd prefer."

Tears blur my vision. This can't be happening. It's exactly what I wanted, but something he could never give me. So, what's changed? Because I don't want his pity. I'd rather spend every night alone than have him feel sorry for me. "You don't have to worry about me. I'm okay," I assure him.

"I will always worry about you, sunshine, but that's not why I want you here in my room." He edges closer so that our bodies are pressed together. "In my bed," he growls.

Warmth coils up my spine, his deep voice traveling into my core. "But why do you want me in here now when you didn't before?"

He slides his hand to the back of my neck, palming it possessively. "Because I was a fucking fool, and I had no idea how much I needed you until you weren't here anymore. And now that you're home, I don't want to spend another night without you, Mia."

"I don't want to spend another night without you either."

"My tesoro," he says with a soft groan as he bends low and seals his lips over mine. Looping his free arm around my waist, he pulls me closer, and I melt into him, opening my mouth and allowing him to slide his tongue inside and deepen the kiss. My pulse thrums rapidly and warmth floods my body. His hands grip my ass and he lifts me with ease, wrapping my legs around his hips and carrying me to his bed. He nestles between my open thighs, pressing his hard cock against my pussy through our clothes. As he rocks his hips, my core contracts with wet heat. Taking my hands, he laces our fingers together, pinning my arms on either side of my head.

"Lorenzo," I groan, desperate for him. The emotional upheaval of the whole day threatens to overwhelm me, and he's the perfect distraction.

He pulls back and glares at me. "In my bed, Mia, you will call me Sir. Understand?"

I gasp, and my racing heart goes into overdrive. Pleasure skitters through every nerve ending in my body. *Sir?* "But you said you'd never ..."

"I was wrong. You still want this with me?"

I take another deep breath. "Yes, Sir."

"Good girl," he growls before he rubs his nose along the column of my throat, inhaling deeply. "You smell so fucking delicious. I don't know how I ever lived without you."

His hands caress my skin as he slowly undresses me. I whimper with frustration, pleading with him to hurry, but the more I beg, the slower he goes. I curl my fingers in his hair, guiding his head lower so that at least his mouth might end up where I want him.

He jerks away and gives me a wicked grin. "I can see I'm going to have so much fun playing with you, sunshine." He tugs my panties off and wetness slicks between my thighs. "Hold out your hands," he orders.

I do as he asks, watching in fascination as he binds my wrists together with my underwear, like he once did in the library.

"Now put them above your head," he commands in a deep throaty growl, and I immediately comply, desperate to please him.

A few seconds later, I hear a soft click and I pull at my wrists. They don't budge. I twist my head, trying to see what he's done.

"It's a design feature," he says with a wicked grin.

A thrill of excitement shoots through me. "You've tied me to your bed?"

There's a wicked glint in his eyes as he tugs on my restraints, making sure I can't move my arms. "More like cuffed."

I arch an eyebrow at him. "Cuffed and tied up with panties?"

"You're going to want to move those hands an awful lot, sunshine," he says with a dark laugh that makes molten wet heat sear between my thighs.

"Have you used them with anyone else?" I ask, unable to stop myself even if it kills the mood.

"No. They were part of the bed when I bought it. I've never used them before."

"And has there been anyone else?"

"No." He kisses me softly. "No one but you."

"There's been nobody for me either," I assure him.

"Oh, I know that, sunshine," he says with a deep growl, and I don't ask him how. Instead I lean against the pillow and watch him trail soft kisses and sharp bites over my entire body.

LORENZO WASN'T wrong about me wanting to move my arms. I pull at my restraints as he teases me relentlessly with his mouth and his fingers and his beautiful big cock, bringing me to the crest of my orgasm before gently easing me back down again. He does it repeatedly, rendering me a trembling, sweaty mess. I beg him to let me come.

"Such a needy little sub," he taunts, sinking his cock inside me once more. How does he have so much stamina? He's already finished inside me twice and he's ready to go again.

Meanwhile, my nerves are fraught with pent-up tension; my entire body sizzles with frenetic sexual energy and all it would take is one tiny spark to set me off like a Fourth of July display. Every cell trembles with the need to come. Perspiration slicks my skin. My heart pounds in my ears, mirrored by the throbbing in my clit as Lorenzo goes on paying it enough attention to keep me on the precipice of eternal ecstasy. Pleasure skitters through me, coiling and whirling but never really taking hold.

"You're so mean." I pant out the words, feeling like I'm about to pass into the afterlife.

He chuckles softly, sucks my nipple into his mouth, and bites hard.

"Please, Sir?" I beg one last time, beyond needy and desperate. "I'll do anything."

"Anything, huh?"

"Y-yes," I scream as another wave takes hold. Will he let me ride it to the end this time?

He drives his cock into me, hitting my G-spot. "Then come for me, tesoro," he commands, and I explode around him, like a billion tiny fire bursts all went off in my body at the same time, each one setting off the next in a chain reaction until they all converge in that one sweet point between my thighs where he's inside me.

I scream his name. My entire body convulses. I drench him. My mind goes blank, drifting into a semiconscious state where all I can feel is contentment and pleasure and warmth. Lorenzo anchors me to reality, growling filthy words in my ear while he slowly fucks me into oblivion.

Lying in Lorenzo's arms a little while later, I'm tempted to purr like a cat. I can't recall the last time I felt as happy and cherished as I do right now. Maybe I never have. Brad swept me off my feet after we met. He promised me the world. But I don't know that I ever experienced this joy with him—not even in the very beginning when things were good.

I press my face against his chest. "That was incredible, Sir."

He murmurs his agreement, dusting his lips over my hair.

"I enjoyed calling you Sir. I mean, I thought I'd be into it because I read a lot about the lifestyle, but I didn't think I'd be *that* into it, you know? It was so hot. And when you did that thing with—"

"You really have an issue with quiet, don't you?" He chuckles.

"Yes, sorry. I have so many questions though."

He yawns. "You also apologize way too much. I'm going to train all of that out of you."

Train it out of me? Why does that fill me with excitement? "You are, huh?"

"Hmm. But right now I just want to lie here with you."

My cheeks hurt from smiling so widely. I can't believe this is how my awful day is ending. "I love lying here with you."

He tightens his grip, pulling me closer so that I'm practically lying on top of him. "Get some sleep, sunshine."

FORTY

Mia looked so peaceful lying in my bed that I left her sleeping. She needs it after what she's been through the past few days.

Sitting in my office, I find my mind drifting to her instead of focusing on work. It felt so good to fall asleep with her in my arms and wake up with her juicy ass nestled against me. I was tempted to wake her up by sliding my cock inside her, but we haven't had any discussions about consent yet.

A soft tap on the door distracts me from thoughts of Mia in my bed. My cock stiffens at the realization that it's probably her outside the room. My men don't knock so quietly.

"Lorenzo?" she calls out, confirming my suspicion.

"Come in."

She walks through the door, a huge smile on her face and her hair still mussed from sleep—the embodiment of my pet name for her. She's wearing a T-shirt of mine, and from the outline of her hard nipples against the soft fabric, little else. I growl my appreciation.

"All of my clothes are still packed away in boxes," she says when she sees me staring at her attire. "This was on the top of your laundry basket. I hope you don't mind."

"Not even a little. Come here." I push my chair back and watch her walk toward me. She looks at the floor rather than at me.

I reach for her as soon as she's within touching distance, pulling her close enough that I can cup her chin and tilt her head up. "Why won't you look at me, sunshine?"

She wrinkles her nose. "I'm not sure of the rules."

"There are no rules. *Yet.* We haven't agreed to them."

She smiles wider. "We agree to them together?"

"Of course."

"Will I need a safe word?"

"Yes."

"I think it should be bananas."

Laughing, I arch one eyebrow. "It can't be bananas."

"Why not?"

"Because it has to be a word that you wouldn't ordinarily say. You say bananas far too often."

Her hazel eyes widen. "I do?"

"Mia." I brush a hand through her hair and tug her head back to the perfect angle. "You are the only person I know who says bananas when they really mean fuck." I kiss her soft lips then release her so she can perch on the edge of my desk.

"I don't *always* say bananas when I mean that other word," she reminds me, a pink blush creeping across the bridge of her nose.

"Pick another."

She presses her lips together and stares at the ceiling. "How about cantaloupe?"

"Why the obsession with fruit?"

With a shrug, she pops a grape into her mouth from the bowl on my desk. "I guess I'm a fruity kind of person."

She's certainly something. My eyes roam over her face. She's entirely serious about her word choice.

"So cantaloupe then? Can that be my safe word? I would never say that usually. I'd just say melon."

"Cantaloupe is fine."

She inches along the edge of my desk, dangerously close. Mia will soon learn that being within touching distance means she's likely to end up with a part of me inside a part of her. She runs a fingernail across the collar of my shirt. "Do you have a safe word?"

"No."

"I read that some Doms do."

"I don't. I'll stop a scene if I think it's too much for either of us."

"Okay. So, do we need to discuss limits?" I pull her onto my lap and silence her with a brief kiss, but as soon as I let her up for air, she's talking again. "I'm sorry, I just have so many questions," she whispers.

"I know, sunshine. How about we go grab some breakfast before we talk any more about this?" I run my nose along her throat, and I swear, she fucking purrs like a contented cat. "Because thinking about all of the filthy things I'd like to do to you while you're sitting here half naked is making me hard as fuck."

She giggles, biting her lip as she runs her slender fingers over the back of my neck. "I guess that's not very conducive to talking then?"

I grab a handful of her perfect ass. "No. If we stay here, the only talking you'll be doing is moaning my name."

Her hazel eyes grow darker and she clears her throat. "That sounds all kinds of hot, but I think we should talk first."

I'm glad she backs away, because I lack the willpower to

force the issue, and I really don't want to fuck this up before we even get started.

Mia sits opposite me, chewing a bite of her pancakes and watching me intently. I can almost hear her brain working, racing with questions.

"You want to talk about how this might work?"

She nods, swallowing her food before she speaks. "Please."

"What do you want to discuss first?"

Her brows pinch together. "I researched Dom/sub relationships, but I don't know where to start. So how about you tell me what rules you'd like to have, and I can say whether I'm happy with them? Is that okay?"

"I only have one rule."

"And what's that?"

"You give me complete control over your body."

She gawks at me. "Complete control?"

"Yes."

"B-but how would that even work? Like you'd tell me what I could and couldn't do all the time? I'd have no free will?"

I run a hand over my beard. "You always have free will. But when I tell you to do something, I'd expect you to do it. No matter where we are or what you're doing. There may be days when I don't ask you to do anything at all. Other days I may feel like controlling every aspect of your day. Or there may be times when you don't feel like making any decisions and you ask me to make them for you."

Deep in contemplation, she rests her fork against her lips. "And in return, what do I get out of this arrangement?"

"You get the freedom of knowing that someone else is always in control. I will always take care of you. Part of my role as your Dom is to know what you need, and giving you that is something I take very seriously. I would never do anything to cause you any real harm."

"Hmm." Her brow furrows. "Can you give me an idea of the kinds of ways you'd exert this control?"

"It's the act of your submission that interests me. Knowing that I have control over you is what I thrive on. I have little desire to police what you eat or wear." She's had enough of that in her life. "But that doesn't mean I won't sometimes order for you when we eat out or occasionally choose your clothes."

Nodding, she leans forward in her chair.

"If we go anywhere and I have expectations about how you're to behave, I'll outline them before we go. If we engage in any kind of play, I will make the boundaries and expectations clear at all times."

"I like clear expectations."

"And there are certain things I'd like to work on with you."

She frowns. "Work on?"

"Yes. Your nervous chattering for one."

Hurt flashes in her eyes. "I thought you liked that I talk a lot?"

"I do, sunshine. I'm not referring to you talking a lot, I mean the babbling you do when you're nervous." I lean forward now too. "I guess it's a trauma response, but I don't think it's from Brad because you said he berated you for talking too much. So I'm thinking it was something before that?"

Her mouth drops open, and she blinks at me for a few seconds.

"If I'm going to be your Dom, it's helpful for me to know what causes you to react to things the way you do."

"Well, you're right about the babbling. My dad was a drunk. I was his little princess. I used to tell him jokes and stories to distract him when he was trying to beat my mom. Sometimes it worked, sometimes not." She shrugs.

The fact she grew up in an abusive household explains a lot about her. But that's a conversation for a different day.

"I also want to work on your low self-esteem."

"I do not have low self-esteem," she retorts.

"No?" I arch one eyebrow. "Why the hell have you only eaten half a pancake for breakfast when I made you three?"

She presses her lips together and mutters, "Touché."

"You want to keep going, sunshine?"

She glares at me. The defiance in her eyes makes my cock hard. "Yes."

"You only need to address me as Sir in the bedroom or if I've instructed you to do so. But I expect obedience and respect at all times. Any failure to adhere to the rules will result in a punishment."

She chews on her juicy bottom lip. "So obedience and complete control? And that includes sex too, obviously?"

"Sex is a huge part of it, yes. And that's why we need to discuss your limits. Hard limits are the things you're not willing to try at all, and a soft limit is something you're unsure about but you'd be open to exploring it if it's handled carefully and considerately."

"So, should I tell you what my hard limits are, because I already know them." She takes another bite of her pancake.

"You have been doing your research."

Nodding, she continues to chew.

"Yes, tell me what your hard limits are."

"I don't think I have many, actually."

I frown. "No?"

"No. Because isn't that what safe words are for? You'll stop if I'm not into something?"

"Yes, that's what your safe word is for, but there must be things you wouldn't even consider trying."

Her lips twitch into a wicked smile. "Ball gags."

That's definitely not where I thought she'd start. "Ball gags?"

"Yup, and I know you have a thing about my constant chattering, so I'm sorry if they were going to feature in your training, but I can't do them." She shakes her head, and her hair falls in soft caramel waves over her shoulders.

Cupping her chin, I brush the pad of my thumb over her full lips. "I have plenty of more interesting ways of keeping you from talking, sunshine."

Her throat constricts as she swallows, but her eyes hold mine and they blaze with fire.

"Anything else?" I ask as I sit back.

"Nothing degrading or humiliating. Like I don't want to be led around on a leash or get peed on. Although I don't get the sense that they're your thing anyway."

I don't confirm that she's right. We'll get to my limits shortly. "Anything else?"

"Anal fisting," she says, deadpan.

"No anal fisting," I agree, fighting to keep the smirk from my face. "So fisting in general is okay then?"

She looks at my huge hands resting on the table and winces. "Okay, maybe no fisting at all."

She's quiet for a long moment.

"Is that all?"

"I think so."

She hasn't given this enough thought. I don't want to dredge up bad memories for her, but better to do it here in the safety of the kitchen than when my hand is wrapped around her throat or I have her bent over my knee. "What about punishment, Mia?"

She blinks a few times and suddenly her eyes are wet with tears. "Like beating?"

Shaking my head, I frown. "There are many different forms of punishment, not just physical."

"Don't ignore me. I would hate that."

"That's not a punishment I would use."

"Is beating?"

I suck on my lip. This won't work if I'm not honest, right? "Not beating. I'm not a sadist. Causing physical pain doesn't get me off, but ..."

"But?"

"There's a very fine line between pleasure and pain, and I like to walk that line. Spanking makes me hard as fuck. Having complete dominance over you makes me even harder. But you do understand that spanking and causing physical pain to illicit pleasure is different than beating someone?"

Her eyelashes flutter, wet with unshed tears. "Yes."

"Is that a hard limit for you?"

"Do you only use your hand?"

"Not just my hand," I admit. "Many things. A cane. A flogger. A paddle. My belt."

Her tanned face pales. "Just don't use a belt."

"Is that a hard limit?" I hope not. I'd love to stripe her ass with my belt.

She wrinkles her nose again, the way she does when she's thinking. "If it's a soft limit, we'd always discuss using one first, right?"

"Always."

"Then it's a soft limit, I guess."

"So spanking in general?"

She gives me a faint smile. "Spanking is fine."

I walk around the table and sit beside her, taking her face in my hands. "We don't have to decide all of this now. We can take it slow and work out what you like as we go."

"That sounds good."

"Do you trust me, sunshine?"

"Yes," she says, without a flicker of hesitation.

"Then know that I will never hurt you. I will never punish you when I'm angry. I consider it a privilege and an honor to have your submission, and if we do this, your safety is my priority. Always."

"*If* we do this?"

"We can just be us. No Dom, no sub. Just me and you. If that's what you want."

She shakes her head. "I want to be your submissive, Lorenzo."

"Why?"

Hurt and confusion flash across her face.

"This is important, Mia. Why do you want this?" I need to know that this isn't about her trying to compete with anyone else or a misguided attempt to please me. If she's not all in on this because it's what she truly desires, it won't work, and I'd rather we have a more conventional relationship than a failed one.

Head tilted to the side, she takes a deep breath. "I've thought a lot about this," she says, her brow wrinkled in a frown. "When I was in Iowa, I looked into the lifestyle quite a bit. It was something I was open to exploring, even if it wasn't with you."

I grind my teeth at the thought of her with another man but force myself to remain silent and let her continue.

"When I was married to Brad, most of my life was controlled by him. What I could wear. What I should eat. How much I should weigh. Who I could talk to. So, shouldn't I want the opposite of that in a new relationship?"

The question is obviously rhetorical, so I remain silent but motion for her to continue.

"But that's not what I want at all. I mean, I want control, but isn't that what this is? Aren't I the one in control here too? I think that was what drew me to Brad when I met him. He always took charge of situations, and I loved that about him. I guess I was attracted to his dominance even though I didn't really understand that back then. And there were so many red flags that I didn't see until after we were already married. *This*"—she waves her hands between us—"feels like an equal partnership way more than any other kind of relationship could be. I choose to give my autonomy to you, and in return you respect my wishes and my feelings. You stop whenever I ask you to. You check in with me. You care for me and my well-being. And *that* is why I want this."

I brush my fingertips over her cheek. She couldn't have given me a more perfect answer if I'd written it for her myself.

"And why do you want this, Lorenzo?" she asks softly, her hazel eyes shining green as they stare into mine. She's so open and trusting. In my world of darkness and deceit, she is an actual ray of fucking sunshine.

"These limits don't mean a lot to me, Mia." My statement is met with a frown. "Your limits do, of course. I will respect them, but there's very little I wouldn't be prepared to do for or to you. I don't enter into this kind of relationship lightly, and I'm not doing it so I can punish or praise or spank you. We could do those things in a conventional relationship too. I told you before, what I want is simply your submission. The very act of you giving up your control is what's important to me."

She climbs into my lap and straddles me, wrapping her arms around my neck. "If you want my submission, you have it. I'm yours."

My cock throbs in my pants as she rolls her hips. There are

two thin pieces of fabric between us, and the heat from her pussy is too fucking distracting.

"My good girl," I growl, running my nose over her collarbone.

"Only if you want me to be." She laughs softly. "But you must have some limits. You said there was very little you wouldn't do, not nothing."

"I have two." I lift my head and look into her beautiful trusting face. "Infidelity is unforgivable. It's the worst breach of trust between two people who have committed themselves to each other. You ever cheat on me and we're over."

She shakes her head. "I would never."

"That means I don't share. No matter the circumstances. You belong only to me."

"I don't want you to share." Her eyebrows knit together in a frown. "Why would you do that?"

"Some people do, especially in the community. Sometimes as a form of punishment, other times because that's a couple's dynamic, but it's not mine."

"Not mine either. So I guess that's a hard limit for me too," she says. "And your other limit?"

"I can't abide petty jealousy. Know that if I'm committed to you, I am yours as much as you're mine. If I talk to a woman, if I make pleasant conversation, that doesn't mean I want to fuck her." It was the thing Anya struggled with most, and it took years for me to condition it out of her. Questioning my loyalty is a big deal for me.

Mia smiles. "No acting jealous if you speak to another woman. Promise. No cheating or sharing."

I slide a hand to the back of her neck, palming it possessively as I wrap my other arm around her waist and pull her closer. "No cheating or sharing isn't just a limit, Mia. I don't do jealousy, but that doesn't mean I don't protect what is mine.

You *are* mine. If another man so much as touches you without my permission, whether you want him to or not, he will die."

"Like ... you'd kill him?"

"Yes."

She darts out her tongue, moistening her lips. My little pacifist is struggling with that concept.

"This is the man I am, sunshine. You sure you want to go all in with me?" Like she actually has a choice. She's already mine, and there's no chance in hell I'm letting her go.

Her eyes flicker over my face and she nestles closer. "I want all in."

So we're doing this. I stand, picking her up with me and wrapping her legs around my waist.

"Where are we going?" she asks, smiling up at me.

"Back to bed to continue working through our terms."

A flush creeps over her neck.

"We still have some issues to iron out, don't you think?" Not giving her a chance to answer, I seal my mouth over hers and carry her upstairs.

FORTY-ONE

MIA

I chew on my thumbnail and bounce on my toes, full of nervous excitement. Lorenzo takes my hand and pulls it away from my mouth.

"I'm excited," I say breathlessly and peer through the windows while I wait for the car to pull up at the front door.

"You remember the rules, sunshine?"

"No nervous babbling. No negativity about myself, and no brushing off compliments." Those are the only rules he gave me for our first time out as a couple. I figure he's taking it easy on me—way too easy, if you ask me—because he thinks I'll struggle to obey his rules. Like I told him, I'm excited rather than nervous, and I can keep my babbling in check for a few hours. As for talking bad about myself, I know I joke about my fat butt occasionally, but I'm a woman confident in her own skin. I can so do this. This submissive thing is a breeze. I'm going to ace my first test.

The car pulls up and Lorenzo places his hand on the small of my back, flashing me a wicked grin, like he knows something I don't. "You ready?" We're going on a double date with Joey and Max, and I'm beyond giddy with excitement. "You remember the other rule, right? The one that's always in play?" he asks, dusting his lips over my neck and making me shiver.

"Do whatever you say without question."

"Good girl."

JOEY PUSHES HER PLATE AWAY, groaning loudly. "I'm so full," she moans, rubbing a hand over her stomach. "That was so much pasta."

Max grins at his wife. "Pretty sure you'll still have room for dessert, baby girl."

"There's always room for dessert, DiMarco." She grins back at him, and he licks his lips.

"Do you two really have to do that in front of me?" Lorenzo asks with a groan. "Can we not have one meal without some kind of sexual innuendo?"

"Says the man who's been feeling his date up under the table all night?" Joey fires back with a pop of her eyebrow. "Don't think we can't see you."

I suppress a smile because she's right, he has been doing that.

Lorenzo narrows his eyes at her. "I wasn't trying to hide it. But Mia isn't Max's little sister, is she?"

Joey rolls her eyes, but Max laughs. "We'll be good, buddy," Max adds when Lorenzo shoots him a look.

I push some chicken from my Caesar salad around my plate. "You had enough to eat, Mia?" Joey asks. Her pasta looked delicious, but I went for the lighter option because I don't want to burst out of the beautiful new dress that Lorenzo bought me— it cost more than I used to earn in a year—and also because this is my first dinner out with Lorenzo. I want to make a good impression.

"Yeah." It's not exactly a lie. I have eaten *enough*, although I could eat a lot more.

I feel Lorenzo's eyes on me. He and Max ordered ribeye steaks, which were massive, and they practically wiped their plates clean.

Joey extends her arm and makes a gimme gesture. "Pass me that dessert menu."

Max rolls his eyes and takes a menu from the empty table beside us. He grabs another one and hands it to me, but I shake my head. "Oh, none for me, thanks."

"You don't want dessert?" Joey asks incredulously. "What was the point of getting that tiny ass salad if not to save room for a dessert as big as a bus?"

"Yeah, well my ass is already the size of a bus, so I have to stay away from sugar and fat," I say, laughing.

Joey rolls her eyes but doesn't question me further. "Loz, you'll order dessert with me, right?"

He takes the menu from her outstretched hand. "Sure, kid."

As we walk out of the restaurant, my cheeks hurt from laughing and smiling. I hug Joey and Max goodbye, and then Lorenzo and I climb into the waiting car. When the car merges into traffic, he presses a button to speak to the driver.

"Take the fastest route home, Tommy," he orders.

"Of course, Boss."

I bite down on my bottom lip, wondering what he has in store for me when we get home. Surely I just aced my first sub mission. I run my hand over the lapel of his jacket. "Tonight was lovely. Thank you."

He gives a subtle nod. "It was, sunshine."

"And I obeyed all the rules, right?"

His handsome face furrows and he shoots me a look that makes an uneasy feeling settle in my gut.

"I know the night's not over yet, b-but—"

He pats his thighs. "Come here."

I straddle him, wrapping my arms around his neck. He pulls my thick hair aside and trails soft kisses over my collarbone. Warmth rolls in my core. He runs his fingertips up my thigh, slowly pushing my dress up.

My breath hitches. He goes on kissing my neck, teeth gently scraping my skin.

"Lorenzo," I whimper, dropping my hips and chasing friction between my thighs.

His tongue darts out, licking the length of my throat as his hands coast higher. When he reaches the apex of my thighs, he yanks my panties to the side and brushes the pad of his thumb over my clit.

My thighs tremble and I gasp.

He lifts his head, his dark eyes boring into mine. "You had two rules, Mia. Can you tell me which one you broke?"

I open and close my mouth like a goldfish, genuinely confused as he goes on softly rubbing my clit. "I know I talked a lot, but I was chatting with Joey about the casino. I didn't babble."

"I never said you talked too much," he replies coolly.

"I-I—" Heat flashes over my cheeks. He's talking about the negativity thing. "I didn't ... Joey said I looked stunning, and I just said thank you ..." Now I'm babbling, and he's making it hard to think with his delicious teasing between my thighs. I did accept Joey's compliment, and Max's, even though it felt strange not to brush them off.

His eyes narrow. "What did you have to eat?"

"A Caesar salad."

CHAPTER FORTY-ONE

He increases the pressure with his thumb, and I whimper. "Why?"

"Because I—"

"Don't lie to me, Mia," he warns.

I swallow down the words that were about to trip off my tongue, not so much a lie as a well-practiced habit. "Because I didn't want to appear greedy," I admit on a whisper while heat and need coil deep in my core.

"Did anyone else at the table appear greedy for eating what they wanted?"

"No, but I ..." I bite my lip, wanting to scowl at him but too distracted by what he's doing with that magical thumb to follow through. "So, I want to eat healthily. I don't get how that's a bad thing."

"It's not, but when you deny yourself an occasional pleasure because of some fucked-up idea that you're fat, it isn't healthy." He rubs harder, swiping the pad of his thumb from side to side.

"I didn't deny myself." I try to snap at him, but my words come out on a moan.

"Did you want dessert? Do you think I didn't hear your stomach growl when I was eating mine? If I take you out for dinner, Mia, I expect you to fucking enjoy it."

"I did enjoy dinner. Just because I didn't eat dessert—" My climax builds to a crescendo, and I throw my head back on a moan. How does he have me so close using only his thumb? Wizard! "I didn't even know that was part of the rules," I whimper.

"It wasn't. But what did you say when Joey asked why you weren't having dessert?"

Oh bananas! Here I was thinking I aced his test. My cheeks burn with shame. "That my ass was fat," I whisper.

He changes the angle of his thumb, sweeping back and forth now. "That it was the size of a bus?"

"I ... I was joking. It's a reflex thing—" I gasp, my thighs and core tightening with my impending orgasm. Just before it hits, Lorenzo stops, slips his hand away, and grabs my jaw, holding my head in place so I have nowhere to look but his eyes.

"It's not a joke, Mia. It's a deeply ingrained, fucked-up belief that I'm going to rid you of."

My breath catches in my throat. "Are you going to punish me?"

His mouth curls into a smirk. "Yes I am."

Lifting me off his lap, he returns me to my seat and places his thumb into his mouth, sucking it clean. I lean my head back and swallow the ball of anxiety in my throat. We spend the rest of the drive home in silence.

CHAPTER
FORTY-TWO
MIA

My legs are actually trembling as I kick off my heels and walk to the closet to take off my dress. Lorenzo sits on the edge of the bed, watching my every move. I wish I knew what was going on in that devious brain on his. When I'm standing in only my underwear, he finally speaks. "Come here."

I take a deep breath and approach him on shaky legs. What on earth does he have in mind? He pats his knee, and my eyes dart between his face and his muscular thighs, spread out as though he wants me to lie on top of them.

"A-are you going to spank me?" I whisper.

"It's the quickest form of punishment I can think of right now, and your ass in that dress has me dying to fuck you, so yeah." He pats his knee again.

I swallow hard.

"Don't make me ask again, Mia," he warns.

With trembling everything, I position myself over his lap, my elbows resting on the bed and my ass in the air. I feel like a naughty teenager.

Lorenzo rubs his rough hand over my ass and pleasure

sizzles through me. Maybe this won't be so bad. He's slapped my ass plenty of times before.

"This is a beautiful ass," he says, right before he brings his hand crashing down on the meaty part of my cheek.

I yelp even though it didn't hurt that badly.

"Not even the warm-up, sunshine." Slapping me harder this time, he continues. "Your panties are still on. Your spanking doesn't really begin until this ass"—he smacks me again—"is bare."

"Then make it start, please." How many times is he going to spank me before the punishment truly begins?

"I'm doing you a favor warming this ass up first." He slaps me again, and unexpected waves of pleasure roll through me. I can't stop the moan that tumbles from my lips.

"Warmed up then?" He peels my panties off, and I press my ass up into his hands, desperate for his touch despite knowing it will hurt.

"You're going to count your punishment, Mia. Okay?"

"H-how many, Sir?" I breathe as wetness drips between my thighs.

"It's your first punishment, so only eight. We'll increase the number over time as you get used to it. You ready?"

"Y-yes, Sir."

He spanks me hard, and I cry out, white-hot need searing through me.

"How many?" he barks.

"One!"

He spanks me again, harder. "T-two," I pant.

"Good girl," he grunts and spanks me again. By the time he gets to number seven, my ass is on fire, my pussy leaking like a broken faucet, and my head spins. The burning sensation is unlike anything I've experienced. Concentrated in that one single place, it stings and throbs, making me needy for him. But

I'm not sure how much more I can take. It won't be long before the balance tips from pleasure *and* pain to only pain.

He spanks me one last time, harder than all the rest, and stars flicker behind my eyelids. "Eight," I scream, gasping for breath. He rubs a soothing hand over my poor inflamed ass, and I press into his palm, longing for his touch.

His hands disappear, leaving me desperate for him. I need to feel him inside me. His cock dug into my ribs the whole time he spanked me, so I expected to be thrown onto my back and fucked as soon as he finished.

"Sir?" I whine.

"Lie on the bed. Face down," he orders.

I crawl off him and do as I'm told. He leaves but reappears a few moments later and rubs something cooling and soothing over my ass cheeks. Although it feels good, I'm still sore and pissed at him. Wrung out but desperate for him at the same time.

"You did well, sunshine," he says softly. "Your ass looks even more beautiful after a spanking."

I don't respond.

"I can't wait to use my paddle and my crop," he says with a groan, squeezing a handful of my ass. "I can't wait to see you striped with welts."

Unexpected tears prick at my eyes and I turn away, but he turns me back to him.

"Don't pout."

"My butt hurts!"

He arches an eyebrow, and I'm sure I see the flicker of a smirk on his lips. *Jackass!* "It was a punishment. It was supposed to hurt."

"You've spanked me before and it never hurt like that."

"This is the first time I've punished you though, right? And will you think twice before you talk bad about yourself again?"

I press my lips together, refusing to give in so easily.

"Answer me, Mia." His hand squeezes my tender flesh.

"Yes, Sir," I gasp.

"So the correction worked then." He does smirk now.

"The correction?" I snap at him, annoyance prickling beneath my skin. "You make me sound like a dog."

All the humor on his face disappears, replaced with a simmering anger that vibrates through every part of him. I swallow hard and my heart rate kicks up at least half a dozen gears. Lorenzo Moretti is a violent and dangerous man, and I played with his last nerve. My blood freezes in my veins as I brace myself for another punishment.

But he pushes himself off the bed and stalks toward the closet. I watch him intently as he takes out two huge blankets and starts to spread one out on the floor beside the bed.

"You think I treat you like a dog?" His tone is calm and collected, but it's so cold that it makes me shiver.

"I never said ..." I swallow again. My heart pounds in my ears.

He nods toward the blanket on the floor. "This is where my dog would sleep."

I blink at him. "Are you suggesting ...?"

"Dogs don't sleep in my bed. You want to accuse me of treating you like my pet, then I'll show you exactly how that would feel. Floor. Now!"

My breath hitches in my throat as I stare at him. He's serious. I should tell him to go to hell. Use my safe word, maybe? This has gone too far. So why do I slip out of bed and lie on the blanket on the floor? Because this feels like a test. Everything feels like a test with him, and I don't want to fail so soon.

Tears prick my eyes and I swallow the emotion knotting my throat. "Don't I even get a pillow?"

He places the second blanket over me, and although he's

mad and this is a punishment, he does it so tenderly that it makes me more emotional. "My dog wouldn't even get a blanket." Then he climbs into bed without another word.

I put my hands behind my head and stare at the ceiling. The blankets are thick and soft, but they do little to negate the hardness of the wood beneath me. This isn't the worst place I've ever slept, but sleeping on the floor isn't the most difficult part of this, at least not for me. It's not being close to him that hurts. Not being able to touch him at all as I drift off to sleep, that's the true punishment. And I'm sure the jackass knows it.

I listen to his steady breathing as I lie in the darkness. Needy for his touch. Wet from his teasing in the car and even from the spanking. His hands on any part of my body make me yearn for him. Is he awake? I bet he fell fast asleep the second his head hit the pillow. *Correction: arrogant jackass!* My back starts to ache and I shift onto my side.

"Sir?" I whisper.

"Yes?" His deep soothing voice cuts through the thick tension like a knife.

I smile because he's awake just like me. Does he miss my touch as much as I miss his? "Am I a bad sub?"

He sucks in a breath, and my heart stops beating while I wait for his answer. "No, just a new one."

I smile wider. "Sir?"

"Yes."

"I'm sorry."

"I know. Get some sleep."

FOOTSTEPS ROUSE me from my fitful sleep. It took me hours to finally doze off on this damn floor. Opening my eyes, I see Lorenzo, fully dressed in his suit and tie. He crouches down beside me. I swear if he pats me like I'm a dog, I'll bite him like one.

But he doesn't. He scoops me into his arms and places me gently on the bed. "What are you doing?"

"Even bad dogs get to sleep on the bed sometimes," he says softly. I feel the retort on the tip of my tongue but amusement dances in his eyes, and I don't want another fight. He takes away my blanket and tucks the duvet around me before sitting on the edge of the bed.

"I'm going to be out all day. I won't be home until after dinner."

"Okay," I whisper. I don't know how to do this yet; how to act normal with him after he spanked me and made me sleep on the floor. I'm used to tension and conflict being resolved with shouts and fists. At least I knew how to handle strife with Brad, even if it was a nightmare to live through. I don't know how to move past this with Lorenzo.

"I missed you," I admit.

He dusts his knuckles over my jaw, and I press my cheek into his hand, desperate for his affection. "I missed you too."

"Did I mess it all up on our first date?"

A deep frown furrows his brow. "No."

"You're not still mad at me?"

He rolls on top of me, his forearms on either side of my head and the weight of his body pressing me into the mattress. "No, sunshine. The point of the punishment is not only to correct the behavior, but to enable us to get past whatever the issue was. Once the punishment is over, it's done with and we move on. No holding onto any negative shit, and if you are holding onto any, then talk to me about it."

"I didn't like sleeping on the floor."

He runs his nose along my jawline and goosebumps prickle

over my forearms. "I know. I didn't like you sleeping down there either."

"I'm sorry."

"You already apologized."

"Hmm. It's an old habit." I shrug.

"Another one I'm going to break," he says before he trails soft kisses over my neck.

I whimper like the desperate little sub he's turning me into. "You smell so good, sunshine."

"So do you, Sir." Catching the scent of his expensive shampoo and his cologne, I moan.

A deep, guttural growl rumbles in his throat. "I have to go."

I wrap my arms around his neck and lift my hips, rubbing along his rock-hard length. "Can't you stay for ten more minutes?"

"No." He nips at my neck and pushes himself up. "Besides, ten minutes is nowhere near enough time for all of the things I'm going to do to you."

A shiver runs the length of my spine.

"After dinner tonight, I want you to come straight to bed and wait for me."

"Naked?" I bite my lip.

He fixes me with a steely glare. "Of course."

"Of course."

"You can shower when you get up today, but that's it. Don't shower before bed."

I frown. "Really?"

"Really." A wicked glint flashes in his eyes. "And no touching yourself."

"W-what?" I stammer. "That's so unfair. I'm a woman on the edge here."

"And whose fault is that?"

Drat! I sigh. "Mine."

"So be good today and I'll take care of you tonight." He gives me a soft kiss on the forehead and stands, straightening his jacket.

"How long will I have to wait for you?" Five minutes will be too long. I need him back in bed with me now.

"As long as it takes."

My lower lip juts out, but I don't want to get in trouble for pouting, so I pull it back in. "Can I read in bed while I wait?"

"Yes."

"Thank you, Sir."

With an unintelligible grunt, he leans down and kisses me, parting my lips with his tongue and making me moan softly into his mouth. All too soon, he pulls away again, leaving me wanting. "Be good, sunshine."

"I will, I promise." Maybe I can do this submissive thing after all.

FORTY-THREE

LORENZO

My heart thumps loudly and my cock aches as I take the stairs two at a time. Mia isn't downstairs, so she must be doing what I asked of her. I've been desperate to fuck her since we left for the restaurant last night, and I might explode if I don't feel her tight pussy around my cock soon.

When I walk into the room, she's sitting up in bed reading, blanket pulled up over her breasts. I can't tell if she's naked beneath there or not. From the looks of the book cover, it's one of the filthy ones that she and Kat like to read.

She looks up and places her book on the bed. "Hey," she says with a sweet smile.

"Hey." I pull off my tie. "How was your day?"

"It was good."

"Did you eat dinner?" My socks and shoes join my tie on the floor.

"Yes. Spinach and ricotta cannelloni." She licks her lips as she watches me undress. "It was delicious."

"And for dessert?" I shrug off my jacket and fold it over the back of the chair.

"I didn't have any."

I walk toward the bed. I need to feel her now. "Why not, sunshine?"

Her cheeks flush a little pink. "Because I wasn't hungry."

I narrow my eyes at her, reading every single emotion on her face as I crawl onto the bed.

"I wasn't. I swear," she whispers.

"I believe you." I fist my hand in the duvet, pulling it down and revealing her beautiful body inch by inch. Her breath catches in her throat and her tits shudder as I expose them to the air. Leaning forward, I suck a hard nipple into my mouth, and she whimpers, threading her fingers in my hair and arching her back. I nip her gently before moving to pay her other one the same attention.

"That feels so good, Sir."

I pull the duvet down lower, over her stomach, resting it on her hips. The scent of her fills the air. "I can smell how wet you are from here. Tell me, was it your dirty book?" I glide my hand up her thighs, and I'm pleased to find her naked for me. She spreads her legs without hesitation, allowing me to slip two fingers between her pussy lips. "Or is any of it for me?"

She stares into my eyes, biting her lip and stifling her soft moans. "It was a little from my book." A flush creeps over her neck. "But mostly for you."

"Yeah?" I dip my head lower, trailing soft kisses over her breasts and down to her stomach as I drag my fingers through her wet folds.

"Yes. I've been thinking about you all day."

"I've been thinking about you too, sunshine. I brought you something."

"You did?" Her voice goes high with delight.

Getting out of bed, I go over to the chair and grab the silver nipple clamps from my jacket pocket. I lie back down next to her and hold them up by the thick chain linking them. "You know what these are, Mia?"

Her tongue darts out, moistening her juicy bottom lip. "Nipple clamps," she breathes.

"You ever had them used on you before?"

She shakes her head, her gaze never leaving the toy in my hand.

I dip my head and run my tongue over one of her hard nipples. "I bought them this morning and I've been waiting to use them on these perfect tits all day."

"Do they hurt?" she whispers, eyes wide.

"Only in a good way," I tell her with a wink, shaking the chain loose so that a clamp dangles from each end. "You ready to try them?"

She nods eagerly. "Yes, Sir."

"That's my good girl."

I don't miss the way her face lights up at my praise. She needs this after last night. We both do. I open the first clamp and bring it close to her hardened bud. She sucks in a breath, intently watching me fasten it onto her nipple, and makes the softest, sexiest little moaning sound.

"You like that, huh?"

She gasps, her neck flushing with heat.

I tighten it a little and the clamp bites into her stiff peak. She whimpers, but a few seconds later she's moaning again. "Still good, sunshine?"

"Y-yes," she pants, licking her lips.

"Keep your hands by your sides. No touching yourself. Okay?"

She presses her lips together. "Mmhmm."

I clamp her other nipple and she squirms when I increase the pressure. She sinks her teeth into her lip now, her fingers twitching on the covers.

I grin wickedly and hook my finger on the chain. Tugging gently, I watch in satisfaction as her back arches off the bed.

"Sir," she whimpers.

"I wonder if I could make you come like this, tesoro?" I tug the chain a little harder and she keens, back arching higher and legs spreading wide.

"Sensitive, are we?" I flick her pebbled nipple with my tongue, lavishing it with attention. Her hands ball into fists and she lifts them off the bed. "Hands," I remind her.

"I know, Sir," she whines.

Sliding my hand across her soft stomach, I cup her other breast, wedging the clamp between the knuckles of my middle and pointer fingers. I squeeze gently and her eyes roll back in her head. "Is this what you wanted?"

"Yes!"

I settle between her thighs, my hard cock encased in my suit pants and pressing up against her pussy. I knew she'd like the clamps, but I had no idea they'd make her this feral.

I roll my hips, rubbing the seam of my zipper over her clit. "Oh, holy cow!" she moans.

"How about we see if we can get you off like this?" I suggest, squeezing her breast harder. "You grind that pussy on me while I play with these beautiful tits."

"Y-yes, Sir."

FORTY-FOUR

My breasts throb with a delicious, heavy ache. I can barely see straight. Wetness slicks my thighs, and I whimper without shame, grinding myself on Lorenzo's hard cock.

"These are fucking beautiful, tesoro," he says, squeezing one of my breasts hard, his tongue sweeping over the other, teasing my pebbled nipple while the toy bites into my skin. Every time I feel like the pleasure can't get any more intense, Lorenzo pulls on the chain between the two clamps, and I enter a whole new sphere of ecstasy.

Pressure building in my core, I rock my hips, rubbing my sensitive clit over his hard length. I've never come from having my nipples played with before, and although I'm grinding against him like a horny she-cat, it's the sweet ache in my breasts that's causing the deep contractions in my pussy. The ones that build and crest as he goes on playing me—like a puppet master literally pulling my strings.

He sucks one nipple into his hot mouth and bites gently, causing me to gasp. "Sir, that feels so good."

"Mmhmm," he murmurs, feasting on my flesh and twirling

the chain between his thumb and forefinger so that it pulls and releases over and over again.

"Can I please touch you, Sir?" I beg, desperate to feel any part of him beneath my fingertips but conscious of his instructions to keep my hands by my sides.

"Only touch me."

I sigh with relief as I grip his thick hair, holding his head in place and pressing into the pleasure of his expert mouth. He rolls his hips, causing the perfect amount of friction against my clit, and as I arch toward him, giving in to the sensations that course through me, he gives the chain one final yank, pulling the clamps off completely. Blood rushes back to my nipples and intense euphoria crashes over me.

"Oh, fu—" My orgasm tears the words from my mouth, cutting off my oxygen as it rips through me. I try to catch my breath, but Lorenzo wraps a hand around my throat. "Hold it in and feel it all."

I clamp my mouth shut and tremors rocket through my body. And when I feel like I'm about to pass out, Lorenzo releases his grip. I gulp air, filling my burning lungs with oxygen.

"W-wow," I pant, several minutes later. "That was incredible."

Raising his eyebrows, Lorenzo winds the chain around the clamps. "I'm definitely adding these to our playtime, sunshine."

"That would be nice, Sir," I purr, fluttering my eyelashes at him.

His eyes narrow. "You're being a very well-behaved sub today."

"I am," I agree.

"Still not going to save you though." With a wicked grin, he jumps off the bed and gets undressed.

CHAPTER FORTY-FOUR

I marvel at the sight of him. All hard ridges and beautiful artwork carved into his skin. "Save me from what?"

"Your next lesson."

"My next lesson, Sir?"

He nods and removes his boxers and pants, revealing his incredible cock standing thick and tall, weeping with precum.

"And what is that?" I ask, full of excitement and a little trepidation.

He crawls onto the bed, trailing feral kisses up my legs, all the way from my ankles to the tops of my thighs. "You'll see."

Half an hour later, I'm wondering if the lesson is orgasm denial. Lorenzo has my legs thrown over his shoulders while he eats my pussy with all the skill and finesse of the genius sex wizard I've always known him to be, but no matter how close I get to the edge, how much I beg and plead and promise to be good, he refuses to let me come.

"Please, Sir!" My entire body feels aflame with desire.

"Not yet," he growls against my flesh. "You need to learn patience."

Patience? Is that my lesson.

"Your cunt is so fucking sweet," Lorenzo says with a groan as he sits up, dropping my legs flat to the bed before he wipes his mouth free of my juices.

I gasp for breath and try not to pout as yet another mind-blowing orgasm ebbs away. Lorenzo leans over me and brushes my hair from my face, and without further warning, he sinks his cock all the way inside me.

"You know how I train my subs to come on command, Mia?"

I'm too consumed with the sweet relief of being filled by him to respond.

"I get them to the place where they're so wrung out and desperate to come that it would only take the slightest amount of pressure in just the right spot"—he rolls his hips, sweeping the crown of his cock over said spot and proving his point—"to have them fall apart at my say so. And eventually there's such a strong association between the words and the orgasm, they will come almost from the words alone, with very little stimulation."

"Like Pavlov's dogs?"

"Are you going to be sleeping on the floor again?"

"What?" He rocks his hips again, and I arch my back, giving into the pleasure he invokes. "I didn't mean—it's a famous experiment," I protest.

"I know what it is," he says with a wicked grin, and I realize he's teasing me.

"You're a jack—"

He cuts me off by slamming into me, making me gasp as endorphins race around my body. "Come for me, Mia."

My body teeters on the precipice of ecstasy, and his words tip me right over the cliff. I fall hard, my climax crashing into me with such force that I shake. He fucks me through every second of it, railing into me as he grinds out his own orgasm.

Pulling me with him, he rolls onto his back.

"So coming on command was my lesson, Sir?" I nestle my face into the crook of his shoulder.

"Well, we laid the groundwork." He laughs softly. "It's not as easy as people think."

"I never thought it would be easy. I assumed it was only in my books."

He brushes my hair from my face and palms the back of my neck. "It can be done with practice."

"I look forward to practicing a lot." I snigger and drape my leg over his hip.

He hooks his hand under my knee and pulls me closer, kissing the top of my head. "Goodnight, sunshine."

CHAPTER
FORTY-FIVE
LORENZO

I stretch my neck and it cracks. Work is busy and that makes me tense, but lucky for me, I have the perfect distraction. I type out a message to Mia that simply says, *Library. Ten minutes.*

Ten minutes later, like the good little sub I'm training her to be, she walks into the room.

"Come here." I nod, indicating the space between my thighs.

Her breathing grows faster as she approaches. She knows what I want. It's what I always want lately, and I can hardly believe I forgot the innate pleasure and power of having sex whenever and wherever. Mia has reawakened something in me that I thought I buried along with my wife.

"Bend over the desk," I order as she steps between my thighs. If she's bothered by the fact that I clearly only asked her in here so I could fuck her, she doesn't show it. Instead, she turns around and does exactly what I told her to do, laying her face flat against the wood. Running my hands up the curves of her juicy ass, I sink my teeth into my lip to stifle a groan and yank her dress up over her hips.

"Spread your legs for me."

She does so without hesitation, revealing the unmistakable damp spot on her pale pink panties. My aching cock weeps for her.

I run my fingertip down her slit, making her shiver. "Something got you wet, sunshine?"

"Y-yes," she whimpers, squirming.

"Have you been touching yourself?"

"No, Sir."

Tugging the cotton aside, I drag my pointer finger through her dripping folds. "Then why are you this wet?"

"I was thinking about this morning." She stifles a giggle. "And then you ordered me in here, and I knew—" I push a finger inside her hot channel and she gasps.

"You knew all I wanted was to fuck you?"

"Yes, Sir." Face pressed against my desk, she pushes her ass back onto my hand and takes more of my finger inside her.

I push deeper, enjoying the sensation of her pussy squeezing me and knowing I'll soon get to feel her pulse around my cock. "And that doesn't bother you?"

She lets out a breathy moan. "Not at all, Sir."

"Good girl." I slide my finger out of her, and every inch comes out thick with her arousal.

She whimpers my name, and my balls pulse with desperation to claim her. My cock throbs and my head spins as every drop of blood in my body rushes south. I fumble for my belt, blinded by an insatiable desire to fuck her until her screams and moans fill the library. I stare down at my compliant little submissive, waiting patiently for her master to fuck her. My belt buckle jangles as I wrench it free from its leather confines.

Mia gasps. Every muscle in her body goes rigid. "C-cantaloupe."

I freeze, my cock straining to be released from my zipper—

aching to be inside her. Sinking into my chair behind me, I silently curse my recklessness. I was so desperate to fuck her that I forgot to take care of her.

She remains locked in place, completely motionless. Taking hold of her hips, I gently tug her toward me, and she offers no resistance when I pull her onto my lap. "Come here, tesoro." She curls her trembling body against me, bringing her knees up to her chest and nestling close.

Wrapping my arms around her, I hold tight and press my lips against the side of her head. "I got you, sunshine." My breath dusts through her hair, dislodging notes of jasmine and citrus. God, she even smells like sunshine and summer.

She doesn't speak but covers her face as tears drip from her jawline onto the silky skin of her chest. I gently take her hands in one of mine and pull them to her lap. "You don't need to hide yourself from me."

She sucks in a deep, bone-shaking breath just before a giant sob rips through her entire body. I pull her tighter and she presses her face to my shirt, soaking the thin material with her tears. Murmuring words of comfort, I let her pour all the hurt and pain onto my chest and wish that I could take away all her bitter memories.

No man will ever hurt her again. And any man who tries ...

My jaw aches, anger and injustice burning through my veins, but something stronger settles in my bones. Her pain leaches into me and awakens a deeper emotion. An instinct I've suppressed for too long snakes its way to the surface, demanding that I remember the man I was born to be. It is my job to protect her, to chase away her demons. I will hold her while she fights this battle raging inside her and help her to realize her true strength.

Because of Mia, I reclaim the man I once was and thought I could never be again. As her tears soak through my shirt and onto my chest and she clings to me like I'm the only anchor in her storm, a newfound peace settles over me. This, right here, is where I'm meant to be.

~

MIA CRIED in my arms for a full half hour before she stopped enough that I risked carrying her to bed. I lay her on the bed and she sniffs loudly, roughly swatting at her cheeks. Lying beside her, I brush away her tears with the pad of my thumb.

"I'm sorry. I hate crying."

I narrow my eyes. "Why?"

"It used to m-make him super m-mad ..." She sucks in a huge breath. "He hated it. He said it was me m-manipulating him."

Anger rolls in my gut, and I wish that piece of shit wasn't already dead. "Crying is a perfectly safe and natural way to release emotion and tension, Mia."

"Hmm." She blinks, staring at the ceiling. Then she rolls onto her side and faces me. "Thank you."

"For what?"

"For understanding what I needed. For not getting mad."

I cup her cheek in my hand. "For that, you never have to thank me, sunshine."

She sinks her teeth into her lush bottom lip, and I have to remind my still-aching cock that this isn't the time. "I just know that you wanted to ... in your office ... I guess I'm not very good at this submissive thing."

A sigh heaves from my chest. I forgot how exhausting and complex training a new sub can be. "Listen to me, Mia. We have a power exchange in our relationship, but that doesn't mean there's a power imbalance. Do you understand the difference?"

Her cheeks flush pink. "Yes."

"There is no circumstance where my needs outweigh yours. There will never be a time when I'll be angry at you for feeling something you have no control over, for not wanting sex, for using your safe word. Never."

Confusion pinches that spot between her brows.

"Using your safe word when you need to is a good thing."

"It is?"

"That's what they're for."

"I guess. I just ... I feel like I keep failing."

I press my forehead against hers. "No, tesoro, I failed you. I forgot about the belt. That's what happened, right?"

"Yes." She breathes the word like a sigh of relief. "I knew you weren't going to use it, I just ... the sound ... it made me ..."

"I know."

"His belt was his favorite thing to hit me with. It had this huge buckle. When I'd hear him opening it ..." She starts to cry again, and I wrap her in my arms, pissed at myself for not realizing that taking off my belt like that might spook her.

"We're going to fix your fear of belts, sunshine."

She looks up at me, eyes so full of trust that my heart beats faster. "How?"

"You'll see," I tell her with a wink.

My phone vibrates in my jacket pocket, interrupting the moment. Fishing it out, I glance at the screen and see it's a call I need to take, but I have no intention of leaving her right now.

FORTY-SIX

MIA

Lorenzo's call didn't last very long and now he's scrolling through his cell phone while I read a scene in my book in which the main character gets railed by three vampires.

A deep ache builds in my core, and I clench my thighs together, jealous of Ophelia Hart and the fact that she's full of dick right now. Why the hell am I reading about this when I have my very own hot, brooding alpha-hole beside me?

I nestle closer and breathe in his scent—so masculine and fresh and intoxicating. He brushes a stray hair from my forehead. "You getting to a good part, sunshine?" he asks with a low growl.

"Why do you ask that?" I whisper, cheeks flaming.

"Because you're rubbing up against me like a bitch in heat."

I open my mouth to protest but close it again, not wanting to lie.

"Read it to me," he orders in that low, smooth tone that turns my legs to jelly.

"I-I can't."

"Why not?"

Will he judge me for reading about a woman being taken by three guys at the same time? Will he think that's what I secretly want? My cheeks burn hotter. "It's like really spicy."

"So read."

I lick my lips. Holy shit! He's going to realize I'm a complete deviant, and then I'll have to start hiding my smutty books from him just like I did with Brad. And I would hate that. I love that Lorenzo isn't the least bit threatened by what I read—although that was before he knew exactly what it was.

"Mia?"

I take a deep breath. Holy bananas. Here goes nothing. "I arch my b-back as Xavier's c-cock stretches my ass. 'You can take me too, baby,' he groans softly in my ear. Axl grips my breast and drags the fingers of his other hand through my dripping sex. 'I can't wait to fuck you w-with him, Ophelia.'" I glance over at Lorenzo, but his expression is unreadable, and I continue reading the spiciest scene in the entire book to my possessive, hotter-than-hell boyfriend, while I get wetter by the second. When I get to the part where the third guy joins the action, Lorenzo makes a noise between a growl and a grunt and flips me onto my back, taking the book from me and tossing it toward the nightstand.

"I had no idea your reading choices were quite so filthy as that," he says with a wicked glint in his eye.

"W-well," I stammer. "Not all of them are, but ..."

"That was fucking porn."

Is he mad? "It's not," I insist. "It has a plot too."

He arches an eyebrow. "It does?"

"They're also saving the world from a mutant vampire race."

"Oh, really?" He pins my hands to the bed and trails soft kisses over my jawline.

"R-really," I pant, lifting my hips and grinding against his hard cock.

"I like how worked up those books make you," he says, moving lower and grazing my neck with his lips and teeth.

"You do?"

"Hmm," he murmurs against my skin. "How could I not like something that makes you this needy, sunshine?"

"I wouldn't say needy," I protest, even though that's exactly what I am.

"No?" He smirks. "What do you need right now, Mia?"

"You," I admit in defeat.

"My mouth? My fingers? My dick?"

"All of you," I groan, arching my back as he rubs his hard length against my pussy.

"My greedy little sub needs more?" He gives a dark chuckle and sinks a finger inside me.

"Y-yuh," I whimper.

He inserts a second finger, stretching me wider. Hot pleasure skitters up my spine. He trails his mouth lower, skating along my breasts and my stomach, and when he moves between my thighs, he takes a deep breath through his nose. "You smell so fucking wet already." He blows a stream of cool air over my clit while slowly fucking me with his fingers and I see stars.

"Sir, please?"

"Tell me what you want, Mia," he commands.

"Your mouth on me," I gasp, rocking my hips and chasing the sweet relief of his tongue on my clit.

"I love how much you need me," he groans against me, and the sound vibrates though my clit, making tremors wrack my body. "You're so close."

"Yes!"

He swirls his delicious tongue over my clit, making appreciative growling noises as he eats my pussy and drives his fingers deeper inside me. He quickly finds my G-spot and applies the perfect amount of pressure.

I squeeze my eyes closed. I'm going to lose control any second, and he knows it. Pleasure and panic course through my body. But I can let go. He's got me.

A deep, throbbing ache grows in my center, and I clamp my thighs around his head as my orgasm builds to a crescendo. He uses his free hand to force my legs back down to the bed, giving him more room to eat me and finger fuck me.

"Sir, I'm going to—" I scream. My climax washes over me like a full-scale tsunami, soaking Lorenzo and the bed. I gasp for breath while my devilish Dom lifts his head and watches me come back down to earth with a wicked glint in his eyes.

He pushes himself to his knees. "You had my fingers and my mouth, sunshine. What's next?" He licks my arousal from his lips.

My chest heaves as I push myself up onto my elbows, my gaze dropping to the bulge in his suit pants. I lick my lips too. I want all of him. "Your dick," I whisper as heat rushes to my face.

He kneels, straddling me. "You want my dick, Mia, you're going to have to open my belt first."

Staring up at him, I swallow.

Amused, he raises one eyebrow. "You want me to fuck you?"

"Yes," I whimper. I want him to fuck me more than I've wanted anything in my life. My entire body aches and screams for him to sate this ever-present need for him.

"So, open my belt," he commands, and the deep, soothing timbre of his voice melts my core.

With trembling fingers, I reach for his belt and tug on the supple leather. The metallic jangle of the buckle is jarring and tries to pull me into an old memory.

"You're doing so well." Lorenzo anchors me back to the present. To him. To us. I tug the leather through the buckle and take another deep breath. "All the way off, Mia," he adds, brushing his strong fingers over my trembling ones.

I nod jerkily and pull it through the loops of his suit pants. The sound of it sliding against the fabric threatens to drown me again, but he keeps me afloat, telling me what a great job I'm doing. When I finally work it free, I smile up at him in triumph.

"You did so good, sunshine." He takes the belt from me, and my blood freezes at the sight of him holding it, but he's ready for me this time. He places a warm hand over my heart. "Relax, Mia."

I nod. I trust him. Lorenzo might be the most dangerous man in Chicago, but he isn't cruel and he would never hurt me. He trails the tip of the leather, warmed by his body heat, over my stomach and I shiver.

"One day, I will show you how good this can feel on your skin, tesoro." Tossing the belt to the floor, he nudges my thighs further apart with his knees, unzips his fly and reaches inside his pants to free his thick cock. A groan of relief tumbles from his lips. I think he's been hard since earlier in his office, yet he's been nothing but patient and understanding. Oh, god, I love him.

He gives his dick a quick tug, groaning as precum seeps from the tip. Oh, bananas. I love him so freaking much.

"You see how fucking hard you make me, Mia," he says with a throaty growl as he nudges his cock at my entrance. I wrap my legs around him, fisting my hands in his shirt and pulling him down onto me.

"Feel how wet you make me, Sir." He drives into me, hard and fierce and all-consuming. My walls squeeze around him. I'm desperate for the relief that being full of him gives. He pulls out only to push back inside with even greater need. I whimper as he slams into me repeatedly, making the headboard crash against the wall. Clinging to him, I ride the waves of the orgasm that's already building. He rolls his hips, sweeping the crown of his cock over my G-spot and causing tremors to vibrate through my body.

"Holy ... Sir," I groan, wrapping my arms around his neck. He buries his face against mine, teeth and lips lashing over my skin. Warm pulses of energy roll through me as he coaxes another climax, this time from deep within me. I cry out when it hits, and it seems to drive him even more feral with need.

He fucks me like a frenzied animal, as though he can't get deep enough inside. His breathing grows heavier as he grunts loudly, railing into me one last time before his hips still. "Fucking Christ," he groans, lifting his head and looking into my eyes. I brush aside a damp strand of hair as he stares at me so intently that my entire body shivers. It seems like he wants to say something, but he holds back, and so do I.

"Was that worth waiting for?" I ask instead, a mischievous grin tugging at the corners of my mouth.

"You"—he kisses my forehead—"are always worth waiting for."

FORTY-SEVEN

MIA

"Your gown is stunning," I say with a soft sigh while Kat tries on her outfit for the charity gala she's attending with Dante, Joey, and Max. Lorenzo and I are on babysitting duty, and I'm a little envious she gets to dress up in a ball gown and go dancing with her husband, but I also understand that going to such a public event together would be a huge deal for Lorenzo. Besides, I'm looking forward to snuggling on the sofa with him and forcing him to watch my favorite movie of all time, *City of Angels*.

"Thanks, honey." She smiles widely. "Dante hates these things, but I'm so excited. Do you know some of the cast of that show, *The Vampire Journals*, are attending? One of them is a patron for the charity or something."

I roll my eyes and stifle a groan. "Okay. You don't have to rub it in, I'm already green with envy."

She laughs softly. "You don't have an envious bone in your body, Mia Melon."

"That was before I realized you might get to meet some hottie vampire actors."

"I, uh. I need to go check on the kids."

"Okay ... Well, I'm going to take a long soak in the bath before I have to report to babysitting duty."

Kat links her arm through mine. "Not to worry, Cinders, one day you'll get to go to the ball."

Kat and I part company at the top of the marble staircase, and I go into Lorenzo's bedroom. My eyes are immediately drawn to the gold ballgown lying on the bed, and I glance around. *Is this Joey's? Is she getting ready here? Did somebody put it there by mistake?*

I wander over to the bed and pick it up. The color is beautiful with the way it shifts depending on the way the light hits it. It's so luxurious, but it seems a size too big for Joey and it's not the right shade for her skin tone. What the hell is it doing here?

"You like that, sunshine?" Lorenzo's deep voice rumbles through the room, followed by the sound of the door closing.

I spin around, still clutching the gown. "What? Yes, but ..." I frown.

"I spoke to Kat and Dante. They're happy for Sophia and Maria to watch the kids tonight, along with some extra armed guards."

Mouth hanging open, I blink at him as he crosses the room and stands directly in front of me. Close enough that I can smell his expensive cologne. "Does that mean ..."

He arches an eyebrow. "You want to come to the ball with me?"

I toss the dress onto the bed and throw my arms around his neck. "Yes, yes, yes," I squeal.

"The hair and make-up lady will be here in thirty minutes, so I suggest you stop rubbing up against me like that."

My cheeks flush pink and I take a step back. "Sorry."

His eyes narrow.

"No, I'm not," I add with a smile. "I love that I make you feel like that."

The corner of his mouth curls up, and he reaches into the inside pocket of his suit jacket. "I have something else for you too." He pulls out a long black box, covered in velvet.

My mouth goes dry. He snaps it open, revealing a beautiful thick gold chain with a sunflower pendant. The petals are made of gold, and the center is a huge yellow gemstone. "Is that a ..." I gape at him.

"A two-carat canary diamond? Yes." He takes the necklace from the box.

"Lorenzo, it's too much."

Shaking his head, he tosses the box onto the bed and opens the clasp on the chain. After looping it around my neck, he fastens it in place. "It's not enough, sunshine."

I brush my fingertips across the sunflower. It's way more snug than any necklace I've ever worn before. My breath hitches in my throat, and he dusts his lips over my ear. "It's not a collar, Mia," he says, answering the question I didn't voice.

I swallow the lump in my throat. "Okay."

He takes a step back, his eyes raking over my body before fixing on my neck. On the necklace that's not a collar.

"Thank you," I whisper. "For the necklace, and the dress. They're both beautiful. You have exceptional taste."

He stares at me with hunger in his gaze. "I agree."

Wetness pools between my thighs and the air becomes charged with sexual tension. I clear my throat. "I should shower if the make-up lady will be here soon."

He licks his lower lip before his eyes meet mine, so dark and full of longing. "I should leave you to it because you're way too much of a distraction."

I smile at him. I love being this man's distraction more than anything in the world.

~

I POKE my head into Kat and Dante's bedroom, and my cousin squeals my name, jumping up from her chair and clapping her hands.

My excitement matches hers, and I charge across the room. We meet in the middle, and she wraps me in a hug.

"Did you know he had this planned when you were teasing me earlier?" I ask accusingly.

"Yes!" She giggles. "I was so desperate to tell you, but I didn't want to spoil the surprise. I'm so excited we're getting ready together."

"Like when we were back in high school," I add, tears filling my eyes as a wave of happiness and contentment washes over me.

"Except that we have actual professionals to make us look good now instead of having to do each other's eyeliner." She laughs loudly. "You were so bad at that."

I snort. "Like you were so much better."

Laughing, she takes my hand and pulls me to sit in the chair beside hers so the hair and make-up ladies can get to work.

I lean back and allow the lady who introduces herself as Lucy to brush my hair. Butterflies swirl in my stomach. I'm sitting here with Kat being pampered, wearing a beautiful diamond. It might not be a collar, but it feels like the start of something special. And the most exciting part of all—I'm going to a ball with the man of my dreams.

FORTY-EIGHT

LORENZO

The smile on Mia's face could light up the entire state of Illinois. From the moment she stepped out of Kat and Dante's bedroom, she's been grinning from ear to ear, awestruck by everything. The limousine, the champagne in the limo. The limo's mini fridge that's stocked with Milky Ways, Three Musketeers, and Snickers bars for the journey home.

She's no less stunned when the limo pulls up at the venue—a hotel built to look like a French castle, the walkway lit by six-foot brass candelabras. It's a stunning sight, but it pales in comparison to the way Mia looks in the dress Kat helped me pick out, with its tight corset top that pushes her tits up and displays them to absolute perfection and the full skirt that manages to cling to her hips and juicy ass just enough to showcase her beautiful curves. She takes my breath away, and it took every ounce of effort I possess not to march her straight into my bedroom when I first saw her.

She holds onto my arm, and I escort her down the red carpet while she looks around the entire time. Eyes wide and mouth hanging open, like a kid on their first trip to Disney World.

Biting back a smile, I allow her a few moments to enjoy her surroundings before I pull her closer, pressing my lips to her ear so no one else will hear. "There are some rules tonight, Mia."

She shivers and it fills me with a perverse sense of satisfaction.

"Yes?" she whispers.

"You will not speak unless you are asked a direct question or I give you permission." She presses her lips together. That's a tough rule for my little chatterbox to follow, but she nods.

"You will not make eye contact with anyone without my permission."

Her gaze drops to the floor, and I grin. That rule can be a difficult one for inexperienced subs to follow without appearing rude, and I know that Mia is a people pleaser at heart. I look forward to seeing how she'll handle it, and my cock throbs at the thought of spanking her for breaking the rule, which she surely will.

"And you will do whatever I tell you to do without hesitation. You understand me?"

"Yes," she replies, full of confidence.

"Good." I blow out a breath, preparing myself for the inevitable stares and questions. This is the first time I've attended a function with a woman since Anya died, and it's a public statement that we are a couple. There will be people from the lifestyle here, and I can already hear the whispers and the gossip about whether I might have taken a new sub. I've had no shortage of offers the past two and a half years. Any single experienced Dom is in high demand in the circles I used to move in, and I'm no exception. But I told them all I'd never take another sub. I meant it when I said it.

My muscles tense. Mia squeezes my arm reassuringly and I glance at her. "Look at me," I command. She turns her head, fixing her hazel eyes on mine. "You ready?"

"Yes, Sir." Her soft purr rolls through my body and goes straight to my dick. Fucking siren.

MIA HAS BEEN nothing short of impeccable tonight. As I expected, there were plenty of people eager to meet her, and she greeted them all pleasantly and respectfully, managing to avoid eye contact with every single one. Even while dancing, drinking champagne, and laughing with Kat and Joey, she has obeyed my rules to the letter.

I'm escorting her back to our table when a familiar voice stops me in my tracks.

"Lorenzo Moretti," she says, her voice a sultry purr. "It's so wonderful to see you." Oh, fuck! I hoped she wouldn't be here tonight.

I turn with my arm locked around Mia's waist, and she's forced to turn with me. "Dahlia," I say with a weak smile. "It's nice to see you too."

Mia keeps her gaze averted from Dahlia's, but I see her appraising the other woman, taking in her perfectly styled dark hair and elegant black gown, as well as the diamonds dripping from her neck.

Dahlia lifts her eyebrows expectantly. My discomfort at seeing my old girlfriend is no excuse for forgetting my manners. I slide my right arm from around Mia's waist and grasp Dahlia by the shoulders, giving her a kiss on each cheek. "You look well."

She runs a manicured fingernail over the lapel of my suit jacket. "And you are as handsome as ever. I'd almost forgotten what that face looked like."

I force a laugh and return my hand to Mia's hip, pulling her toward me again. "This is Mia."

CHAPTER FORTY-EIGHT

"Mia?" Dahlia extends her hand. "Delightful to meet you."

Mia extends her hand and smiles widely, being careful to avoid eye contact. Dahlia shoots me a knowing look and touches my arm. "It truly is wonderful to see you back out here." She gives me a kiss on the cheek and says goodbye to both Mia and me before disappearing through the crowd.

With my hand on Mia's back, I guide her through the crowd, searching her face while we make our way to our table. She continues smiling, her eyes sparkling with delight as she looks around the huge ballroom with wonder, despite having already been here for three hours. But then she glances at me, sinking her teeth into her bottom lip.

"Something you'd like to say?" I ask her.

She nods, avoiding my gaze.

I sigh inwardly. I knew she was too good to be true. She's going to bitch about me talking to Dahlia. "Then say it."

"May I look at you?"

"Yes."

Her hazel eyes appear green tonight, sparkling under the bright chandeliers. "Your friend was so lovely. Did she know Anya too?"

I scan her face and don't find a trace of jealousy or envy, only genuine curiosity. "Why do you ask that?"

"It just seemed like she did, from the way she spoke."

My heart constricts. "Yes, she knew Anya too. Although it took them a long time to become friends."

She tilts her head to the side, regarding me with curiosity. "Why?"

"Dahlia and I used to date. She was my first sub." I narrow my eyes, waiting for the inevitable change in her demeanor.

Mia's eyes widen, shining with delight and intrigue. "That's ... wow, I love that," she says the last part softly as she scans the crowd.

"What?" I ask her with a frown.

She blinks at me, as though the answer is obvious. "She was so nice. It makes me feel like I know a little more about you is all."

I continue watching her for any sign that she's bullshitting me, but she remains her usual happy, heart-on-her-sleeve self.

I arch an eyebrow at her. "You only met her for a few minutes, how can you know if she was nice?"

"Her whole vibe was good." She shrugs, but then she gives me a wicked grin, running her hand over the buttons of my shirt. "Are you telling me she's not nice? Are my spidey-senses off?"

"No." The corners of my mouth tug into an unexpected grin. "She's a good person."

"Well, I'd love to get to know her better—if that's a possibility? I guess it must be hard to see your old friends when you're here with me."

Fuck me, this woman is too perfect for words. She waits for my response, her tits heaving every time she breathes, and my cock twitches in my pants. "Go to the restroom and take off your panties."

She stares at me, her cheeks turning pink before she looks away. I cup her chin in my hand and tilt her head up. "Look at me." Her gaze fixes on mine. "Do I need to ask you again?"

"No," she whispers.

"So go do it and come straight back here to me."

She nods and turns to obey. I watch every step she takes as she disappears through the crowd to the powder room.

CHAPTER
FORTY-NINE

MIA

I walk out of the powder room, panties stuffed inside my purse, my heart racing wildly as I scan the hall for Lorenzo. I'm not sure if he's mad at me or not. One second we were talking and the next he went all bossy alpha-hole on me.

I've only taken a few steps toward where I left him standing a few minutes ago when he moves in front of me.

He leans close, lips against my ear. "Where are your panties?"

"In my purse."

"Good." He takes hold of my elbow, nods at one of his men, Tito, to follow us, and then leads me to a staircase at the back of the room that's blocked by thick velvet ropes with a *closed* sign. Lorenzo simply lifts the ropes and walks up the stairs, leading me with him while Tito trails behind.

My heart beats faster, and I glance around, wondering why he's bringing me up here, why Tito is coming, and what will happen if we get caught. When we reach the top, Lorenzo turns to his guard. "Make sure nobody comes up here."

Tito nods and turns to face the stairs. Lorenzo takes my

hand and pulls me along the narrow hallway until we reach a balcony that overlooks the ballroom.

Looking out at the crowd, I gasp. The view is incredible from this vantage point. A few people glance up and see us, and I instinctively shrink back, aware we shouldn't be up here, but Lorenzo is right behind me, pressing his body against mine so I'm pinned to the waist-high wall and unable to move.

He pulls my hair aside and dusts his lips over my neck. "Don't you like being up here?"

"Yes," I breathe as heat coils up my spine. "But are we allowed to be here?"

"We're this charity's biggest donors, we can be wherever the fuck we want."

"Then I love it. I love being able to watch everyone."

"And how do you feel about them watching you?" he asks, his voice dropping an octave. It's dark and tempting and wicked as sin.

Then he's lifting my skirts, pulling at the layers of fabric, revealing my bare legs inch by inch. "W-watching me?"

He drags his teeth along the back of my neck as he pulls my dress higher, exposing the tops of my thighs. "Watching you while you come on my cock."

I inhale sharply, sure I misheard him. There must be at least two hundred people down there.

His fingertips brush my bare ass cheeks, and I shiver. "You want them to watch us?"

"I want them to look up here and have no idea that I'm fucking you," he says with a dark chuckle. "I want you to come in front of all these people, sunshine, but I don't want them to know a thing about it."

"I-I—h-how?" I stammer. The wall hides us both from the waist down, but surely they'll still be able to tell. They'll see him railing into me. See my face change when he forces an orgasm from my body.

He glides his hand over my hip and down between my thighs. "Open," he commands, and I spread my legs wider, allowing him room to rub my clit in slow, teasing circles. "I'm going to slide my cock inside your tight cunt and rub right here"—he presses firmly on the sensitive bud of flesh, and my eyes almost roll back in my head—"until you come for me. And while I'm doing that, we're going to see if you can make me come with just your hungry little squeezes."

Heat floods my entire body as I look at the sea of people below. Will they really have no idea what we're doing? Or will it be completely obvious that I'm being fucked while they're dancing and drinking champagne?

"I'm going to open my belt," Lorenzo says softly, preparing me so I don't freak out at old memories again.

I bite down on my lip as he tugs open his belt, his other hand still between my thighs.

"I'm so fucking hard for you," he says on a deep groan. "Are you wet for me?"

"Yes, Sir," I whimper, feeling able to use that title while we're alone.

His teeth graze the shell of my ear. "You're turning into such a good little sub, Mia."

The tip of his cock presses against my opening and I gasp. "Hold onto the wall while I get inside you," he orders.

I brace myself against the cool brick, my fingers gripping the edge tightly as he pushes his thick cock inside me. Our height difference is much less pronounced in my six-inch heels and he's able to fill me without it being obvious to the crowd below. He grunts as he sinks all the way in, making wet heat rush between my thighs.

Oh god. Knowing that people can see us is so hot.

"Fucking Christ, you are wet, sunshine. Soaking for me." He groans loudly in my ear, his hips stilling as he fills me up completely. He starts to rub my clit again, using the pads of his fingers to coax warm waves of pleasure to rush through my core and thighs.

I press my lips together, careful not to speak unless he gives me permission. But I so want to moan his name as his cock throbs inside me.

"Squeeze my cock. Make me fill you with my come."

I squeeze and release, my pussy walls pulling him deeper and eliciting guttural growls from his throat. Over and over again, I grip his cock with my inner muscles.

He increases the pressure on my clit. "Holy fuck, tesoro."

Glancing at the scene below, I see that nobody is paying us much attention now, and I allow my mouth to fall open on a soft moan.

"You're doing so well, Mia. Being such a good girl for me."

A whimper falls from my lips, and I bite my cheek to stop any further sounds from escaping.

He nuzzles my neck, biting down on my sensitive flesh, then soothing the sting with a sweep of his tongue. My pussy ripples around him and he grunts in appreciation. "That's it, sunshine. Come for me in front of all these people."

With his permission given, the orgasm floods my body, washing over and through me in long, undulating waves. I clamp my lips together and rock on my heels, my back pressing against his hard chest. He snakes an arm around my waist, pulling me close as I squeeze him deeper. With an Italian curse, he fills me with his cum. "Holy motherfucker," he groans, sliding out of me and causing wetness to slick my thighs.

Gripping the wall, I suck in a stuttered breath while he lowers my dress and fastens his pants. My head swims as I come down from the high, but I manage to focus on the crowd.

Nobody is looking. Nobody except Lorenzo's friend, Dahlia. She catches my eye and raises her glass of champagne in a silent toast. I swallow hard. Did she see? Does she know?

I glance back at Lorenzo. He's looking at Dahlia too, and the change in him is instantaneous. He grabs hold of my hand. "We're leaving," he growls.

His jaw ticks, his muscles tense. I want to ask him what's wrong, but I don't want to upset him further. Is he mad because Dahlia knows what we were doing? Did I do something wrong? Draw too much attention? He remains silent as he hurries down the stairs, my hand still clasped in his. We almost bump into Tito, who waits obediently at the foot of the stairwell.

"Tell Dante and Max I'm taking the car. I'll send it straight back for them," he snaps.

Tito nods and slips away through the crowd, and I swallow the knot of anxiety currently lodged in my throat as Lorenzo pulls me out of the building like it's on fire. I did everything he asked of me. This can't be about me, can it? Is he upset about Anya's friend seeing us together that way?

As soon as we're alone in the back of the car, Lorenzo sinks against the seat and wraps an arm around my shoulder, pulling me close. He presses a soft kiss on my forehead, and I lean into him, loving the comfort and warmth of his body. He doesn't seem mad at me, but his jaw is still clenched and he's stiff with tension. I wish he'd let me in and tell me what's going on with him.

"Are you okay?" I chance asking a question. The rules were for the ball, right? Not for he and I alone in the car.

"I'm good, sunshine," he assures me. But he says nothing else, and I spend the rest of the drive wondering what went wrong.

FIFTY

LORENZO

As soon as the car rolls to a stop, I open the door, too impatient to wait for the driver. Mia's hand is clasped in mine, and I pull her out with me, hurrying up the path and into the house.

My jaw aches. I stretch my neck, trying to ease the tension there, and quicken my steps, desperate to get her to my room. Mia's heels click along the marble floor as she breaks into a slight jog to keep up with me. She stumbles, and I curse out loud before scooping her up. Holding her against my chest, I take the stairs two at a time, forcing her to wrap her arms around me to maintain her balance. Her breathing is heavy—stuttered—and it makes those cock-achingly perfect tits jiggle.

"Sir?" she whispers, her voice uncertain. I walk inside my bedroom and kick the door closed behind me before striding toward the bed and setting her on her feet. My pulse races, thundering like a prize-winning stallion. My cock is painfully hard, leaking precum in my boxers. She was fucking perfect tonight. She *is* fucking perfect.

I need her more than I need my next breath.

I brush her honey-blond hair back from her face and cup

her chin in my hands as I draw a deep breath. Her full pink lips part like she's about to ask me what's going on, but I seal my mouth over hers, sliding my tongue inside and tasting her sweetness. Everything about her is good and light. She's the perfect balm for my wretched darkness.

She whimpers and I swallow the sounds, kissing her so hard that she's unable to breathe, but I don't let up. I can't. I slide my hands to her back and find the concealed zipper of her gown. The dress falls away, exposing every delicious curve to the cool air, and the shimmery fabric lands in a pool at her feet, leaving her naked except for her heels. I pull her closer, warming her with my body heat. Her tits press against me, her nipples pebbled.

Lifting her, I wrap her legs around my waist and crawl onto the bed. Only when I have her beneath me do I break our kiss, taking the opportunity to look over her beautiful body.

"Sir?" she says on a breathy moan, arching her back and rubbing her pussy on my cock through my pants.

"You're so fucking beautiful, tesoro," I groan against her skin, lips dusting over her neck and collarbone as I make my way down to her delicious tits. I suck her nipple into my mouth and bite down on the turgid peak until she cries out. Sweeping my tongue across the tip, I soothe the sting of my bite, then move to the other one and do the same. She curls her fingers in my hair and presses herself into my hungry mouth. I fight myself for control. If I'm not careful, I will end up devouring her whole, permanently marking her perfect body for all eternity.

She mewls and whimpers as I work my way down, over the soft curves of her stomach. My lips graze her thighs, still sticky with our cum, but it's her essence that floods my senses, the scent of her arousal that makes my mouth water.

My aching cock weeps to be inside her. I swirl my tongue over her clit, soaking up the taste of her juices. When I growl against her sensitive flesh, a shiver ripples through her body. She bucks her hips, pressing her pussy into my waiting mouth, and I suck and lick her wetness from her, feasting on her cum until my balls burn with the need to fill her.

Holding myself up on one forearm, I tug open my belt with the other. Her hands fist in the collar of my shirt. "I want to feel you, Sir," she pants. "Feel your skin. Please?"

I push up onto my knees and start to unbutton my shirt. Her deft fingers soon join mine and she tugs at the buttons with a desperation that mirrors my own. Once that's out of the way, she unzips my pants and, without warning, slips her hand into my boxers and squeezes my cock at the base.

"Fuck!" I get rid of my pants and boxers, along with my socks. Being propped up on top of her makes it so much more difficult, but I can't tear myself away from her delectable needy body.

With a seductive smile, she wraps her slender legs around my waist and tugs me closer, and I press the crown of my cock against her drenched opening. She hisses out a breath, clawing at my back and shoulders as she tries to pull me inside her.

I hold back, teasing us both despite our urgent need. I want to take my time, savor every single second with her.

"Please, Sir?" The sound of her begging shoots a bolt of pleasure through me. I trail kisses over her collarbone, inhaling the smell of her sweet skin as I roll my hips and sink so deliciously deep inside her that I almost come on the spot.

She cries out, the sound so full of relief that I feel it in my soul. I suck a tender spot on her neck and pull out of her slowly before sinking back in.

"Oh god," she whimpers. Her nails rake down my back and break the skin, but I don't feel the sting of her scratches. I feel nothing but the deep, soul-cleansing euphoria of being inside this woman. Nothing exists outside the two of us. She is everything. Where I begin and end.

And when I crash my lips against hers, taking her breath as I take her body—while she claims my heart and my goddamn soul—I slowly rock my hips. Her hot, wet channel squeezes my cock like she never intends to let me go.

"Fuck, tesoro," I groan in her ear. "Sei fottutamente perfetto."

She cries out, clinging to me desperately. "I love you, Sir!"

Her words steal the breath from my lungs. Her juicy lips open on a moan as she comes hard for me, milking me for all she's worth. I plow into her, drawing out her orgasm while I grind out my own. My head spins with the force of it. I roll my hips against her, spilling every last drop from my balls into her sweet cunt.

Completely spent, obliterated by the love of this woman, I collapse on top of her, my head buried in the crook of her neck. The high starts to ebb away, and as it does, I'm hit with the realization that I just *made love* to a woman who isn't my wife.

FIFTY-ONE

MIA

A current of cold air makes me shiver, and I roll to the middle of the bed, seeking Lorenzo's warmth. Disoriented, I open my eyes and see him perched on the edge of the bed, his head in his hands. Waves of pain radiate from him, and my heart drops through my stomach.

Climbing out from under the covers, I crawl across the bed to him and slide my hands over his shoulders.

"Don't." The way he shrugs me off and his harsh tone hit me like an arrow through my heart.

"What's wrong?" I ask softly, terrified of his answer.

"This," he says with a snarl. "This is all wrong."

"Lorenzo, don't ..."

Rocketing off the bed, he spins around to face me. "Do *not* fucking tell me what to feel, Mia."

I flinch at the hostility in his tone. "I wasn't going to."

He runs his hands through his hair. "I'm sorry. But this—us. It can't work."

"But it does work," I remind him.

"But it can't!" he yells, morphing into a man that I don't

recognize, and I flinch. "I can't do this, Mia. I'm sorry." His tone is softer now, his head hung low—in defeat.

Climbing off the bed, I go to him and cup his face in my hands. "You *can* do this. I know you're feeling things, but just talk to me—"

"It's no good." He steps back and sneers. "You need to get the hell out of here. Get the hell away from me. You were right when you said you deserve more than I can offer."

Fighting tears, I stare into his eyes that are so full of shame and sorrow. "That was before I knew you were capable of—"

He scoffs. "Capable of what? Of loving you?"

Goddamn this stubborn asshole. "Yes!" I shout back.

His mouth twists in a cruel sneer. "You think I could ever love you as much as I loved her, Mia? You will never be her. You will never be good enough. Is that how you want to live your life? Always second best?"

I recoil, no less wounded than if he'd punched me in the face. In fact, a punch to the face wouldn't have hurt so much. Tears stream down my cheeks. I don't think there's any way back from what he just said.

Lorenzo knows it too. He turns around and storms out of the room, slamming the door behind him.

FIFTY-TWO
LORENZO

S itting at the piano, I stare at the keys. My fingers hover over them, poised to play, but it's like they've forgotten how. I slam the lid down and rest my forehead on the cool polished wood.

I need to think. To breathe. To stop the walls from closing in around me. But it's no less than I deserve.

An image of her face torments me. Mia Stone, the woman I tore to pieces because I'm a selfish asshole who can't give her what she needs. I can't give her what she deserves. Mia should have every single thing her heart desires—just as long as that something isn't me.

Except I could grant her everything she wants, couldn't I? The wedding and the kids and the happily ever after—the entire beautiful fucking future I dreamed of last night after I made love to her like she was the other half of my fucking soul. We could have everything together. But why should I get a happily ever when Anya couldn't have hers? What gives me the right to a joyful future with Mia when I promised my wife on her fucking deathbed that I would never love anyone else ever again?

CHAPTER FIFTY-TWO

Anya's letter healed me in ways I never expected, but I can't give myself permission to move on. I can't offer another woman the future I was unable to provide for my wife ...

And I can't do it for Mia.

She was so perfect last night. I saw people watching us, and I know that they saw it too—how right we looked together, how fucking incredible she looked on my arm. Like everyone forgot that another woman once occupied that place. They forgot my beautiful Anya. But worse than that—I forgot her too. Not once did I think of my wife last night, and the weight of that guilt is heavy enough to crush me.

What if I stop thinking about her altogether? What happens to her then? What if I forget the feel of her skin against mine? The scent of her hair. The sound of her voice. How she curled up on my chest whenever she was tired. Who will remember all of those things about her if I don't? If I stop thinking about her every day, she might be lost forever.

Balling my hand into a fist, I curse the day I met Mia Stone. Rage is an emotion I know how to deal with. Anger is all I'm good at now. If I'd never met her, I wouldn't have made love to her last night. I wouldn't have broken her heart.

I wouldn't have betrayed the only two women I've ever loved.

And I never would have felt my own heart shatter for the second time.

FIFTY-THREE

MIA

K at places a reassuring hand on my shoulder. "He'll come around, Mia," she says softly. "You looked so happy together the night of the ball."

I know we did. Because we *were* happy. I have no idea what happened to turn the man I love into the world's biggest jackass. "I don't think so, Kat," I sniff. "He said some awful things." The memory of his words slices a fresh welt across my heart. I haven't told Kat exactly what he said. I couldn't bear the pain of repeating them, and I'm too ashamed of thinking I could have a future with a man who sees me that way.

"Besides, I've waited too long already. He had all day yesterday to come and talk to me." My cheeks flush at how I stupidly sat in his bedroom for hours, hoping he'd rush back in and beg my forgiveness. Tell me it was all some awful mistake, that he didn't mean any of those horrible things he said. "But I haven't seen him at all. It's like I don't even exist anymore. I'm done, Kat." I dry my face with a tissue from the box she hands me.

The agony of Lorenzo's betrayal is so acute that reliving his unforgivable words renders me almost numb. It's as though my brain knows that to allow myself to feel the pain of those words would be too much for me to bear all at once, so it won't let me. Instead, I remember snatched pieces, and I recall the hurt. The soul-crushing hurt of him eviscerating my heart all over again.

For a few hours after it happened, I even convinced myself that he'd come to me and somehow take back those terrible things he said. But of course he didn't. Lorenzo Moretti might just be the most damaged and stubborn man I've ever known. He's either beyond redemption or I pity the woman who eventually decides to stick around long enough to help him work through his pain. Because he's a selfish son of a bitch, and if he was right about one thing, it's that I deserve so much better.

I roll back my shoulders and swallow down a fresh wave of sorrow. "I found a few apartments nearby. Would you come look at a few with me? I have some savings and ..."

Kat pulls me into a hug. "Whatever you need, honey. I'm here for you."

FIFTY-FOUR

LORENZO

I stare out the window without seeing anything. Since the night of the ball, I've felt like I exist in a void. Walking around in a body that doesn't belong to me.

I don't realize I'm not alone until she speaks. "You're a gigantic asshole, you know that?"

I spin around. "What?"

Kat stands in front of my desk, holding my nephew on her hip and glaring at me with contempt. "I said you're an asshole."

I lick my lips and sigh. I have no desire to get into an argument with her, especially not when she's right.

"If I didn't love you so much ..." She shakes her head when I don't give her any response other than a blank stare. "That being said, can you look after Micah for me? Dante took Gabriella and Marco to see Toni."

I scowl at the mention of my half sister's name. We've never had a great relationship, although it's certainly improved since our father died.

"I'll be back in a few hours, but there's some expressed milk in the fridge if he needs any."

"Where are you going?"

"To help Mia look for an apartment. I'd take him but it's hot out and he gets a little cranky in the car lately."

Mia's looking for an apartment? I swallow the question down without asking it. It's for the best. She needs to be far away from me before I fuck up her life more than I already have.

"So will you?" she asks again, and I realize I haven't answered her.

"Sure." I take Micah from her arms, and he curls his chubby fingers in my beard and giggles.

"Thanks," she says softly, her eyes shining with unshed tears.

I glare at her in warning. "Don't, Kat."

"I didn't say anything." She kisses her son on the cheek. "Be good for Uncle Loz, baby."

Then she walks out of the room, and I'm sure she calls me an asshole again under her breath.

Drool runs down my nephew's chin, and I wipe it with the pad of my thumb, which he tries to suck into his mouth. I arch an eyebrow at him. "You think I'm an asshole?"

"Dada," he replies.

I look into his dark brown eyes. So innocent and trusting. A vise clamps around my heart and squeezes.

"Dada," he says again, sucking his chubby fist into his mouth.

And I see it all again. Mia at the ball. My dream from the other night. My legs buckle, and I sink to the floor with Micah in my arms, fighting to breathe like someone just sucked all the air out of the room.

"Dada. Dada," Micah chants, clapping his hands and squealing. Images flash through my head. Mia in her sexy-as-fuck heels. Mia being the perfect submissive. Wearing my collar. Wearing my ring. Children with Mia's honey-blond hair and sparkling hazel eyes ...

"Dada," Micah coos, resting his plump little cheek against my chest.

"No, baby." I kiss the top of his head. "Not me."

The realization that it *could* be me hits me like a forty-ton truck.

My heart pounds, threatening to explode through my ribcage. Kat's right, I am a gigantic fucking asshole. I destroyed Mia because I allowed my guilt to consume me.

I look down at my nephew's smiling face. I thought I could never have what my younger brother has. That I could never have a family of my own. But why can't I be called Dada or Daddy for real?

The only thing stopping me is this soul-crushing guilt. Finding the strength to get off the floor, I go to my desk and grab the envelope containing my wife's letter. As agonizing as they were for me to read, I can't imagine the pain she must have felt when she wrote these words. Jealousy was Anya's one major flaw. After I put in a ton of effort to prove my commitment and devotion to her, she eventually trusted my loyalty. Still, a small jealous streak remained. How hard must it have been for her to contemplate the notion of me loving someone besides her? My incredible wife rose above her grief and fear, and even her jealousy, to urge me to keep living, proving what I already knew to be true. Anya's kind heart and compassion outweighed all her other flaws combined. And she loved me just as much as I loved her.

Cradling my nephew against my chest, I stride out of the library and find Kat in the hallway, fixing her purse over her shoulder. Mia, standing beside her cousin, looks up. Her eyes lock on mine, and the expression on her face almost breaks me. There's no light left, not even a flicker. I stole it from her. Without taking my focus off Mia, I hold Micah toward Kat and tell her that I can't watch him.

I see her frown from the corner of my eye. "What? Why? Is this because I called you an asshole?"

Mia glares at me, her jaw set.

"No. It's because you're not going."

"Oh, for goodness' sake," Kat says with a sigh.

I drag my eyes away from Mia for a second. "Can you give us a moment?"

"No," Mia snaps.

"Please?" I say to Kat.

Rolling her eyes, she sighs again. "I'll be in the den if you need me," she tells Mia before giving me a pointed look and walking away.

"Kat?" Mia shouts after her, but my sister-in-law ignores her. "Fine." She huffs and stomps toward the front door.

An armed guard stands nearby, and he looks at me for guidance. I shake my head. "Sorry. I can't let you leave," he says, stepping in front of Mia and blocking her path. She spins on her heel, her hazel eyes blazing green with fury.

"I am not your prisoner, Lorenzo. Let me out of this house right now."

"No."

"What the ..." Pressing her lips together, she draws a deep breath through her nose. "I can't even deal with you right now."

"Leave us." The guard nods politely and goes outside. At least Mia doesn't try to bolt after him. She crosses her arms over her chest and taps her foot on the marble floor, refusing to look at me.

"Mia?"

Pursing her lips, she tilts her head toward the ceiling.

"Look at me."

Her throat constricts as she swallows.

"Now."

She lowers her gaze to the floor, but she turns her head in my direction.

My heart pounds so hard, I'm certain she must hear it. Can she not see how fucking brutal this is? "Please, sunshine. Please look at me."

Her head lifts, eyes flickering over my face before they land on mine. "What do you want from me, Lorenzo?"

"Stay."

She snorts. "Stay?"

"Yes."

Her eyes narrow, confusion and anger pulling her beautiful face into a scowl. "Why the hell would I do that?"

"Because I need you."

"No." Shaking her head, she glares at me. "You don't get to do that. Not now. Not after I begged you to talk to me. Not after those things you said. Two days I've waited for you to tell me that you didn't mean it. For two days, it felt like my heart was being torn apart. Two days, Lorenzo! You could have asked me to stay at any point. Could have told me you needed me. But instead, you ignored me and left me alone when *I needed you*."

A thick knot of regret threatens to choke me, but I manage to swallow it down. "I needed time. To process."

"Bullshit!" she bellows, angrier than I've ever seen her. "You needed time to wallow in your own misery. Well, I am done watching you shred yourself to pieces with guilt. Done waiting for you to wake up and realize that loving somebody else doesn't mean you loved her any less." She swats away the tears dripping down her cheeks. "I'm just done."

The pain in my chest nearly brings me to my knees at her feet. "Mia, please?" She can't be done. "I can't let you walk out of here."

She shakes her head. "You can. You don't have a choice. The

time to ask me to stay was two nights ago, Lorenzo. You're too late."

I open my mouth to argue, but she cuts me off.

"Goodbye, Lorenzo."

This time I don't stop her.

FIFTY-FIVE
LORENZO

Where the hell is she, and how the fuck could I just let her walk out of here like that? Did I learn nothing from what happened the last time I let her leave? But I thought she'd take a few hours to cool off and be back behind the safety of these walls before nightfall.

I thought I had time to win her back.

Placing my hand on the wall, I gulp air, but I can't get enough oxygen inside my lungs to stop the burning fire in them. There's a gaping hole in my chest where my heart should be. She put it back together piece by piece without me even noticing, and now she's taken it with her.

I slam my fist against the wall. Where the fuck else does she have to go? I know who will know. Leaving the library, I stalk around the house until I find Kat in the den watching TV.

Dante walks into the room behind me carrying two glasses of wine. He stares at me, eyes narrowed in concern when he sees the murderous look on my face.

I ignore him and focus on my sister-in-law. "Where's Mia?"

She doesn't look at me. "I'm not telling you."

I scrub a hand through my hair and glare at her. "Where the fuck is she, Kat?"

"Somewhere she doesn't want you to know about," she says with a casual shrug, not taking her eyes off the TV.

My hands clench into fists, but I bite back the angry retort on the tip of my tongue. I need to rip someone's head off. Now.

Shooting me a warning glare, Dante sits beside her on the sofa and places the glasses of wine on the table. She lets out a frustrated sigh when he turns the TV off.

"Kat." Cupping her chin in his hand, he forces her to look at him.

"She doesn't want to see him, Dante," she insists.

He frowns. "You really think that's true, kitten?"

She rolls her eyes.

"Kat?" His voice drops an octave.

She glances at me. "Why can't you just leave her be? Let her have a little space before you break her heart again?" she snaps, and the reminder of how much I've hurt her cousin pierces me like a surgeon's blade.

"I'm not looking to break her heart, Kat. I need to tell her ..." I swallow the words. Mia should hear them first.

My tormented expression must give me away because she offers me a faint reassuring smile. "She's in the presidential suite at the hotel."

"Our hotel?"

"Of course."

Thank fuck for that. She's safe and easy to find. "Thank you, Kat."

"If you hurt her again ..." She scowls.

"I won't."

She continues to glower at me, and the icy look in her eyes actually makes me a little nervous. This woman knows her way around a scalpel.

287

"He said he won't hurt her, kitten." Dante pushes his wife against the sofa cushions and silences any further concerns she might have with a kiss. I'll have to thank him for distracting her later. I've got more important things to do right now. Like begging the woman I love for her forgiveness.

FIFTY-SIX

MIA

"So apartment hunting was a bust, huh?" Joey perches on the edge of the sofa in my hotel room. Well, it's not a room so much as a huge suite that I'm sure costs more a night than I've ever made in a month. I saw four places today and none of them were suitable. Kat said I should come back "home" to the mansion, but when I told her I couldn't bear to face him, she insisted I stay here instead.

"Yeah. There's not a lot available for my budget." I have money in savings from my time in Iowa, but it won't get me far. "I'll find somewhere soon though. I promise."

Frowning, she shakes her head. "You can stay here as long as you need to."

"I can't. You must be losing what, like a thousand bucks a night letting me stay here? I'd be happy in any room."

"Actually, this is one of the few available rooms tonight. We keep suites like these open for our exclusive celebrity clients and high rollers, and we don't have any in town this week. Besides, you're family. You only get the very best." Her warmth and generosity nearly bring me to tears.

"Well, I'll be out of here as soon as possible. I have a bunch of apartments lined up to see tomorrow too. I'm sure one of them will be a good fit ..." How can anything compare to the life I thought was mine just a few days ago? The future I imagined with her brother. God, she looks so much like him.

"Lorenzo is a jackass." She pushes to her feet and gives my shoulder a gentle squeeze. Is it so obvious that I was thinking about him? She regards me with curiosity. "But I saw the way he looked at you the other night. If you want him, Mia ..."

"What?" I blink at her.

"If you want him, he's yours. My brother doesn't fall often but when he does, he falls hard. I've only ever seen him look at one other woman the way he looks at you." She leans down and places a soft kiss on the top of my head. "I have to get home or Max will send out a search party. Ring the desk for anything you need."

"Thanks, Joey."

"My pleasure."

At a loss for what to do with myself, I pace around the spacious suite. I tried meditation earlier, but I couldn't clear my mind. Every time I closed my eyes, all I saw was Lorenzo's face. Asshole.

A knock at the door makes me jump. Kat called a little while ago and said someone was on their way over with my things.

Smiling, I open the door and his familiar face twists in a triumphant sneer.

My heart drops through my stomach. Oh god. How did he—

"Thought you could hide from me forever, Mia?"

Adrenaline thunders around my body. I can't breathe. Can't get my body to cooperate with the message screaming in my head—*close the fucking door!* He takes the opportunity to push his way inside my hotel room. I stagger back, but he catches my wrist, his brutish grip sending a sharp pain up my forearm. The memory of his touch makes my skin crawl, like a million scurrying ants have taken up residence.

I try to wrench from his grip. "G-get your h-hands off me."

He holds tighter, pulling me toward him. The smell of cigarettes invades my nostrils. "What? You used to love the way I touched you." He runs a fingertip down my cheek and I shudder. Closing my eyes, I take a deep breath. I'm safe. I'm in the hotel. There's security here.

I blink and focus on his face. "What the hell are you doing here, Jake?" I spit his name because I dislike this man almost as much as I did his brother.

An arrogant smirk on his face, he pulls a pair of cuffs from his belt. "Taking you in on suspicion of murder, darlin'." He twists my wrists behind my back and roughly slaps the restraints on me.

My head spins. He knows what I did to Brad? Am I going to prison for murdering a cop?

"Wh-what the hell are you on about?" I stammer, afraid my guilt is written all over my face.

He grabs my hair at the nape of my neck and pulls hard, forcing me to look at him. "You know exactly what the hell I'm talking about, you cheating whore." A globule of his saliva hits my cheek. I try to wipe the vile substance onto my shoulder, but he holds my head firmly in place and brings his face close to mine, his foul breath making me gag. "Brad went looking for you and never came back. You might have the rest of the world convinced you're some sweet little angel, but you and I know the truth, don't we, Mia?" He shoves me down the hallway. "We both know you're a liar and a bitch who'd fuck anyone over just to save her own skin."

"No, Jake, please." He knows that's not who I am. He

knows me.

"Jake, please?" he whines, mocking me with my own words. "Save it for the station, sweetheart, because you'll be confessing to my brother's murder before the night is over."

He releases his grip on my hair and grabs my elbow, his thick fingers digging into my skin as he drags me along the hallway to the elevator. I glance around, hoping that a Moretti guard will be there, but we're alone.

A sob wells in my throat. I guess this is what I deserve after all. I did kill Brad. I plunged that knife into his neck, and I'd do it again. The elevator doors ping open. One of Lorenzo's men steps out and frowns at us, and my heart leaps with hope.

"Tommy!" His name leaves my lips like a prayer to the heavens.

He trains his eyes on Jake, teeth bared like a protective dog. "What the fuck do you think you're doing?"

Jake pulls his badge from his pocket. "Back off, asshole. Mrs. Mulcahy here is under arrest."

Tommy reaches around to his back, where he keeps his gun in a holster. Oh god. "Tommy, don't! He really is a cop. Can you just let Kat know what's happened to me? Please?"

His eyes flit between me and Jake.

"That's right, fucker, do as the lady wants and back the fuck off."

He grinds his teeth, likely torn between wanting to protect me and the knowledge that any attempt to free me from this situation would cause a load of trouble. "Please, Tommy. I'll be okay, can you just let Kat and ..." Swallowing, I stop myself from saying Lorenzo's name. "Can you just let Kat know what's happened?"

He nods but continues glaring at Jake.

"That's a good boy." Jake gives a sinister laugh and shoves me into the elevator.

CHAPTER
FIFTY-SEVEN
LORENZO

I 'm almost at the hotel when a call comes through from my sister.

"Hey, Joey."

"Are you driving?"

"Yeah."

"Fuck," she mutters, almost inaudibly.

The hairs on the back of my neck stand on end. "What is it?"

She clears her throat before answering. "Mia's been arrested."

She must be mistaken. My Mia? Arrested? "What the fuck are you talking about?"

"Tommy just called Max. Mia was arrested ten minutes ago. The cop had a badge. He was legit."

Every breath of air feels like it's being sucked from my lungs. "She was arrested?"

Blood thunders through my veins. "What the fuck for? Who was this cop?"

"I don't know, Loz. Tommy said he was an asshole. He took her out in cuffs and the hotel manager saw him put her in a car."

"And nobody fucking stopped him?" I shout.

"What could they do? The guy was a cop."

"Fuck, Joey!"

"I know. Max is already on the phone to Dante and Kat. We'll find out where she is. I'll call Drake. He'll—"

"Fuck Drake. I want Nathan James on the next fucking plane to Chicago."

"Okay. I'll get Max to call him."

"I'll call him myself." He's not going to jump on a plane at the drop of a hat for just anyone, but he will for me.

"Okay. Head back to the mansion, and Max and I will meet you there."

"I need to know where she is," I growl, anger surging through every cell in my body.

"I know, Loz, but until we find out what precinct she was taken to, there's nothing we can do. We need to work on this together. This is the cops we're talking about. We can't solve this our usual way."

"Fuck!" I slam my hands against the wheel. I never should have let her leave the fucking house.

"I'll see you soon, Loz. We'll fix this, okay?" Joey says reassuringly. "We'll get our girl back."

I can't even think about how scared she must be. How I should have been with her. Then at least she'd have a hot-shit lawyer sitting by her side right now.

I bark an order to my car's hands-free system to dial Nathan James. It takes him seven fucking rings to answer me.

"Lorenzo?"

"I need you in Chicago. Now."

"What's going on?"

"My girlfriend ..." That word sounds so fucking wrong—it's not enough for what she is to me. I clear my throat. "She's been arrested."

CHAPTER FIFTY-SEVEN

"For?"

"Not sure. Probably for the murder of a cop."

"Fuck, Lorenzo. Where's Drake?"

"I don't want your fucking brother, Nate. I want you."

He sighs, and I can almost hear the cogs ticking in his brain. "The jet's at JFK. Give me a few hours and I'll be there. But have Drake filled in by the time I get there. He can do what needs to be done until then."

"I'll call him now," I say.

"See you in a few hours."

FIFTY-EIGHT

MIA

J ake manhandles me into small room and shoves me into a chair.

"I get a phone call, right?"

"You're lucky you're even walking, bitch. You know what we like to do to cop killers around here?"

"And do you know what my lawyer will do when he finds out you didn't give me my phone call?" I snap back, full of bravado and a confidence that I don't feel. But I was married to a cop for nine years. I know my rights—well, some of them at least. Every nerve in my body is frayed beyond belief. Even my eyelids are trembling with fear. I killed Brad and I'm going to go to prison for the rest of my life.

"You got a lawyer?" he says with a sneer.

I don't. But the Morettis do, and I know Kat and Dante will help me. "I'm sure you're aware that my cousin is married to Dante Moretti. And if you're not familiar with that name, I'm sure your buddy here can fill you in." I nod toward the cop with gray hair and matching soul patch who greeted us when Jake brought me in.

His eyes go wide as he looks at Jake. "You should probably get her that phone call."

Jake presses his lips together, anger flashing across his face. "What the fuck?" he mumbles.

Soul Patch steps toward Jake. "I said I'd help you out, man. I didn't know the Morettis were involved in this. Give her the phone call and you can hold her until one of their lawyers gets here." He walks out, leaving Jake and me alone.

"I know you fucking killed him, Mia."

"My phone call?" is all I say in response.

Jake uncuffs me and hands me a telephone. But he stands over me, watching the entire time. I hold the plastic receiver to my face, praying that Kat answers.

"Hello?" The sound of her voice almost makes me cry.

"Kat," I blurt out. "I've been arrested."

"Mia, honey," she says with a huge sigh. "We hoped that was you. Are you okay?"

"No," I sniff.

"Have they hurt you?"

"No. I'm just—they've arrested me on suspicion of murder, Kat," I whisper.

"We'll get you out of there soon, okay? But I'm going to pass you over to Dante's lawyer real quick. His name is Drake James."

I don't want to talk to a lawyer; I don't even want to talk to Kat. I need to hear his voice. "Is, uh, is Lorenzo there?"

"I'm here, Mia." His deep, calm tone cuts through my internal chatter, soothing all those frayed nerves. Even after everything, his voice alone gives me comfort. Kat must have me on speaker. "Listen to Drake. He's going to have you out of there real soon."

"Mia, this is Drake," an unfamiliar voice says. "Don't say anything. I'll be there soon. Okay?"

"Okay."

"We've got you, sunshine," Lorenzo says softly. *Sunshine.* The memories invoked by that word have me fighting off tears.

"Tell me where you are and exactly what the cop who took you said."

"I'm at the Fourth and Beacon precinct. He said he was bringing me in on suspicion of murder." The force of Jake's glower has me whispering that last word again.

"What's the cop's name?" Lorenzo growls.

"J-Jake Mulcahy."

"Brad's brother?"

I glance up at Jake and wish I hadn't because the pure venom in his glare makes me want to throw up. "Yes."

"Goddamn motherfucker!"

"Is Jake a Boston cop?" Drake asks.

"Yeah."

Another round of curses and grumbling come from Lorenzo and someone else, maybe Max or Dante.

"Hang tight and I'll be there as soon as I can. You can't be under arrest, Mia, because a Boston cop has no jurisdiction in Chicago," Drake assures me. "Say nothing. You understand me?"

"Y-yeah," I mumble, but I don't fully comprehend what he's saying. I'm not under arrest?

"It will be okay, honey. I promise," Kat assures me.

"Okay," I agree, but it won't be. I killed Brad and Jake must have found out. As much as I despise him, he's a good cop. He'll never let his brother's disappearance go unresolved. It's only a matter of time before he's able to charge me for real.

298

HE'S BEEN ASKING me the same questions for almost an hour now. I've refused to answer a single one, and my continued silence is met with increasing agitation. Jake bangs his fists on the table. Pulls at his hair. Snarls in my face, so close that his spittle flecks my cheeks. After my phone call, he cuffed me to the table, so I'm unable to move and unwilling to talk. He should know that a little Mulcahy rage isn't going to intimidate me—I lived with it for ten long years.

My head hurts so much.

Sunshine. Sucking in deep, even breaths, I repeat the word to myself.

"Could I please get a drink?" I ask. My throat is bone dry and I feel sick.

"When you start answering my fucking questions," he says with a vicious snarl.

I glower at him. "I'm pretty sure it's not common practice to deny prisoners a glass of water."

"Common practice," he spits. "I should fucking—"

The door bursts open, and a tall, handsome man with impeccably styled hair and one of the finest suits I've ever seen strolls into the room.

"Take the cuffs of her. Now," he demands, his tone even and calm but full of authority, like he's used to people doing exactly what he says.

Jake glares at him.

"You usually restrain innocent citizens you bring in for questioning, Detective?" he asks. "Unless you want to find yourself on charges for kidnapping, I suggest you take the cuffs off her right now and let her go."

"Fucking lawyers," Jake grumbles under his breath, but he unlocks the cuffs, and I rub at the red marks they left on my wrists.

"Kidnapping?" I blink at the guy in the suit in confusion.

"Ms. Stone? I'm Drake James." He shoots me a wink. "Detective Mulcahy here has no jurisdiction to arrest you in Chicago. No warrant. No grounds at all to detain you here against your will." He returns his attention to Jake. "And you can make damn sure your superiors back in Boston will be hearing about this."

"I have every fucking ground," Jake says with a snarl. "And there will be a warrant. Soon." The amount of menace in his voice makes me shiver. "Enjoy your freedom while you can."

Drake takes my hand and helps me up from my seat. Wrapping a protective arm around me, he escorts me to the door, then stops and glances at Jake. "Threaten my client again, Detective, and I'll have you charged with harassment. Enjoy that badge while you can."

Jake glares back at him, the vein in his forehead pulsing. He's not used to being told what to do, much like his older brother.

My legs shake as we walk down the corridor of the station. I can't believe it's over ... except it isn't, really. There's no chance in hell that Jake is ever going to let this go.

"You okay?" Drake asks as he opens the door onto the street.

"Yes. Thank you for that." I glance behind me, making sure Jake isn't going to come after me with an arrest warrant. "You were so good in there."

He shrugs. "That was nothing. You should see my older brother in action."

"No, you were super impressive. Thank you."

"Just doing my job, Ms. Stone."

"Please, call me Mia."

"Mia." Smiling, he guides me down the street. "Mr. Moretti is waiting in the car for you."

Despite everything, my heart fills with joy. Lorenzo came! Drake opens the car door, and I struggle to hide my disappointment.

Dante reaches for my hand and pulls me into the idling car. "Come on. Let's get home," he says with a soft smile that I can't help but think is full of pity. Am I really so pathetic? I settle into the back seat and Drake climbs into the front beside the driver.

"You run into any trouble at all?" Dante asks him.

"Nope. None," he answers, eyes fixed firmly ahead.

"So, I wasn't under arrest at all?" I ask.

"No," Drake replies.

"We'll be home soon. There's no sense in you having to relive this whole ordeal twice." Dante pats my shoulder. "Unless you need to talk about it right now?"

I shake my head and stare out the window. I don't want to talk about what just happened, but I would like to know why the hell his cowardly older brother isn't here instead. He really wasn't joking when he said I'll never mean that much to him.

Tears sting the corners of my eyes.

Dante sighs. "You know I couldn't allow Lorenzo come to get you."

I turn and blink at him. "What? Why not?"

"Because he would have stormed into that station and probably shot the cop who arrested you, as well as any others who got in his way."

"You think?"

Shaking his head, he lets out a dark laugh. "Have you met him?"

Relieved that Lorenzo didn't choose not to come, I sit back and close my eyes for the rest of the drive.

Kat is the first to rush out of the house and greet me when the car pulls up outside the Moretti mansion. She hauls me into her arms for a fierce hug, then steps back and checks me over. "Are you okay?"

"I'm fine," I assure her.

She hugs me again. "I was so worried about you."

301

"Me too." Joey wraps her arms around both of us.

A throat clears.

Stepping back, Joey and Kat glance at each other awkwardly and follow Dante and Drake into the house, leaving me standing outside with Lorenzo. I look down at my feet.

"Mia?" His tone is commanding and deep, and despite myself, I look up at him. His dark eyes smolder with emotion. I can't do this. Not again. "Did they hurt you?"

I subconsciously rub my wrists. "No."

He walks down the two steps separating us and stands right in front of me, so close that I feel the heat from his body. He takes my hand and I jerk it back. The memory of his fingers on my skin is too much.

But he holds tight, inspecting the red skin on my wrists. "Who the fuck did this to you? Jake?"

"It's fine. It was just the cuffs."

"He put you in fucking cuffs?"

"That's kind of what they do when they arrest people, Lorenzo."

"But he didn't fucking arrest you. He had no warrant."

I shake my head. This is all too confusing. Every part of it. The whole thing with Jake, and now this with Lorenzo. I hate that I seek his comfort, hate that I can feel how much he cares for me even after those awful things he said. This would all be a lot easier if he acted like that uncaring asshole from the other night.

A thick vein pulses in his neck as he goes on staring at me and holding onto my wrist. "I'll fucking kill him."

I jerk my hand away. "Is that your answer to everything? Destroy it?" I swallow down the sob that wells in my throat. We both know I'm no longer talking about Jake.

His eyes flash with pain. "Mia." My name is spoken like a

plea, but I have no idea what he's pleading for. He destroyed everything we had together.

"You killing Jake isn't going to help me, Lorenzo. In fact, the only way you can help me is by staying away from me." Brushing past him, I walk into the house.

WITH A MUG of chamomile tea warming my hands, I recount exactly what happened at the hotel and everything Jake said to me in the interrogation room.

Drake's brother, Nathan, seems to take charge, asking me questions and probing for more information, not letting up even after Lorenzo scowls at him. Nathan James is a formidable character. Tall and dark and muscular, but leaner than the Moretti brothers. He wears casual slacks and a white polo shirt, but every inch of him screams power and control.

When I've gone over my account at least three times and Nathan has asked me dozens of questions, Lorenzo stands and clears his throat. "It's late," he says pointedly to Nathan and Drake. "There's nothing that can't be discussed in a day or two, after Mia's had a chance to rest."

I glance sideways at him, thankful for his intervention.

"Of course." Nathan stands and Drake follows suit. "I have to fly back to New York for a hearing tomorrow, but I'll be back in Chicago by Wednesday. I'd like Mia to come in and we can discuss everything in more detail then." He glances at me and I swallow. I guess that means we'll be talking about the fact that I actually did murder my husband. I'm sure Lorenzo has told them both that already, but they probably need to hear the full story from me. Isn't that how these things work?

Lorenzo agrees and pulls Nathan into a brief hug. "Thank you for coming."

"Any time. I'm just glad I wasn't needed tonight," Nathan says, slapping Lorenzo on the back.

Once everyone else is gone and Dante finally persuades an anxious Kat that she needs to get some sleep, I find myself alone with Lorenzo. I can't help feeling like this is a setup. I've felt his eyes on me all night long. I hate that I still find more comfort in his presence than I do with anyone else, but he can't undo what he said.

I fake a yawn and stand. "I guess I'll head to bed as well. Goodnight." Lorenzo stands too, and as soon as I open the door, he's right there behind me. His closeness has goosebumps popping up all over my body.

With one hand above my head, he closes the door and blocks my exit, his body heat warming my back.

"Lorenzo. I'm tired. Please just let me go to bed," I say with a heavy sigh.

He brushes the hair from the nape of my neck with his free hand, and my skin quivers at his touch. "Can we talk?"

My thighs tremble, but I suck in a deep breath. *Stay strong, Mia. You can do this.* "I-I have nothing to say to you."

He moves closer until his warm breath dances over me. My core contracts with pulsing need. "Then listen."

Listen?! How fucking dare he! I spin around so I'm facing him. "I don't want—"

He grabs hold of me, one hand in my hair and one on my ass, and seals his mouth over mine, pushing me back into the door. My treacherous body wants to melt against him, but I slam my fists into his chest. It has no impact. He's an immovable wall. He doesn't even flinch. Instead, he deepens the kiss, pulling me tighter, and despite my anger at him, wet heat pools between my thighs.

But this can't happen. He doesn't get to kiss or fuck me into submission.

Struggling, I try to shove him back, but he holds me in place with his undefeatable strength. I bite his lip, drawing blood, but he simply licks it off and goes back to kissing me. Beating against his chest, I strain to get away from him, but he pins me with the weight of his body and captures my hands in one of his, securing them above my head. I could say my safe word, that would make him stop. He'd never break that trust, right? So why can't I bring myself to mumble that one word?

Why are my eyes closed and my legs trembling? Tears stream down my cheeks. I don't know what to think anymore. I want him, but he's not mine. He'll never allow himself to be mine. I wrench my lips away and rasp, "Cantaloupe."

Gasping for breath, he releases me, a pained expression taking over his face. "Mia. Please?"

Tears blur my vision, and I swallow the words that my heart wants me to scream. I cannot let this man rip my soul apart again. I won't recover from it a third time. "No, Lorenzo. It's too late. There's nothing you can say."

Fumbling for the door handle, I'm relieved when it turns with a soft click. He stares at me without blinking as I slip out of the room and get as far away from him as I can.

FIFTY-NINE
LORENZO

"They have a sister, Michaela," I tell Drake James as we go over everything related to Mia's arrest last night. "I had an ex-fed looking into her, but her records were sealed tight."

"Yeah?" he mumbles, and I imagine him furiously taking notes. I fill him in on everything I learned from Lionel before he died. "I wonder what Jake's role in it was?" I rub my hand over my jaw. "At the very least, he's implicit in any cover-up."

"Hmm. I'll run it by Nathan when he flies back in the morning and we'll get one of our guys on it. Pretty sure he knows some hot shot hacker in Manhattan."

"Is there anything else from the cops? Is Mia at any risk of getting pulled in for questioning again?"

"It's unlikely but not impossible. Seems Mulcahy had nothing but his own hunch to go on. Some old buddies of his work at the precinct, and they let him use an interrogation room to scare Mia into a confession. Thankfully she was smart enough to keep her mouth shut. But the guy's a rottweiler. He's not going to let this go, Lorenzo. The most important thing is for Mia not to panic and do anything stupid. Even if he does try to rattle her cage again, he doesn't have any evidence, and knowing you, there's no evidence to find."

"I'll rattle his fucking cage," I say with a snarl.

Drake sighs. "You know you can't touch him, right? Not with all of this going on?"

"I know," I assure him, even as plans for torturing and killing that fucker race through my head.

"So you'll tell your girl he has nothing on her and she needs to keep a clear head, yeah?"

"Yeah." Except she's not my girl any longer. That reminder makes my chest ache.

"Bring her in tomorrow when Nathan's back and we'll go over everything with a fine-tooth comb. Make sure we have every base covered."

Ending the call, I lean back in my chair. At least Mia will be forced to spend a little time in my company tomorrow. I'll be damned if I let anyone else take her to see the James brothers. She's avoided me all morning, leaving the kitchen under the pretense of needing the restroom when I walked in for breakfast, and then she never returned.

What can I expect after those things I said to her? The memory of the pain on her face tears my heart in two. How the fuck do I ever take something like that back?

I walk out of the study and bump into her, almost knocking her off her feet. Reaching out, I grab her forearm to steady her, but she jumps back like my touch scalds her skin.

There was a time when my touch set her skin on fire for a different reason. I clear my throat. "I just spoke to Drake. He said you have nothing to worry about for now. Jake has no evidence to connect you to Brad's death. Looks like he was on a fishing expedition." I don't tell her that I agree with him about her ex-brother-in-law not letting this go. I imagine she already knows that.

"Thanks," she says, without looking me in the eye.

"We'll still have to go in and see Nathan and Drake tomorrow. So they can make sure everything is properly dealt with and this won't bite you in the ass in the future."

She continues to look anywhere but me. "Fine."

I want to grab hold of her and shake her. Fine? Nothing about this is fine. I'm falling to fucking pieces here, Mia! But that's not her fault, is it? I had her in the palm of my hand and I forced her to fly away.

CHAPTER
SIXTY

MIA

I slap my book down on the table next to me and groan. The whole situation with Jake weighs heavily on my mind. Despite Lorenzo's assurances earlier, I'm sure my ex-brother-in-law is going to rock up here any minute now with a warrant for my arrest. I can't even find any pleasure in reading. Living vicariously through fictional characters isn't as much fun after having my heart broken by a man who did things to my body that put every book boyfriend to shame.

Damn you, Lorenzo Moretti!

As though I've conjured him with the strength of my thoughts, he walks into the library, a large brown envelope tucked under his arm.

"Oh ... I thought you were with Kat and Joey. I'm sorry, I was just—I'll go to my study."

"It's okay." I stand and smooth my dress over my thighs, not missing the way his eyes follow my hands. "I was just leaving anyway."

He glances at my discarded book. "That one not filthy enough for you?"

Despite everything, I smile. It's like I can't not smile in his presence. He's so annoyingly lovable. Infuriating and lovable. "Something like that."

He rakes his gaze over my body, unashamedly drinking in every inch. I'm wearing his favorite yellow dress. Was that a conscious decision? Because no matter what went wrong between us, I still feel more alive when I'm near him than I ever have in my life. And I hate it. "What happened, Lorenzo?" The words tumble from my mouth before I can think about the can of worms I'm opening.

His eyes drift upward, locking on mine. "What do you mean?"

I swallow hard. I shouldn't ask this of him. Not now. But I need answers. Maybe then I'll be able to truly let him go. "That night after the ball? It felt like everything was perfect, and then ..."

"Mia." His chest strains against the buttons of his shirt with the force of his sigh. He walks toward me and places the envelope on the table next to my book.

"Tell me the truth," I plead with him.

He tucks a strand of hair behind my ear, and I press my cheek into his palm, subconsciously seeking the comfort of his touch. "It was a perfect night, Mia. So perfect. You were fucking perfect."

I frown. "So?"

"I saw it." The tears swimming in his eyes render me mute for several seconds.

"Saw what?" I ask, finding my voice.

"Our future."

"And was it that bad?"

He shakes his head and pinches the bridge of his nose.

My head swims with confusion. "No?"

His eyes blaze, fiery and dark. Goosebumps break out all over my body. "It was fucking glorious. I saw you standing at an altar with my ring on your finger. I saw us on our honeymoon on some tropical beach. You were wearing the tiniest fucking bikini imaginable." His Adam's apple bobs. "I saw us old and gray with our kids and our grandkids."

Winded by his revelation, I suck in a harsh breath. "And you don't want any of that?" I ask, my heart shattering into a million tiny pieces.

"I want every single fucking second of it."

I blink, my eyes blurry with tears. "But?"

He palms the back of my neck and presses his forehead against mine. "I couldn't give it to her, and she deserved it. So fucking much. All of it."

"W-why are you doing this to me?"

"I'm not ..." He shakes his head and drops to his knees, staring up at me, his own tears staining his cheeks. "I'm so sorry, Mia. I didn't mean any of those awful things I said. You were right, it was all guilt and self-loathing. I was hating myself for finding happiness without her, and I took it out on you. And even though what I said and the way I acted was unforgivable, I'm selfish enough to ask you to forgive me anyway."

"So why couldn't you just admit that when I asked you? Instead of tearing out my heart?"

His eyes fill with immeasurable pain. I want to drop to my knees and wrap him in my arms, but I can't give in that easily. I deserve so much more. And he's the one who taught me that.

"Because I was truly happy the other night, Mia. You make me so fucking happy. I made love to you like you were the only woman in the entire world. And then I saw our future together so clearly, it was all mapped out for us, as though it was exactly what I was supposed to do with my life. I was consumed with guilt for wanting that life—for wanting to give *you* that life when I couldn't give it to her."

"Y-you really want all of that? What you saw? With me?"

"Fuck yes. I want all that and more."

I rub my throbbing temples. This is all too much. He's scrambling my brain with his smooth words and sex appeal. "But why didn't you just tell me that?" I repeat, still unable to comprehend why he couldn't be honest with me. "Why didn't you talk to me? I needed you to let me in and you shut me out."

"Kat was right, I'm an asshole. It was only when I knew I'd lost you that I realized I can't live without you. I'm far from fucking perfect, and I know I'll make mistakes. I'll still feel guilty sometimes, but I promise to never shut you out again. I'll always be honest with you from now on, even if it hurts. I swear. You'll never be second best, sunshine. I'll remind you every single fucking day how much I love you."

Heart pounding, I blink at him. "Y-you ... you love me?"

He stands and wipes the tears from my cheeks with the pads of his thumbs. "So fucking much. With everything I am. I am yours, Mia. Every part of me, even the broken ones. You're way too fucking good for me, but if you'll have me, I will never let you spend another second of your life doubting how much I love you."

My heart aches to tell him what he wants to hear, but I'd be a fool to trust him with it again, wouldn't I? "What if I let you back in, and you ..." A shuddering sob forces me to pause, and I shake my head. "I can't take that risk."

Placing a fingertip under my chin, he forces me to look at him. "A very smart woman once told me that love is *always* worth the risk."

Damn him. Using my own words against me. Without warning, the emotional upheaval of the whole week slams into me and I sway on my feet, but his hands on my hips hold me steady. What kind of person would I be if I didn't give him another chance after he bared his entire soul? Not the kind of person I want to be.

I wrap my arms around his neck. "I love you too, Lorenzo Moretti."

His lips find mine and he kisses me so fiercely that my head spins. Melting into his embrace, I allow myself to be dominated and claimed by him. It feels like coming home.

I rub myself against his rock-hard cock, chasing the deep connection that I've only ever felt when our bodies join together. With frantic motions, he pulls at my dress, bunching the material at my hips. His hand delves between my thighs, tugging my panties out of his way. When he slides a finger through my wet folds, my legs almost buckle, but he holds me up, wrapping his free arm around my waist.

"Need you ... so fucking bad." He kisses me deeper, grinding his hard length against me.

"I need you too," I gasp, feeling for his button and zipper and tugging them open. Reaching into his boxers, I wrap my hand around the base of his thick shaft and squeeze, eliciting a guttural groan from deep in his throat.

He's holding back. "Fuck me," I murmur into his mouth.

He wastes no time lifting me onto the piano and wrapping my legs around him, not breaking our kiss for a single beat as he tugs my panties aside and sinks all the way inside me. His tongue swirls against mine and he rails into me, claiming my mouth and my body with the same intensity.

I claw at his back and shoulders, trying to take him deeper, desperate for him to sate the ache inside me the way that only he can. With equal frenzy, he squeezes my ass in one hand while the other roams my body as though he's reacquainting himself with every curve. His heavy breathing morphs into animalistic grunts, my moans turn to eager whimpers.

"Fuck!" He changes the angle so he can go deeper. My back arches as he rolls his hips, sweeping the tip of his cock over the sweet spot inside my pussy that makes me want to do anything for the promise of the bone-shattering orgasm he's about to deliver.

I wrench my lips from his, unable to kiss him and breathe at the same time for much longer. "Please, Sir!"

"Oh, tesoro, you know I love it when you beg." The vibration of his words against my ear shoots electric pleasure up my spine. His abs and thighs clench tight as he tries to stave off his release, but I want him to lose control right along with me.

I dust my lips over the shell of his ear, and in the most seductive voice I can muster while being nailed into oblivion, I say, "I'd do anything for your cock, Sir."

"Holy. Fuck. Mia!" he roars, slamming into me. My walls contract around him, milking his thick cock and coating him with my slick release. He buries his head into my neck, breathing heavy and muttering in Italian.

SIXTY-ONE

I carry her upstairs to bed, my cum dripping from her and a satisfied smile on her face. As soon as the bedroom door closes behind us, I finish undressing her.

She walks backward, and I follow her step for step, herding her toward the bed. My eyes roam hungrily over her beautiful body. It's been three days since I saw her naked, but it feels like forever.

"Take off the underwear." I pull off my shirt.

"You're very impatient tonight, Sir," she says with a soft laugh, her skin flushing pink.

Grabbing her at the nape of her neck, I pull her tantalizingly close and tilt her head, forcing her to look up at me. My free hand coasts down her back to palm her juicy ass. "I know it was all my own fault, tesoro, but that doesn't change the fact that I have lived without this beautiful body for three whole days." Her soft pink lips fall open on a moan. "And I intend to spend as long as it takes to reacquaint my hands, my mouth, and my cock with every single delicious inch of it."

Dipping my head, I sweep my tongue over the plump bow of her lips and squeeze her throat gently. She sucks in a stuttered breath. "So take off your fucking clothes and lie on the bed."

After I release her, she stares at me while slowly stripping off her bra. I try to maintain eye contact, but I see her reaching for her panties and I'm done for. My gaze drops, and she lets out a triumphant laugh and peels away the small scrap of fabric, well aware that I'm watching every move she makes. By the time she stands up straight, her glorious naked body on full display for me, I'm hard as fucking iron. Then my little temptress sits on the bed, leans back on her elbows, and inches toward the pillows. I finish undressing, eyes fixated on her sweet pussy—my heaven on fucking earth.

Acting coy, no doubt just to push my fucking buttons and make me harder than I already am, she crosses her legs as she scoots back.

I scowl at her. "No. Let me see my pussy, sunshine."

Smiling mischievously, she opens her legs a little wider.

"All the fucking way, Mia."

She rolls her eyes but spreads her legs wide for me, letting me see her juicy cunt dripping with our cum. "I know what you're doing, tesoro."

"And what's that, Sir?" she purrs the last word.

I crawl over her, running my nose from her ankle up her calf and all the way to the apex of her thighs. Damn, she smells so fucking good. I need to taste her, but I need to deal with her attitude first.

She whines with frustration when I pay no attention to the space between her thighs but instead keep moving. Planting my forearms on either side of her head, I bring my face close to hers. "You're trying to test me to see if I'm feeling guilty enough about what I did the other night that I won't punish you for misbehaving."

She narrows her eyes at me in defiance.

CHAPTER SIXTY-ONE

I press a soft kiss on her forehead. "And the answer is no. Behave yourself or I will spend the rest of this long night taking my fill of your entire body, and when I'm done, I'll leave you wanting."

Her hazel eyes flash with defiance and desire.

"I'll bring you to the very edge while I suck and lick and fuck you. Over and over. Even when you cry and beg me like the needy little sub you are, I'll keep you there on that edge ... never letting you get off."

"You wouldn't," she breathes.

"Oh, I would, sunshine. It's my favorite kind of punishment, and I know many, many ways to deny you a release."

"But Sir ..."

"And I am so looking forward to seeing you all wrung out, on your hands and knees, begging for me to let you come. So, what's it to be? Are you going to be a good girl for me or am I going to get to use this beautiful body all night?"

She sinks her perfect teeth into her juicy bottom lip, her face flushing with heat.

"Mia?"

"I'll be good ..."

I narrow my eyes at her. "But?"

"You using my body all night sounds kinda hot."

"It will be." I kiss her, swallowing the soft whimpers she makes as I grind my hard length against her wet pussy lips.

SIXTY-TWO

"Come here, sunshine, I'm not done with you yet." Lorenzo grabs my hips, pulling me up so I'm on my knees with my head down and my ass in the air.

"I c-can't ... anymore ..." I pant. Every part of my body aches and trembles.

He leans over me, his hot mouth resting against my ear. "I told you I was going to use this body all night long. Did you think I was playing?"

"No, Sir."

"I won't ever give you more than you can take, but you can use your safe word any time you need it."

"Uh-huh," I whimper.

"What is it, Mia?" he whispers, his warm breath dusting over my damp skin and making me shiver.

"Cantaloupe."

"Good girl." He drags his thumb through my wet folds, scooping up my arousal with the tip.

"Sir?"

"Yes?"

CHAPTER SIXTY-TWO

I chew on my lip. Will he be annoyed if I make him say it again?

He leans over me, cupping my chin in his hand and tilting my head back so he can look at me. "What is it?"

"Can you tell me again?" I whisper, tears pricking unexpectedly at the corners of my eyes.

He smiles and my heart bursts. "I love you, tesoro."

"I love you too, Sir."

He lets my head drop back to the mattress and rubs a soothing hand down my ass. "I know you do." Then he spanks me hard, causing white-hot pleasure to burn through my core. I whimper with need as another orgasm starts to coil deep in my center. I stopped counting how many times he made me come when I got to four. They just keep rolling over me one after the next until I can barely remember my own name.

His hand spanks my tender cheek again and I yelp, pulling my legs toward my body but unable to move much. He tied my wrists and ankles to the bedposts a while ago, spreading me out like a giant cross but with plenty of give in my ropes that he can still flip me over whenever he wants. The man is a machine. A hot devilish machine with the body of a demigod.

"Sir," I whimper after he spanks me again, harder this time, and I have no idea how it's even possible that my body continues to crave him when I'm so completely wrung out and exhausted. I'm sticky with cum—his and mine—the sheets are soaked, and I'm pretty sure I've passed out at least twice. But I still push my ass back, needy for more of whatever he's willing to give.

"You have such a beautiful ass, Mia." He pushes his thumb, slick with my cum, into my asshole.

"Oh, fuck." I hiss out a breath as my muscles clench around him. He spanks me over and over while he fucks me there, slowly working his thumb in and out, and I teeter on the edge of a sex-induced coma.

He sucks in a deep breath. "You're so tight here, tesoro. Have you ever been fucked here before?"

"Yes," I admit.

"Did you enjoy it?" He pushes his thumb deeper, making me moan.

"Sometimes," I whisper when I regain my ability to speak coherently.

"You think you can take my whole cock in your ass right now?"

The words come out without thought. "Yes please, Sir."

"You're being such a good girl for me tonight, so much cum I don't think I even need the lube." He slips his thumb out of me, then to my shame and delight, he scoops our cum from between my thighs and uses it to coat his cock. Grabbing hold of my hips, he positions the crown at the seam of my ass.

He pushes in a little and I groan as he stretches me wide open. "Okay, sunshine?" he asks.

"Uh-huh."

He waits, allowing my body to adjust to his size before he pushes a little deeper.

"So fucking tight," he says with a growl as he massages my G-spot with his finger and sinks further into my ass.

"Sir!" Waves of unending pleasure roll through me.

"Almost there. You still okay?"

"Y-yes," I whimper. "I can take more."

"Yeah?" he grunts, his free hand gripping my hip so tightly, his fingertips bruise my soft flesh, but I don't care. I'm going to be covered in his marks tomorrow, and I'll remember how good he made me feel making every single one.

"Yes please!"

He rewards me by sliding all the way inside. I almost

crumple to the mattress, but he holds me upright, stilling my body while he pushes deep. "Jesus. Fuck!"

I whimper and mewl like a feral kitten.

"So fucking good."

I murmur something unintelligible, incapable of forming coherent words. And when he slips a second finger inside me and starts to fuck my ass and pussy at the same time, I go nuclear. He curls the tips of his fingers, pressing against that spot that he finds so damn easily, and I lose all sense of space and time. Wave after wave of euphoria overpowers me and a tsunami of cum rushes between my thighs.

My body shakes and shudders, and he finally allows me to drop to the mattress, pressing me down with his weight as he goes on fucking my ass. I try to focus on his words. On the sounds he makes when he comes apart a few moments later, but I'm floating somewhere between reality and oblivion, unable to get any rational sense of where I am. There is only warmth and happiness and a deep-seated contentment.

"You're okay, sunshine." Lorenzo's soothing voice anchors me to reality, and I blink to find myself lying face up, free of my restraints. I feel blissfully cozy and there's a soft warmth between my thighs that I can't work out. "You coming back to me, tesoro?"

I focus on his hands. The warmth is a washcloth. He's cleaning me up. Washing our cum off me. The fabric beneath me is dry now too. I wiggle my ass a little. The duvet is gone and I'm lying on the dry sheets.

"That feels nice." My eyes flutter open.

Lorenzo kisses my stomach. "You did good. Are you feeling okay?"

"Hmm," I murmur. "Better than okay."

"Good girl," he repeats, peppering soft kisses over my abdomen while he cleans me up. Then he pushes himself up from the bed, and I whimper at the loss of his warmth. My eyes shutter closed again. The bed dips beside me and I smell a familiar scent. Jasmine and lemon.

His hands glide over my calves, smoothing my favorite body lotion into my skin and working his way up to the tops of my thighs. "What are you doing now?" I ask softly.

"Making sure your skin doesn't dry out. I just gave you a bed bath." He chuckles.

"You're so considerate, Sir."

"It's all part of the service."

"Hmm. Fuck me into a coma and then take care of me after?" I giggle.

He playfully nips at my thigh. "It's called aftercare. I'm surprised it never came up in your extensive research."

"Oh, it did. I just didn't think it would feel this good." I practically purr the last word.

He rubs his hands over my hips and stomach. "I didn't think anything could feel this good again." His voice is thick with emotion, and it makes my heart ache. I reach for him, pulling him to lie down next to me. He goes on massaging my skin with lotion while he nuzzles my neck.

"I'm glad you took a risk, Sir."

"So am I, tesoro."

SIXTY-THREE
LORENZO

I wake with her still asleep on my chest. My muscles tense instinctively, my arms banding tighter around her in case this is a dream.

She snuggles closer, and I drop a soft kiss on her forehead. Her eyes flutter open. "Morning, Sir," she breathes, and already my cock is twitching. How the fuck does she do that?

"Morning, sunshine."

"I love waking up next to you."

I brush her hair back from her face. "Me too. I'm so glad you're home."

"Hmm." She sinks her teeth into her luscious lip, and it makes me instantly hard.

But I don't like that look on her face. "What does that sound mean?"

"This doesn't really feel like my home is all," she admits.

I look around the room, the one I shared with my wife. She's right; I've done nothing to make Mia feel like this place belongs to her. "What would it take to make it feel like your home?"

She shrugs. "I don't know. It's such a big house."

"It's about to get bigger too. Dante convinced Max to move back here with Joey, but only if they can build their own wing."

"Wow! A whole wing."

"Well, everyone needs their privacy, I guess. Although most of this wing is barely used now. After Anya's cancer went into remission the first time, we moved to Italy for a few years and this part of the house was locked down. We came back when she got sick again, but we never really opened it back up."

She rolls onto her back and stares up at the ceiling, a soft smile on her face. I love that she allows me to talk about Anya and doesn't make me feel bad about it. "That's such a shame. It's an incredible space."

I prop myself up on one elbow and search her face. "You could bring it back to life."

"I could what?"

"Why don't you make this part of the house ours. Mine and yours."

"But how?"

"However you want."

"I couldn't. I'd be too scared of changing something I shouldn't. Besides, I don't need a wing. But maybe a room? Where we could watch TV alone sometimes? Somewhere private. The library is supposed to be for everyone, and I spoke to Kat about a reading corner for the kids. So I don't think we can keep using it as our own personal ..." She bites on that damn lip again.

"Fuck den?" I suggest.

She laughs out loud. "Our bang palace?"

I dip my head and nip her shoulder, making her squeal as she goes on giggling. "Yeah, we definitely need some space of our own."

She flutters her eyelashes at me. "It would be nice to have somewhere to watch you work while I read."

CHAPTER SIXTY-THREE

"Read your porn?"

"My cli-te-ra-ture," she says, enunciating each syllable.

"Maybe I'll make you read it to me while I'm working." I roll on top of her.

Her chest and neck flush with heat. "I'd like that a lot, Sir."

"And between reading your porn, you can renovate this entire wing so that you feel like it's your home as much as mine."

She opens her mouth. "I said—"

I kiss her, refusing to let her argue with me. I need her by my side every second of every day, and it's safer for all of us if we live in this mansion. My free spirit will be able to spread her wings, but that doesn't mean I'm not going to protect her while she soars.

SIXTY-FOUR

MIA

"The James building?" I ask as we walk up the marble steps to the huge glass doors.

Lorenzo straightens his tie and nods.

"They have an entire skyscraper named after them?"

"It's their building," he replies, glancing around the street, always on alert.

"Wow! They must be super rich to own a whole building, and I bet that's not just here in Chicago, right? Did you say Nathan is from New York? I bet he has his own building there too. And where else? I heard there were four brothers. Do you know—"

"Mia." Lorenzo squeezes my hand. "It'll be okay."

I swallow down a thick knot of anxiety. "Sorry."

He lifts my hand, brushing his lips over my knuckles. "Stop apologizing."

"Sor—" He shoots me a warning look, and I clamp my lips together.

A man holds the door for us, and Lorenzo guides me into the building, his hand placed reassuringly on the small of my back. "Mr. James is waiting for you, sir," the man says.

"Thank you." Lorenzo leads me to the elevators on the other side of the building. As we near them, a smartly dressed woman, about my age, stops in front of us.

"Lorenzo, it's so wonderful to see you." She leans in and kisses him on each cheek, leaving a cloud of expensive perfume behind.

"Melanie, how are you?" he asks, giving her shoulder a light squeeze with his free hand, keeping mine clasped in his other.

Even in sky-high heels, she has to crane her neck to look up at him. "I'm wonderful," she says, giving me only a cursory glance. "I heard a rumor you were back on the *scene*."

"Well, you heard wrong," he replies curtly but politely.

"Oh?" She blinks at him, fluttering her eyelashes and running a hand over her perfectly styled blond hair. "So, you haven't taken a new sub?"

"Not that it's any of your business, or the kind of information I want to discuss in a public lobby ..."

I lower my gaze to the floor, feeling unexpectedly wounded over the denial that's about to come from his lips. Maybe I'm no longer his sub? We didn't discuss the specifics of our relationship last night. "I haven't *taken* a sub, but perhaps you're referring to *Mia*." He pulls me closer and possessively wraps his arm around my waist. "My future wife."

What the ...

Melanie's face flushes as crimson as the elegant dress she's wearing, and she opens and closes her mouth like a goldfish. I feel equally stunned by his revelation, but for the sake of appearances, I gaze adoringly up at Lorenzo and almost melt into a puddle when he winks at me.

"We should go," he says with a polite nod. "It was ... interesting running into you."

"You too." She still doesn't acknowledge me. "Perhaps you could come to the club some time?"

He narrows his eyes. "Only if Mia would like to. Perhaps you should ask her?"

Melanie makes a sound like she's choking on her own breath. "Of course, Mia. We'd love to see you at the club some time."

"Maybe," I say with a genuine smile. I have no idea what *the club* is, but I want to go.

"We really need to go, tesoro," Lorenzo says to me, guiding me into the elevator and leaving Melanie staring after us.

The doors close and I press my body against his. "Your future wife?"

He rolls his head from side to side, stretching neck. "Aren't you?"

"I, uh, well. We never discussed it."

"I told you what I saw. What I wanted," he says matter-of-factly.

"I know, but that's not exactly discussing it, Lorenzo."

Sliding his arms around my waist, he pulls my body close to his. So close that I feel the heat from him even through my coat. He dusts his lips over my ear. "You will be my wife, Mia."

Not will you, but you will. Arrogant son of a ...

"Won't you?" he growls, and the sound of his voice makes me shiver.

"Is that your idea of a proposal?"

"Not even close." The corners of his lips curl into a smile.

"I'm technically still married," I remind him.

"I know, and in a year's time you can apply for divorce on the grounds of desertion."

I sigh. "If I don't end up in prison for life first."

He holds me tighter, and I bury my head against his chest. "I would go to prison myself before I let you spend a single day in one," he says softly.

What does he mean by that? He'd take the blame for Brad's death? "No! I would never let you do that."

"Neither of us are going to prison, sunshine." He brushes my hair back from my face. "Trust me."

"I do trust you, but I killed him, Lorenzo," I whisper.

His dark eyes narrow. "You protected yourself, Mia."

The elevator comes to a stop and the doors open with a soft ping, signaling the end of our conversation.

Drake James's office is bigger than my first apartment. Floor-to-ceiling windows, shelves upon shelves of journals and awards. There's an enormous glass desk in the center that could easily accommodate six people but is currently home to Drake and his brother.

Nathan and Drake welcome us both and we take a seat on the comfortable sofas in the corner of the room.

Nathan pours us all a glass of water. "I'm sorry we couldn't meet yesterday. But I'm here for today and I can fly back any time you need me to."

"I appreciate you doing this on such short notice, compagno," Lorenzo says.

"You know I'd do anything for you, buddy," Nathan replies, and if I wasn't feeling so nervous and desperately trying not to babble, I might ask what that was about.

Nathan leans forward in his seat, hands steepled beneath his chin. "Tell me everything. From the start."

Lorenzo squeezes my hand in his. "Tell them, sunshine. Anything you say in here is completely confidential."

I sip my water and take a deep breath, my hands trembling. Lorenzo squeezes again, his solid presence calm and reassuring, but I'm about to confess a murder to two men I barely know.

Nathan and Drake listen intently while I tell them about leaving Boston and the events that led to that awful day in Iowa.

"And you disposed of the body?" Nathan asks Lorenzo without even a flicker of discomfort, as though they're talking about disposing of some trash, which I guess isn't entirely inaccurate.

"Yes."

"No trace?" Drake asks.

"The body was incinerated. His ashes were dumped in the Chicago River. There's nothing left to trace," Lorenzo replies confidently.

Nathan bobs his head. "And the knife? The house? Mia's clothes?"

"The knife was melted down and recycled. Mia's clothes were incinerated too. And the house was forensically cleaned by my best men. Max oversaw it all."

Nathan licks his bottom lip, his brow furrowed. Then he glances at his brother who nods back at him. What was that nod for? My gut swirls with so much anxiety that I feel like I might throw up. Do they think I'm evil?

Nathan fixes his eyes on mine. "Well, it's difficult to have a murder trial when there's no body or other DNA evidence to prove that a murder took place, but I doubt that this guy is going to stop digging into this, so I think we need to focus our efforts on—"

"Wait," I interrupt him. "What about other evidence?"

Nathan regards me with curiosity. "Such as?"

"Maybe somebody saw him drive to my house? I used a different name, but what if they put me in a lineup and one of my customers can identify me? What if—"

"Mia?" Lorenzo lifts my hand to his lips and kisses my knuckles.

Closing my eyes, I take a deep breath.

"All that would prove is that you lived in Iowa for a few months. You've never officially denied that. Even if there was absolute proof that your ex-husband visited you at your house—"

"There isn't. Max swept the entire area for camera footage, but there weren't any near the house. It's one of the reasons I chose that neighborhood," Lorenzo interjects, confirming my suspicion that he was the one responsible for overseeing my move. God, I love him so much.

"Even if there were, it's all circumstantial, Mia. I think we focus our efforts on convincing your ex-brother-in-law to let this thing go. There's no evidence to connect you to a murder or even a disappearance. Unless there's something else you haven't told us."

"Not about that, no."

Nathan frowns. "Is there something else we should know?"

I fidget in my seat. "I-I'm not sure it's relevant."

Lorenzo narrows his eyes at me. "It's relevant, Mia."

I swallow hard. I never wanted him to know about this. Oh god. Will he hate me now? "I ... Jake and I ..." Every muscle in Lorenzo's body goes rigid. "We had an affair," I whisper, overcome with shame.

Lorenzo rubs his free hand over his beard and sighs.

"When was this?" Drake asks.

"About f-four years ago."

"Did Brad know?" Nathan probes.

I steal a glance at Lorenzo, but his eyes are closed.

"God no. He would've killed him. It only lasted about three months." I swallow the huge knot of shame and guilt that sticks in my throat. "He knew what Brad was like. He would sometimes come see me when Brad was working a double. One time, after a bad e-episode ..."

"Episode?" Drake asks with a frown.

"After that piece of shit beat the fuck out of her," Lorenzo answers for me, his voice rough with anger.

"Y-yeah. Well, Jake came over and helped me get cleaned up. He took care of me, and it had been so long since anyone had been so nice to me …"

I swear I can taste Lorenzo's rage. He vibrates with fury. I keep tight hold of his hand, refusing to let him go, and he makes no attempt to pull away.

"He kissed me, and well …" I don't want to say the words out loud in front of Lorenzo and these two smartly dressed lawyers. "We were together a few times after that."

"Who ended it?" Drake asks.

"I did."

"Why?" He probes further, and Lorenzo mutters a curse.

"I was scared we'd get caught. I didn't really like him that way. It was just nice to be taken care of after, you know?" I take a long drink of my water, and when I glance up again, I want to hide from the looks of pity I'm getting from Drake and Nathan.

"You're a hell of a woman, Mia." Nathan smiles and shakes his head. "I'm surprised you didn't kill that fucker way before you did."

Drake snorts. "I would have."

"Mia doesn't believe in violence," Lorenzo adds quietly. "She feels guilty about ending that twisted fuck's life."

Nathan frowns at me. "It was you or him though, right?"

"I guess so," I admit.

"That's self-defense, not murder. Had Lorenzo not protected you by disposing of the body and getting you out of that house, I still would have had you out within twenty-four hours."

"He's right," Drake agrees. "But right now, we need to deal with Jake and the added complication of him maybe still having some kind of torch for you. Did he take the break-up well?"

Recalling that awful day, I shake my head. "He was furious.

He threatened to kill me. Then tell Brad and all my friends what a whore I was."

"Jesus fucking Christ," Lorenzo mutters. He must be so disappointed in me. Infidelity is his hard limit.

"I knew he wouldn't do any of that though. He was too worried about what Brad would do if he found out."

"Just let me fucking deal with him," Lorenzo says with a snarl.

Nathan shakes his head and gives Lorenzo an exasperated look. "He's a cop. A decorated detective. You can't use your usual methods, buddy. Especially not after he's been accusing your girlfriend here of killing his brother. We need to be smart about this."

"So what the fuck do you suggest?" Lorenzo snaps.

"Well, I'm betting any guy who would take advantage of his brother's wife and then call her a whore because she breaks it off isn't the stand-up guy everybody thinks he is. I'm sure that with a little digging, we can find some leverage on this prick," Drake says.

"Agreed. We'll get our best guys on it. And we'll have someone look into the sister too. Maybe that's an avenue worth exploring. But the further you stay from this guy, the better," Nathan warns Lorenzo.

Grumbling, Lorenzo agrees. "But I'll kill the piece of shit if I ever see him again."

I squeeze his hand, but he still doesn't look at me.

"How about for now you let us do our thing and try not to kill anyone in the meantime?" Nathan stares at us, his eyebrows pointedly raised.

Lorenzo stands, pulling me up with him. "I'll do my best, but no promises."

WE'RE in the elevator by the time I pluck up the courage to raise the issue of my affair. Lorenzo leans against the wall opposite me, his jaw set.

"I'm sorry," I choke out on a sob.

I don't even finish taking my next breath before I'm wrapped in his huge arms. "What the hell for, sunshine?"

My chest heaves as I cry. I've tried my best to forget about those months with Jake and pretend they never happened. I feel so much guilt for breaking my marriage vows. While it was nice at first to have someone to care about me, he soon became as possessive and demanding as his older brother. I lived in constant fear of Brad finding out, but Jake made it hard to say no to him. "I-I know you hate cheating, and I … Jake and I were never—" Another sob steals the rest of my sentence.

"Hey." He smooths my hair back and kisses the top of my head. "That prick took advantage of you when you were at your most vulnerable. That was not cheating, it was an extension of his brother's abuse."

I bury my head against his chest, comforted by his warmth, his familiar smell, but most of all, by his understanding. "So, you're not mad?"

"Not at you, Mia."

"I thought you were disappointed in me."

"Never." He kisses my head again. "But we really need to work on your self-esteem because those Mulcahy brothers made you believe that you're worthless. When I'm done training you, you'll believe me when I tell you that you're nothing less than perfect. You understand me?"

My cheek brushes against the soft wool of his coat as I nod my agreement.

"That's my good girl."

SIXTY-FIVE

MIA

I place my hand on the door and shivers of both excitement and trepidation shoot through me. Lorenzo sent me a text message asking—no, instructing—me to meet him in the bedroom. He went out with Dante for a few hours when we got back from our appointment with the lawyers, and despite spending a lovely afternoon with Kat and the kids, I still feel a little wobbly. Reliving my affair with Jake and having Lorenzo learn about it at the same time really shook me. And even though he told me it changed nothing between us, I crave his reassurance. He truly has turned me into a needy sub.

With that thought in mind and a faint smile on my face, I enter the bedroom. He's sitting on the bed wearing only his suit pants, legs spread wide as he stares at me. I close the door behind me, and my pulse thrums an erratic beat.

"Come here, sunshine," he orders in his signature low growl that rumbles through my bones. I walk toward him, the wooden floor warm beneath my bare feet. As soon as I reach him, he nods, indicating the space between his thighs. "Kneel."

I drop to my knees at his feet, licking my lips in anticipation, and a grin tugs at the corners of his mouth. "Turn around."

I do as he instructs. What wickedly sinful ideas are going through his head right now? He surprises me by running a brush through my hair. I close my eyes and sigh with contentment. Once he's finished untangling it, he begins to braid my hair into a thick plait. He's efficient at it too, securing the end with a hair tie when he's done.

He gently taps my shoulder, indicating I should turn around again, and I shuffle on my knees until I'm facing him once more. "Where did you learn to do that, Sir?" I ask with a pop of one eyebrow.

"Not where you think. Our mom died when Joey was three. I had to braid a lot of hair."

The image of him braiding little Joey's hair warms my heart.

Lorenzo's dark eyes fix on mine. "I have a gift for you."

Warmth settles in my core, and any lingering doubts I had about this morning melt away.

He cups my jaw in his hand, rubbing the pad of his thumb over my cheekbone. "It's not just a gift though, tesoro." His eyes narrow. "It's something much more. A commitment."

I blink in confusion. I'm the one on my knees here, so this can't be a proposal.

My entire body trembles when he pulls a square velvet-covered box from behind his back and snaps it open to reveal a stunning white-gold choker. Tears prick at my eyes. On closer inspection, I see it's a series of thick links that fit so perfectly together that they look like one piece of metal. Each link has a sunflower or a sun delicately engraved on it, so fine that they can only be seen from up close.

The center link is set with a large canary diamond and the fastening at the back has a small heart-shaped padlock. It's the most beautiful piece of jewelry I've ever seen.

"Is that a ..." I swallow the emotion welling in my throat, worried I might cry and spoil the moment.

"It's a collar, sunshine. I want you to wear it, but I also want you to think about what this means before you say yes. I can wait if you need time."

A collar means he's my Dom and I belong to him. What is there to think about? "I know what it means," I whisper.

"Do you?" He arches an eyebrow at me. "Because once you put it on, you don't get to take it off so easily."

I glance at the choker again. So intricate and pretty.

"You can take it off to shower or bathe," he says, reading my mind, "but once you wear my collar, you belong to me. It's like a wedding ring. Off or on, you're still my sub. Twenty-four seven."

Sucking in a deep breath, I try to calm my galloping heart. "With the same rules we have now?"

"Yes. But we can revisit the rules anytime you want."

"An equal partnership?"

"Yes."

"Where I do whatever you tell me without question?"

He smiles widely, and the sight makes my heart, and my pussy, flutter. "Yes."

I suppress a grin. "If this is a proposal, shouldn't you be the one on your knees?"

The sound of his laugh fills the room. I don't think I've ever heard him laugh like that before. "For *that* proposal, you can be sure I'll be on at least one knee, sunshine."

Butterflies swirl in my stomach. He tucks a loose strand of hair behind my ear, his face growing serious again. "Know that this means more to me than any marriage proposal. I can wait to make you my wife, but I don't want to wait any longer for this."

"Well, you kind of have to wait to make me your wife seeing as I'm technically still married." I regret the words as soon as they leave my mouth. Brad has no place in this conversation.

But if the reminder of my ex-husband bothers Lorenzo, he doesn't show it.

He places his hand on my cheek and rubs his thumb over my bottom lip. I stare up at him, drinking in every single thing about him. I love him so much it makes my heart ache. "Mia Stone, will you wear my collar?"

"Yes Sir, I would love to."

His chest heaves as though he was holding his breath waiting for my answer—like there was ever any doubt that I would say yes. He takes the choker from the box and fastens it around my neck, clicking the lock into place before sitting back with a satisfied smile on his face.

I run my fingers over the stone on the front. The choker is surprisingly light and comfortable—two things I'm sure he took into consideration when he chose it.

"If it's not to your liking, I'll have them make you another."

"I love it. It's perfect." My cheeks flush with heat. "But where is the key?"

He indicates the crucifix around his neck, and I notice the small gold key nestled behind it. "Right where it belongs."

I whisper his name on a breath. How long has he been planning all of this? Can this even be real?

"Take off your clothes." The air in the room grows thick with supercharged sexual energy.

Bowing my head, I reach behind me and lower the zipper on my dress. I take it off, along with my underwear, all under the heat and scrutiny of Lorenzo's intense gaze. When I'm done, I resume my former position at his feet. He cups my chin in his strong hand, tilting my face up, and runs the tip of his pointer finger over my collar. "From now on, this is all you wear in my bed unless I give you permission to wear something else. Understand?"

"Yes, Sir."

His eyes twinkle with delight. "And when I tell you to be ready for me, this is how I want you. Naked, with your hair up in a braid or a ponytail."

"Of course, Sir."

"Now how would my little sub like to thank Sir for her collar?" he asks, his tone deep and smooth.

I glance at his hard cock, currently straining at the zipper of his pants, and lick my lips. A wicked chuckle escapes him. "That's my good girl." He unzips his fly and frees his thick shaft from his boxers.

I bring my mouth close to the tip, already wet with precum, and breathe in his masculine scent. My pussy clenches as I swirl my tongue over the crown, and a deep groan reverberates through him. He wraps my braid around his fist and uses it to hold my head in place while he slowly feeds me his entire length. "You look so beautiful wearing my collar and sucking my cock."

"Mmm," I murmur around him, my tongue darting over his length as I squeeze his thighs.

"Fuck, you do that so well." He relaxes his grip on my hair, allowing me more control. I take full advantage, sucking him all the way into my mouth. With the crown of his cock lodged in my throat, I inhale deeply through my nose and swallow.

"Jesus fucking Christ, Mia." His fingers tighten around my braid once more, tugging at it, and the sharp sting in my scalp spurs me on. I swallow again, and his animalistic growl travels straight to the aching spot between my thighs.

I moan around him and the vibrations have him shouting out my name. Before I can swallow again, he pulls his beautiful cock from my mouth. "Tongue out," he commands, and I do as he tells me, waiting for his release like his needy little sub.

Gripping the base of his shaft in his free hand, he pumps twice before warm ribbons of cum streak over my tongue and drip down my chin. He looks at me through half-closed lids, his chest heaving. I smile triumphantly, loving that I can make him lose control.

"Swallow, sunshine." I do as he instructs, savoring his taste. He swipes the pad of his thumb over my jaw, his eyes sparking with unrestrained desire. I ache for him, desperate for his touch. My chest heaves as I pant in anticipation, and he flashes me a wicked grin. "Get dressed. Time to go to dinner and show off your pretty collar."

SIXTY-SIX

LORENZO

Fastening the buttons of my shirt, I don't let my gaze fall from her perfect body for even a second. My cock's already twitching at the sight of her, despite the amazing blowjob she just gave me. But of course I'm hard; I collared her. I want nothing more than to throw her down on our bed and claim every inch of her until she has no memories of her past life, remembers nothing but me and my body.

But I want to show her off too. Let our family see how beautiful she looks wearing my collar. She smooths the fabric of her dress down over her hips and flutters her eyelashes at me.

"You ready, sunshine?"

"Ready, Sir," she says, her voice a soft purr.

I squeeze her ass and guide her out the door.

Dante, Kat, Joey, and Max glance up from the table when we walk into the dining room. And when I pull out Mia's chair for her to sit, they all seem to notice the thick white-gold collar around her slender neck. Kat gapes openly and Dante gives her a discreet nudge. My younger sister breaks the silence.

"Mia!" she squeals. "Is that a collar?"

Mia brushes her fingers over the choker, her cheeks turning a deeper shade of pink as I take a seat by her side.

"Yes," she replies confidently, giving Joey a huge smile.

Clapping her hands, Joey pushes back her chair and throws her arms around Mia's neck. "I'm so happy for you both!" Looking at me with tears in her eyes, she mouths, *love you.*

"Me too," Max says, giving me an approving nod. Meanwhile, Kat continues to gape at us with her mouth hanging open.

Dante chuckles. "You're staring, kitten." She closes her mouth, but her narrowed eyes remain fixed on me.

"Are you okay, Kat?" Mia asks sweetly.

"Of course. It's just …" Kat frowns, her gaze flicking to the jewelry at her cousin's neck.

"It's a collar?" Mia finishes for her.

Kat frowns. "It's … I mean …"

"Katerina," Dante says in a firm tone.

She turns and glares at him. "It's just unexpected is all."

I don't buy it, and neither does my brother. He rolls his eyes and turns back to me. "Congratulations to both of you."

"I HAVE a little business to take care of, sunshine. I won't be long. Go wait for me upstairs," I tell Mia after dinner.

"Don't be long, will you?" She presses her curves against me and makes my cock twitch at the thought of fucking her while she wears my collar.

"I'll be real quick," I assure her, giving her a soft kiss on the lips before smacking her on her ass and sending her upstairs.

Sitting down at my desk in the library, I fire up my laptop and read through emails while I wait. She doesn't keep me waiting long. "I knew you were alone so I didn't knock," Kat says as she makes her way toward me.

Closing my laptop, I rest my hands on the lid. "I was expecting you."

She gives me a faint smile. "You knew I'd come, huh?"

I raise my eyebrows. "You love your cousin and you want to make sure my intentions are honorable."

She takes a seat opposite me. "Now you're making me sound really stuffy and old fashioned, Loz."

"You're the one worried about your cousin's honor," I remind her.

She fixes me with that famous Kat Moretti glare I've come to love. She is more than a match for my strong-willed, headstrong younger brother. "Not her honor. Just her heart."

I lean back in my chair. "I wish you'd had the chance to know Anya before she got sick."

Kat blinks at me, unaccustomed to me using my wife's name in her presence—in anyone's presence.

"She was vibrant and challenging and full of life." Emotion clogs my throat.

"She was all of those things when I knew her too," she says sadly.

"She was a mere shade of those things after we came back from Italy," I recall with a faint smile. "But before the cancer took hold, she was really something. A force of nature."

Kat brushes a tear from her cheek.

"Dante told me how when you first met the two of us, you thought she was afraid of me." I laugh at the absurdity of that notion.

She gasps, eyes wide. "He told you that?"

"Yup."

"She just seemed so ... so small in your presence. At least that's what I thought at first."

"Our relationship changed as she grew sicker." Icy fingers of regret clamp around my heart. "It became necessary to take a greater degree of control. Perhaps too much."

"No, Loz," Kat says, reaching across the desk and placing her hand over mine. "My first impression was all wrong. Anya was never more alive than when she was with you." She swats another tear from her face. "You took care of her and allowed her to make her own decisions right up to the end. You were the finest husband and partner she could have wanted."

I give her a nod of appreciation.

"But Mia isn't Anya," she adds, wincing as though the words pain her.

It's my turn to frown now. "You think I don't know that?"

The sound of the door opening distracts us both. Mia glances between Kat and me, her eyes narrowed with confusion. A split second later, she walks straight toward my desk, head bent low as she avoids looking at my face, and drops to her knees at my feet.

"I'm here and ready to serve you, oh mighty one," she says deadpan, eyes on the floor.

Out of the corner of my eye, I see Kat's horrified expression, and I have to bite my lip to stop myself from laughing out loud. Fucking siren!

Instead, I cup Mia's chin in my hand and tilt her head up until her gaze meets mine. Her eyes dance with amusement. "Behave, sunshine, or I'll make you start doing that for real."

"I couldn't help it." She giggles and jumps up from her knees. "The look on Kat's face is worth it."

Kat glares at her cousin. "That wasn't funny, Mia."

Mia perches herself on my lap and wraps her arms around my neck. "Well, why are you in here grilling Lorenzo about my collar when you could've just come and spoken with me?"

Kat's tongue darts out to wet her bottom lip as she glances

between Mia and me. "I just wanted to make sure he's not pressuring you into this."

"Kat!" Mia admonishes.

"She's only worried about you, tesoro. That's not a bad thing," I say softly.

"Exactly," Kat agrees.

"I think Kat's worried that you're a little too feisty to be my sub." My statement is met with an eye roll from both women.

Mia turns serious. "I know this might seem absurd to you after what happened with Brad, but this isn't about me losing control, Kat."

"It's not?" she asks.

"No. It's about me *choosing* to give up control, and that's an entirely different thing."

Kat frowns, seemingly unconvinced. "But you're allowing someone else to control your life. To tell you what to do. I don't get it."

"Okay." Mia chews on her lip and thinks for a moment. "Let's say you were in here alone and Dante came in and told you to get on your knees. With no other explanation. He just unzips his fly and says do it. Would you?"

Kat's cheeks turn pink, and I clear my throat, wishing I wasn't here for this part of the conversation.

"Well?" Mia presses.

"Yes, if we were alone, of course, but that's because ..." She goes quiet.

"Because you trust him? You know he's not going to do anything you don't want him to?"

"Yes," Kat replies quietly.

"That's what this is." Mia laces her fingers through mine. "Pure and simple trust. That's all."

I squeeze her hand.

"You trust Lorenzo, right? You trust me?" Mia asks.

"Of course."

"Then trust us to know what we want."

Kat nods, tears pricking at her eyes. "You're right. I'm sorry. It's none of my business."

"Mia's welfare is your business, Kat," I assure her.

"Yours is too," she retorts, her brow furrowed.

"Yeah, I know." She and the rest of my family were the only reason I managed to put one foot in front of the other for the past few years. "But I've got her now. You can trust me to take care of her."

"And I've got him," Mia adds with a triumphant smile.

Kat's eyes swim with unshed tears. "I see that." Her voice cracks on the last word and she clears her throat. "And I'm sorry if I overstepped."

I shake my head. "You didn't."

"I was just worried about you both, but I can see how happy you are. And ..." She swats away a rogue tear. "And I'm glad you found each other."

I mouth *thank you* and she acknowledges it with a nod before leaving and closing the library door behind her.

Alone with Mia, I turn her on my lap. She straddles me and runs her fingers through my hair, a half-smile playing over her mouth as she sinks her teeth into her juicy lower lip. "You got me, do you?" I ask with an arch of one eyebrow.

Her eyes narrow. "Yes. I get to take care of you too, don't I?"

I tilt my head to the side, eyes raking over her face and down to her beautiful tits that are pressed against my chest, but I don't answer.

"I think we need to revisit my hard limits, Sir, because you not allowing me to take care of you is a big one."

I pull her closer and trail soft kisses down her neck that make her squirm. "Too late now, sunshine, you're wearing my collar," I tease. She gasps loudly, feigning indignation as she rolls her pussy over my already hard cock.

"I might go on sub strike." Tilting her head back, she allows me better access to her throat. I take full advantage, trailing my teeth along her sensitive skin, my lips brushing over her new neckwear.

I pull down the zipper on the back of her dress. "You're unionized already?"

"I'm starting my own union."

Slipping the dress off over her shoulders, I growl when it falls to her waist. "Now that I would love to see."

"You would, huh?"

"Hmm." Moving lower, I pull her bra down so I can toy with her hard nipples. I roll one between my finger and thumb, making her whimper and grind her pussy on me. Flicking my tongue over the other one, I bite back a smile when she moans my name. "I can just imagine the punishments I could dole out for your strike. They would make the spanking you're about to get upstairs for your little stunt with Kat look like playtime." I sink my teeth into her juicy flesh.

"But you thought that was funny," she whines, pressing herself into my mouth in search of the delicious blend of pain and pleasure. "I saw you trying not to laugh."

Fisting my hand in her hair, I tilt her head so she's looking at me. "It was very fucking funny." A victorious smile spreads over her face, and I can't help but grin back at her. That smile of hers is fucking infectious. "And that's why I'm going to let you come after I'm done punishing you."

SIXTY-SEVEN

LORENZO

S itting on the edge of the bed, I reach up and cup Mia's jaw in my hand. "Take off your clothes and get on your knees." She does what I ask without a second's hesitation, quickly pulling off her dress and underwear before dropping to the floor and looking up at me expectantly. Such a good little submissive already. I run my fingertips along her collar, and a primal urge to throw her down and fuck her senseless washes over me, but I resist it. "Your collar wasn't the only gift I bought you today."

Her hazel eyes shine with delight. "It wasn't?"

I reach for the black box beside the bed. Opening it, I take out the piece of fabric and hold it up for her to see. She sinks her teeth into her luscious bottom lip, making me envious that I'm not biting on it right now instead, but we have plenty of time for that. As soon as I lean forward, she dips her head slightly, allowing me to tie the blindfold. Sitting back, I admire her while she waits patiently for whatever I have planned next.

Reaching into the box again, I pull out a pair of leather cuffs. Mia tilts her head, like she's straining to hear what I'm doing. "Hold out your arms." She does as I ask, a smile playing on her lips as I wrap the first cuff around her left wrist. "You're unusually quiet tonight, sunshine."

"I don't want to miss any instructions, Sir."

"You do know you're still going to be punished for that stunt with Kat downstairs, don't you?"

My little siren grins. "Yes, Sir."

I grin too. Her little joke on Kat was hilarious, and the look on my sister-in-law's face was priceless. I have no intentions of actually punishing Mia for it, but that doesn't mean I won't have fun with her. "You won't be smiling when I'm done with you," I warn her.

"I know, Sir."

I wrap the second cuff around her right wrist. Standing, I help her up. "Come with me." I walk to the other side of the room, pulling her along with me. The metal hook has been in the ceiling for years, and I've used it plenty of times in the past, but never with Mia. I bought the new chain to go on it earlier today, and she was so focused on getting her collar and then sucking my cock, she must not have seen it, which was exactly what I'd hoped for.

I join the cuffs with the metal fastenings and lift her arms to attach them to the chain overhead. She flinches at the rattling sound but doesn't pull back from me. Instead she allows me to shackle her to the ceiling without any resistance. Finished securing her, I run my hands down her arms and sides and she squirms, pressing her lips together, but a giggle escapes. I don't bother to hide my smile—one of the perks of her being blindfolded is that I don't have to mask my facial expressions.

I grab the belt I bought for her and trace the soft leather tip over her hip bone. She shivers under its touch. "This is for you to wear, tesoro," I reassure her and slip it around her waist.

"Oh?" she breathes as I fasten the top half in place. No

doubt she can feel the additional straps and knows this isn't a regular belt, but she doesn't ask questions.

"This part," I say, holding up the piece at the back, "goes through here." I slide the leather between her thighs, and she sucks in a deep breath. Her nipples harden further and her skin blooms with heat. I suppress a laugh and fasten it to the front. When I'm done, I step back and admire her for a few seconds.

"What is it I'm wearing, Sir?" she asks softly.

"It's a wand belt." I walk back to the bed and take out another gift.

"A wand belt?"

"Yeah." I plug the new toy into the wall and her mouth opens wide at the sound it makes. "You know what a wand is, right?"

Her cheeks flush pink. "Yes."

I hook the head of the toy into the straps between her thighs, dusting my lips over the skin of her neck and making a shiver run the length of her body. "This part holds the wand in place while my hands are busy doing something else."

Panting, she squeezes her thighs together and presses the bulbous head of the toy between them.

And as for what I'll be busy doing ... I take her final gift from the box and smack the leather paddle against my hand. With a loud gasp, Mia squeezes her thighs tighter together. Goosebumps break out all over her body.

I trail the paddle over her breasts, gently tapping it against her hard nipples. She moans. "You know what your final gift is?"

"Is it a paddle?"

I trail it further down her body before giving her a quick swat on the ass with it. She yelps. "Clever girl."

I take a few steps back. Absolute fucking perfection. Her flawless tits jiggle with each breath. I drink in every part of her.

Every line. Every curve. Every scar. But it's not her beautiful body tied up and ready to be used however I want that makes me feel like I can't breathe. It's how she waits for me. So patient. Wearing my collar. Unable to see or free herself. Nipples hard enough to cut diamonds. Legs trembling from standing on her tiptoes. Skin flushed with heat and anticipation, and not a single ounce of fear.

After everything I've done to her, after the way I pushed her away and those awful things I said, she still trusts me completely. Not only with her body, but with her heart too. The realization floors me and makes my cock harder than an iron bar.

"Sir?"

I realize she's listening to the silence and probably wondering what the hell I'm doing. "I'm just admiring my property, sunshine. You look so fucking beautiful wearing my collar."

"I feel beautiful wearing your collar," she says, and the smile that follows nearly knocks me on my ass. It's sweet and pure and everything she is. And everything I'm not. But I will spend the rest of my life trying to prove myself worthy of that smile.

Coasting my hand over her stomach and down her ass, I walk behind her. "Your ass is going to look even more beautiful when I've striped it with my paddle."

She opens her mouth, but I spank her with my palm before she can speak, hard enough to make her squeal. I slap her other cheek just as hard, but this time she moans and rocks forward on the balls of her feet.

"Where did I tell you to wait for me after dinner, Mia?" I spank her again.

"U-upstairs."

"So why did you come to the library?" Smack.

"I d-didn't know it was a rule, Sir. I th-thought ..." I bring my palm down on the fleshy part of her behind and the sound makes me groan. She yelps.

"Thought what?"

"That it ... was a ..."

I spank her again. "A what?"

"A suggestion," she whispers.

I press my lips to her ear. It wasn't a rule, but then this isn't a punishment. Not even close. I slip two fingers inside her and she whimpers. "You're already wet, sunshine. Are you enjoying this punishment a little too much?"

"I'm sorry, Sir. I can't help it."

"You can't help getting wet when I spank you?" I smack her ass again while I drive my fingers in and out of her.

She groans softly. "N-no, Sir."

"Maybe I need to be a little tougher on you, huh?" I don't give her a chance to reply before I pull my fingers from her pussy and spank her with the paddle.

"Ow!" she screeches, rocking forward and causing the chain to take most of her weight. I glance up at her wrists, making sure the cuffs are secure and not too tight. It's been so long since I've shackled someone new to my ceiling, and back before I was married and I used to do it with many different women, it was a fine balance to cause enough discomfort without it being so unbearable that the scene ended too soon. This position can cause considerable damage if not done properly. I would never risk Mia's safety, so I intend to be careful to watch her for signs of distress.

The sound of the paddle colliding with her perfect ass makes my cock weep to be inside her. I rub a hand over her reddened cheeks, kneading her soft flesh to soothe the sting and add a different kind of pain.

She leans back, pressing her ass into my hands and I smile

at her high pain threshold. I give her four more sharp smacks with the paddle, then stop. Stroking her back, I drag my teeth over the skin on her neck. "You're doing so well, sunshine."

"Thank you, Sir," she says, breathless.

"I'm going to give you a little break for a few minutes, okay?" I kiss her shoulder and step away.

"Why? Where are you going?" she asks, a faint hint of panic edging into her voice.

"I'm right here. Just taking off my shirt."

She lets out a relieved sigh.

I pull off my shirt and toss it into the hamper, watching her intently as I do. Her ass is a delicious shade of pink, but she still has a sweet smile on her face. Taking the remote control from my pocket, I switch on the wand between her legs. She jumps, letting out a small shriek that makes me chuckle.

"Oh god," she pants as the toy vibrates against her clit. Her heels drop to the floor and she allows the ceiling hook to take most of her weight, which will help her aching thighs but will make her arms burn more. I turn the wand setting down until it's only a gentle thrum and she purrs contentedly.

"You having fun there without me?"

"I'd much rather have fun with you, Sir." Stepping up behind her, I cup her breasts. She leans into me, rubbing her back against my chest and her ass over my aching cock. "I love feeling your skin on mine, Sir."

"I know, tesoro." Kissing her neck, I continue kneading her breasts, rolling her nipples between my thumb and finger. She moans. My cock throbs. Her breathing gets shallow and fast, and I step back from her, giving her ass a hard smack with the paddle.

"Oh, fuck," she pants.

"Don't forget this is supposed to be a punishment," I tease, then deliver another hard slap on her ass.

She groans, pulling at her restraints as her body chases release.

I turn up the setting on her wand. The increase in pressure makes her mewl with pleasure, so I spank her again, harder than before, enough to take the edge off the euphoria from the vibrations pulsing directly on her clit.

"Sir, please?"

I bring the paddle down on her ass again, loving the way it marks her exquisite skin. "You know your safe word, sunshine."

"I don't want it to stop, I want to ..." She gasps, frustrated and desperate and needy.

I trail my fingertips down her spine, making her wriggle. "What do you want?"

"To come, Sir," she pleads.

"But this is a punishment, remember?" I bite down on her neck and suck hard enough to leave a mark. My mark.

I spank her over and over again. Sometimes hard. Sometimes soft. Sometimes in quick succession and sometimes leaving ten or fifteen seconds between each blow. I grab her ass cheeks, kneading and pawing her sensitive skin to soothe the sting or to make it hurt a little more. And I turn the vibrations of the wand up and down to counteract the pain I inflict on her. She begs me to let her come each time I bring her close to the edge, whimpering while tears stream from her eyes, but she takes everything I give her. We're both panting from the effort and perspiration covers our skin. I'm hard as fucking stone.

When her ass is crimson and she's close to the edge once more, I turn off the toy and throw the paddle onto the floor. She drops her head and her entire body sags, mostly held up by the chain attaching her wrists to the ceiling. She whimpers when I remove the wand from the fastening between her thighs, and I take the belt off her too, careful with the leather against her sensitive flesh. She stands before me in only my collar and the blindfold.

"How are you doing, sunshine?"

She tilts her chin up, her pink cheeks stained with tears. Fuck me, she's beautiful. "I'm good, Sir."

Slipping my hand between her thighs, I slide two fingers through her soaking folds before dipping them into her tight pussy. "You took that spanking so well." Her smile grows wider. "You remember the first time I fucked you, Mia? When I didn't make you come? And you thought that I couldn't do it?" Her throat constricts, a flush creeping across her face at the memory. "And now you've spilled your cum all over this house for me. I know your body so well, I can tell exactly when you're about to lose control. The way your greedy cunt spasms." I sink my fingers deeper and her muscles ripple around them. "The way your legs start to tremble. Your breathing gets faster and shallower." I trail soft kisses along her collarbone and she whimpers. "The skin right here turns a very particular shade of pink."

"S-Sir?" She tries to sink further onto my fingers but can't because of her restraints.

"You want to know something about our first time? You felt so *fucking* good. I lost myself in you. And I've been losing myself in you ever since."

I sink my teeth into the soft skin on the side of her neck, causing her to moan loudly. Her legs tremble as her orgasm grows dangerously close again, and I slip my fingers out of her, sucking them clean while she whimpers in frustration. "A part of me knew from that very first time that we'd end up right here. Even when I was pushing you away, some part of me knew we'd wind up like this one day. You wearing my collar." I caress her throat and her chest heaves. "You being completely mine. Mine to control. Mine to use." I tweak one of her hard nipples.

"Sir," she whines, tears running down her face.

"Mine to care for. Mine to worship." I dust my lips over hers, taunting her with the promise of a kiss, then pulling back. "Who do you belong to, Mia?"

"You, Sir," she whispers.

After unzipping my fly, I slip one arm around her hips and free my cock from the confines of my suit pants. I grip the base and squeeze. Her arms must be aching, and she's probably approaching the limit of what she can take, but how do I not fuck her right now, when she's tied up and desperate for me? I rub the crown of my cock on her clit and her entire body shudders. She leans into me as I lift her, wrapping her legs around my waist and positioning my tip at her entrance. She's so fucking hot and inviting that it nearly kills me not to plow straight into her, but she's so dangerously close to the edge that it might just tip her over, and she doesn't get to come—not yet.

"Please, Sir? I need you."

"You have every single part of me, sunshine. All of me. Always." I sink halfway inside her and groan at the relief of her hot, wet pussy.

Tremors wrack her body and cause her to jerk on the chain. I glance up at her arms, aware of the ache that must be burning through them right now. "You're doing so well. You take your punishments like such a good fucking girl." I sink deeper and she coats me in a rush of slick heat. "So fucking good." I groan out the words as warmth coils up my spine. My head spins with the effort of not nailing her into next week.

She throws back her head, grinding herself onto my cock while she chases the orgasm I've been denying her. I sink all the way inside her and suck a pebbled nipple into my mouth, biting down hard enough to make her cry out and giving her the perfect amount of pain to take the edge off her pleasure and keep her teetering on the brink.

"Lorenzo," she whimpers, her mouth open as her chest heaves with the effort of breathing.

Keeping one arm banded tightly at her waist, I reach up and free her wrists from the hook on the ceiling. She drops her head against my shoulder. Her hot breath on my neck makes all the tiny hairs there stand on end. With my dick still inside her, I carry her to the bed and lay her down. And when I slide out of her a second later, she lets out a sob.

"Where are you hurting, sunshine?"

She sniffs. "My arms."

I rub my hands up and down her arms, gently kneading her muscles to soothe the ache and encourage blood flow. A few moments later, her breathing evens out and her chest stops heaving. "You did so well, tesoro."

A grin tugs on the corner of her lips. "Thank you, Sir."

I take off her blindfold. She blinks, adjusting to the light, and when her eyes finally find mine, she rewards me with a heart-stopping smile. "You're so fucking beautiful, Mia." I run my fingers over her collar and tug it gently, making her gasp. "And you look even more beautiful wearing this."

She flutters her eyelashes. "I love wearing your collar, Sir."

I dip my hand between her spread thighs, enjoying the way her eyes roll back when I toy with her wet pussy.

"You wear it so well. You're fucking perfect, you know that?" I sink two fingers into her and her back arches off the bed. "I have no idea what I did to deserve you."

She writhes, her body fighting for the orgasm she so desperately needs. Her lip trembles, but she holds my gaze. "You have it all wrong, Sir. You might have lost yourself in me, but I found myself in you."

I swear someone just punched a hole through my chest and

put my heart in a vise. I take a deep breath to replace the air she stole from my lungs. If I wasn't already on my knees for her, I'd drop to them right now and worship this woman for the rest of my life. "Jesus, Mia." Slipping my fingers out of her, I position myself between her thighs and drive my cock into her instead, unable to resist being inside her for a second longer. "You feel so good."

Circling my neck with her arms, she wraps her legs around my waist, trying to pull me closer even though there isn't a millimeter of space between us.

"So do you," she whimpers, nails clawing at my back.

"You think you deserve to come, sunshine?" I growl as I nail her to the bed.

"Yes. Please?" Her hot cunt squeezes me tight, and I slam into her, rolling my hips so that the crown of my cock sweeps over her G-spot, giving her the release she's been craving for the past hour.

She cries out when she comes—a sound that's ripped from deep in her core, filled with relief and euphoria—and she soaks us both with her cum. It runs down her thighs as I carry on driving into her, drawing out her pleasure while I chase my own. I bury my head against her neck, sinking my teeth into the skin just above her collar, and fuck her harder than I've ever fucked anyone in my life.

I never thought I'd have anything like this again … and I almost lost her. Almost let her slip through my fingers. But she's mine now. She will be mine forever.

I thrust into her one last time. "Mine," I growl as I fill her with my cum, grinding every single drop from my balls into her sweet cunt.

Rolling onto my back, I pull her with me so that she lies on top of me. Her eyes are closed and she's practically purring like a kitten. I gently squeeze her ass and watch her face for any signs of discomfort, but she just smiles. The aftercare can wait a little while.

I brush her hair back from her damp forehead. "That's another duvet that needs to be dry-cleaned."

"And whose fault is that, Sir?"

I press a kiss to the top of her head. "I guess I do make you come kind of hard, huh?"

She laughs. "So hard."

I stare down at her beautiful face. So peaceful and content. "What we just did, Mia, did that feel like a punishment?"

"No, not even a little," she says with a contented sigh. "More like funishment."

"Funishment?" I bite back a laugh. "I guess it was."

"It was hot, Sir."

My cock twitches at the fresh memory. "I'm glad you could tell the difference between real punishment and playing like we just did."

She lets out a sigh of pure contentment. "I knew all along. I could tell by the devious look in your eyes when you pulled out that blindfold."

Reaching out, I grab the duvet and pull it over us both, wrapping us up in our own little cocoon. Then I close my eyes and listen to the sound of her steady breathing. Just a few minutes and I'll get us cleaned up and get her ass taken care of. But right now, I don't want to do anything but hold her. Only the two of us in our own tiny part of the world where nobody else can touch us.

"I love you, Sir," she whispers, rubbing her cheek against my chest.

"I love you too, sunshine." The words come so easily to me, like some universal truth that I've known all my life. Suddenly an image of Anya's face drifts into my head—my other universal truth—and instead of the pain that usually accompanies her memory, there's only a sense of peace.

Mia's breathing grows deeper, and I tighten my arms around her, wanting her as close as possible. I really should get us cleaned up, but her body's so soft and warm, and it feels so fucking nice lying here with her. I never want to move.

SIXTY-EIGHT

MIA

Lorenzo pops his head into the den where I'm playing with Kat and the kids. "Nathan and Drake want to see us at their office, sunshine."

"Oh." I bite my lip and cast an anxious glance at Kat.

"Drake says its good news," he assures me.

Kat squeezes my arm. "And Lorenzo won't let anything bad happen."

Less than an hour later, I'm seated next to Lorenzo in Drake James's office. Anxiety and trepidation shudder up my spine, but Lorenzo squeezes my hand, and I'm reminded that he and the James brothers are on my side.

"Sorry to keep you waiting," Nathan says as he and Drake walk in.

"You said you have some good news?" Lorenzo asks.

"Some very good news. We found the sister," Nathan answers with a smirk.

"The sister? The one you told me about? The one who disappeared?" I ask Lorenzo. "What does she have to do with anything?"

Lorenzo nods but keeps his focus on Nathan. "You found her? How?"

"One of my new clients back in New York happens to be the best hacker in the country. She found her for me. Michaela Mulcahy is now Callie Stretton, and she lives in Nevada."

"And did you manage to speak to her? Did she tell you what happened? Has Jake been covering for his big brother all these years?" Lorenzo asks.

Drake clears his throat. "How about we let her answer that herself?"

"Herself?" I gasp. "You mean she's here?" I grip Lorenzo's hand tighter. I'm not sure

I want to meet Brad and Jake's sister. What if she's as awful as they are?

Lorenzo squeezes my hand in return. "I'm right here, sunshine," he assures me, then turns his attention back to Drake. "She was willing to come here after hiding for so long? Why?"

"She's an advocate for women's rights. She runs some charity in Nevada. I gave her an overview of the situation and she was keen to help. She's on the level, I swear."

"You want to meet her?" Lorenzo asks me.

"Do you think she can help us?"

"I think she might have some information that we could use to keep Jake off your back until I find a more permanent solution," he replies. I don't ask what his permanent solution is—I already know. I make a mental note to remind him that he can't go around killing cops.

"Then yes, I'd like to meet her."

"Brad and Jake abused her too, Mia," Nathan says. "Her motives align with ours, I promise you that."

They abused her? Their own sister? I swallow down a bubble of anxiety as Drake leaves the room. A few seconds later, he comes back with a woman who looks to be in her early thirties and is wearing the coolest pair of purple boots I have ever seen in my life.

She chews on her lip, and I feel her nervous energy from across the room. I guess she has even more reason to be anxious about this meeting than I do.

"Callie?" I say with as wide a smile as I can muster.

"Mia, right?" She gives me a faint smile in return.

"Yes." I instinctively jump up from my seat and pull her into a hug. Thankfully, she's a hugger too, and she hugs me right back. "Thank you so much for coming."

She laughs nervously, tucking a strand of auburn hair behind her ear. "Anything I can do to save any woman from those toxic pieces of shit is my pleasure."

The sadness in her eyes makes me want to cry. I didn't have any siblings, but Kat was like a sister to me growing up. She has a brother, Leo, and he was always kind of an asshole, but I can't comprehend how anyone could hurt their own sister.

When introductions have been made and Drake's secretary has provided everyone with a hot drink, the four of us wait for Callie to speak.

"I guess I'm the one with all of the answers then?" she says with a wry laugh.

"We have some for you too," Nathan tells her.

"You said Brad is dead, right?" she asks.

He gives her a curt nod.

"Good riddance to that piece of shit," she mutters.

Lorenzo leans forward in his chair. "Can you tell us what happened to you, Callie?"

She takes a sip of her coffee and rests the mug on her thigh. "That sick fuck beat me and raped me," she says matter-of-factly, as though she's told this story many times.

"Brad?" Lorenzo asks.

"No." She shakes her head. "Jake."

"Jake?" Lorenzo frowns.

"Yeah, I told my parents, and they both just let it happen," she says with a shrug. "He was like our dad's golden boy, and he got away with murder—probably literally in the case of our mom."

"You think it was Jake who killed your mom?" Nathan asks, while I listen in shock.

"I wouldn't put it past him. He was a sick, twisted fuck."

I squeeze Lorenzo's hand and try to stop my entire body from shaking.

"Jake? Not Brad?" Lorenzo asks again.

"The semen found on Janice Mulcahy's body belonged to Jake," Nathan cuts in. "We got access to all the sealed files."

Holy crapballs. What the hell kind of family did I marry into?

"How old was Jake then, like fifteen?" Lorenzo asks.

Nathan nods. "That's why his files were sealed too."

I fight the urge to be sick. "Semen? You mean Janice? Brad and Jake's mom?" Lorenzo squeezes my hand tighter. "So she was abusing Jake? Having sex with him?"

Callie snorts. "He was raping her too. I told you, he's a twisted fuck." How is she so calm about all this?

Lorenzo takes a deep breath to compose himself before he speaks again. "What happened when you were thirteen?"

"I got pregnant. Best thing that ever happened to me," she says with a derisive laugh. "That's when people started to believe me. Child services whipped me out of there and I never looked back. I found out about my mom's death when I was seven months along, and I haven't seen a single one of those fuckers since."

"What happened to your baby?" I ask.

She smiles softly. "He was adopted by a great family. He's

doing really well. Just finished college. I don't see him, but I get updates."

I return her smile, glad that she seems to take comfort in that.

"Did you know that Mike Mulcahy wasn't your father?" Nathan asks her.

"Not back then. I didn't find that out until a few years ago."

"Who was your father?" Lorenzo asks. I can't believe I had no idea about any of Brad's messed-up past. "He have anything to do with how hard it was to access those records?"

"Yep. Seems my dear old mom had an affair with a guy named Foster Carmichael," Callie replies.

Lorenzo frowns. "Why do I know that name?"

"He was a big deal in New York in the nineties and early 2000s," Nathan explains. "Before he started pissing off the wrong people. But back then he was a big fish with a lot of government pull. Family values were a major foundation of his campaigns. He couldn't afford the scandal if word ever got out that he'd had an affair and a kid with a married woman, so he had the whole thing buried deep."

"I figure good old Mike knew all along that I wasn't his kid, which was why he allowed Jake to do what he did," Callie adds. "And my mom was bullied by him her whole life."

"Where does Brad fit into this though?" I ask, finally finding my voice. "Jake always seemed a little afraid of him."

"I guess he was." Callie shrugs. "Brad was always a bully too. He was the one person Jake could never push around, and while Brad didn't actively participate in any of the shit Jake did to our mom and me ..." She shakes her head.

"He didn't stop it either. And he was the one person who could have exposed Jake's secrets." Drake finishes for her.

Callie nods. "Exactly."

"But what does all this mean?" I ask. "Callie, you can never let Jake know who you are now. You'd be putting yourself at risk, and maybe even your son too."

"My son is very well protected, I assure you. And while I have no desire to see that piece of shit again, he has the entire Boston police force on his side. Oh yeah, I've kept tabs on him. If he wants to pin Brad's murder on you, he won't stop until that's what he's done. I will happily do whatever I need to if it means preventing him from ruining your life the way he tried to ruin mine." She pulls a brown envelope from her purse and hands it to Nathan. "But I hope this is enough and that it never has to come to that."

Nathan slides the envelope across his desk. "This is Michaela Mulcahy's written statement of everything that happened to her and her mom, and it's sure as hell gonna be enough to get Jake to back down."

I lean back in my chair, my entire body trembling as her words sink in. I thought I knew Brad and Jake. And I knew they weren't good men, but now that I know the true extent of the things they're capable of ...

"I will never let him anywhere near you again, Mia," Lorenzo says, his voice calm and reassuring.

I swallow the huge knot of anxiety balled in my throat. I know I'm safe with Lorenzo. He'd protect me from harm even if it meant hurting himself, but if Jake is determined to have me arrested for murder—one that I actually committed—I have no idea how he can stop that from happening. Not unless he can persuade Jake to drop it.

"So we confront him with the information and warn him that if he doesn't stay the fuck away from Mia, we'll make sure Michaela's statement goes public?" Lorenzo's question is met with nods of approval from Drake and Callie.

CHAPTER SIXTY-EIGHT

"I'll go to trial to see that sick fuck suffer if I have to," Callie adds.

"Don't do anything stupid, buddy," Nathan warns Lorenzo. "I can speak with him. Lay it all out on the line right here in my office."

"That sounds like a good plan." I don't want Lorenzo getting himself into trouble.

Lorenzo turns to me. "No, tesoro. I will look him in the eyes when I threaten his life if he ever comes anywhere near you again. It's not up for negotiation."

Callie grins. "I wish I could be there to see it too."

"So, it's settled then? You'll speak to him yourself?" Nathan asks Lorenzo. "And I mean *speak*."

"I'll be good. I'll take Dante and Max," he replies with a hint of a smirk.

Drake laughs. "He's gonna shit his pants."

"Good." Callie stands and sets her coffee mug down on the table beside her. "I have to catch that plane back if I'm gonna make my meeting later."

"Of course. Thank you so much for coming, Ms. Stretton," Nathan says, standing to escort her out.

"Thank you for flying me here on your fancy private jet," she says with a chuckle. "Not every day a girl gets to see one of them."

I jump up and give her another impromptu hug. "Thank you so much, Callie. For everything."

"My pleasure, honey. I hope he leaves you in peace now." I smile at her, trying to think of something appropriate to say back, but she winks at me. "I found my own peace a long time ago, don't you worry about me."

Nathan returns to the office after escorting her out and grabs his coat. "If you don't need me for anything else, I have a whole fuckload of shit to deal with in New York."

"Thanks for everything, compagno." Lorenzo wraps the other man in a hug. "I owe you."

Nathan hugs him back. "You will never owe me, buddy, and you know it."

SIXTY-NINE

LORENZO

"You sure we can't just tie him up and torture the sick fuck to death?" Max asks as we duck across the road to Jake Mulcahy's house under the cover of night.

"Don't give him fucking ideas, Max," Dante says with a sigh.

"Hey, I'm good with the plan," I assure him. "No sense having to dispose of a cop's dead body when we have enough information to scare the fuck shitless." I'm not lying; I will stick to the plan. But I intend to deal with the twisted piece of shit my way in the future.

"Kitchen light's on. You think he's in there?" Max asks as he and I jog around to the back of the house while Dante goes to the front. We climb over the fence and drop to the grass below with a soft thud.

Max grins. "Well, let's go say hello."

We break in through the back and find Jake Mulcahy bent over his kitchen table, eating a microwave lasagna when Max and I stroll into the room. "What the fuck?" he snarls, scrabbling to get up and reach for his gun on the counter. But Max is too quick. He has Jake in a headlock before the prick can even get off his ass. We pull his arms behind his back and make short work of tying him to the chair.

Once he's secure, Max releases his hold on Jake's neck. "Who the fuck do you think you are?" he seethes, wrestling against his restraints.

"You know who we are," I remind him as I take a seat.

"You won't get away with this. I'm a fucking decorated cop," he spits.

"We haven't done anything we need to get away with, Jakey." Max perches on the edge of the table. "Not yet, anyway."

"We only want to talk." That's bullshit. I want to rip his fucking throat out. But not tonight.

Dante walks into the kitchen, placing the lock he's just removed from Jake's front door on the table. "You might want to get that looked at. Came right off in my hands."

"Fuck you!" Jake snarls.

Max backhands him across the face. "Don't ever speak to Mr. Moretti like that again, fuck-nugget."

Jake spits blood on the floor and glares at us with contempt. The stupid fucker doesn't know how lucky he is that he'll still be breathing when we walk out of here.

"Like I said, we only want to talk," I repeat.

"So talk," he snaps but there's a tremor in his voice now. As though he's only just realized the severity of his situation.

"I want you to stay away from Mia," I start.

"She killed my fucking brother," he says, his voice dripping with venom.

I glance at Max, and he punches Jake in the mouth. We agreed I wouldn't lay a finger on the horrible fuck in case I couldn't stop.

"As I was saying, you will stay away from Mia. You will drop this bullshit about your waste-of-oxygen brother, and you will never even think her name again. Understand?"

Beads of perspiration trickle down his forehead. "And if I refuse?"

"How about I cut you open from scrotum to nose, fuck-nugget?" Max asks, kicking Jake's chair and making him flinch.

"You'd never fucking get away with it," Jake insists. "I'm not some street punk you can make disappear."

I made your brother disappear, you stupid fuck! The words want to roll off my tongue, but I hold them back. I'll tell him when I return for his life. "I think you'll find we can make anyone disappear," I say instead. "But fortunately for you, my colleague here won't need to gut you like a fish to stop you from talking."

He eyeballs me but doesn't say anything.

"All we have to do is release the statement your sister gave us. All about what a warped, evil little fuck you are. Your life as you know it would be over."

His face turns whiter than the fridge directly behind him.

"Michaela's even willing to press charges should we ever need to provide you with a little more encouragement. You know there's no statute of limitations for rape in Boston, right?"

"You're lying," he snarls, but his lip wobbles and he's sweating profusely now.

"No. We had a good chat with her. And of course there's DNA evidence of your crimes. Did you know she had your child? A son. He knows nothing about the depraved fucker who sired him though."

"Fuck you!"

I push my chair back and he flinches. I need to cause him a little pain, just so he has a taste of what's coming to him one day. I grab his limp dick and squeeze. He wheezes and tears spring to his eyes. "Drop the vendetta against Mia or I *will* release that statement. And if she ever has to see your ugly goddamn face, hear your voice, or if anything happens to her because of you for the rest of her days"—I squeeze harder, tempted to pull the goddamn thing off with my bare hands— "we will come back here and we will slice off every single part of your anatomy piece by fucking piece. Until you're nothing but a head on a fucking torso. And then I will pour battery acid into your fucking eyes and watch you burn from the inside out, you disgusting fuck! You got me?"

Unable to speak from the pain of having his junk crushed, he nods.

"Good." I walk out of his kitchen before my restraint snaps, leaving Max and Dante to untie him. Glancing back at the house, I swear that I will return. And next time I'll come alone.

SEVENTY

MIA

L orenzo slips an arm around my waist, giving me a reassuring squeeze as we move past the thick velvet ropes that lead to The Peacock Club. I resist the urge to chew on my lip, not wanting to ruin the lovely make-up that Joey helped me with.

"No need to be nervous, sunshine," Lorenzo says softly in my ear, his warm breath sending a shiver along my spine. "I'll take good care of you."

"I know," I say with a smile. "I think I'm like excited nervous though, you know? This is my first time in a club like this."

"Glad to hear it," he says with a wink. "You remember the rules once we're inside?"

"Only address you as Sir. Don't talk unless you give me permission, and do anything you say without hesitation?"

"That's my girl." He dips his head and gives me a sweet, lingering kiss.

"Can I ask you something though, Sir?" I purr, running a hand down the lapel of his finely tailored and incredibly well-fitted suit.

"Of course."

"Why the no talking rule tonight? Is there a specific reason?" The nervous chattering rule is a constant, and I've almost cracked that particular habit, but not talking at all, even when someone speaks to me, is completely new.

He gives me a wicked grin, his eyes crinkling at the corners, and skims a hand down to my ass.

"What?" I frown.

He dusts the knuckles of his free hand over my cheek before cupping my jaw and tilting my head so he can look into my eyes. "It's because, my feisty ball of sunshine, despite you being so full of fire and defiance, you're actually turning into a very well-behaved little sub."

My entire body floods with heat at his praise.

"I had to get more creative and make some rules that you might actually break."

My breath catches in my throat. "So you can punish me?"

"Exactly."

"So, are you saying I'm a good sub, Sir?"

He presses his lips close to my ear again. "You're my perfect sub, tesoro."

"Thank you," I whisper, basking in his praise, just like he's taught me.

My head may as well be on a swivel once we get inside the club. It's one of the most beautiful places I've ever seen. All glass and chrome and plush velvet. Lorenzo told me it's under new ownership and they renovated and changed the name. Whoever the new owners are, they obviously have impeccable taste. The club is packed, and we have to thread our way through the crowd to reach the VIP booths at the back.

Mouth hanging open in fascination, I admire the costumes and outfits of everyone I see. My jaw drops further when we pass two people having sex on a table about two feet away from us.

Lorenzo tugs on my hand, pulling me through the mass of bodies, and I stumble after him in my heels. Instead of continuing toward the back of the club, he leads me to a crowded spot with a single seat available at a table. Two men and a woman are already sitting there, and they acknowledge him with a nod. Lorenzo sits in the empty chair. Confused, I frown. Am I supposed to sit on his lap?

Lorenzo glares up at me. "On your knees."

I blink at him.

"Do not make me ask again."

My heart rate kicks up as I sink to my knees. What the hell is he doing? He grips my jaw in his hand. "You want to stare at people, sunshine. Maybe I should show you how that feels."

I open my mouth to speak but close it again. No talking.

"Oh you're going to want to open that mouth again." He unzips his fly. "Because it's going to be full of my cock in a few seconds."

I quickly glance around the room, noting the growing crowd, but I'm not surprised. Lorenzo Moretti is a big deal in these circles. And he's about to teach his new sub a lesson on her first night here. I want to tell him that I wasn't staring to be rude, but I can't, and I guess it doesn't matter because it was kind of rude. But now I get to be the one who's stared at while I suck Lorenzo's cock. Holy bananas! I'm not sure I can do this. Not here in front of everyone.

"Eyes on me," he orders as he reaches inside his suit pants. "You look at anyone other than me while you're sucking my cock and you'll be spanked in front of all these lovely people too."

I swallow the thick knot in my throat and nod faintly, keeping my gaze fixed on his.

He palms the back of my head, threading his fingers through my hair. Then he leans close, lips dusting over the shell of my ear. "And you know I'm looking for any reason to spank you, sunshine."

"I'll be—" *Crap!*

"And there it is." He chuckles wickedly, sitting back and pulling his cock from his pants.

My entire body trembles and my eyes brim with tears, but I keep my gaze fixed on his. Searching my face, he leans forward again and cups my chin in his strong hand. "I should have reminded you that your safe word still works in here, Mia," he says, his voice low. "Anywhere. Anytime. No matter what the rules are. You understand me?"

I stay quiet, my stare fixed on the side of his head.

"You have permission to speak."

"I understand, Sir."

Seemingly satisfied with that response, he leans back again and I train my eyes on his. I can do this. No matter who's watching or what happens, I trust this man in front of me more than anyone else in the world.

I see him squeezing the base of his shaft in my peripheral vision. "Show all these good people how well you suck my cock."

I plant my hands on his thighs and dip my head, dropping my gaze to his beautiful cock, weeping with precum. Swirling my tongue over the crown, I collect it all before I wrap my lips around him. He keeps his fingers tangled in my hair, pushing down and forcing me to take more of him into my mouth. Lorenzo stays silent but the people around us murmur appreciatively. I don't know if I can do this. All I have to do is say that one word and all this will stop. But then what happens? We go home and maybe never come here again?

"You're doing so well," he groans.

I am? I focus on him. His scent. The power in his body. His taut thigh muscles beneath my palms. Then the soothing sound of his voice as he goes on telling me how well I'm doing. Pleasure and warmth wash over me as I suck him harder, taking him deeper until he's inside my throat. I swallow, and his groan rumbles through him and into me. Yeah, I can do this.

"You got yourself a wonderful new sub, Lorenzo." I recognize the soft purring voice. It's the woman Lorenzo introduced me to in the lobby of the James's building.

Lorenzo tightens his grip on my hair. "Sure fucking did." Close to losing control, he grunts the last word.

Wetness floods my panties at the thought that they're watching him as much as they are me. This is actually kinda hot. I'm about to make the most powerful man in the city lose control in this room full of people. How many women can say they get to do that? Just one. Me.

Spurred on by that realization, I inhale through my nose and swallow again, squeezing his thick cock in my throat. "Holy! Fuck!"

I look up to see him gazing down at me, eyes dark and full of so much love and desire for me that my heart almost bursts with happiness. Now there's nobody here but me and him. This is all about us and no one else.

"You suck my cock so fucking good," he groans, holding my head still as he drives into me. I keep my eyes on his and open my throat, accepting every drop of the cum that he feeds me. Trailing my tongue along his shaft as he slowly slides out of my mouth, I lick him clean.

Saliva drips from the corner of my mouth and he wipes it away with his thumb. The woman who spoke earlier sits on his left. She leans close to talk to him, but his attention remains on me. "You did so good, sunshine."

I gaze up at him with adoration. I love him so much, love that he knows exactly how far to push me.

"Don't forget her spanking, Lorenzo," the woman says with

a dark laugh, and my heart sinks. I'd forgotten about that. How did she even hear what he said to me? Has she been here the whole time?

Lorenzo tucks his cock back into his pants and zips himself up. Then he takes my hand and pulls me up from the floor and onto his lap.

"Melanie, you remember Mia?" he says to the woman on his left.

Ah, yes. Melanie.

"I certainly do. And I don't think I'll be forgetting her any time soon." She arches an eyebrow, and my cheeks flush in response.

Lorenzo skims his hand over my ass. "She is unforgettable." He winks at me, and I practically melt into him. Then he gives me all his attention. "Let's go find our booth."

He sets me on my feet, and Melanie watches us intently. I can tell she wants to ask why he's not spanking me like he promised, but I doubt she—or anyone, for that matter—would challenge him so openly. He squeezes my hand tightly in his and we weave through the crowd once more until we reach the private tables at the back. A bouncer shows us to our booth, and I slide along the plush suede bench seat with Lorenzo immediately following me.

"You can speak freely in here, Mia," he says as soon as we're seated.

"That was super hot." I blurt the words out before he changes his mind about the speaking thing.

His eyes narrow. "You like being watched?"

"I didn't think I would, but ..." My cheeks flush bright red. "I loved that everyone was watching us. That they ..." I trail off, suddenly self-conscious.

A smirk tugs at the corner of his lips. "That they what, sunshine?"

Biting my lip, I stare into his dark eyes. "They would know I belonged to you."

His smile widens and he brushes his fingertips over my cheek. "Yes you fucking do. Is that all you enjoyed about it?"

Damn! He knows me so well. "No," I admit with a shy grin. "I also loved that they were watching you come. I bet a lot of them would have loved to have been on their knees for you, but I'm the only person who gets to do that."

Without warning, he crashes his lips against mine, palming the back of my neck and holding me in place while he tongue fucks my mouth. When he breaks our kiss, I gasp for air. "I think more people wanted to be me," he says, his voice low and husky. "Because you are the perfect little sub. The perfect woman."

Heat pools in my core. "Sir." I breathe out the word.

"But you're still owed a spanking. Over my knee, now."

"Here?"

He smirks. "I can take you back out there and do it in full view of the entire club if you'd prefer?"

"No, no. Here is good." I shuffle onto the seat and lie over his knee, resting my elbows on the soft suede bench with my ass in the air.

He pushes up my short dress, tugging on the soft fabric until it sits snugly around my waist. He rubs a large, strong hand across my ass, and I purr in contentment. Then he slaps me hard, four times over my panties. I yelp when the last one lands, just as a couple walks past our booth. I freeze as my cheeks burn with shame, but they don't linger.

"People aren't allowed to stay and watch up here unless they're invited," Lorenzo assures me, and I relax again. He pulls my panties over my ass cheeks and rolls them halfway down my thighs. "How many times should I spank this beautiful ass tonight?" he asks me.

I think of the appropriate number. Too high and I will have given myself an unnecessarily sore ass—at least more painful than I would have had. But too low and he'll double the amount as further punishment. "Fifteen?" I suggest.

"That's a little harsh, sunshine," he says with a dark laugh. "But if you insist."

Dammit!

I brace myself for the first blow, and he brings the flat of his palm down hard over the meaty part of my butt cheek. Ow! I press my lips together and wince as he spanks me again.

"Your ass looks beautiful when it's red from a spanking." He slides a finger into my pussy and I whimper shamelessly. "Jesus, fuck, Mia, are you this wet from sucking my cock or from being spanked over my knee?"

"Both, Sir."

He spanks me again while he gently finger fucks me, and hot pleasure coils in the pit of my stomach, making me achy and needy for him. "Sir," I moan.

"My needy little sub. So desperate for a fucking."

He goes on spanking me, making me wetter with every blow. I had no idea pain could cause this kind of pleasure, but the brand of pain that Lorenzo Moretti doles out is nothing short of exquisite.

Lorenzo makes the last slap the hardest. The sound of his palm hitting my flesh is so loud, even in the noisy club. It stings like a mother too and I flinch, but then he rubs his warm hand over my sensitive reddened skin and I arch into the pleasure.

"You take my spankings so well, sunshine. Such a good girl for me."

"Thank you, Sir."

He tugs my panties all the way off my legs before pulling me up and spinning me around so I'm straddling him, my red ass on display to anyone who might walk past.

He grazes my jaw with his nose, inhaling deeply and making my organs melt like chocolate in the sun. "Did I tell you how beautiful you look tonight, tesoro?"

"Yes, Sir. Before we left the house."

He slips his hands beneath the fabric of my dress, rubbing his fingertips over my lower back. "I do like this dress on you."

"Thank you," I whisper. Joey helped me choose it. It's short and form-fitting and black. It seemed like the perfect choice for my first visit to the club.

"I still prefer your yellow one though," he says with a smirk.

"Is that so?"

He nips at my jaw and a shiver runs down my spine. "Yes. You're going to wear that and nothing else the next time we come here."

He slips a hand between my thighs and drags two fingers through my dripping center. "With no underwear?" I whimper, rocking my hips against him. I need him inside me so bad.

"That's right. I want to be able to slide my hand under your dress while we're walking through the crowd and feel my wet pussy." He slips a thick finger inside me.

"S-Sir," I moan loudly, rolling my hips and riding his finger.

"What is it, sunshine?"

"Please ... fuck me."

"A demanding little sub tonight, huh?" He laughs darkly.

I drop my hips, sinking deeper onto his finger as he works it inside me. "I always need you, Sir."

"You want me inside you here at this table?"

"Yes, please." Hot pleasure tingles in my thighs.

"Then take my cock out," he orders while he goes on finger fucking me.

With trembling fingers, I work his zipper down and reach inside his boxers. He's as hard as stone, his skin hot and smooth as I wrap my hand around the base of his shaft and squeeze.

"Fuck," he mutters. "You have any idea how much I love your hands on me, tesoro?"

"Not as much as I love yours on me, Sir."

He slips his finger out of me. "Slide onto my cock, Mia. Take me all the way into your sweet cunt. I'm gonna fill your pussy with my cum like I did your pretty throat."

He tucks my hair behind my ears and stares into my eyes. "Maybe I'll fill you with something else too, huh?"

Molten heat sears in my core, and my breath hitches. I had my coil taken out a few days ago. No more birth control for me. "I would love that, Sir."

His eyes twinkle with mischief and delight. "So what are you waiting for, sunshine?"

I shift my hips, angling myself so that the crown of his thick cock is pressing at my opening. Then I look into his eyes, smiling as I sink onto him and see them roll back. Every solid inch of him fills my pussy. My walls ripple around him. I'm so close to the edge already from all the things he's done to me tonight. "Fuck me," he says with a throaty growl. "I'm gonna lose my mind if you don't stop squeezing me like that."

I press my forehead against his, wrapping my arms around his neck as he snakes his around my waist, taking control of my movements. "I'm sorry... can't help it...you feel so good inside me," I pant out each word as warm pleasure rolls through my body, threatening to overwhelm me at any given second.

"I'm going to fuck you like this out there for everyone to see next time we come here. Would you like that?"

"Y-yes," I mewl as white-hot pleasure sears between my thighs.

"Yeah?" He rolls his hips and sweeps his crown over the sensitive spot deep inside me.

"Please, Sir."

"Say my name, Mia," he commands, the deep timbre of his

voice rolling through my body and settling into my bones, soothing my very soul.

"Lorenzo!" My climax washes over me in a long undulating wave.

He pulls me tighter and fucks me through every second of it, his mouth hot against my ear. "I got you, sunshine."

I rest my head on his shoulder, completely spent. He nuzzles my neck, slamming into me one final time while he groans my name.

I pant for breath, and he rubs soothing hands down my back before pulling my dress down to cover my bare ass. "You good?" he asks softly.

I lift my head and look into his handsome face. "Yes." I smile contentedly.

He smiles back at me. "You're so fucking beautiful."

I curl my fingers through his thick dark hair. "Thank you, Sir. You're very beautiful too."

He kisses me softly, slipping his tongue into my mouth and making me moan again. I cannot get enough of this man and the things he does to my body. His hands coast up my back, fisting one in my hair as his kiss grows deeper and more passionate. I grind against him, and he breaks the kiss and lets out a dark laugh. "You're insatiable, my little sub."

I bite my lip and flutter my eyelashes. "For you I am, Sir."

He looks down at the crotch of his pants, stained with our cum, and I blush. "Your lovely suit," I whisper.

"There isn't a suit I own that you haven't stained with your sweet juices." He trails his lips over my neck. "And that's exactly how I like it."

"Can I ask you something, Sir?"

"Anything."

"Why didn't you spank me out there in front of everyone?"

"I told you I'd spank you in front of everyone if you took

your eyes off me when you were sucking my cock. You didn't. Your spanking was for talking without permission, and I never said where I was going to do that."

"Well, I'm glad you did it here instead."

He runs his nose over my jawline. "I know."

Warmth settles into every cell in my body. He knows. That was why he punished me in our private booth instead. "Sometimes I think you can read my mind, Sir."

"Not your mind. But I can read your body. The look in your eyes. Every single movement you make. Every shaky breath. Every tremor and tremble. Every flicker of emotion on your face tells me exactly what I need to know."

"I wish I could read you like that," I say with a soft sigh.

"I'm pretty sure you read me better than anyone else I know. You always know what I need. *You're* always what I need."

"You're all I need, Sir. I love you so much. I can't believe this is my life now, when for so long it was so ..." A sob wells in my throat and a single tear rolls down my cheek.

He wraps his arms tightly around my waist, pulling my body flush against his. "You deserve it all, sunshine. I'd hang the moon for you if you asked me to."

I sink my teeth into my lip, staring into his deep brown eyes. "Well, every girl deserves a man who looks at her like he would hang the moon for her."

I seal my lips over his, kissing him softly until he groans into my mouth and his cock stiffens between us. I roll my hips, taking control while he'll allow it, which I know won't be for long. But that's the man I love. Lorenzo Moretti is my partner. My lover. My Dom. My best friend. My everything.

CHAPTER
SEVENTY-ONE
LORENZO

NINE MONTHS LATER

My sneakers squeak on the wooden floor as I creep along the hallway, but the sound is drowned out by the noise of the TV. The game's on. Patriots vs. Colts. Ten more paces until I reach the den. This isn't the first time I've been here. I know the kind of tiles used to decorate the bathroom, and I know the brand of whiskey the owner drinks and how frequently he drinks it. He downs at least half a bottle during every Pats game. I know that the glass coffee table he uses to hold his bottle of Jameson is from Ikea. I had one just like it in a warehouse yesterday, before it got smashed to pieces and tossed in the dumpster of a local Turkish restaurant by one of my men. Wrapping my gloved hand around the thick shard I kept, I pull it from my pocket.

Slipping into the den, I see the half empty bottle of whiskey on the table and the empty glass sitting beside it. I swallow a knot of regret. I wish I could drag this out. Oh, the pleasure I would take in peeling the skin from his bones while listening to the music of his agonized screams. I'd gouge out his eyeballs and force them down his throat. Let him know who's responsible for every agonizing second of his death while I draw out his pain for as long as I can. Sadly, this needs to look like a suicide.

I quietly step up behind him, although he's too drunk to even hear me. A part of me hopes that he has good instincts and will spin around and confront me because then I could legitimately beat the fucker to death with my bare hands. But his eyes remain glued to the screen, and he curses the Patriots' receiver for dropping the ball.

I'm so close I can smell the whiskey on him and see the strong pulse in his neck. Grabbing his jaw, I tilt his head back before he can process what's happening.

I pull his head back far enough that I can look into his eyes. "Remember me, you sick fuck?"

He makes a grab for me and I don't flinch back. I'm wearing all-black combat gear, the kind that doesn't leave fibers behind. He can struggle and pull at my clothes all he wants. It won't change the outcome of his night.

"This is for Mia and Michaela, you evil fuck." I snarl as I slice the shard of glass across his carotid artery. "You're going to die just like your piece-of-shit brother."

He makes a final grab for me, then clutches at his throat, sputtering and coughing. A river of blood pours down his neck, soaking his football jersey, and I hold onto him as every drop of life drains from his body. Once he's dead and his eyes go dull, I let go and he falls forward.

Taking the shard, I position his hand around it. Then I grab the bottle of whiskey, raise it high and drop it onto the coffee table. It crashes through the glass, shattering it into pieces. I don't have a note, but I do have the unredacted sealed files and Michaela's permission. I place them on the sofa beside the brother who made her life a living hell. Hopefully he's about to spend the rest of eternity in his. Between his family history and the presumed guilt over what he did to his little sister, I have no doubt his death will be ruled a suicide. But if the detectives suspect even the slightest hint of foul play, I'm covered. I happen to know the new Superintendent of the Boston PD—Pete Hayes.

SEVENTY-TWO

LORENZO

Hands stuffed in the pockets of my suit pants, I stand in the hallway watching her. So fucking beautiful.

"You know this is supposed to be girls only, right?" Max walks up beside me, bumping my arm before he stops and stares too, watching my sister the same way I watch Mia. We stand here in silence, each of us transfixed. I swear Mia's smile could light up the entire city. My sunshine.

"I knew this is where you two would be," Dante says with a roll of his eyes as he comes up on my other side, cradling his sleeping son in his arms. "Can't stay away, huh?"

"Well, you might be an old hand at this, but it's kind of new for us," I remind him.

"Never gets old though, bro," he replies with a genuine smile as he stares at his wife.

Max turns and looks at my younger brother, cocking one eyebrow. "Surely you're not going to make that poor woman have any more of your giant babies after this one?"

Dante flashes him a grin. "I want at least one more."

"You want five kids?" I ask.

"I want six, but Kat says five, so..." He shrugs.

CHAPTER SEVENTY-TWO

"What about you, Loz? Will this be the first of many?" Max asks me.

I stare at Mia. Her face glows with such joy that I wonder how I ever got so lucky. Pregnancy looks good on her, but we've already agreed on our number. "One more," I reply.

"Joey says she'll wait to see how much of a tiny demon our first one is before we decide on more." Max laughs.

I glance at my sister, hand resting protectively on her swollen belly and her eyes shining with joy. "She may change her mind. She's young."

Dante snorts. "If your daughter is anything like her though ..."

Max's eyes widen with horror. "Fuck. I'm never gonna know a second's peace again, am I?"

"You wouldn't have it any other way," Dante replies with a grin. Kat is pregnant with their fourth child and despite our father being a monster, my younger brother has taken to fatherhood like he was born for the role. I only hope that it comes as naturally to me. "So, which baby do you think is going to arrive first?"

Mia, Joey, and Kat fell pregnant within weeks of one another, hence the three-way baby shower currently being held in our mansion. Our dining room is full of thirty giggling, excited women and my fiancée outshines every single one of them.

"Mine and Joey's," Max replies instantly. "She's due first."

Dante laughs. "First babies never arrive when they're supposed to, compagno."

"They don't?"

Dante shakes his head.

I blow out a breath at the reminder that I'm going to be a father in a few weeks. And an uncle to two more babies. Joey and Max have their own wing in the house now too. And call me sentimental, but I like all of us Morettis being under one roof. "We're gonna have three newborns under one roof."

Dante puts an arm around my shoulder, cradling his son with the other. "You're going to be an amazing dad."

"What if I'm not?"

Max bumps my arm again. "When have you ever not been good at anything?"

At that precise moment, Mia looks up and catches my eye. She flashes me one of her beautiful smiles, the kind that she reserves only for me. *Love you*, she mouths.

I swallow the words on the tip of my tongue. She knows I love her. Everybody knows. Max wraps an arm around my shoulder now too. "I'm so fucking proud of you," he says quietly, but loud enough that Dante hears him and he squeezes my other shoulder.

I'm proud of me too. After Anya died, I thought there was no life for me at all. I certainly didn't imagine I would experience any of this. There was no doubt in my mind that there could be no one else for me. And then I met my Mia. A woman who's impossible not to fall in love with. There's only so long you can stand in the sun before succumbing to its heat. I'm not sure anyone else could have melted my ice-cold heart the way that she has. And now she's giving me a son too. She is fucking everything.

SEVENTY-THREE

MIA

I lie back on the bed, running my hands over my swollen belly.

"Did you have fun today?" Lorenzo asks, opening the buttons of his shirt.

"I had such a wonderful time! It still feels strange to have so many genuine friends ..." I swallow down a knot of unexpected emotion. I was always a very sociable and confident person when I was younger—prom queen in high school, president of my sorority in college. But Brad never allowed me the luxury of friends. It might have ruined his good guy image if they got too close and saw one too many bruises or cuts. But Lorenzo encourages me to do whatever it is that keeps me true to my real self, and that includes making friends through work, at The Peacock Club, in my prenatal class. He supports every single thing I do, even encouraging me to start up my own aromatherapy business when I wasn't sure I had what it took. Now the business is thriving—I'm thriving. With his love and support, I can conquer the world.

He stops undressing and lies on the bed beside me, brushing his fingertips over my cheek. "You have lots of friends because you're a beautiful person, inside and out, tesoro," he says softly, so perceptive to any change in my emotions.

"Thank you. For everything," I whisper, a tear pricking at the corner of my eye.

"No." Shaking his head, he slips a warm hand over my swollen belly. "Thank you, sunshine. I could live one hundred lifetimes and never repay you for what you've given me."

This man has no idea how incredible he is. He is perfect for me in every single way. "Well, you could start by taking that shirt off. I was kind of enjoying the show before you stopped."

His eyes narrow as they lock on mine. "You were?" His voice drops an octave, becoming a deep growl that rolls through my core.

"Yes, Sir."

"You want to play, sunshine?"

My heart rate kicks up a gear. Hell yes, I want to play. Being heavily pregnant has not hindered our activities even a little and Lorenzo is very creative when it comes to thinking up new ways to tease, punish, and pleasure me. "Please, Sir."

He drags his bottom lip through his teeth, a wicked glint in his eyes as they roam over my nearly naked body. His hand on my belly dips lower, slipping beneath the waistband of my panties. "What the hell should I do with my needy little sub tonight?"

I rock my hips, leaning into his strong hand and silently begging him to slip it between my thighs. "Shall I make you work for your pleasure?" he asks, low and husky, before he trails his lips over my breasts. He sucks a sensitive nipple into his mouth, biting gently on the hardened bud and making me whimper. I curl my fingers in his hair.

"But I've been good, Sir," I whine.

"Mmhmm." He releases my nipple from his sinful mouth. "Did you accept all of the compliments you were paid today?"

CHAPTER SEVENTY-THREE

I roll my lips and screw my eyes closed as he directs his attention to my other breast. So many people told me I looked beautiful and glowing today, and I accepted their kindness with a smile and a thank you, resisting the urge to brush off or refute their assertions. "Yes," I breathe out the word. "I promise."

He lifts his head and stares into my eyes. I would never lie to him, and he knows it. "That's my good girl."

My cheeks flush at his praise. I love Lorenzo's punishments and his teasing, but when he rewards me for being good—well, that's a whole new level of ecstasy. His lips trail higher, skating across my collarbone and up my neck. He nips at the skin around my collar, making me mewl and writhe beneath him.

"You like wearing my collar, Mia?"

"Yes, Sir. You know I do."

He drags his teeth over the delicate skin of my neck. Then his hand finally slips into my panties, and he circles the pad of his middle finger on my clit. "You like the whole world knowing you belong to me?"

I arch my back as pleasure warms my core. "Y-yes."

"You have any idea how hard it makes me knowing that you're mine to do with as I please?" He sinks a thick finger inside me and I cry out, pushing my head back against the pillow. "Do you, sunshine?" He adds a second.

"Yes, Sir."

"I wonder what part of you I should fuck tonight, huh?" he asks, smiling against my skin as he works his fingers deeper.

"Every part of me," I tug at his hair, desperate for more of him.

"A greedy little sub too."

"Greedy for you, Sir."

"Damn fucking right you are," he grunts, rubbing his palm over my clit and massaging my pussy walls with his skilled fingers.

EPILOGUE

LORENZO

THREE YEARS LATER

Stretching my neck, I stare at my reflection in the mirror.

"You look handsome, Daddy," Luca says. My eyes find his in the mirror. His are deep pools of brown—full of happiness and trust. Three years old and, along with his two-year-old sister, Raven, the apple of mine and his mother's eye.

"Thanks, son," I say, flashing him a smile in the mirror that makes him giggle. "Not as handsome as you though."

"And not as beautiful as Mommy," he adds with an assured nod.

"No, definitely not as beautiful as your mommy."

The door bursts open and Max walks through it, carrying the three-month-old Maximo Junior in the crook of his arm. "You not bolted yet, Loz?" He gives a wicked laugh and slaps me on the back.

"Fuck you," I mutter quietly so Luca doesn't hear me.

Max smiles at my reflection. "You look good, compagno. You okay?"

I slide my finger beneath the collar of my shirt and roll my neck again. "Why does everyone keep asking me if I'm okay?" He's the third person in the past half hour who's asked me that.

"Because it's a big day." His eyes meet mine in the mirror.

I know what they're all thinking. It's taken three long years and a hell of a lot of red tape to get us here. Who would have thought that getting a divorce from a dead man could be so difficult? Before I can reply to Max, Dante bounds through the door with two kids in his arms and another six scurrying around his feet. My daughter runs to me, clambering up my leg until I lift her and pull her close. She squishes my cheeks together and I press a soft kiss on her perfect little nose.

Max rolls his eyes. "How did we wind up with all the tiny demons in here?"

"They followed me," Dante says with a shrug. "I'm like the Pied Piper or something. Besides, there are blow dryers and perfume and way too many people fussing around in that room. The kids are better in here with us, where there's a giant ass TV."

I place Raven on the floor to play with her brother and cousins. Maximo glances around the room, still holding onto Maximo Junior while his daughters, Bella and Jess, take control of the TV remote. "How in the hell did we end up with all these kids?" he asks with an exaggerated sigh. "I mean they outnumber us by far too many for my liking."

Dante looks around the room at all of our kids laughing and playing together and a smile spreads across his face. Ten cousins all growing up in one house—it can get rowdy. They adore one another, and although they fight and squabble constantly, they fight for each other as much as against. They're going to rule the fucking world together once they're all grown. And nobody knows besides us yet, but Mia and I are about to add one more to the brood. We didn't plan a third, but I spend so much time inside her, those odds were never going to be in our favor.

"So, how you doing, brother?" Dante asks.

I roll my eyes, but before I can snap at him for asking that fucking question, the door opens again. "Jess, please don't take off your dress, sweetheart," Joey says, spying her daughter about to pull her beautiful yellow dress off over her head.

"I hate dresses, Mommy," Jess whines. "I want to wear a suit like the boys."

"I know, baby, but it's only for a few hours," Joey replies sweetly.

"You should have let her wear whatever she wanted." My niece is every bit as headstrong as her mother.

"She told me yesterday that she wanted to wear a dress!" Joey throws her arms in the air. "The child is a law unto herself."

"Sounds like someone else I know," Dante says good-naturedly, giving our sister a kiss on the cheek.

"Hey!" Joey playfully swats his chest.

Max wraps an arm around her, their son drifting off to sleep cradled against his chest. "You look beautiful, baby girl."

"Thank you," she says, her cheeks flushed.

"What are you doing in here anyway?" Dante asks. "Did Mia send you in here to make sure Lorenzo wasn't having a breakdown?"

I scowl at my brother in the mirror.

"Nope." Joey shrugs. "That woman is as cool as a goddamn cucumber."

Dante laughs. "She kinda has to be to put up with Lorenzo."

The three of them start talking about the ceremony, but their chatter fades away and becomes white noise. I feel a heaviness in my heart that I was expecting, but it rankles just the same.

"I need to see her," I say, interrupting their chatter and making the three of them stare back at me through the mirror.

"Who? Mia?" Joey asks with a frown.

"Yes."

"You can't. It's bad luck," she insists.

"I need to see her, Joey. Make it happen."

She blinks at me. "Lorenzo? Are you—"

"Just do it. Please."

"Okay. Okay. I'll think of something." She gives me a reassuring smile, but Max and Dante watch me with concern.

Five minutes later, I'm standing in the pantry with the door open waiting for my bride and under strict instructions from my kid sister that I will, under no circumstances, step out of this tiny room and look at Mia before the ceremony.

Her soft footsteps approach and my heart beats harder in my chest. The scent of her perfume makes my cock twitch. I'm so tempted to go out there so I can pull my fiancée into my arms, but I made Joey a promise.

"Hey you," she says softly. Her shadow falls across the floor, and I figure she's leaning against the wall right outside the door.

"Hey." I reach my hand out for hers, and she laces her fingers through mine. Her skin is warm and soft like silk.

I swallow the thick knot of emotion stuck in my throat.

She squeezes my hand tighter. "She would be proud of you, you know that, right?"

Tears prick at the corners of my eyes. This woman has such a beautiful fucking soul, and I don't know what I ever did to deserve her. How many women would comfort their husband-to-be on their wedding day because they thought they were thinking about someone else? "I love you," I rasp.

"I know."

"You have any idea how much restraint it's taking to not pull you into this pantry with me and kiss you?"

"Only kiss me?" She giggles softly.

"Well, it would start with a kiss at least."

"And within two minutes I'd be bent over with my beautiful wedding dress around my waist?" she whispers seductively.

"Don't be putting ideas in my head, sunshine." Visions of her bent over with my cock inside her later aren't enough to shake this uneasy feeling I'm carrying though. I lift her hand to my lips and brush them across her knuckles. A deep sigh rumbles through my chest.

"It's okay for you to think about her, Lorenzo. I'm thinking of her too."

"You are?"

"Yes. I'm grateful to her for making you the man you are today, and I always will be. I've been thinking about her all morning. What her dress was like. How excited she must have been to marry you."

Thinking about my first wedding day, I smile. Me thinking about Anya isn't an issue for Mia, I know that with my whole heart, but not talking to her about it is. It's a mistake I made a long time ago and never will again. "She wore a white silk dress," I say, picturing her walking down the aisle toward me. "The corset was tied so tight she almost fainted at the altar."

"Were you nervous?"

"Fuck yeah." I laugh. "My father had all but disowned me. Anya's family did the same to her. But nothing had ever felt so right before."

"Are you nervous today?" she asks softly.

"No. Not even a little," I admit, pressing a soft kiss on her knuckles. I've never been so sure of anything as making this woman my wife. "You?"

"Nope."

"Kind of feels like every single moment in my life was supposed to lead me right here. To you. To Luca and Raven."

"And the accidental jellybean," she whispers.

"Yeah, and him too."

"Him?"

"I got a feeling." I shrug.

She chuckles lightly. "Me too, actually."

The silence hangs between us for a few moments. "I didn't ask to see you because I was thinking about Anya."

"You didn't?"

My heart sinks and I close my eyes. "No."

"Then what is it?" she asks, her voice tinged with concern.

"I have something I need to tell you. But I need you to know that I did what I did for me, tesoro. It shouldn't stain your conscience."

"You killed Jake," she says—a statement not a question.

"You knew?"

"I suspected it was no accident. I figured you'd tell me when you were ready."

"I don't want to have any secrets when I make you my wife. I shouldn't have kept it from you this long." I squeeze her hand tighter and brush my thumb over her knuckles. "But I didn't want you to feel any guilt about what happened because it was between me and him, not you. Then a few days later, Luca was born and, well, there never seemed to be a good time to break your heart."

"You're not breaking my heart. I understand why you did what you did. I get now why a man like you can't let those kinds of things lie. And it's okay. The way you protect the people you care about is one of the million things I've grown to love about you."

"Thank you, and not just for this. Thank you for loving me, sunshine. For giving me Luca and Raven and the new little guy.

For bringing me joy beyond anything I could've imagined ever having again. And thank you for thinking about Anya today. It means everything to me."

"She's a part of you, Lorenzo, and I love all of you."

I know that she means that too. There isn't a spiteful, cruel, or jealous bone in this woman's entire body. "I love you too, sunshine. Are you okay?"

"I'm perfect."

"Yes you are."

She laughs. "I didn't mean—"

"I did." I'm seconds away from pulling her into this room with me. "You're better than perfect, Mia. You're fucking incredible. You and our children are everything to me, you know that, right?"

"You're everything to me too, Sir."

I can't stand not having her in my arms for a single second longer. Closing my eyes, I pull her into the pantry with me.

"Lorenzo!" she squeals as her body crashes into mine.

"I've got my eyes closed," I tell her, wrapping my arms around her waist and savoring the heat of her body through my shirt.

"Me too," she giggles. "I don't want to see you until I'm walking down the aisle."

I dust my lips over hers and she shivers in my arms. "We'd better make this quick before Joey comes in here and busts us."

"So kiss me, Mr. Moretti."

"With pleasure, Mrs. Moretti." I seal my lips over hers, licking across the seam until she opens wide for me, allowing me to slide my tongue inside.

MIA

Apart from the days Luca and Raven were born, this has been the most incredible day of my life. I almost cried when I saw Lorenzo and our son waiting for me at the end of the aisle. And then Lorenzo turned and looked at me, and his face ...

I wipe away a tear as I recall the amount of happiness and love in his eyes. Since the night he gave me his collar, I have never once doubted his love for me, but to see it so raw and primal today nearly made my knees buckle before I reached him. This day has been difficult for him in some ways. Unlike mine, his first marriage was a happy one. Anya was the love of his life, or at least she was *a* love of his life, because I know that I am too. He used to feel guilty for loving me, but now he sometimes feels guilty for still loving her and I wish he wouldn't. His loyalty and passion are two of my favorite things about him.

Someone places a glass of champagne in my hand, and I accept it with a smile. As soon as their back is turned, Lorenzo switches it out for his empty one, giving me a knowing wink. At eight weeks pregnant with our third child, alcohol is definitely off limits for now, which is fine at this huge wedding reception, but later, when it's just close family in the kitchen, it won't be so easy to hide. Apparently, an intimate get-together in the kitchen with just the siblings, and Max and Kat of course, is a Moretti family wedding tradition.

Looking around, I can't help but sigh at the sight of people dancing and laughing, Raven and Luca playing with their cousins while Joey, Max, Dante, and Kat keep an eye on them for the evening. Lorenzo Moretti isn't a dancer, but he happily took the floor with me for our wedding song, and now I'm content to sit beside him with his arm draped around my shoulder. As long as he's by my side, I'm happy and at peace. It's hard to believe that a man so dangerous and violent is the man who makes me feel safer and more cherished than I ever have in my life.

"You feeling okay, sunshine?" he asks, searching my face with narrowed eyes.

"Never better," I assure him.

"Good, because I have a surprise for you." He takes my hand and pulls me up from my chair and the music stops abruptly. Lorenzo grins down at me, but I'm too confused to smile back. Then the opening bars of "Bright Side of the Road" play, and I swear my heart actually skips a beat.

Lorenzo gestures to the dance floor. "Will you dance with me, Mrs. Moretti?"

"This ... it's ..."

"Our song." He guides me toward his siblings, our children, and our nieces and nephews on the dance floor and wraps his arms around my waist. I giggle when he dips me, and when he pulls me back up and we begin dancing, a dreamy sigh falls from my lips.

"You hate dancing," I remind him.

"But I'd do anything for you, sunshine." He gives me a soft kiss on the lips.

"Daddy!" Raven demands, pulling on the leg of his suit pants.

He rolls his eyes and scoops her up, keeping one arm around my waist as he rubs his beard against her cheek, making her giggle. Luca sidles up to me, curling his little hand in mine and shaking his hips to the music.

"He definitely got your rhythm," Lorenzo says.

"You have pretty good rhythm yourself," I reply with a wicked grin.

His eyes darken and then he winks at me. We dance to our song, surrounded by Dante and Kat with their kids, and Joey and Max with theirs, and Toni joins us too. When the chorus kicks in, we all sing along, even my Lorenzo. I place my free hand over my stomach, delighted over our family growing bigger. This must be a fairytale, right? No one could ever possibly be *this* happy.

Lorenzo presses his lips against my ear. "I love you, sunshine."

My smile widens. Yes, a person truly can be this happy. "I love you too."

Are you eager for a little more Lorenzo and Mia? Want to know if they ever cure her fear of belts? Then you can sign up for a bonus extended epilogue here by contacting Sadie on Facebook or Instagram.

The Moretti's might have their HEA, but there's someone out there who wants to take it from them. Turn the page to get a sneak peek at Keres. Coming Spring 2024 or preorder here

KERES (PREVIEW)

I kill the bike's engine and it purrs to a stop. Lifting my visor, I train my gaze on the house a few hundred yards ahead. The Moretti Mansion cuts an imposing figure against the midnight sky. Lorenzo, Dante, and Joey Moretti sleep soundly in their beds, surrounded by opulence and grandeur while the rest of us have to forage for the crumbs they leave behind. So arrogant in their belief that they have the right to be safe while the rest of the world burns outside their gilded walls.

They should enjoy their privileged existence while they still can. No amount of armed guards or iron gates will keep them safe from me. Moretti blood runs through my veins too, and I won't stop until every last one of them is erased from existence.

Preorder Keres now here

Now that Lorenzo and Mia's story is done, are you ready to get to know their friends, the James brothers a little better?

You can meet them all in Sadie's upcoming Manhattan Ruthless series.

Book 1 is available for preorder now. You can get it here or on Amazon.

You can also preorder Sadie's next release, a standalone why choose romance, The Perfect Fit, here or on Amazon

Also by Sadie Kincaid

Want to know more about the Irish Mafia in New York and their connection to the Bratva? If you haven't read New York the series yet, you can find them on Amazon and Kindle Unlimited

Ryan Rule

Ryan Redemption

Ryan Retribution

Ryan Reign

Ryan Renewed

New York Ruthless short stories can be found here

A Ryan Reckoning

A Ryan Rewind

A Ryan Restraint

A Ryan Recon

A Ryan Revelation

A Ryan Halloween

A Ryan Christmas

A Ryan New Year

If you'd prefer to head to LA to meet Alejandro and Alana, and Jackson and Lucia, you can find out all about them in Sadie's internationally bestselling LA Ruthless series. Available on Amazon and FREE in Kindle Unlimited.

Fierce King

Fierce Queen

Fierce Betrayal

Fierce Obsession

If you'd like to read about London's hottest couple. Gabriel and Samantha, then check out Sadie's London Ruthless series on Amazon. FREE in Kindle Unlimited.

Dark Angel

Fallen Angel

Dark/ Fallen Angel Duet

ACKNOWLEDGMENTS

Wow, this book hurt! For anyone who's experienced the visceral, soul-destroying grief of losing someone who's supposed to be a part of your life forever, I hope that I did Lorenzo's story justice.

As always I would love to thank all of my incredible readers, and especially the members of Sadie's Ladies and Sizzling Alphas. My beloved belt whores! You are all superstars. To my amazing ARC and street teams, the love you have for these books continues to amaze and inspire me. I am so grateful for all of you.

But to all of the readers who have bought any of my books, everything I write is for you and you all make my dreams come true.

To all of my author friends who help make this journey all that more special.

Super special mention to my lovely PA's, Kate, Kate and Andrea, for their support and honesty and everything they do to make my life easier.

To the silent ninja, Bobby Kim. Thank you for continuing to push me to be better. And to my amazing editor, Jaime, who helped me dig into a lot of stuff I didn't want to, to make Lorenzo's story happen.

To my incredible boys who inspire me to be better every single day. And last, but no means least, a huge thank you to Mr. Kincaid— all my book boyfriends rolled into one. I couldn't do this without you!

Printed in Great Britain
by Amazon

54605816R00239